ICA[RUS]
AND THE
WING BUILDER

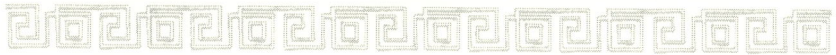

To

Caroline,

Thank you for being my reader.

Robert William Case   06-30-15

Robert William Case

THE
JOURNEYS
OF
DAEDALUS

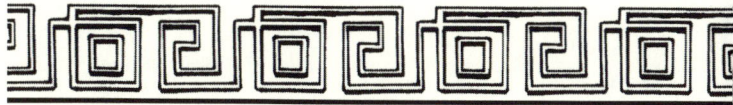

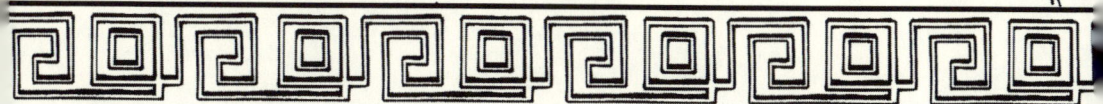

N

TROY

LESBOS

ANDROS

ATHENS

TENOS

SAMOS

KEA

MYKONOS

IKARIA

NAXOS

SIFNOS

RHODES

MELOS

KALLISTE

KARPATHOS

KRETE

KNOSSOS

MALIA

PLATANOS

PHAISTOS

ZAKROS

Kalliste
Productions, LTD

PUBLISHED BY KALLISTE PRODUCTIONS Ltd.
P O Box 140581
Edgewater, Colorado   80214

For information about purchasing books in quantity, promotion, or presentations, please contact Kalliste Productions, or call 303-947-3408.

Library of Congress Cataloging-in-Publication Data
1. Fiction / Historical 2. Minoan Civilization – Fiction 3. Fathers and Sons – Fiction 4. Folklore & Mythology / Icarus 5. Folklore & Mythology / Daedalus
ISBN 978-0-9894770-9-3

Cover art by Benjamin Hummel © 2014
Book Design by Cherished Solutions, llc.
www.cherishedsolutions.com

Manufactured in the USA
First Published June 12, 2014

To Marceil,
for sharing this journey with me.

CONTENTS

GLOSSARY OF NAMES, PLACES AND THINGS

Aadam – Young mariner on the *Pelican* – The name means first born.

Abraxas – Friend of Aella – The name means magician or deceiver.

Aegeus – King of Athens and husband of Aethra – In classical mythology he was the father of Theseus and the King of Athens during these times.

Aella – Mother of Talos – The name means woman of the whirlwind.

Aethra – Queen of Athens and wife of Aegeus – In classical mythology she was the mother of Theseus and Queen of Athens.

Agapios – Student and friend of Daedalus – The name comes from the Greek word agape which means higher love.

Andreas – Mariner on the *Pelican* – The name means strong and manly.

Androgeous – Minoan prince – In classical mythology he was the oldest son of King Minos and Queen Pasiphae.

Ariadne – Minoan princess, the daughter of Minos and Pasiphae – In classical mythology she was the wife of Dionysus, the god of wine, and remembered for urging Daedalus to mark the way through the labyrinth for Theseus and the Athenian slaves with a large spool of twine or thread.

Avram – Young wrestler from Malia – The name means elevated one, or father of many nations.

Daedalus – The Wingbuilder – In classical mythology he is remembered as the first person to fly on wings of his own design, the builder of the labyrinth, and the father of Icarus.

Deena – Villager and friend of Naomi – The name means one who is judged.

Demitrious – Icarus' friend in Knossos – The name means lover of the earth.

Dianna – Friend of Ariadne & Phaedra – The name means heavenly or divine.

Filia – Servant of Naucreta – The name means devoted one.

Galen – The healer on the last island in the chain – The name means calm.

Georgios – The baker – The name means worker of the earth, farmer.

Icarus – Son of Daedalus – In classical mythology he is remembered as the eternal youth, the one who flew too close to the sun on wings made by his father.

Kalliste – A magnificent volcanic island paradise in the center of the Aegean Sea. Before the devastating eruption, it was the spiritual center of the Minoan empire. The name means the most beautiful. The same geographic location is known in the English speaking world as Santorini. To the Greeks, it is known as Thera.

Krete – The island home of King Minos and the commercial hub of the Minoan empire. In the English speaking world of today, it is commonly written as Crete.

Meltemi – Perennial afternoon winds of the Aegean region, which bring cool air out of the north from mid-May through mid-September - Writers of classical mythology made many references to these reliable and sometimes, formidable winds.

Minos – The Minoan sovereign and husband of Pasiphae – In classical mythology he was the king and ruler of the island of Krete during the height of the Minoan civilization.

Naomi – Villager, friend of Deena, and wife of Salim – The name means beautiful or delightful.

Naucreta – Befriends Daedalus and Icarus in Knossos – In classical mythology she was a courtesan in the court of King Minos.

Nikolaos – Captain of the *Pelican* – The name means victor of the people.

Orichalcum – A Minoan word for the ore and metal which, when alloyed with copper, becomes bronze. Today it is commonly known as tin.

Orion – The hunter, the defender – In classical mythology Orion was one of the primordial Titans, a famous hunter. According to legend he was killed by a scorpion.

Panos – Mariner on the *Pelican* – The name means holy man.

Pasiphae – Minoan queen and wife of Minos – In classical mythology she was the Queen of Krete and the mother of Androgeous, Ariadne, Phaedra, and the minotaur.

Phaedra – Younger sister of Ariadne and daughter of King Minos – In classical mythology she was both the daughter of the Minoan king and the wife of Theseus, the Athenian prince.

Phaestus – Fisherman – The name means happy or lucky man.

Philothei – Young woman in Athens – The name means beloved of God.

Platanos – The small fishing village – Also the name of the large and ancient trees commonly found in the center of small Kretan towns and villages.

Salim – Fisherman and friend of Icarus – The name means peaceful one.

Talos – Son of Aella – In classical mythology he was the gatekeeper or protector of Krete.

Thalia – Daughter of Xanthus – The name means blooming or flourishing.

Theseus – Leader of Athenian slaves on Krete – In classical mythology he was the son of Aegeus and Aethra, the prince of Athens, the husband of Phaedra, and the slayer of the minotaur.

Xanthus – Mariner on the *Pelican* – The name means handsome man.

Zavier – Mariner on the *Pelican* – The name means new house.

PROLOGUE

Long ago, on a verdant island in the middle of an azure sea now called the Mediterranean a man named Daedalus designed and built wings. Naturally, inevitably, he had to test them.

On that momentous sun-filled day he stood on a ledge of earth and stone beneath a cloudless sky, long cumbersome wings of his own design draped across his arms, shoulders, and back. The wind was steady and strong and blowing directly into his bearded face. It was a perfect day for flight. But he stood on the ledge of earth for a long while, anxious and uncertain, staring out at the distant gray fusion of water and sky.

The harness and wings carried an unnatural bulk and he constantly shifted his weight to compensate and keep his balance. If he slipped now or was knocked off his feet, the fall onto the rocks and dirt would likely damage the wings. He had labored too long, journeyed too far for that. So he leaned forward with bent knees, opposing the wind's power and keeping his weight over his feet.

Far below and before him, as far as he could see, sparkling waves reflected the sun's warmth and light. The majesty of the seascape called out its siren song, clear and serene. High on this remote perch he could not help but feel it. The attraction was irresistible, enticing him into the sky. As he stood on the shared boundary between the sea, sky, and land, it pulled on him as if his ears were at the center of his heart. But once again he was able to shake his head and look away, shifting his weight and keeping both feet firmly on the ground.

How long do I stand here, waiting?

In silence, Daedalus turned his gaze back toward the sea, compelled to feel the power of the sky just one more time where the wind caught under the wings and the uplift began. He rotated his shoulders and held the wings fast. The steady breeze blew across the outstretched wings, its energy flowing through them into the muscles of his shoulders and back. It teased and taunted him, assuring him that now was the best of times—possibly the only time there would ever be—for making this essential leap of faith.

He leaned forward once again and braced against the force, testing the limits of his fragile equilibrium. Once more he opted for the safety of the rocky ledge. But this time, and before he could look back down to the earth beneath his sandaled feet, a burst of windblown sand struck his face and chest. Instantly he closed his eyes and shifted one foot back for balance, squaring his shoulders into the gust, the wings fully extended.

The wind did not relent. It tore across the surface of the wings. Uplift gripped at his shoulders and spine. And now instead of struggling for balance the wingbuilder pushed hard against the earth, up and away from the rocky ledge. Heart pounding, he dove into the sky. At the apogee of the leap he hung suspended, balanced between time and the jagged rocks of the shoreline below. Gravity, it seemed, had released its hold. Filling his lungs with an intake of breath, he willed his chest forward into an awkward glide, arms and wings outstretched, reaching for the currents of air. Daedalus soared.

The moment was sublime, the splendor of flight on wings of his own design. The sky responded, greeting him with a mighty thermal, lifting him into its invisible spiral, and carrying him into the cerulean heights far above the island. Sweat streaking down his face, he banked away like a great soaring bird. It was a dream realized. He felt so alive, his heart singing with joy, so loud and so strong. He never wanted it to end.

His flight took place before 1620 BC, give or take a few years either way. The geology of the region provides the proof. A major technological achievement such as this could only have taken place during the blossoming of an advanced and ancient civilization. The people providing this cultural milieu were the Minoans, the Sea People, and in their time they ruled the Mediterranean, right up until the explosion of a picturesque island volcano located in the geographic center of their nation and the destructive tsunamis that followed. Much of their legacy still lies buried on a barren island called Santorini beneath many meters of volcanic ash and pumice. But in their time and before the catastrophic eruption, the same island was known as Kalliste, "the most beautiful."

At the time of this first flight, Kalliste was an island like no other, a fertile oasis in the midst of a deep green salt-water desert. Unquestionably volcanic, from a distance the island had the shape of an enormous cone made asymmetric by multiple craters that formed the broad peak. Occasional wisps of vapor or smoke were commonplace from the fresh-looking lava flows near the summit. Where the slopes became gentle, the land was very fertile, supporting every kind of growing plant that was pleasing to the eye, the tongue, or to the nose. And in the island's remote places, fissures descended deep into the igneous rock, many of them filled with alternating bands of gleaming precious metals. Kalliste was an ever-blossoming garden and the most beautiful of places.

The mountain began as upwelling magma deep within the earth. The magma's immense volume was itself a by-product of the incredible heat generated by the subduction of the African Continental Plate beneath the Aegean Sea Plate. From these depths, white hot liquefied earth gradually rose upward, intruding into shallower levels of the earth's crust and forming mammoth underground vaults of pressurized molten rock, rich in rare dissolved minerals. Struggling to contain the pressure below, the overlying crustal rock buckled and heaved. Earthquakes were regular occurrences. When the pressure grew too great, the magma flowed upward, surging through broken rocks and onto the sea bottom as lava, birthing an undersea mountain. Sustained by the slow moving fountain of lava, one day its smoldering pinnacle pierced the surface of the Mediterranean in a boiling froth. Kalliste was born.

Even then, the lava kept coming from multiple vents, both under the sea and above it, building the island out higher and larger. As the molten rock cooled and hardened, it shrank in size, causing cracks and vents to appear. Sea water entered, producing clouds of steam, hot springs, and a perpetual source of fresh water for the entire region.

Four thousand years ago, the Minoans had a different explanation for the origin of their island paradise. They believed in the venerable natures of the Sky, the Sea, and the Land. They believed that the Lord of the Sky once ordered two eagles to fly to the opposite ends of the earth and then return. The place where their paths crossed marked the center of the world. There, the Gods of the Sea and Land took human form, male and female. They fell in love and, being gods, their passions resonated deep into the earth, liberating the Fire that lay at great depths within the planet. The island of Kalliste was born.

The Minoans believed themselves to be the descendants of that union, rightful heirs to Kalliste and all of its bounty. There, the Earth Goddess held dominion over the land and all that grew or dwelt upon it. She and a cast of supporting goddesses were the masters of transformation and change. They were the embodiment of art, the hunt, and the home. They lived deep within the earth. Throughout these islands, priestesses of the goddess presided over ritual celebrations of birth, harvest, and death, honoring the natural cycles of life. Wherever they ventured, the priestesses and their retinue of earthmonks were a protected class. To honor all of their beneficent gods, generations of Minoans created elegant shrines throughout the islands. The finest was a jewel-like temple, overlooking the bustling harbor of Kalliste. The feminine priesthood ruled Kalliste, the spiritual center of the nation.

Masters of shipbuilding and sailing, the Sea People created a maritime empire. In that realm, their spiritual provider and protector was the God of the Sea. In their beliefs, he had enclosed Kalliste all around with concentric rings of land and sea. No ship could enter or leave its deep harbors without first passing through a narrow spiraling canal between towering rock walls. Skilled archers from the nearby community were always available to command these readily defensible cliffs.

Directly south of Kalliste, and a long day's journey away, lay the island of Krete. This southern neighbor was not of volcanic origin. Nor was it blessed with great mineral wealth or hydrothermal waters. Krete's blessings were its enormous land mass, a large population, and its proximity to the ever blossoming garden of Kalliste. Its rulers were patriarchs, direct descendants of the God of the Sea. In the time of Daedalus, Krete was ruled by Minos. He lived in an elaborate palace at the center of a large city named Knossos.

In many ways his island was the perfect counterpoint to volatile Kalliste; for the bedrock of Krete was formed from ancient limestone and other sedimentary rocks, the kind that accumulate very slowly in quiet, deep marine waters. Limestone characteristically weathers and erodes into steep cliffs, narrow canyons, and caves, and the rugged mountains of western Krete are filled with this karst topography. In eastern Krete, the elevations are less pronounced. Here, the Minoans built populous cities, and lived in multi-storied dwellings with beautifully painted walls and running water. Cobblestone roads passable in all seasons connected their cities, cultural centers, and harbors.

Daedalus, the inventor, and his son Icarus were part of this thriving civilization, making their home on Krete. There, the father dedicated much of his adult life to engineering and development projects for the king, and also to raising his son. But civil engineering projects for King Minos were not destined to be Daedalus' life's work. His masterpiece was to design and build working wings; his legacy, to become the first person to fly.

It was a feat of such renown that their story survived, orally transmitted from one generation to another for more than a thousand years and long after the rise and fall of the Minoan Empire. Finally, a poet and writer named Ovid, born in 43 BC, created the written record of this first flight that has survived into the present day. His book was an epic narrative, embracing all the gods and myths of the day; and he was not even Greek. Ovid was Roman. Following the publication of his *Metamorphoses*, Daedalus and Icarus became legends, and their story a source of inspiration for artists, scientists and writers into the present day. Many believe that his story inspired Leonardo da Vinci, born in Italy in 1452, to study the wings of many different flying things, and to dream of his own flight.

According to Ovid's ancient telling of the tale, Daedalus created two sets of working wings from the feathers of seabirds and wax, one for himself and one for his son. It was also written that when the father presented this remarkable gift to Icarus, he delivered an infamous warning. It went something like this:

"Icarus, listen to me. This is important," the father cautioned as he fitted the harness to his son's strong back. "The feathers of these wings are held together with wax."

The youth looked away, admiring the intricate weave of the feathers. Already his chest and shoulders were filing out. Anyone with eyes could see the makings of the man inside, waiting to emerge.

"If you fly too high, the wax will surely melt in the sun's heat," Daedalus continued, searching his son's face.

Icarus nodded, still looking away.

Placing his hands on his hips and moving to face his son, Daedalus said in slow, measured words, "If the wings break apart, you will fall out of the sky and crash."

"OK," said Icarus, raising his voice and frowning.

"Tell me that you understand!" Daedalus demanded.

"Father. Of course I understand," he replied in slow measured tones, simultaneously giving his father's forearm a squeeze.

The geological record is irrefutable. Sixteen hundred years passed between the actual creation of the wings and the writing of Ovid's manuscript. In that very long span of time, there were countless opportunities to embellish, modify, and also to forget parts of the story. His charge was to write a story that would appeal to the audiences of his day. The result was a distillation of thousands of accounts of the tale into one. It was rudimentary at best. And in Ovid's version of the story, "foolish Icarus forsook his guide." He ignored his father's warning, soared too high, and his wings broke apart. Icarus fell into the sea.

But what if Ovid, the original king of drama, got it wrong?

What if Icarus survived?

What if Icarus fell, but did not fall?

What if Icarus made his way to a fertile and inhabited island where he not only survived—but thrived?

And what if Daedalus, the inventor of the wings, finally has his day in the sun, to tell the rest of the story?

PART I

Athens

For Minos acquired a fleet and dominated most of what is now the Greek sea. He ruled over the Cyclades and was the first to plant colonies in most of them, after expelling the Carians and installing his own sons as rulers. As one might expect, he also cleared the sea of pirates so far as he could, so that more revenue might come in to him.

Thucydides I,4
Athenian general and historian
460 BCE - 395 BCE

CHAPTER ONE

There have always been stories, told in gatherings like this one.
        Stars filled the sky, but to see into their splendor I had to step back, away from the glow of the fire and separate from the audience of young and old, families and friends. A chill advanced up my spine with each step. Far from the campfire I tipped my head back, taking in the fullness of the night sky. It was so beautiful I had to sigh and with the exhale a stream of vapor flowed upward, condensing right before my eyes and merging into the starlight.

        I was nervous as usual. In storytelling, there was always a before, during, and after. The afterward was my favorite. It would all begin soon enough. Agapios, my young student and friend, was warming them up with jokes and vignettes. He was so natural in front of the villagers. That was his strength. Mine was experience. I had a message to deliver and a deep mellifluous voice to carry it. Tonight I would bring both. I would make the story memorable. Looking back toward the firelight I watched Agapios standing before them, his gestures big and purposeful. I watched him give a knowing look to his wife, pause and then pick up again in a slightly different tone. It was the start of my introduction.

        "But, you've heard that story before and I'm tired of telling it, so I'll spare us all." Agapios paused, giving the laughter time to fade. "On the other hand," he continued, pointing toward me, "Daedalus over there has a story that I'll never tire of hearing. In fact, I think it's telling is a fitting cap to tonight's victory celebration." The crowd began to applaud and Agapios joined in. When it naturally faded, he placed his arms and hands together and gestured into the crowd, indicating where a path should begin to open. Limping on his club foot, Agapios stepped toward me, and I began my entrance, taking on the role that at this point in life had become my calling. "Here he is ladies and gentlemen, Daedalus, a man for all seasons, the man who held at bay the mightiest army and navy on earth with the words of a simple story."

"Victory!" declared Agapios to a cheering crowd. "Victory over Minos!" Leaning in close, he spoke directly to the children, "And if we're fortunate, maybe he'll include the part about teaching his young son to fly. So, if our storyteller gets lost in the telling and forgets any of your favorite parts, you must remind him nicely, saying, 'Pleeeeease!'" The children nodded earnestly, while chuckling adults shifted in their seats, getting comfortable for the story. Turning back toward me, he asked, "So what do you say, old friend? Do you have it in you tonight to tell us about how someone creates a legacy like building wings?" Raising his arms like a monster, he continued, "Or to tell us about big, bad, angry King Minos? Or," he said, softening completely, "to tell us about the mystery, the romance, and the intrigue that propelled a young fisherman's daughter into the role of queen and ruler over an entire island?"

Ready to respond to his introduction I started to inhale, but before I could begin.

"Great!" Agapios interrupted, flashing a smile in my direction.

I could see that Agapios wasn't quite ready to give up the attention. I used the time to look out into the faces in the crowd and make a few connections.

"Tonight we are in for a special treat," Agapios continued. "Every once in a while someone comes along possessing uncommon creativity, uncommon intellect, and uncommon wisdom. And that person builds buildings or paints paintings or sails seas. Impressive to some, those things are to each of us gathered here tonight fickle and fleeting. That's because we're spoiled. When we see a building, we only want to climb on top of it to get a better view. When we see a painting, we only hope to see one specific image. When we hear that the ships have returned, we only want to learn how far the news has spread. But tonight, the wingbuilder himself is here to educate and to entertain, motivate and inspire!" At this, the

gathering sounded as one body, offering tremendous applause and vocal
encouragement. Even the children anxiously jumped up and down, despite
not exactly knowing why everyone was so excited. Putting his hands in the
air, Agapios regained control. "So tonight, let us give our full attention,"
he paused, "to Daedalus, the man who flew on wings of his own design."

As I walked to the spot held open, another brief round of applause
erupted. How many more times would I be able to tell this story? I
wondered. How many more days would I have in this world? Rather than
a limiting vision, these ideas caused me to want to do the story justice even
more. I wanted to make it unforgettable.

CHAPTER TWO

L ike everyone else my journey began at home. Home is the place for beginnings, the place for receiving—from family and community—the lessons of who we are. And it is only by leaving it, by leaving this nest, that we discover our own creative influence over the man or woman we can become.

My own story began in a homeland far from these islands within a city at the center of a rim of mountains that surrounds the fertile plain of Attica. Much like it is today, back then Athens was a large clustering of houses, markets, and shops, all surrounded by an outer protective wall. Standing nearly a full stadion above the channel of a clear, sparkling river that curves around its base a prominent limestone bluff still rises from the center of it all. From the earliest of times, these cliffs were widely known as a natural fortress or citadel, a gathering place to occupy or to ponder the passing of the sun and stars. On top, there are caves for shelter, percolating springs, and a commanding view of the surrounding fields and forests of pine, cedar, and cypress all the way to the distant sea.

Many times I followed the winding course of the river through the rocky foothills to a source on one of the broad peaks overlooking the valley. If one was prepared, leaving the city to trek into the mountains was to enter a luminous world of immense diversity. There are endless varieties of wildlife and birds, inspirational vistas and even the possibility of stumbling across a vein of silver or copper. From these summits the faraway sea stretches like a silken carpet, offering glimpses of pale, sun-baked islands, distant shadowy mountains and the chance to dream.

From certain peaks you can see the stand of cypress trees and where the bend in the river marks where my small eclectic house on the eastern side of the city used to be. Even as a young man I did not need or want a lot of land or living space. The house was built into the flank of a low hill. The wood beams and stone walls were made to last. It had a simple elegance and a sense of privacy. Shade trees protected the small stone courtyard from the summer's oppressive heat. There was even a raised platform built against the wall of the house, with a pallet bed for sleeping in the cool air and listening to the river sounds. I missed that house after we left.

On moonless nights I was often content to sit on the courtyard and gaze into the canopy of starlight, listening to the lively current flowing past. And when the moon interfered with my stargazing, I could stoke up the fire pit and test different ores for the hot flowing metals they sometimes produced. Alchemy was more than a hobby. In those days I was an architect and builder by trade and well known in Athens for inventing new tools to make the work easier. Even King Aegeus knew of and requested my skills from time to time.

One spring evening I fell asleep on the pallet bed after staying late in the city. Outside of the warm blankets the wind was rising, but within the dream I found myself inside the narrow twisting corridors of a large windowless structure. Angry voices shouted in the darkness. They were after me, or rather, the valuable amulet hanging from my neck. In the dream I was much older, and for some reason it was clear that I had just flown like a bird. The men chasing me knew about my flight. They believed that the amulet contained the powerful secret.

"There he is," someone yelled. "Get him!"

Crouching low, I took off at the shout, and immediately tripped over a large rock. Mocking laughter followed. I rubbed my hand against a rising bruise and listened. All that I could hear was my own breath. And it was slowing. I followed the curves of the passage, wondering if I was fleeing from or moving toward my pursuers. My eyes had grown accustomed to the darkness. Then I heard something very close. I stopped. There it was again, a kind of whooshing sound. Starting off once more I took three steps right into a wall and my heart sank. Wearily my hands moved along the vertical surfaces. Finally there was an opening. The passage continued to my right, the tunnel abruptly turning back on itself. I clutched at the amulet and kept going.

Finally, a wisp of moving air cooled my face and for the first time I felt a sense of hope in that dark place. In the distance, walls became visible and I picked up the pace, making for the luminescence. My quickening steps took me across a threshold and out into the light. Directly ahead the wooden rail of a balcony blocked my path. There was only enough room to leap. Arms extended, legs pumping, I fell through the air, once again grasping for the amulet, and awoke into a brilliant flash of lightning.

Heavy droplets of spring rain were falling all around, mixing with the sweat of my back. Breathing hard I sat up and unconsciously rubbed my hand across my breastbone. The deep blue amulet from the dream was not there. Gathering my blankets and pillow, I ran for the house. During the night a squall line of thunderheads had rolled across the plain of Attica, blanketing the valley in a ponderous darkness. I lay wide awake for a long while, listening to the thunder and the driving rain from the warmth of my stone-walled cocoon. The next thing I heard was a loud thumping, somewhere close by.

Chapter Three

The next morning I awoke to an urgent pounding on the door. The day felt fresh and clear. Standing at my door was a messenger from King Aegeus. I was to accompany him to the palace. The roof of the palace was damaged and leaking.

As I said, the king had relied upon my help in the past. Early on in my career, I was fortunate to have the opportunity to show him a model I had constructed, which demonstrated an innovative way to elevate the large vertical columns for placement in the long load-bearing walls of the new temple. He liked it so much that I was put in charge of that phase of the project. There were many detractors, other artisans mostly, who said that the technique was flawed, and that I was too inexperienced, too young for the job. But I knew I was right, so with a little bit of luck along the way I completed the project as promised, and in time for the solstice festival. I have been the king's architect and engineer ever since.

"Good morning, my friend, come in!" said the aging king, smiling down at me. He was tall and stooped and wore a cloak of blue over his dark embroidered tunic.

"Good morning, my king."

"You won't believe what has happened to my beautiful home," King Aegeus said, beginning the slow tour through the high-walled rooms of the palace.

"How did this happen?" I asked.

"The storm, last night!"

"Was it lightning?"

"Was it ever!" Aegeus replied, emphasizing each word. "You know what the winds are like up here on this bluff, don't you? It woke me even before the rain started. I lay in bed for the longest time, listening to the rumbling overhead, and wondering how Aethra could sleep through it all. Daedalus, you must have heard something of it."

"The storm interrupted my sleep as well," I agreed. "Of course, my home doesn't have this kind of exposure to the elements, or the view."

"Crrrack!" the king said, growing increasingly theatrical. "The rain began slowly enough, but then the lightning started. Thunder boomed. You could hear it coming closer and closer. The rain came down in sheets, pounding on the roof, unrelenting."

I was happy to listen. It always appeared to me that the king enjoyed being able to recount events to a man he respected and was not in competition with. I could only imagine that men in his position get very lonely.

"Is the prince alright?" I asked. "Was he awake during the storm?"

"Last night was intense. Young Theseus ran into the room and dove under the covers. He was sobbing and couldn't stop shaking. I could feel him jump after each clap," the king continued. "Aethra was able to soothe him though. She is marvelous. She held him tight and kept telling him what a great hero he would become someday. For my part, I told him that it was just a bad dream. Theseus shook his head, no. Tears were flying."

"The gods themselves paid a visit last night," I replied.

The king looked at me and smiled. "We lay in the bed, listening to the storm, counting the seconds between the lightning bolts and the crashes of the thunder. The intervals grew shorter and shorter. Then the hair on the back of my neck began to rise…And I threw my body over top of the boy and his mother."

"It was a lightning strike!" I guessed, rewarding his storytelling.

"Daedalus, the sound was like a colossal roar. The walls shook. I could actually hear the wooden beams ripping apart."

"How terrible!"

"Stone and clay tiles came crashing down. We lay there helpless, clinging to each other."

"It's a miracle no one was hurt!"

"The fates were indeed kind. This could all have been so much worse."

"Where is Prince Theseus now?"

"Gone. Aethra and Theseus have left. She's taken him to Troezen to stay with her parents for a while."

"That's probably for the best."

"And just look at this," the king said, making a dramatic gesture with his arm and pointing into the open archway. Sunlight and blue sky blazed in, illuminating a pile of stone and rubble directly underneath a large hole where the peak of the roof belonged. Next to it stood the bed covered with dust and dirt but mostly unscathed. Servants and slaves moved through the debris, carrying away the larger pieces one by one. Others soaked up black water that pooled on the stone and tile floors.

His story complete, the king just stood there, shaking his head in disbelief. I inspected the damage. While we talked and planned the repairs, the sun rose higher, drying everything, especially the remaining roof tiles.

Next I climbed the ladder through a hidden access portal onto the roof, and paused, admiring the incredible view. The entire city was spread out before me, a complex of houses and markets, surrounded by farms, fields and pastures. Far in the distance, the pure blue sea seemed to beckon. Beyond that, I could just make out the roan mountains of the Peloponnesus where Theseus and his mother were bound.

With a sigh I turned my gaze back to the surface of the roof. The damage was significant. In order to reach the ragged opening in the roof, I walked carefully across the exposed beams and tile, discerning from the lay of it how and where to step so that the tile would not break under my weight. Reaching the edge, I peered over. Slaves still moved about in the room below. I tried to collect my thoughts work through the steps to rebuild the roof and then the necessary repairs to the room below. But I kept imagining a young boy playing with a toy bird in the sun.

CHAPTER FOUR

When I was much younger certain women wielded a power to distract me from my work or my studies with a well-timed glance or nod. For a brief intense time one in particular became a flaming passion and the most compelling aspect of my life. In those days I often enjoyed eating at midday in the square under a huge platanos tree. It was there that I first noticed the expressive face and the graceful walk, the long dark hair exquisitely wrapped around the urn that she carried on her shoulder. As she approached, she met my stunned gaze with lively dark eyes and an exquisite half-smile. Everything about that woman captivated me. I knew that I had to speak with her. Something in the way she looked at me told me that she understood and felt exactly the same way.

For the next three days I returned to the well and waited in the hopes of seeing her again. No luck. Finally, on the fourth day she returned. And she noticed me with a smile composed somewhere between a laugh and silence. I rushed at the opportunity and introduced myself. She told me that her name was Philothei, which means "beloved of god," and that she often went to the nearby well for water for her family.

For a long while afterward we met like that in public places, until one beautiful afternoon when we slipped away together for a long walk along the sparkling river, accompanied by a much younger and easily distracted sister. It was there in the flowers by the river bank that Philothei opened her heart to me. We decided to build our home in that very spot together.

Inspired and in love, I planned the project relentlessly. During our walks together I would describe the house and courtyard in vivid detail, all within earshot of the clear, flowing water. And she agreed. I had even saved a few pieces of gold and silver. The land was available. We could begin right away. Her parents would have to approve.

Of course, the little sister could not, would not keep our secret for long. When she told their father, he was furious. His decree: "This could not be." He and her mother had made other arrangements. Without any warning, the love of my life was quietly sent to an aunt's home in another city, far away.

I had already begun the work on the house, and for the longest time I had no idea what had happened. I alternated between laboring on the house and frequenting the places where we might meet. I sent many messages; they were never answered. Time seemed stuck.

Each passing day felt as long as a cycle of the moon. And the moon had cycled many times without any word from her. Then, one day, the house nearly complete, I finally learned from one of her friends that Philothei was married and living in another city. On that day my heart fell into pieces. The beautiful garden I thought that I had found was suddenly empty and barren.

That winter I returned to my work, and found some measure of comfort there. I rededicated my energies into my career and building projects. Eventually, I convinced myself that if I had a contribution to make to my community, it would be through my work. And I began to grow comfortable living alone in the eclectic home, built for two from my own design.

Most of Athens' skilled craftsmen made and sold their pottery, earth and metal-working tools, and other trade goods in the same section of the city. I had a workshop there. The king had given me the task of reconstructing the palace roof, and it was from this neighborhood that I assembled the crew of able and experienced workers to complete it. They had already erected the scaffolding around three sides of the palace. The next day the repairs could begin in earnest. A large table filled the center of the workshop. Along one side it was covered it with an assortment of detailed models of wood and metal. One of the workers was a strong and enthusiastic apprentice named Talos. The youngest of the crew, he loved to linger and play with the models. He was also eager to prove his worth.

"Daedalus, can I be too early tomorrow?" Talos asked me the day before the work began on the palace.

I laughed at his exuberance and replied, "No, Talos. Show up as early as you like. Just be careful."

That night another spring rain fell long and steady, the kind of storm that farmers welcome. Finally it stopped.

Not long afterward, Talos bolted down the remains of yesterday's bread and walked out into the stillness of early morning. There was something in the air that day, a strange metallic smell. On his way to the palace he stopped to fill his water bag from a local well. The water level was much lower than the day before, and that made no sense at all, not after such a hard night's rain. But he did not tarry by the well. He had plans for the day, things to do.

Before sunrise, he had already traversed the winding trail up to the palace. There was the scaffolding, erect and complete. All alone, he raced along the wet planks, not stopping until he reached the top. There, the air seemed cooler and damp. The sun was just pushing its way over the soft eastern hills. But instead of that fresh clear morning smell that follows after a storm, there was that strange metallic smell again. The view was magnificent. He felt proud to be part of the work crew, invigorated and alive. Full of that youthful energy and pride, he returned to the ground and picked up the first load of tools and building tiles. He balanced the extra weight easily in his well-muscled arms and carried the burden up the irregular steps until he reached the top once more. From there it was one long breath and a broad step onto the roof. He moved diagonally across the steep pitch, carefully placing one foot in front of the other on the wet tile. Just a little further and he would reach the place where the roof was ripped apart. There he could rest, put down his load and shake out his arms.

At the surface, the earthquake was a relatively minor one. In the early morning hours, few would be awake even to notice. Talos certainly noticed.

CHAPTER FIVE

"You're him," said the woman in a faraway voice. "The one I've been looking for, waiting to speak with."

It was early, just after dawn. A woman shrouded in black stood outside my workshop. I didn't even notice her at first, not until she started walking toward me, taking a path sure to intersect my own. Her steps were quick and resolute, her anger palpable. I had no choice but to stop and look into the bloodshot eyes that seemed directly responsible for finger that now pressed into my chest. Her dark pupils fixed onto mine. It was a face no longer young and it was aging quickly.

"Talos was my son," she said, tilting her head one way and then another, as if she were boring into me.

"The guilt has been picking my flesh from my bones," I replied, looking from her eyes to the black cloth that draped across her shoulders. "I'm relieved to finally meet you."

"Why was he all alone up on that roof?" she demanded. "My beloved son! Why so early in the morning? He died alone! Why was no one there to help him? He was barely sixteen…and you don't even care! You've done nothing! Nothing!"

The words struck me like a hammer. In those few words she negated all my social skills, pushed past all my defenses. I had no idea what to say, or do.

"Where were you?" she hissed, closing the distance between us.

I just stood there watching her, unwilling or unable to speak. She pounded my chest with her closed fist as she let out a primal wail. That's when the people from the neighborhood began to from their doors and windows.

"Why wouldn't you talk to me yesterday?" She screamed, the other fist banging into my chest.

I took a backward step.

"Or the day before!" she continued, following me relentlessly and raising her fist for the next blow.

"I didn't know who you were, or how to find you," I replied, pushing her hand away.

"Found your voice, have you?" the mother replied, making a fist with the other and shaking it at me.

"Wait," I pleaded. "First, tell me your name."

"Aella," she screamed, her fist morphing back into a pointed finger, "And what are you trying to hide?"

"Nothing," I protested, my forehead starting to sweat. "I'm not hiding anything." But I couldn't look at her and say it. All that I could see, all I could feel was the wall of anger she was directing at me. Part of me wanted to run away, or at least find something to hide behind. People were coming out of their houses to feed on the drama. I had to defend myself, say something.

I blurted out, "I don't really know what happened that day." Trying to be logical I said, "And you're right, I wasn't there. It must have been very early."

"He was doing your work!" she said stridently, hands on her hips, her eyes on fire.

"He was," I agreed. "But he really shouldn't have been out on that wet roof, alone."

"Now you're saying that it was his fault!" she screamed, pointing her finger right at my chest.

"No," I said, wanting to sound calm. My heart pounded away inside my chest. "I'm saying it was an accident."

"He went out onto that roof because of you!" she angrily retorted. "You're the one who told him to do it!" Her hand lashed out toward my face, fingernails extended. Someone in the crowd gasped.

Twisting, I barely avoided the slash of those nails. Then I stepped in and grabbed her by the shoulders. The muscles were thin and bony. She jerked and twisted, trying to free herself, but I held on until she went limp. When I loosened my grip she shrank away from the contact, sank to the dusty ground, and wept.

In the midst of the crowded street I stood and watched the grieving mother. I felt the eyes of the onlookers all around. I knelt down beside her and reached out again, trying to place a comforting hand on her shoulder. Aella shrugged it away. I reached into the pocket of my tunic, pulled out a leather bag and emptied the copper and silver rings onto the ground in front of her. She didn't move or make a sound. Standing up and backing away, I waited and watched for what seemed like an eternity. Finally someone from the crowd stepped up and added a small piece of copper to the pile. Then Aella lifted her head and nodded, thanking him, dry tears streaked across the aging face. Several more followed in turn, and then the crowd began to disperse. Without another word between us, I turned and walked away.

Nothing was quite the same again.

Aella continued to grieve. A stooped figure shrouded in black, she shuffled through the streets. She was always muttering to herself and asking for alms. To those who lent a sympathetic ear she would lament the tragic loss of her son. If her audience showed enough interest, she would quickly launch into a condemnation of the man she believed was responsible for his death, me. For her, everything about it was suspect. She blamed me for not being there. She accused me of intentionally sending the youth into danger and heedlessly causing his death. As she told and retold the story, the scope of her drama grew.

Many listened. One in particular nodded in full agreement, stroking his stubbly beard with one hand and then contributing additional detail. Abraxas could often be found lounging in the nearest shade, rubbing his good hand across his rather large belly. Abraxas and I had a history. For a time he was employed as an unskilled laborer on a building site where I was engineer. That ended when the foreman caught him stealing one of my tools. Now, he had a jagged scar that ran the length of his forearm; an ancient injury of unknown origin, which he claimed kept him from doing anything else with his life.

After hearing her story, Abraxas put his arm around Aella and told her that a great wrong had been done. Over warm tea, he explained to her that on the day before her son's fall, he had seen the master builder out on the roof of the palace, loosening and breaking tiles. At the time he had wondered why anyone would weaken the roof like that, knowing that others would soon be walking across it, in order to make the needed repairs. Not long after that, Aella and her new friend told their tales together to anyone who would listen. And together, the story began to take on a life of its own.

I admit, back then I was not a brave man. I had no interest in seeking out and comforting a grieving mother. Nor was I proficient at telling my own story to rebut hers.

In fact, the drama was wearing me down. If someone did ask me about Talos or the fall, I easily became defensive. These were opportunities to explain, but instead my replies were too often curt and unresponsive. "How could I know what happened on the roof? I wasn't there," I would say. Or, "I build roofs. I don't destroy them." And I spent more and more of my time behind the walls of my workshop or home, waiting it out and hoping.

Aella would not let go. She proclaimed that my new found silence was proof of my guilt. When I ventured out for a meal or a walk, I could sometimes hear people I had never met maligning me in conversation. In due course their story reached all the way to the king's advisors. Among them there was a man with a certain amount of influence who had long coveted my land and my house by the river. He took up Aella's cause. And it was not long before a call for justice for the boy had spread among the nobility.

To the citizens of Athens, my guilt had become a foregone conclusion. Wherever I went, someone was ready to stare or point a finger in my direction. Worse still, my craftsmen no longer showed up for work. And certainly no new work came in. It was as if a strong wind had come out of nowhere, to blow away the habits and routines of my life.

One day a messenger from the king arrived at my door.

Gratefully I accompanied him to the high place above the city. The sun shone down on the trail as we walked, bathing the cliffs in a soft golden light. At last I felt a lightness of spirit. Everything seemed different, the sky more beautiful, the scent of the faraway sea. Even the air felt cleaner filling my lungs.

The king met us at the door. We talked in the anteroom. When I brought up the reconstruction of the roof, he changed the subject. When I tried to ask for his assistance with the ongoing slander by a member of his court, King Aegeus was not interested. He said that unfortunately, his time that day was limited.

"Then, why did you summon me?" I asked.

"Daedalus, I have a new job for you, an assignment."

"You mean, other than finishing the roof reconstruction?"

"Yes, a rather challenging one, something with great potential."

"I don't understand," I said, frustrated to see that even King Aegeus couldn't overcome the will of the mob.

"And I haven't had the chance to tell you what it is," Aegeus snapped back. Pausing to reconnect the king continued, "Daedalus, I have a proposition that I believe will solve all of our problems."

"Tell me then," I replied, curious indeed to learn about our shared difficulties.

"You have so many interests, so many skills. You are the perfect fit for this undertaking."

I just nodded.

"I want to you to journey to the Minoan capital and learn everything there is to know about this new material they have in such copious supply."

"Is it metal?"

"All I can tell you is that it shines like the sun and makes their breastplates invincible to our arrows," King Aegeus replied.

"You want me to leave Athens?"

"Yes, and soon. Several of their merchant ships will be arriving before the new moon. You are to be on one of them when they leave."

"You've made these arrangements."

"No, they are not expecting you. If you went as my ambassador, nothing would come of it. Their brutish king would see you as a spy. His name is Minos. You wouldn't be allowed access to anything of any real value. For this assignment to work you cannot be seen as my agent. So, be a merchant. Be an artisan. However you accomplish it, is up to you. "

"Why me? Why now?"

"Their galleys are already en route; because of your knowledge of alchemy, because of all your skills, and most of all, because your country needs you! Daedalus, in this entire city, you are the only one I can trust to complete this complex mission. If you can learn the secrets of this new metal, and return to teach them to us, then I promise you, you will become one of Athens' greatest heroes."

"Thank you for the compliments, but I would prefer to have my life back."

"You may not realize this, but I consider you a true friend. I know of your troubles and sympathize. As your king, I understand that you have enjoyed an illustrious career as an architect and inventor. Daedalus, you deserve more than just to be remembered for the lethal fall of a careless youth."

"I certainly agree with that."

"I'm offering you a chance to redeem yourself," said the king.

"But I've done nothing wrong!"

"I know that," said the king, his tone softening. "That is why I want to compensate you as well."

"What kind of compensation?" I asked skeptically.

"Come with me, Daedalus, I want to show you something."

He led me from the anteroom, past a warrior guard and into his private study. Shutting the door behind us, the king opened the latch of a stout wooden box and lifted the lid. It was full of small disks of tarnished metal. "One quarter talent of silver," he said, "from the mines at Laurium."

I had never seen so much wealth in one place. Smiling, King Aegeus picked one off the top and handed it to me. I rubbed it between my fingers and felt a rough design stamped on its face. Looking closely, I saw a winged owl with bulging eyes.

"Fine workmanship, don't you agree?" the king continued. "I want you to have that one, Daedalus, to compensate for the losses you are facing…and to speed you on your way to Knossos. Upon your return with the knowledge I seek, a quarter talent of Laudian silver, much like this one, will be yours. I give you my word."

CHAPTER SIX

As I walked home through the remains of the sun-filled day, the weight of the silver disk weighed down the pocket of my tunic.

"How many money changers are there in this town?" I muttered, frustrated with my whole situation. "And now when I need one, there are none to be found."

Out of nowhere, a stone struck me squarely on the shoulder. The impact rocked my bones with a hard jolt. I lurched forward, twisting. A second one whooshed past my ear, just wide of its target. Turning quickly I saw two young men running towards me, more stones in their hands. A third was bent over, re-arming, and an angry crowd surged behind them egging them on, yelling and cursing.

I ran. At the first corner I turned and dashed down a cobblestone street, then another. Then another corner and another, until the jeers and shouting grew faint. Yesterday I would never have believed that I could still run like that. Tears welling up in my eyes, I quickly slowed and bent over at the waist, hands on my thighs, chest heaving. A welt was rising on my back. The hamstring of my right leg, unused to such exertion, refused to take any weight. My breath returning, I slowly hobbled toward the river and home, cursing my luck, the crowd, and my life.

"Damn you!" I cried out to no one at all. "I've spent a lifetime building this city. Now you throw pieces of it at me."

Exhausted, I limped through the courtyard gate. All I wanted was to be alone, completely and desperately alone. Throwing open the sturdy entryway door, I stepped inside and set the wooden brace across the jamb. An unfinished mural decorated the wall opposite the door, the beginnings of a bright seascape commissioned long ago. I threw myself onto the soft pallet bed that sat across from the hearth's cold ashes and felt my aching body sink into the stillness.

Sometime during the night I awoke and rekindled the fire.

"Why? How did this happen?" I asked no one. "How could my entire life have gone so wrong, so quickly? Aaaaah," I moaned, the hamstring refusing to take any weight. "Those weren't people today. They were animals, a mob! Those fools could have killed me!" I wrapped myself tighter into the soft wool of the blanket, staring into the growing flames of the fire. "I don't deserve this!" I growled. "It isn't fair at all!" On it went, while I tossed and turned in the firelight. Then I remembered the silver coin in my tunic.

That night a dream came, but not in the usual way. Not the kind that rises up out of one's own unconscious. It was as if this one came upon me from the outside, stealing upon me in my slumber and taking me by surprise. There was a sense of transport, of being taken away so swiftly and with such acceleration that my arms and legs, even my neck and head were immobilized. But before I could even react, there was a sound. Soothing and calm, a mellifluous voice called out to me from somewhere very close, explaining just how peaceful and safe the situation was. As if carried by a blade stabbed directly into my heart, the voice became all I knew. I soon gave in to its persuasion. Simultaneously, I understood that I was not alone. I had a companion, and we were steadily moving together across a great distance.

The song continued. Some remote part of me was tempted to squirm free and twist my head just enough to see who or what had the ability to communicate in such pure, clear tones. But I couldn't move, not at all, not without first waking up. The dream was far too pleasing for that. So I gave my will over to the voice. Yet there were still sensations of awareness in my hands, fingers, arms, and legs. I could feel the insides of my skin like never before. And I assured my conscious mind that as soon as we began to arrive somewhere, I would quickly turn and see whatever it was that held me fast.

When the voice finally faded, I tried to move an arm, a hand, even a finger, but there was no response. There was stillness all around. It was quiet and serene. I could feel it. But I could not open my eyes. So I waited in the solitude, emotions neutral and my mind alert. I could imagine myself inside a shadowy, warm place, with something like firelight flickering on craggy walls. It felt humid, even moist, and far too warm for a cave. There were smells of sage and garlic, reminding me of home.

They were no restraints, yet I remained completely immobile. Listening into the stillness, I realized that I was not alone. There were movements around me, like shadows moving into the space and filling it. I could sense other eyes looking at me and I wanted to speak, to make a sound, some kind of greeting. But my lips and tongue and breath would not move in that way.

But before I could feel any frustration, the voice returned, explaining in those same tranquil tones that there was no need for words. To reinforce the point, the image of an amber slab of polished stone appeared in my mind, growing larger, as if coming closer. A message began to appear upon the tablet's face, formed from words and letters moving as if they were alive and written in a language I did not recognize. Then the voice explained that the writing told of a promise, a pledge intended only for me; that I would one day have the opportunity to receive a great and wondrous gift. It had to potential to set me apart from all other men.

"What will it be?" my mind raced. "How will I know it? When?"

"Too many questions," replied the voice in patient, understanding tones. "Calm yourself. If the gift is great, then why isn't that enough?"

"Enough of what?" I persisted.

"For you to agree."

"To do what?"

"Only to be open and willing to receive it," said the soothing voice without a hint of haste. "It is quite simple. Once you give your word, then the pledge becomes a covenant. It will become part of you, even though your conscious memory of all this will quickly fade once you return to your home. When it is time, you will understand. But know this, if any of this is to be, then it must be your choice. No one is forcing you. If you do not agree, then you will simply return to everything that you have grown accustomed to, without any appetite or interest in being or becoming anything more."

"How can I agree to anything when I am unable to speak, unable to move?"

"The same way you ask these questions," the mellifluous voice replied. "Make a choice. Make it soon."

"Tell me, how will I recognize this gift? How will I know when the time comes?"

"Why do you assume that you are capable of understanding the answer?" replied the voice. "It is time for choosing."

"Alright," I said, still wanting some kind of guarantee.

"I can tell you that this gift cannot appear until you are ready. That much I can promise you. There will be signs, omens along the way. It is up to you, it is your responsibility to notice them. And when the gift presents itself, you cannot be too busy or too fearful, or offer some other excuse."

My restless mind still perseverated.

"Do you have enough trust in yourself to give your word, without first having what you think are all the answers?"

In my heart I wanted very much to agree. It was a deep attraction, a longing for the ineffable offering. Then I looked once more into the incomprehensible jumble on the face of the tablet. The meaningless designs transformed into letters that I recognized. They formed words that were clear and simple and meaningful, commemorating our agreement, where before there had only been confusion.

Focusing on the now filled slab, I tried to make a conscious memory of the words, reading and rereading them, as they faded into the half-light. The shadows that had once surrounded me receded into the warm stillness; just as my body once more accelerated away, head and neck immobile, held in place by the familiar force. The voice returned, coming out of the depths of the stillness, deep and rich, and with soothing words, calming and congratulating me for what I had accomplished. Now, more than ever, I wanted to turn and see my companion, to learn the source of the sounds and discover how my body could be held so completely still.

I willed myself to twist around and look. But before the joints of my head and neck could engage, I was back at home, lying in the tangle of my blankets. The voice was gone and with it, the sublime blend of power and tenderness that had held me so secure. My body lay motionless, the muscles and bones still holding onto the memory of immobility. My eyes felt sealed shut, but cool air and my own bedding's familiar texture reassured me. There was no hurry to open them—no hurry to move again. I understood somehow that once I did, the memories of the dream and the covenant would begin to fade. Until then, it was all clear and vivid, and unlike anything I had ever experienced before. I lay back and listened for the sounds of the river, remembering the flow and sensations of the dream. I thought about being a secret agent for King Aegeus and for the first time thought that it might actually be possible. There would be no more sleep that night.

CHAPTER SEVEN

During the time period of this story, there were many islands to the south and east filled with other people, other monarchs. Far away on Krete, the largest and most populated of these islands, one of the kings sat sprawled across the cushions of his high-backed chair. More wakeful than asleep, the deep set lines and creases of his expressive face memorialized many years in office. Large hanging oil lamps illuminated the richly imperious and elegant space. Behind him, majestic griffins surveyed the room from a huge wall mural, painted in deep reds, blues and yellows—the colors of the island.

The evening's festivities over and complete, the king still wore the white ceremonial robe, edged with glittering gold thread. The garment's milky color dramatically offset the deep brown hue of his skin. Only hours before he had presided over yet another ceremony, a very long one.

"What did I even say? Something about planting olive trees in rows and cultivating them like grape vines," the king remembered, chuckling to himself. "Now, grapes," he said aloud, looking towards a dozing servant. "That is a subject more to my liking."

After all the speeches, the toasting, the countless morsels of olives and flatbread, more awards and more toasting, sleep still eluded him. He rose from his cushioned chair to cross into the adjoining courtyard and pace the length of the patterned rug. Alone, even at this late hour, he carried the bearing and dignity of his office. It was not long before the servant awoke.

"Does the king desire something?"

"Yes, my red cloak."

Outside, the light of the full moon was so bright that it cast shadows on the empty streets of Knossos. The palace was a complex of structures designed to house a community of people. A shadow of its former self, many floors within the multi-storied complex of living spaces had collapsed. Walls had caved in, crushing people, artwork, and other treasures indiscriminately. Walls and apartments can be rebuilt and restored, but all the rest was lost. More than two cycles of the sun had now passed since the last major earthquake, yet so much work remained. The lack of progress was baffling. Many still lived in tents on the edges of the city and made do with lifestyles that had few of the amenities of life before the quake.

Even the roof of the palace was damaged, possibly beyond repair. The dome and oculus of his megaron, an architectural marvel of both beauty and purpose, had fallen and broken apart. It was an elegant, domed portal bringing light and energy into the huge space. There was majesty and magic in the room when the moonlight streamed in and the dancers whirled. These qualities made it the perfect place for feasts and celebrations, ceremonies and dances. The quake had transformed it into a pile of rubble. Minos feared it would never be the same again. There was so much more work to be done. How to know where to start?

"Where is the progress?" he shouted at the moon, now low on the horizon.

His emotions drained and spent, the king returned to the colorful gardens of the courtyard and made his way back to the huge, intricately carved chair with the gold inlay. He slumped into the cushions. Once, this seat of Minoan power had occupied an imposing presence inside the megaron, something unique among all the monarchs of the Great Green. There, Minos had held court, bestowed his blessings, and dispensed his justice. Now, with a jagged rent in the ceiling, the power of his office was leaking away. These days he had to make do with conducting his councils outdoors under wicker canopies with nature as witness. His throne, the seat of power, was just a rather large ornate chair inside an elegant courtyard. And that was so very much like the courtyards of all the other royalty, on all the other islands.

"When did it become impossible to build a domed roof with a hole in the middle?" Minos asked no one in particular. In the nearby courtyard, his sleeping servant awoke for the second time that night.

"My accursed engineers are idiots or fools!" the king complained. "Their grandfathers knew how to build a dome!"

The stoop-shouldered servant approached the throne room and waited just inside the threshold.

Minos looked up and said, "Someone somewhere must have the answer."

CHAPTER EIGHT

Still limping I walked outside into what was left of the dark night. The moon was already down, but I easily remembered the soothing voice. It made me sigh to think about it. I had found something inside the dream that was good, a transcendent spark for carrying forward into the day and beyond. Otherwise it might have been easy to fall back into the drama of yesterday's encounter with the mob. Recoiling at the memory, I pushed on through the chill of early morning darkness. "To hell with the mob, I'm a free Athenian man," I said. "I will go when and where I please." Then with a wistful smile, continued, "And where exactly will that be?"

Certainly I had to sail away from Athens. But I was only beginning to understand all that it would entail. I had been on small boats before, but never beyond the sight of land. First, I would walk by the shore, smell the air and observe the ships. Then, I would talk with the people who used them for their livelihood.

I left the quiet outskirts of the city for the well-worn road to the harbor. It was a long way, but there was still time to reach the seashore while the city slept. It felt good to be out in the open air, and better to feel a sense of purpose once more.

Surely there would be someone willing to talk about seaworthy ships heading for Krete, their cargoes and their crews.

These thoughts and more filling my head, I came to the top of a low sandy ridge and there it was, spread out before me. The merchant ships sat together, half in and half out of the still, dark water. On the opposite side of the harbor, five of King Aegeus' war galleys floated on the water, tied to a large wooden pier. Many smaller fishing boats and rowboats were scattered about in groups, pulled up onto the sand. All along the shore smoldering fires dotted the beach. They were surrounded by clusters of sleeping mariners and piles of cargo, netting, and ropes. I sat down on the ledge of a nearby rock, wide awake and planning my next step.

My swollen shoulder beginning to throb again, I tried to visualize myself on a ship with a strong and reliable sail, traveling from one island to the next under a brilliant blue sky. In my hand was a stout bag with two of my favorite inventions, the plumb line and the saw. I imagined the ship's captain or someone on the crew, massively muscled and watching me, rubbing his chin and coming to the obvious conclusion: that a man of wealth and means was departing Athens for a very long time, and taking all of his valuables with him. The shoulder throbbed even more. That's when I knew that I couldn't leave the island without some sort of disguise.

Alone and cold, I let out a soft moan and buried my face in my hands. All the fatigue that had gripped me after the run-in with the mob came rushing back. I just sat there unable to move, continuing a weary vigil, and certain that I was quite alone. My eyes no longer saw the ships on the grey green water. They were turned inward again, seeing only darkness and gloom.

All around the daybreak was quiet and still, except for my occasional sobs. I was completely unaware of the young boy watching from the shadows, behind a nearby cypress tree. He was studying his prey and waiting, like a condor circling in the sky. He couldn't possibly have seen my eyes or even my face. But he would have surmised that I didn't smell drunk and had no apparent wounds. With some luck I might even be good for a cooper ring or two.

It must have taken some courage for him to begin moving in, step by step, every sense alert, poised and ready to flee at the first sign of danger. He was so much smaller then. The young boy stealthily approached me, stopping out of arms' reach. There he stood, one thin arm extended out, palm upward. More than once he shuffled his feet to make some noise, but I did not stir. Then the boy sniffled a little. With a jolt, I lifted an arm up to cover my head and ward off a blow. The boy jumped. But he resisted the urge to flee. Instead he stepped forward again, extending his open palm a little more, arm outstretched.

Sheepishly, I lowered my arm and smiled at the intruder, looking him up and down in the dim light. I could see the bare feet, the skinny arms and legs covered with red sores and bites.

Wanting to sound as relaxed as possible, I looked at the sad face and asked, "Who are you? What are you doing out here in the cold, early morning hours?"

The boy shrugged. With a beseeching look he returned my gaze, pushing his open hand forward a little more and saying nothing. Just one moon cycle ago, I would have easily overlooked his dirty young face. There were scores of unkempt urchins roaming the countryside and streets of Athens, most of them with huge dark eyes and disheveled black hair, much like this one. But that morning I still had the bruises from my encounter with the mob. And there was something engaging about the boy's face, something that made him stand out. My heart swelled inside my chest. Today, instead of being too busy, I felt compelled to start a conversation with the skinny, affectless boy who had appeared out of nowhere.

CHAPTER NINE

I guessed that he was about seven or eight. He probably didn't even know his own age. By the look of him, no one had been around to keep track of birthdays for a long time. Still, he hadn't said a word. His dark eyes were focused on the ground, avoiding my gaze. I smiled again and softly asked, "When did you last eat?"

Again he shrugged. His hand stayed outstretched.

So, I persisted. "Where's your home? Your mother? Your father?"

Another shrug in reply.

"Who takes care of you?"

Finally he raised his head and replied, "Please." When he turned his head away, I realized what it was that seemed so endearing. In profile, his nose had a prominent bridge, giving it the appearance of being curved or slightly bent. It was just enough to resemble the beak of a hawk and looked so incongruous on that small face. I motioned for the boy to come closer, but he warily kept his distance, watching and waiting. I pulled out the leather pouch from the inside pocket of my old tunic and opened it, filling my own palm with flattened rings of copper and silver. I wrapped my fingers around the coins, enjoying the small smile that crept across his dirt-smeared face. Slowly, I reached out and held my closed hand slightly above the boy's palm and released the coins in a steady rush. He quickly cupped both hands and deftly caught each one.

"Nice catch," I said.

The praise and the coins now his, that same hook-nosed, dirt-smeared face broke into a smile. Then he turned and took off running, just as fast as his legs would carry him.

"Wait!" I called out after him. "What's your name?"

The fleeing boy did not look back.

CHAPTER TEN

The boy gone, I proceeded to walk toward the ships. There I saw a grizzled boatman, his skin the color and texture of a used water bag. He leaned against a rock bench, snoring peacefully in the morning sunlight. Hands folded across his middle, he had the arms and shoulders of a titan. The contrast between us was remarkable. Only one of my shoulders was enlarged, and that, from the swelling of large bruise. I could barely raise the arm. Clearing my throat, I sat down and woke the old salt to ask if he could recommend someone to take a curious city dweller on a tour of the harbor. Looking around and stretching, he replied with great candor that there were many fine rowers who could ferry trade goods and passengers from the shore out to waiting boats and back again for a price.

"But," he continued with a glint in his eye. "If you're looking for someone who can put more than three words together to form a sentence, pull a boat through water, and explain the intricacies of seafaring and trade—all at the same time—then I'm you're man."

Stepping spryly, he easily dragged a nearby boat off the sand and into the shallow water. I limped alongside.

"Just tell me everything then," I said, climbing in while he steadied the craft, "I want to know all about the ships and the crews, where they are going and how they do all that they do."

The calm blue water was dotted with skiffs, barques, and galleys of all shapes, sizes, and states of repair. The old man had something to say about each of them, and matched his prose to the rhythm of the creaking oarlocks. Gulls circling overhead added a chorus. He seemed to enjoy having a willing audience, and I listened contentedly, musing about the past and dreaming about the future.

His eyes on the land, the boatman could not see the line of large galleys coming into view just beyond the headlands, their sails bellying in the breeze.

"There will always be a need for oarsmen," I said, thinking out loud, "but the power of the wind is the way of the future."

"Of course, there will always be rowers!" declared the old boatman. "It's the way of the sea. Even the biggest galley needs rowers to steer by."

I just smiled, my mind still wandering. In the light of this new day, King Aegeus' challenge actually seemed possible. Sitting in the small oarboat with this ancient mariner and with everything in Athens going from bad to worse, I was beginning to understand the allure of the open sea. Somewhere beyond the horizon, distant lands were calling with promises of opportunity and adventure. It was an irresistible attraction, and I found myself willing to believe that I was ready to leave Athens behind.

"Have you ever rowed on a large galley?" I asked, hoping to kick off another story.

"No, thank you! I'll not set foot on one."

Frowning at his response, I asked the obvious, "Why is that?"

"Can't swim," said the boatman without a moment's hesitation. "I've always figured that if I can't see the bottom from where I'm seated, then I'm on the wrong boat. I'm happy right here on this patch of shoreline."

I quickly changed the subject. "What about those three?" I asked, pointing towards the sea.

Shipping his oars the boatman turned and looked.

"See the broad beam," he replied. "Those ships are hauling cargo. They're merchant ships, and from the size and look of them, Minoan. Once they land this little harbor will become a much busier place with as much work as this old oarsman can handle," he said with a wink.

"What do you mean?" I asked.

"It's the beginning of their trading season," he replied. "All winter those ships were refitted in safe harbor at Kalliste or Krete. The barnacles were scraped and the crews rested. The ships are well-laden now with the best the Minoans have to offer. Last year one of their merchants even showed us a disk of pliable metal. He shaped it into a small bowl with a hammer and bare fingers. It was almost effortless. Everyone wanted to touch it."

"What was the metal called?"

"I don't exactly remember."

"Do you know if anyone purchased it?"

"It wasn't for sale, at any price. And there were many who asked. I do remember that much."

"Could it have been orichalcum?" I asked, hopefully.

"The name?" he asked. "I don't recall that he gave it a name. But that one's a mouthful."

"Was it copper?"

"No. Everyone knows copper! This was something very different," the boatman sharply replied. "Give it a rest would you? I've told you everything I know."

"It's just that one day I hope to study this metal myself."

"I'm sure you will," replied the oarsman, turning the boat to offer us both a view of the approaching galleys. "Maybe you should ask them about it." While we watched, the ships came in closer, looming large. "In no time at all, those three will be lined up on shore and the beach arrayed with trade goods. Many from the city will turn out to meet them. It will all make for a fine show."

The immense ships cut through the water. I couldn't take my eyes away. I counted fifteen oars pulling as one along the closest side of the first vessel. It was close enough to make out a symbol painted on the sail. They beckoned and inspired, offering a passage toward the solutions to all my difficulties.

"In this little skiff, we'll give them a wide berth," the boatman said, squinting in the direction of the shore.

"You're the boss."

"Do you see the flying pelican painted into the fabric of the first sail?"

"So that's what I'm seeing."

"For sure they're Minoan. That's the *Pelican,* a fine ship and crew; not a soft-bellied puker among them. They've visited our harbor a time or two."

"What's their story?" I asked.

"The captain is named Nikolaos. Calls his ship the *Pelican* because of the ways she can glide over the water. The way he tells it, he has sailed that ship from Samaria to the boot of Italia, to Carthage and beyond, all the way to the edge of the earth."

"Why would anyone want to travel beyond the Great Green?"

"Why indeed."

"Well, I want to meet that man," I declared. "Does Captain Nikolaos take passengers?"

"For the right price. He'll carry merchants and travelers. I've watched more than a few leave for distant Krete. Don't recall seeing any return though."

"What's that supposed to mean?"

"I'm not sure what it means," replied the boatman. "Maybe you're the one to figure it out."

While we completed our circuit of the harbor, the galleys closed the distance to the beach. I paid the boatman, said farewell, and found a good vantage point from which to watch their approach. A small cluster of Athenian warriors stood nearby. All were armed with some variety of shield and weapon. Some had clubs, others spears. Most wore breastplates of leather or padded linen.

I watched as a bare-chested man with a long pole stood at the very front of the closest ship, scanning the sea bottom. Occasionally he would call out to someone standing in the rear. Then in precise accord all the oars along one side lifted out of the water, their blades glistening in the sun. The tiller man deftly brought the ship about one hundred and eighty degrees. I watched two seamen scramble to ship the large oar. Then stern leading, all oars pushing, the large ship beached itself in a gritty roar, scrapping across the sand and stones of the waterline. Fascinated, I stayed and watched the next two Minoan vessels complete the same maneuver, one on each side of the lead ship. Together, they took up a sizable portion of shoreline.

Brown skinned crewmen scrambled over the sides, filling the air with greetings and shouts. Already a crowd was assembling and I quickly joined them. A few mariners were already there to greet us, setting up a perimeter around the beached ships. I heard the creaking sounds of wooden holds being opened. Oarsmen shipped and dried their blades and then stowed them away.

A man wearing a saffron colored robe climbed down from the deck and began inspecting the *Pelican*'s hull. Encircling his ample waist was a finely tooled belt of silver and leather with the curved scabbard of a large knife protruding into plain view. Two others clad in similar robes joined him on the shore, and they soon entered into a robust conversation.

"Every time we enter this port I am reminded that it is better to trade with one another than fight," said the stocky leader. "We cannot grow through war. Commerce is the key. We must keep that in mind, especially in dealing with the Athenians."

The other captains nodded their agreement.

"Offload the lumber and stack it to form a perimeter," said the first man. "Once it's gone, the ships will be easy to refloat."

"How long can we expect to stay?"

"Our welcome usually sours in three days. Let's be out in two."

"What about defenses?"

"Breast plates and long knives for the sentries," he responded. "Archers will back them up; one on each bow and another on the stern. Tell them to keep their quivers in plain sight."

CHAPTER ELEVEN

A warren of makeshift stalls and carts began to form at a respectful distance from the galleys, selling all manner of food, clothing, and trinkets. By evening, the beach swelled with entertainers and onlookers, buyers and sellers. Vendors arrayed their jewelry and amulets on small blankets spread across the sand. Astrologers and soothsayers hawked their talents. Wine merchants appeared. Women with painted faces stood along the edges of the activity, casting for a longing look.

I stayed for hours that evening, eating and drinking a little more than my fill, watching and listening. Heady with wine, I bargained with an astrologer over the price of a glimpse into my future, and walked away without purchasing. Instead I resolved to create a new life for myself on Krete or someplace better. That's when I noticed the young boy from the day before, the one with the hooked nose. He was sitting on his haunches in the sand by a merchant's blanket, studying an assortment of knives. One in particular had his eye. The handle was carved from the antler of a deer, the blade made from sharpened bone.

"A good choice," the merchant said, nodding approvingly.

Keeping a close eye on the transaction, I walked to a nearby stall where another vendor was cooking marinated pieces of lamb on long skewers. The smell was tantalizing and I bought two. Wasting no time, I returned to the blanket on the sand where the negotiation was taking place.

"Where does a poor little beggar like you get the money for a fine knife like that one?" asked the merchant sympathetically.

"None of your concern," replied the boy, rubbing his finger along the edge.

"We can talk about reducing the price…" the knife seller paused with a greasy smile. I didn't like his tone at all. "If you know what I mean," he continued. So I moved over toward the young boy.

Right away the boy dropped the blade back onto the blanket. "Such a fine knife would only be asking for trouble. I'll come back when I'm big."

Jumping up to leave, he turned and bumped right into me. Unintentionally, I blocked his retreat. Intentionally, I held out the flavorful meal.

"So we meet again," I said in a friendly voice. "I thought you might like something to eat."

I handed him the skewer.

While the young boy eagerly reached out and took it, I placed my free hand on his back and steered him down the beach.

"Let's walk over to the big ships while we eat these, OK?"

"All right," said the boy, smacking his lips as he devoured the morsels. We walked together toward the Minoan galleys.

"What's your name, son?" I asked.

"Icarus," he replied without hesitation, wiping his hand across his ragged shirt before presenting it to me. "My name is Icarus."

"Do you live around here, Icarus?"

"Sometimes…"

"I see," I replied thoughtfully. "Icarus, my name is Daedalus. I build and invent useful things. Would you like another skewer?"

"Sure!" replied the boy with enthusiasm, and we headed right back toward the food vendor's stall.

"You woke me from my stupor the other day," I continued. "You helped me when I needed it. That's worth something to me."

"You already gave me the copper coins," replied Icarus.

"Yes, I did. And those are yours to keep. I hope you still have some of them."

"Yes, thank you, Sir."

"You don't have to call me Sir," I replied, purchasing two more skewers. "Come on. Let's go back to the boats. I want to ask you something.

It's important."

As we walked I explained to the boy about my desire to travel on one of the ships to a distant island called Krete. I would be leaving very soon. My plan was to travel disguised as a blind man. That way, most everyone on the ship would leave me alone and not suspect that I had any valuables. I planned to hide in plain sight, as a way to keep myself safe from brigands, thieves, and other bad men.

Icarus nodded in agreement.

"Tomorrow I will need a guide," I continued. "Once I'm in disguise I'll need someone to lead me down to the ships and assist in the search for the right person for the negotiation."

"That's all you want?"

"Yes, and I'll pay you."

"How much?"

"There is one more thing," I paused, thinking it over. "If you promise to call me uncle, I'll pay you a silver ring when I'm safely off the beach."

"You've got a deal, Uncle."

"That's great," I said and we shook hands. "So tell me a little something about yourself, Icarus. What do you like to do?"

"I like to fish," Icarus replied, looking around and stifling a yawn.

"That's interesting," I said, trying to keep the conversation going. "Fishing is something that I always wanted to learn about. Maybe someday you can show me how it's done."

Icarus was becoming restless and I had already run out of questions. We decided to meet at noon the next day by the cypress tree at the harbor overlook. I said goodbye, wondering if I would ever see him again.

CHAPTER TWELVE

When I arrived the next day the sun was already high overhead, filling the air with heat. To my relief Icarus was already there, throwing rocks at a target only he could see. In my hand I carried a stained and dirty cloth, my attempt at a blindfold. With the other I waved to the boy and called out, "Hello." He walked right over to meet me and with an earnest look, pointed toward a ridge on the far side of the port. "That's the place you were asking me about," he said.

"What place?" I asked.

"My home," he answered softly. A craggy promontory, neither wide nor high, separated the Athenian harbor from the small fishing community where Icarus was born. We walked together past the bustling docks. No one seemed to recognize me. Soon it was clear that we blended in nicely. Icarus led the way to a well-worn path that traversed up the barren incline and meandered across the crest. On the far side the sea was full of tiny isles and reefs until the rocks gave way to a calm stretch of deeper water and a sandy cove for fishermen to safely land their boats.

High above the water, one- and two-room white and graying hovels dotted the hillside. The original inhabitants had dug into the rocky slope to build their homes with the lowest room carved directly out of the rock. Subsequent owners might cut deeper into it, creating capacious, cool living spaces for the hot summers. For the ambitious an additional room of mortar and stone was sometimes stacked on top. The flat roof served as either an extra room in good weather, or a trap for rain water in bad.

We walked together along the common quay of the village. "Is there something in particular you want to show me?" I asked.

"That's the one," Icarus said, pointing at a single-level hut with crumbling outer walls, fading into gray. He took off toward it.

"Is anyone living there?" I called out, rushing to catch up.

"Not now," Icarus said and pushed on the door. Cockroaches scurried from the light as he stepped inside and scanned the room. "It wasn't always this way," he said tearfully. For a long time he stared at the shelves carved out of the rock next to the fireplace. He told me how his mother's ceramic pottery and herbs had once filled the space. Now there was a fetid smell, the room damp and peeling. Rat pellets littered the floor.

Placing one hand on his shoulder, I pushed him gently back outside into the warmth and light. Sobbing, he followed me out of town and back up the ridge trail. At the highest point, the trail curved around a large striated rock with a fine view of the Minoan galleys. The other side of the rock offered some shade and an ideal spot for conversation and remembering.

"You can tell me about this place, if you want," I said.

In truth, Icarus didn't have many memories of his own father. Mostly he remembered what his mother had said about him. That he was handsome and strong, and a fine fisherman who knew exactly which birds would lead him and his boat to the best fishing grounds. He always brought home fresh fish, octopus, or crab for their dinner, until the chilly autumn day with the sudden storm. That night, his mother wept and moaned on the sleeping pallet. Icarus remembered going alone to forage for wood in the rain, to keep their hearth fire burning. And he remembered praying to the sea god for his father's safe return just the way he and his mother had done many times before.

"But he never came back," Icarus concluded.

"I'm sorry about your father," I said. "How long did you and your mother live there together?"

"That's all right," he said. "Just us?"

"Yes."

"I don't remember exactly; maybe two or three sun cycles."

"What was it like, just you and your mother?"

"It was fun. We did everything together. We had everything we needed too, especially in the summers. In winter, it was wet and cold, and sometimes we ran out of wood. But we always found more."

"Who taught you to fish?"

"She did. With this line and barb," he said, reaching into his tunic and proudly pulling out the first of his keepsakes.

"Can I see it?"

"It was my Da's," Icarus said with no small amount of pride. "But she was the one that taught me where the fish would come to feed, how to catch an octopus, and how to turn the stones for crabs."

"What else did you eat?"

"Greens and roots. Sometimes seaweed. She would mix them all together with olive oil and lemon. Even when there wasn't a lot of it, we always had food," the boy said proudly. "She kept a large pot of dried beans in the cellar. In the spring we planted them. Life was very good then."

"Your mother sounds like a fine person. Your father, too," I said. "I'm so sorry they're gone. What happened to her?"

Icarus looked away and said nothing. I knelt down to eye level and waited.

"They took her away."

"Who?"

"Bad men," he said, beginning to sob again.

"Who? Did you know them?"

"Three men! I don't know who. Scary men. They came at night. I remember they had clubs and knives, dirty beards. Their chests bore leather patches. One of them in particular had wild eyes," he recounted, pausing. After a moment, he repeated, "They were very bad men," choking on the words.

"Yes, they were," I agreed.

"It was dark. We were asleep on the pallet," Icarus said, tearfully.

"I'm so sorry she's gone," I said, turning enough to place an arm around the boy's thin shoulders.

No one said anything for a long while. Only after Icarus composed himself did we walk along the trail until the gathering on the beach came into view. I pointed to the galleys and shared a little of my own story. I repeated my intention to travel to a distant island called Krete, and my plan to become a builder for their king.

"Hope is a very important thing to hold onto," I began. "For many reasons it is time for me to leave Athens. I do have to leave. But I have great hopes for the future. Hope may just be the key, for both of us," I continued. "Icarus, will you please think about something? There's room enough for both of us on that ship, if you choose to come along. You can come too and be a blind man's guide. I can use your help. It's up to you."

The dirty, tear stained face looked up but said nothing.

I stood up and placed my hands on his shoulders. I said, "It's a lot to think about. But if you do decide to come on this adventure, I promise to do everything I can to keep you safe." Pausing to look into the dark eyes, I continued, "You don't have to give me an answer right away, but those ships are leaving soon. When they do, I'll be gone. Let's go back down there together and see what we can learn about this voyage."

CHAPTER THIRTEEN

Leaving the fishing village behind us, Icarus and I returned to the docks. We paused to fashion the stained sash into a blindfold and place it over my head. Then Icarus led me carefully through the crowd and down to the water. Several times people stopped us and asked if we needed help. Each time I turned in the direction of the voice and explained that we were interested in traveling to the island of Krete. Each time, I asked for help finding Captain Nikolaos of the *Pelican*.

It was not long before we found a talkative know-it-all who was eager to explain in considerable detail how much he had always wanted to travel to Kalliste. We talked for a while and then followed him to the line of ships where he introduced us to a young sentinel named Lucas. In the prolonged silence that followed I guessed that a muscular unmoving mariner was sizing Icarus and me up. Uncertain and growing anxious, I cleared my throat and asked if anything was wrong. "Nothing's wrong Uncle," Icarus replied. "We just have the same nose, the sailor and I."

"Handsome lad you're traveling with," said the heavily accented voice. Even behind the blindfold I easily imagined a smiling young face, winking to the boy and showing off his profile. Then Lucas said, "See over there? The man in the yellow tunic, pacing back and forth? He's the captain, the man your uncle wants to see. Understand?"

"Yes sir," Icarus answered, guiding me away from the sentinel with the aquiline nose, the crook of my arm in his hand.

Following his next prompt I spoke right up and said, "Hello to you, sir. Are you the captain of this ship?"

"Today, I am Nikolaos the trader, a friend to all," he replied, his manner instantly engaging. "When we depart this place tomorrow or the next day, then will I become the captain of this fine ship. He can be an entirely different fellow, depending upon the circumstances and demands of the job."

Even behind the blindfold I could feel his presence, his gaze, like he was leaning into the conversation.

"Right now, I am the visitor—a guest—in your country, and a very satisfied one at that," he said. "How can I help you?"

"Welcome to Athens, trader Nikolaos," I began, "and hello. My name is Daedalus. I am a traveler, seeking a cure for my blindness."

"How can Nikolaos be of service to you, Daedalus?" he replied, with what sounded like a smile. "If it's travel you seek, the *Pelican* is a fine ship. She has a fine, strong sail and a good crew. Together we can cover great distances on the wind, just like the soaring bird she is named for. Our oarsmen are the finest, anywhere. We have crossed the Great Green many times, this ship and I."

Icarus tugged insistently on my arm.

"Uncle, wait!" he said sharply.

I turned towards Icarus, and then smiling an apologetic smile, returned my speech to where I remembered Nikolaos to be.

"Excuse me, Captain," I said. "I must have a word with my guide." Together we turned and walked away out of earshot. I bent down so that Icarus could whisper into my ear.

"I want to come too," he said, in earnest.

"You're sure?"

"Yes."

"Once this ship leaves the harbor, there's no going back."

"I know that," Icarus said. "And I want to come."

"OK," I said smiling. "Then let's go tell him." I squeezed his hand as we walked and whispered, "You've made a good choice, Icarus." We walked together, back to the waiting captain.

"We need passage for two."

"This is good, because we often take passengers. And we are loading a cargo of wool and dyes to deliver to the islands to the south. Krete is the last one in a long chain. Along the way lies Kalliste. He's a fortunate man, one that chances to see that most beautiful island even once in this lifetime." The captain paused, as one does to admire a painting. "The boy, he will never forget it. The islands of the Great Green are all mystical, but Kalliste is the queen of them all. Where exactly are you bound for?"

"How much for my nephew and me to travel all the way to Krete?"

Nikolaos hesitated as if he were thinking of a number. "I feel that I may have offended you with my comments about 'seeing' the mystical island. That, and because of your condition, I will give you a very good price."

"How much?"

"For the boy, nothing," the captain replied. "How much could he eat anyway? He can sail with us at no charge. And for you, blind traveler, the price is one silver ring."

I didn't even question the price. I simply nodded in agreement.

Captain Nikolaos went on to explain that with fair winds the voyage to Krete would last at least four days. "Can you be ready to depart at first light?"

"We'll be here."

Chapter Fourteen

On the island of Kalliste, far to the south of mainland Athens where Daedalus and Icarus were about to spend the evening dreaming of brighter futures, the monarchs of the ten-island Minoan empire were gathered for their summit. Their first day was always the most challenging one. But the agenda was a matter of law, passed down to the first kings by the God of the Sea. It was inscribed on the pillar of orichalcum still standing in the courtyard of the gardens of his great temple at Kalliste. They had the shared and sweaty task of finding, isolating, and capturing a large and dangerous quarry.

Three of these island leaders had already worked their way behind the beast and set their looped snares. Each one waited in the thick foliage, their saffron robes indicating their positions. The rest maneuvered the beast towards them, taunting him, calling out, and waving their arms overhead. They made themselves as imposing, evasive, and willful as possible. The angered bull pawed at the ground and snorted. He pranced for them. He charged. He threw his head, brandishing the dangerous horns. He ducked and weaved. And sometimes he backed toward the waiting snares.

In the end it was Meriones, childless king of Naxos, who tripped his running noose at just the right moment, slipping the loop of the rope up and around the hind leg of the massive bull. Almost at once the animal stopped in his tracks. The massive shoulders drooped and he glowered at his tormentors. Behind the beast and to his right, another sovereign dropped her brightly colored robe to the ground and stepped out from behind the brush, her long stave balanced firmly in both hands. She moved in quickly, focused on reaching the bull's flank before he realized what was happening. Minos approached from the other, timing his movements to match hers. It was a dangerous sort of dance, one that abruptly ended as the two monarchs slipped their running bowlines around the thick muscled neck and, in precise accord, gripped the massive head from opposing sides. A few more loops were quickly applied. The sovereigns had him. A runner was dispatched with the news.

Now their task was to guide the hobbled bull all the way to the temple, a distance of many stadia. Almost at once spectators began to gather. Children ran ahead, marking the way with flowers. At the outskirts of the city a phalanx of priestesses joined, leading the procession in ceremonial headdress and attire. Cheering crowds lined the way. The long layered skirts of the bare-breasted priestesses swayed back and forth in front of the subdued animal, subtly directing him onward. Head bowed, the tired beast was led all the way to the grounds of the holy temple, where the crowds would not enter.

At the center of the site stood a holy temple dedicated to the Earth Goddess and the God of the Sea, accessible only through an enclosure of gold. Once inside, the hunting party passed serene lakes and streams, gardens and flowering trees of all varieties, completing a circular path. It led to an elaborate patio of red and black stone laid out in the design of a spiraling labyrinth. In a circle of bare earth at the center of the labyrinth the high priestess waited. A single pillar of stone as thick as the most ancient of trees stood behind her. It was covered over with a malleable sheet of gray orichalcum. Clustered nearby sat her retinue of earth monks and other followers, already in meditation. There, the exhausted bull was sacrificed with a blade of well-honed bronze. His warm sanguine life-force spurted from the severed artery, spattering on the pillar's sacred inscriptions, the bronze skin of the priestesses, and the saffron robes of the nobility. The sacred blood became a steady flow—all of it sacred—and was collected within a large copper bowl recessed into the darkening earth.

Later that evening the sovereigns would gather in circle and celebrate their collective victory over a common foe, one more physically powerful than any one of them alone. They would toast one another with golden cups filled with a deep red mixture of wine and the blood of the bull. Then, gathered around the embers of their sacrifice, the individual kings and queens would air their claims and complaints. They consulted about their common interests. And in the end they would settle their differences. For it was only by renewing their respective pledges of cooperation, mutual support, and defense that their individual islands would receive the blessing of the Goddess.

Such was their law, their constitution. It conferred upon each sovereign absolute authority over their home island, but required a return to Kalliste, the beautiful one, on alternating fifth or sixth cycles of the sun in order to renew their vows and receive the blessing. With that, the rulers could return to their home islands and tell their citizens that their communities would continue to prosper in harmony with the earth. It was a source of hope for all who lived in the shadow of the active volcano, one that infused Minoan life with a sacred balance.

Before meeting in circle, the rulers cleansed themselves in the hot springs and ritual baths. Their bodies were oiled and massaged. Each received a beautiful purple robe of the finest quality, and the freedom to spend whatever remained of the day at their leisure. Many rested. Minos of Krete wandered alone toward one of the hot springs. This was his third gathering, and he was still among the younger participants. Meriones was participating in his fifth, the queen of Rhodos her seventh. Physically, she was the oldest and most fragile of their select group. No one blamed her for hanging back while the bull was maneuvered and trapped. Her strong point was in verbal acuity. Many referred to her as its queen, and she reveled in the notoriety. It would fall on her shoulders to develop their agenda and then lead the discussions that followed. Every gathering Minos would envy her skills, but then he would return to Krete where the memory faded. The maritime fleets were his to manage. With those assets under his control, it was difficult for him to find the motivation needed to discipline his skills at oratory. Her people would always be dependent upon his ships and the commerce they carried. It was all part of the proper balance.

PART II

Voyage to Kalliste

Some of their buildings were simple, but in others they put together different stones, varying the color to please the eye and to be a natural source of delight…Whatever was to be found there…they dug out of the earth in many parts of the island, being more precious in those days than anything except gold. There was an abundance of wood for carpenter's work, and sufficient maintenance for tame and wild animals…for there was provision for all sorts of animals…

In the center was a holy temple…surrounded by an enclosure of gold…All the outside of the temple…they covered with silver. In the interior of the temple the roof was of ivory, curiously wrought everywhere with gold and silver and orichalcum…

Also, whatever fragrant things there are now in the earth, whether roots, or herbage or woods, or essences which distil from fruit and flowers, grew and thrived in that land; also the fruit which admits cultivation, both the dry sort which is given to us for nourishment…and the fruits having a hard rind, affording drinks and meats and ointments, and a good store…which furnish pleasure and amusement…and the pleasant kinds of dessert, with which we console ourselves after dinner…all these that sacred island which then beheld the light of the sun, brought forth fair and wondrous and in infinite abundance.

Critias 114-116
Written by the Greek philosopher and mathematician Plato.
424 BCE - 348 BCE

CHAPTER FIFTEEN

Early the next morning, we returned to the harbor. Our steps were short ones. Sandpipers on the shoreline searching for breakfast would take one look at us, and understand that there was no need to hurry out of the way. My tunic was heavy and unobtrusive. Over one shoulder I carried a large satchel. Inside was everything I was willing to carry into our new lives on Krete. Much of the previous evening had been spent packing it, and also on sewing gold nuggets and silver rings into the folds of my garb.

Icarus narrated the entire scene for me in as much detail as a young boy could. The galleys were floating now, freed from their perches on the sand. Surrounding them like bees to a flower, much smaller rowboats waited impatiently for a turn at the ropes. Icarus described how a large hoist now stood at the end of each ship with a rope dangling down into the water. Whenever their loads shifted the small boats rocked precariously, thumping into whatever was nearby. Sailors shouted and cursed. I could hear the gulls overhead shrieking, tirelessly watching and waiting for their share.

"Over here!" a boatman called out, responding to the furtive steps of a blind man led by a young boy walking toward the sea. "Are you the ones taking passage on the *Pelican*?"

"Indeed, we are," I responded, relieved to get my bearings from a voice, other than one that belonged to yesterday's wizened old oarsman.

"You're doing so well, Icarus. Now that we're in the sea, don't let go. Just keep pointing me toward the boat," I said, stepping into the water's cool embrace.

"A little further," said the boatman.

Leaning into the boy's guiding hand for balance and drawn to the sound of the voice, I clumsily felt my way until a steady hand gripped my upper arm.

"First, let me take your bag," said the voice.

"Nephew, are you with us?" I asked.

"I'm here, in the front." Icarus replied.

"From this moment on, son, it's called the bow," corrected the rower, as he helped me to step over the side and settle into the low wooden bench.

"Icarus, you did well getting us here," I said, meaning every word. We were finally boarding the ship that would take us away from the turmoil of Athens. Unable to actually see much from behind the blindfold, I could still sense the separation. Instead of being elated, I felt melancholy. I could picture myself standing on some kind of shadowy threshold. It was the beginning of a long journey together. I hardly knew the boy. I had no idea how to watch over him, teach him anything, or even to care about him. But together, we were crossing a sea. We were headed to a different land and about to see a whole new culture. Maintaining this blind man's role for the whole crossing would be a challenge.

Chapter Sixteen

Captain Nikolaos stood on the stern deck, one arm casually draped across the steering oar, watching the last of the small cargo boats off-load. Directly below him, within the hold, seamen arranged large packages of pottery bound in protective layers of sheep hide and dried bark. Interspersed were clay amphorae filled with wine and dyes. And there were bows, shields, and breastplates of bronze. It was clear even to Icarus that all of it had to be stowed with an eye to proper balance and then the deck restored.

As the last of the rowboats pushed away from the larger ships, Icarus clumsily stepped onto the rope ladder and began the awkward climb. Above him the crew member of the *Pelican* patiently waited. The sailor's task was to intake the passengers, help with their bag, and then show them to their place on the foredeck.

When Icarus climbed over the rail, I heard him exclaim, "Uncle! There's another boy here."

"Welcome aboard the *Pelican*. I am Aadam," the young sailor said, first in clumsy Greek and then in Minoan. "What is your name?"

Icarus was glad to find someone even close to his own age among the crew. And after a few stammers the younger boy found his voice, introduced himself, and asked, "What do you do on the ship?"

"Whatever I can to be useful," Aadam replied, stepping to the rail to steady me as I climbed over the rail.

Activity all around, Aadam led us to a prepared spot on the fore deck. It was a windy place where Icarus could see most everything and both of us could stay out of the way. I could hear a rope being coiled and stowed. Others worked to close up the hold. Shuffling feet signaled that the rowers had taken their places at the oar ports. Beneath their seat they secured whatever personal gear they possessed and settled in against foot braces mounted to the ribs of the ship. It was my first time on such a large ship. Everything was very close and compact, and I was very curious. I wanted to see the faces. More than that, I wanted to remove the blindfold and watch. I opted for being unobtrusive. So I listened, sniffed at the air, and asked Icarus to continue to describe everything, as long as it was interesting.

The last of the deck planks were finally set into place, securing the holds. Right away I heard the sound of footsteps and imagined the tall crew chief moving forward along the center line. His presence felt like the point of calm in the storm of activity. Apparently it only took a nod of the crew chief's head to inform the captain that all was ready to be underway.

"Stand by the sail!" the crew chief (Orion we later learned) called out in a deep resonant voice, audible over the surrounding din and well beyond the confines of the ship.

"Ready the oars," he commanded, followed by the sounds of stout wooden poles grinding against their oarlocks. The unifying sound of thirty oars rising out of the water and holding as one was breathtaking.

"Pull!" the crew chief called. On command, the blades struck the water in precise accord. Placing his hand on the lead oarsman's shoulder, Orion delegated the chore.

"Pull!" a second voice took up the rhythm. "Pull for home!" the lead oarsman shouted, establishing the tempo. Somewhere a third voice began slow song, marking the rhythm. Others took it up and the merchant galley slid across the water, gliding serenely toward the open water beyond the harbor. The sail was set and a light favorable breeze began pushing us even faster away from Athens. Icarus stood at the rail, watching the water break against the sides and ripple across the clear depths.

"The captain wants you to make yourselves comfortable here," said Aadam, smiling at the passengers. "You are our guests. If there is something you need or want, you have only to ask." Turning to leave, he pointed at the sail, unfurled and catching the wind, directly behind us. Aadam spoke the word "pelican" in Minoan and was gone. In great detail, Icarus described the way the strong square of linen filled with the breeze and stood out against the deep blue sky. It had to be the same brown and red and larger-than-life sized pelican I had noticed the day before, a colorful complement to the sky and sea. He played with the word Aadam had taught us, repeating it several times and I listened closely, doing my best to mimic the sound of it.

CHAPTER SEVENTEEN

The *Pelican* was underway. The ship and crew were heading toward their home. The weather was perfect. Our boarding and departure were without incident. Icarus and I were sailing into the unknown.

Turning to him, I said, "Just before we climbed into that rowboat, there was a moment when we could have changed our minds and turned completely around. We could have returned to our old lives, but not anymore. This adventure has officially begun."

I paused, expecting an answer. When he made no reply I continued, "I'm glad you're along."

"Me too, this is exciting!" said Icarus.

Hearing Icarus' genuine enthusiasm, I realized that I was alone with my regrets.

"I've been hoping for something like this for as long as I can remember," said Icarus, jumping to his feet and taking two quick strides to the opposite rail. "I did not like Athens, not anymore. Do you remember the day we first met?"

"Yes, of course, it was at the place overlooking the sea. What were you doing awake at that hour anyway?"

"I went there to watch the ships," he answered. "I used to pretend that someday I would be sailing away on one."

"You never told me that."

"My mother was taken away on a big ship. Maybe she's somewhere ahead of us, hoping I'll find her."

Even blindfolded, I could sense his movement from the sounds of his feet and direction of the words as they were spoken. I remember being fascinated that he was so intent on leaving. I yearned to be young again, and unaware of the fear of the unknown.

The first day aboard the ship was a long one, filled with hot sun, salty air, and time. I can't deny, though, that there was more than a touch of sadness inside my chest. I had spent my whole lifetime in Athens. I could not will the memories away, and still had regrets about the way things could have been or should have been.

As the *Pelican* followed the rocky coastline, I often asked myself, "Am I doing the right thing? Did I make the right decision? Was it wrong to invite the boy, a child with no real understanding of the consequences of his decision?" When I carefully examined the progression of events that led to our meeting and departure, however, there was no doubt in my mind that the decision to leave was the right one.

I became bored. There were many ways to feel the motion of the ship, but none of them included watching the land pass by. I wanted to see sunlight sparkling on the water. There was almost no one to talk to besides the boy. I toyed with the edges of the blindfold, sorely tempted to pull it down. I just wanted to get a glimpse of the shoreline, or see what Icarus was doing.

I pulled up on the bottom edge; just enough to recoil from the blast of light and heat that replaced the darkness.

I recommitted myself to the blind man's role, vowing never to give away any more visual cues of my disguise, not for the rest of the voyage.

Icarus did great though. He certainly played his part, keeping me company as guide and nephew and happily chatting away. It was late afternoon when he reported that the mainland was curving away and fading into the northern horizon. The *Pelican* did not alter its course. There would be nothing ahead but blue sky, open water, and the wake of our sister ships. Much to Icarus' delight a pod of dolphins appeared swimming alongside, showing off their glistening, sleek, and gray sides. I heard him run down the deck for a closer view. He was gone for what seemed like a long time. When he returned Aadam was with him, and they described in great detail how the dolphins crossed repeatedly in front of the bow. Aadam assured us that it was a sign of good fortune ahead. It reminded me that I still had to decide whether to treat the journey as a way to make a fresh start, or to do King Aegeus' bidding.

"I can already see the next island," Aadam said, pointing at the horizon. "If you squint and look right over there, you can see the gray mass rising above the water. It is called Kea. There's a good harbor and fresh water. We have a settlement there."

"Will we camp there tonight?" I asked.

"Unless something is not right and the captain wants to go on."

Never interrupting Aadam as he spoke, it was clear that Icarus much admired the older boy and had already made up his mind to be more like him.

They waited together on the bow, watching the distant land grow larger. Icarus willingly described the scene. Slowly our landing developed into barren hills and craggy ridges, white with seabird dung and nests. A circular bay appeared. Inside its calm expanse, two Minoan galleys were already at rest. When the sea bottom became visible, a sailor came forward carrying a long, notched pole. He scanned the bottom and occasionally plunged it into the sea, calling out the depth.

Already I could smell the smoke of cooking fires and hear the sounds of people milling about on the beach. Icarus' delicious detail of the passing scene constantly surprised me. My stomach growled in response, a gentle reminder of how long it had been since our last meal. Behind us, several seamen were taking in the sail.

Back in charge for the landing, Orion's voice called out and all the starboard side oars came up out of the water in unison. The rowers on the opposite side started to chant, keeping to their rhythmic strokes. The ship swung around in a sharp turn. I could almost see the pilot leaning into the steering oar. When the prow pointed away from the land, all oars splashed back into the sea and I felt them pushing this time, driving the large ship toward the beach. In the stern two seamen lifted the large steering oar from its mount and set it on the deck.

"Icarus, come with me," said Aadam, tugging on the sleeve of his tunic. "You'll want to see this. It's fun," and he rushed off to the stern rail, Icarus hard on his heels.

Alone now, I listened to the jeers and calls from the men on the beach. The *Pelican*'s oarsmen shouted back in response, pushing hard at the oars and driving the curved hull toward the shore. A crowd stood clustered near the point of impact. They clapped and cheered, urging the *Pelican* on.

"Hold," called out the crew chief, and on both sides of the ship the oars lifted out of the water. Stillness gripped the ship while it coasted, but only for a brief time. It was broken by sudden deceleration and the sound of timbers groaning and scraping against pebbles and sand. We came to an abrupt halt, held, and then rocked a bit to one side.

A great cheer went up all around. I had to stand and join in. Unsteady at first, I held onto the rail and looked in the direction of the smells of food and land. I was in no hurry. But when a small hand touched my arm and led me to the rope that descended to the pebbled beach, I felt relieved and truly happy for the first time that day.

CHAPTER EIGHTEEN

Icarus and I had completed the first leg of our journey. Krete was still far to the south. There, on the southern shore of the island, two young girls walked together in the lingering heat through a field bursting with red, yellow, and lilac-colored blossoms. Their mothers had sent them out to gather greens for supper. These two friends, however, had a different idea. Many of the adults in their small village were probably sleeping at that time of day. Supper was still a long way away. Long dark hair swaying across their shoulders, the girls moved among the poppy anemones, gathering blossoms amidst the hummingbirds, butterflies, and bees. I know these things and tell you about them because some day, Icarus will marry one of them.

Older by several cycles of the sun, Naomi halted by a patch of sweeping magenta, picking only the fullest of flowers. Around their waists the girls wore aprons, each one soiled and stained, each one uniquely their own. Deena looked down into the riot of color that overfilled her makeshift basket. She ran her fingers and hands through the bright petals. Slightly ahead, Naomi stopped her humming and called out to her friend, asking if she was ready.

"Almost," Deena replied.

"No, now," called Naomi, breaking into a run.

Gripping the folds of the cloth together, Deena ran to catch up.

Their trail led down to the river bank and a grove of palm trees. It was a lush and intensely green place this time of year. Naomi slowed, allowing her friend to catch up, and they splashed barefoot into cool water at the finish. Their laughter filled the air of the small river valley. Far in the distance, peaks of gray and brown disappeared into the thin white clouds that patched a serenely blue sky.

Never releasing the hems of their aprons, the two friends playfully followed the river upstream through sweeping curves, pools, and shallows into a narrow gorge, a natural labyrinth cut by erosive forces through the limestone bedrock. Sandbars and shallows marked their course as they splashed their way through the shallow river. Already they could hear it, the constant roar of the falling water. They were going to the hidden pool beneath the cascading water that poured out and over the large cleft in the rock. In this season, at this time of day, the sun was directly overhead, pouring heat into the canyon and warming the air above the cool water to a very inviting temperature. It was fresh water, pure and clean to the skin, not at all like the salty residue that always came from the sea.

Ripples spread across the sparkling surface of the pool and a low mist filled the air. Off to one side and away from all the motion and sound there was a calm corner of relatively still water. Clapping their hands in delight and exchanging gleeful smiles, they laughed the way that only two girls sharing a secret can. They opened their aprons and the colorful contents poured out, creating a large mound of beautiful, bright blossoms that floated on the surface. In the heat of the blazing sun, they stripped out of their dull gray skirts and blouses and stealthily entered the shallow water. Linking arms they gently stroked the water's surface, pushing back against the downward flow and adorning themselves in an array of color and fragrance.

The two girls played in the refreshing pool, committed to their secret adventure. One by one the blossoms slipped away into stronger currents. Then the sun slipped past the edge of the gorge, the temperature dropped, and it was time to leave—while the memories were still good ones.

CHAPTER NINETEEN

Eyes shut and still half-dreaming, I lay back on the sleeping skin and sorted through the memories of the first day out of Athens. It was cold. I reached for the soiled blindfold to rewrap my head and adjust it to cover my eyes. In the distance I could plainly hear the sounds of men gathered around a cooking fire. But there was also another sound, close by, the sound of a young boy humming.

"Icarus, is that you?"

I felt a small hand on my shoulder, prodding me to rise. "What is it? Do you feel like talking this fine morning?"

"It's too cold for talk," Icarus replied. "Come on, get up."

"What's the hurry?" I asked, sitting up and rubbing my face with my hands.

"Just come. It's warm over there. Besides, this giant rock is no place to be left behind."

"Well, then, what are we waiting for?" I asked, rising to my feet. We made our way toward the low voices, Icarus pushing on my elbow, guiding me toward the smells of fire, food, and men.

I could hear that someone was helping Icarus acquire a portion of the food. Next, someone pushed a wooden bowl into my hands. I breathed in the aroma. It was filled with a nameless stew, greasy and brimming with hunks of stringy meat. There was a piece of dry bread. It all tasted wonderful.

With dawn just beginning to break, the captain announced his plan to reach the island of Sifnos before nightfall. The crew was quick with its approval. Already some were gathering their belongings. Icarus told me that Orion and a few oarsmen had already boarded, climbing up the ropes left dangling over the side. They dropped a rope ladder over the side for us. Aadam was quick to grab one end, pushing down with all his weight on the bottom rung. He signaled for Icarus to ascend. I followed, climbing one gangly step at a time. As my hands reached the rail, I heard Orion's welcoming bass voice. Before I could even respond, strong hands gripped my shoulders and armpits, lifting and dragging me over the rail and onto the deck. Dizzy in the knees, I struggled for balance. More hands reached for my shoulders and back. My heart started to race.

What if one of them feels the weight of the nuggets sewn into the fabric?

"Something troubles you this morning, my friend?" Orion asked, displaying great attentiveness.

"Just a rough landing is all," I replied, forcing a smile in his direction. "I'm alright now." I brushed my hands down the front of my tunic, trying to look composed.

"You are a good man," said Orion in his full voice, giving me one more clap on the back.

I had noticed the day before that he had a way of connecting with each person on the crew. He knew everyone by name. He even seemed to know the names of their wives and children. Even a blind man could see that everyone looked up to him.

"Go and wait by the mast while we free the ship," Orion directed Icarus. "Grab onto something fast and keep an eye on your Uncle," he instructed. "Make sure he's holding on. Once we're clear you can make your way forward."

On both sides of the ship, rowers quickly stowed their gear and readied the forward oars.

"Free the ship," Orion called out and two complimentary forces responded.

On board, the forward oarsmen struck their oars into the water and pulled. Back on shore a host of well-wishers set their shoulders against the stout wooden sides and heaved as one against the great weight. In one surge the wooden ship lurched forward. Feet digging against the sand, the crew roared their collective determination. The keel responded, scraping across the strand. The oars kept up their rhythm. Crewmen cursed and shouted, and the *Pelican* picked up speed, slowly sliding away from the sandy perch and finally floating free. Again I felt like cheering.

As we left the bay, the sun rose to greet us. The wind came up and held. I could tell that we were in open water again, and making good time. From the direction of the warming rays, I knew that we were headed southeast.

Pleased with the morning's progress, Captain Nikolaos came forward to talk to his passengers. "What you witnessed this morning, the ease with which we packed everything away and made our departure, that doesn't just happen," said the captain in earnest. "It takes a lot of practice, and no one on the Great Green moves a ship full of men and cargo better than him," Nikolaos went on, proudly pointing to his crew chief and gesturing for Orion to join us. "He doesn't talk that much about it, but before seeing the light and becoming a trader, he'd sailed on Minos' warships for many seasons, chasing down pirates and smugglers."

"Pleasure in the job puts perfection in the work," Orion responded modestly, slightly uncomfortable with all the praise.

"And," the captain continued, "He's a very good man to have at your back. You see that leather guard on his wrist? Not many targets avoid the reach of his long bow."

"Every time the captain gets a new audience he brings out his tall tales," Orion said, smiling.

"I have watched him punch an arrow through a pirate's chest from at least one hundred paces away," said Nikolaos. "Not even the Amazons can shoot so far with that kind of accuracy. It was quite a sight to see."

"I do favor the bow," agreed Orion, "and long arrows."

"And not just any bow," said the Captain. "He's been known to sleep with the one he has stowed below this deck."

Then Nikolaos launched into his story, without even a pause.

"They were on course to ram us, three fast galleys off the coast of Phoenicia."

"It was long ago," interrupted Orion.

"But I've only told it several hundred times," responded Nikolaos, grinning at his friend. "Orion gets his long bow and walks out to the fore-deck, right here where we're sitting. He takes his bow, fits an arrow, and looses a single shot. The arrow flies across the water and takes out the pilot of the closest one. That ship makes a sudden turn and right away, the next one runs into it, disabling half of the oars. The captain on the second ship is furious.

He's a short fellow like me, only red faced, hairy, and rather slow in the head. He orders his bowmen to shoot a few volleys. All their arrows fall short. Now the captain's enraged. He stands up on the rail of his ship, holding a rope in one hand and waving a dagger with the other. He's screaming at us, and so preoccupied that he doesn't even notice when Orion takes a second shot; one that shut him right up. It was the stuff of legend."

"What happened then?" asked an eager Icarus.

"Their ships all split up. We followed the closest one for the rest of the day. Caught up with her too, beached and abandoned."

"What did you do?"

"What any good Minoan mariner would do to free the sea of pirates," said Orion.

"Aye," replied the captain. "We took her stores, torched the ship and left, quick."

CHAPTER TWENTY

On the second day at sea, Icarus was no longer content to just sit on the bow and watch. He wanted to move about the ship and spend time with Aadam. The young Minoan sailor had found two spare lengths of rope and showed his newfound friend several useful knots. Now, Icarus wanted to show his mentor how fast he could tie them.

That morning, I, too, was restless. To break the day's tedium I began to walk the narrow wooden decks that ran the length of the ship, at first with Icarus and then alone, making my way cautiously along the rail. By midday, there was no breeze. The heat had driven me back to the shade of a small awning a sailor had rigged across the bow. That's where Aadam and Icarus found me, and told me about the plan to land on the next island and take a break from the heat.

Everyone went ashore and relaxed in the shade of a thicket of trees and greenery. I'm certain that it was a lovely spot. There was a little river, soaking its way into the pebbles of the anchorage. Not that I actually saw much of it.

Icarus was too enamored with Aadam not to follow him back aboard the ship. The older youth showed Icarus the bench where Xanthus rowed. Icarus eagerly sat on the smooth planks and ran his fingers along the distinctive grain of the oaken oar. Aadam surmised that the generous older man would not object. Icarus looked out through the oar port toward the blade and the spot where it disappeared into the clear shallow water. He wrapped his fingers around the smooth grip, imagining what it would be like to feel the boat surge ahead with every stroke.

"I'm going to be a sailor someday," Icarus said solemnly, extending one leg as far as it would go, straining his toes forward to reach the foot block mounted to the ribs of the inner hull. Aadam smiled, remembering a time long past when he had sat next to Captain Nikolaos on this same ship, in another port, and had done exactly the same thing.

"Come here," instructed Aadam. "You'll want to see this too." Icarus quickly followed to the hold along the aft deck where most of their weapons were stowed, curved knives, breastplates, and arrows. Never had he seen so much metal before in one place. "It's all right to look, but not to touch," Aadam cautioned. "That's what Orion says."

When the wind picked up, we were underway again. I listened patiently to Icarus' tale, all about his private tour of the galley. When he left again, I started another slow shuffle along the deck. Hearing something, I stopped to listen. It was the sound of low, intermittent thumps against the outer planking. Something small and wet tumbled onto the deck near my feet. I knew right away what it had to be, and quickly groped along the wooden boards for a breathless, flopping creature. I sympathized with the one shimmering fish out of an entire school, enabled or empowered to somehow thrust itself through the surface of the water into the light and air. Most of his brethren would stay behind in their watery school. In my mind only a very few had the tenacity, the luck, or the force of will to leap out of the water. Of those that did, most fell back into the sea unharmed. It seemed unjust that the one able to leap the highest and to clear the rail of the *Pelican* should also be the one to sputter and die there, for lack of breath. I wanted very much to save that fish. First I had to find it.

That's the way Icarus found me. Without a word he dropped to his knees and began running his hands over the planks. "What are we looking for?" he asked.

"Do you see a small flying fish?" I replied. "Just a moment ago one flew over the rail and bounced at my feet."

"They do that sometimes, when the tuna chase after them," he said.

"What! Tuna? How do you know about such things?" I asked, delighted to learn more about the boy.

"I just know it. My father was a fisherman," Icarus replied, sounding defensive. "You knew that."

I stopped searching and rose to my knees. "That's right, you did tell me that."

The young boy reached a skinny arm behind a clay amphora and pulled out his quivering quarry.

"Found him," Icarus said proudly, standing up at once and flinging the desperate creature back into the sea.

"Well done," I said, clapping my hands and rising to my feet. I reached out clumsily towards him, wanting to place a reassuring hand his shoulder. My gesture missed the mark. "You know, it's all right if you want to talk about him," I said gently.

"Or maybe Aadam told me about them. I'm not sure."

"That's not what I meant."

"I really don't remember my father. But my mother talked about him sometimes."

"What did she say?"

"That he went out in his boat one day to catch fish for us. There was a storm. That he didn't come back."

"Well. I'm sorry about your father. And thank you for helping me with the flying fish."

"Sure. I'm going to go find Aadam now."

"I'll be on the bow watching for dolphins," I said, laughing at my own joke.

"How are you going to do that?" Icarus wondered out loud.

In fact, it wasn't all that long before another pod of dolphins did appear, swimming along before the bow. An excited Icarus ran forward to watch and describe, in great detail, their color and number. I listened with genuine interest.

It was such a relief, such a pleasure, after so much time living alone to feel a sense of companionship. In this watery place with my self-imposed blindness, I was learning to breathe again, to slow down. It was a rich, satisfying moment, one that I remember still hold close to my heart.

Later in the day, Icarus spotted the hazy outline of another island, just visible on the horizon ahead. He spoke of brown and gray hills with alternating splashes of green and milky white beneath a clear, deep blue sky. Fishing boats and ships of different sizes appeared, and he could see a rocky cliff, shrouded in white, jutting straight up out of the sea. As the *Pelican* drew near I could hear the sounds of the birds, circling above us, screeching to each other. Finally the starboard oars turned the ship smartly around that cliff into the entrance of a great, curving bay, one that penetrated deep into the island. Sandy beaches and a cluster of white-walled buildings filled the harbor at the far end.

"Welcome to Sifnos," said the captain, coming toward us from behind the sail. "Quite a difference, isn't it, compared to the sleepy, run-down port we left behind in Athens?" I could feel a mischievous wink as he said the words.

"Athens has nothing like this!" agreed Icarus.

"And if good fortune continues to smile on us, tomorrow you will see how much Sifnos pales in comparison to our home port of Kalliste," replied the captain, his voice beaming with pride. "Once you see Kalliste you may never want to leave. It is a paradise of green in a sea of deep blue, with lakes, waterfalls, and hot springs. Every time that I bring my ship through the outer ring and into the harbor, it is so much more than just coming home. It feels like returning to the center of all things. I love it there."

After a thoughtful pause he concluded, "But, then I leave again every spring when the trading season begins. So what does that tell you?"

"It tells me that you are a poet as well as a trader," I answered. "It makes me wish that I could see your island for myself."

"Thank you, my friend," replied Nikolaos with a contented smile. "A good trader wears many hats. As your captain, I invite you and Icarus to gather with the crew around our fire on the beach tonight. There will be many local people about, mystics and merchants selling anything and everything imaginable."

"Thanks for the invitation, or is it a warning?"

"It is both, of course," the captain replied. "Or you might want to consider a small side trip. The hills and ridges above the island are a splendid place to watch the sunset. If there are no clouds, Kalliste may be visible. Sometimes at night, when the Goddess is restless, the summit glows orange and red. If she becomes really upset, then the mountaintop can throw fire high into the air."

"Captain, have you ever seen it throwing fire?" asked a curious Icarus.

"No, for me the mountain only rumbles and shakes. Aside from that, she has always been a comforting presence."

"Let's climb the ridge tonight!" said Icarus, enthusiastically.

I turned toward the eager youth shaking my head, "I can't go hiking with you. I would only slow you down. Besides, the entertainment on the beach sounds more to my liking. Are some of the crew going?"

"What about Aadam?" asked Icarus.

"Zavier is leading the hike. You know him, the tall one with the truly large shoulders. These ridges are a popular destination and he is an easy man to follow. Others will go. Go ask Aadam about it," Nikolaos suggested.

Turning toward me, he continued, "Do not be anxious. There is security in numbers and we take care of our passengers. It is only the smugglers and pirates that need worry."

"Icarus," the captain said, "Your task is to make a good memory and then safely return to us. Agreed?"

"Yes sir. I will do exactly that," he replied, immensely pleased to be included in an outing with the crew.

CHAPTER TWENTY ONE

Several ships and many hundreds of mariners were camped on the beach that day. Mostly the crews of the different ships formed ragged circles around their own campfires. The evening air seemed to fill with the sounds of games of chance, drinking wine, and the occasional fight. There were many performers, moving from one group to the next, passing a hat, and entertaining their listeners with lyres, sweet voices, and rhythm globes. A number of local women had gathered, and the sounds of laughter and conversation drifted across the beach.

I sat near the warmth of the *Pelican's* fire, enjoying the challenge of listening to the sounds and the voices without seeing the faces. The more watered wine I drank the more certain I was of the features and expressions of the person I was listening to. Mostly I wanted to be awake when Icarus and the hiking party returned. Finally he did, safe and sound, and dragging his tired feet across the sand to our space near the fire.

With his return, my long day's journey into night was over, and I, too, fell into a deep and restful sleep. In the dream that followed I found myself walking away from a windowless stockade made of logs, down a trail-less hill toward a narrow river. I followed it downstream through vast woodlands until it led to a verdant meadow covered in blooms of anemones, asphodels, and wild gladioli. The sky was the blue of a bluebird's wing. Directly overhead, the sun shone down upon the crown of my head. In quiet solitude I walked into the field. A prominent hill stood in the center covered with soft grasses, their tops blown over by the steady breeze. I walked completely around the base, and then began climbing in an ascending spiral path, circling around the flanks. After reaching the top, I gazed in each direction, finally stopping when I could feel the force of the wind directly into my beard. Suddenly, a quickening—a vibration—moved through me like a shiver. It spread from my head, to my chest and arms, down into my legs, and even into my toes, passing through me like an electrical current continuing into the ground. And the earth answered back with a surging pulse rising from each blade of grass beneath my bare feet.

The shock of it twisted me around so that the wind was now full onto my back, arousing a strange and yet familiar yearning. Instinctively, my arms rose up over my head, elevating my back and shoulders toward the sun. The rotation continued, my left knee rising. The wind was full in my face again. I didn't yet realize that the big toe and ball of my right foot were the only parts still in contact with the grassy earth. Then my palms turned skyward. I no longer felt the ground beneath my foot. I spiraled steadily upward, arms extended but hardly moving, as if I could ride a thermal like the graceful soaring bird.

I rose effortlessly, moving upward into the light and warmth of the sun, feeling relaxed and at peace, right until the moment when I looked down. I expected to see a small mound directly below, but I was much, much higher than that. The hilltop was blurred into the broader expanse of field and trees. Turning my eyes toward the horizon I felt the tension ease, and continued to spiral upward, trusting in a ride that became more sublime with each second. Far below, the field became a small rectangle in an expanse of green woodlands. Beyond it, I saw rocky cliffs and beaches, all rising up out of an azure sea.

When the entire island was visible below, my ascent began to slow. Without pretense, I seemed to have reached a balance point. I gave myself over to the opposing forces, extending my arms as if there were great wings on my back and shoulders. Quite by accident, the wings found a place of elegant equilibrium, an invisible zone where two forces of attraction canceled one another. Within it, I could soar like an albatross or a great condor. It was so much more than just floating. Within this stable and narrow band, I could fly. So I banked and soared, but all the time losing altitude, as I glided back toward the earth in a slow descending arc.

So much excitement and wonder packed into a single glorious

dream, but somehow and somewhere I would eventually and inevitably land. Looking out toward the horizon, I considered whether I had the elevation to glide out beyond the shoreline and end the flight in a water landing. Surely that was the best option. But as soon as the thought of landing entered my head, the dream began to unwind. Already, I had lost too much altitude. There was nowhere to go except back toward the field where the flight originated. I would have to make do with its soft earth.

I began measuring the momentum of my downward glide against the steady and rapid approach of the land, rising up fast to greet me. Once more the rolling green of the hills became tall, individual trees. The meadow was in my line of sight, and I willed the winds to hold on long enough for the momentum to carry me there. It was coming up fast, directly ahead. Then the trees beneath me opened into the rich expanse of green.

Instinctively I dropped my legs and rotated my arms back, begging the wind to help slow the descent. In that moment I imagined how the young condors must feel on their first landings. There certainly was a lot to learn, and once a flight started, it had to have a finish. Just before the collision, I cradled his arms around my head, shielding myself as best I could. Suddenly, the grass, soft dirt, and sand separated into a dark furrow that enveloped my body and drained away the forward momentum. Finally, my body halted half-in and half-out of the earth. And I was still alive.

Dazed, and brushing sand and dirt from my face, I pulled myself out of the furrow that had opened in front of me. Blinking furiously, I stood up and looked back for the point of impact. But the dirt, the grass and the trees were all gone. There was only starlight filling the night sky.

Once more I was on my back fully awake and lying on a sleeping skin on a beach somewhere, surrounded by snoring sailors. Every cell of my body tingled, alive with the memory of the flight. It was simply the best, the most exhilarating dream I had ever had or ever could have. And rather than lose the memory of it, I lay there in the sand, recounting each scene and sensation. When dawn began to break, lighting up the eastern hills, I was still lying there, awake and lost in the memory of the dream. All was quiet. I stood up and made my way across the beach, searching for some solitude. When I reached the shore I skipped and then danced, reveling in the majesty of soaring through the sky. Already I hoped for the coming day to pass quickly, just on the chance that the flight dream would return again the next night.

CHAPTER TWENTY TWO

All the next day the *Pelican* continued southeast on the prevailing wind accompanied by the steady beat of the oars. By mid-afternoon the air was hot to breathe.

"Icarus how was the hike yesterday?" the captain asked, coming forward, checking on the passengers. "Any fire on the mountain last night?"

The young boy had been so exhausted on the return trip that he could hardly keep his eyes open. But rather than complain, he had collapsed on the trail. Zavier, the giant, had carried him the last few stadia, all the way to the spot where I had lain out the empty sleeping skin.

"No," replied Icarus. "But we saw Kalliste far away. It looked like an enormous ring of land with a mountain in the middle. Clouds covered the top. If there was any fire coming out, I sure couldn't see it."

"It is often that way," said Captain Nikolaos. "The mountain seems to make its own weather."

"Kalliste!" the pilot called out and a roaring cheer went up in reply. Orion's voice responded with a rhythmic chant in their strange native Minoan tongue. The oarsmen took it up, incrementally increasing the pace. Icarus watched in silence as the island grew in size and depth. From beyond the ship the only sounds came from the occasional gulls circling overhead.

"From a passing ship, who would ever guess that behind that wall

of rock, there is a smoldering mountain covered over with an ever-blossoming garden?" the captain posed. "All tended by a cadre of priestesses and
earth monks sworn to serve the Goddess."

"Who are the earth monks?" Icarus asked.

"To be a priestess or an earth monk is a calling. That's all I can tell
you; except to say, that if the mountain is quiet, then they must be doing
their part."

"And why would anyone want to become one?" Icarus asked.

"How far until this wall of rock opens up for us?" I asked.

"Let me tell you a little story about this island and our nation,"
the captain responded, his voice deepening, the sounds almost hypnotic.
"Many generations ago when our people were very young, there was an
earthquake. In those days the island was completely covered over with trees,
birds and animals, and not nearly so many people. It was a very large earthquake and came in the depths of the night. Just as the shaking began to
subside, a tremendous, thundering roar filled the air. It went on and on as
if the entire island was splitting apart. The stars and the moon were blotted
out of the sky, and the air became hot and full of the smells of burning trees
and sulfur. Sizzling brown rocks fell from the sky. Some tried to flee in their
boats, but they could not leave the land. Everywhere they looked the sea
was steaming, densely covered over with floating rocks. There was nothing
to do but pray and comfort the dying."

"Then what happened?" asked Icarus, entranced in the story.

"After a very long night the sky became lighter. In every direction,
the sky was heavy and dark. The sun was barely visible. There was only
enough light to see that the top of the mountain was gone. What was left
was completely burned and barren, and pillars of fire spewed like fountains
from the new summit."

"And that incredible noise, it had to be the sound of the mountaintop blowing apart," I guessed.

"Yes, the gods were most displeased," agreed Nikolaos.

"Apparently so."

"The story does not end on Kalliste," the captain earnestly
continued. "A great wall of water went out that night. It smashed into
the ships and the harbors, destroying everything it touched. The salt water
swept across the farm lands, destroying the fields, the grape vines and the
olive trees. For many cycles of the sun, there was no new growth."

"How terribly tragic!" I said.

"Yes. It was a great tragedy, one that affected all of the islands.

From those ashes, though, the first kings were able to see the benefit of forging the alliances that became our Minoan nation. To this day we have been willing to keep them. Now there are hundreds of priestesses and earth monks on all of the islands, keeping the rituals alive." The captain paused to look into the faces of his audience. "And Kalliste is a garden once again."

Then he stood with a nod and headed back to the stern.

"How much longer before we can see Kalliste?" Icarus wondered aloud, eager for something different.

"The cliffs are a natural sea wall. They seem to go on and on," answered Aadam, leading against the rail.

"Until we fall off the edge of the world?"

"These walls have turned away many faint-hearts," Aadam replied. "You saw them last night from the top of Sifnos."

"They were smaller then and a long way off."

"And now we are close up. Too close to see the mountain or anything else inside."

"Anything would be better than this," complained Icarus.

"Aye," Aadam agreed, "But the rest of the voyage is something you don't want to miss."

"So there is a way inside?" asked Icarus.

"You could swim over and climb. Many have tried. A few have actually done it."

"That's not what I mean. Besides I can't swim."

"There is a single break in this ring of cliffs," Aadam continued, ignoring the question. "By boat, it is the only way inside. It's narrow. If you fall asleep or even blink, you might sail past and miss it."

I sat nearby, listening quietly to the exchange. It had been a long day with little activity. The sun was far to the west and low in the sky. Time itself seemed to have slowed down.

"That looks like flames coming out of the top of the cliffs," said Icarus.

"Something is burning?" I asked. "I don't smell anything."

"You're seeing one of the lighthouses," replied Aadam. "The ship channel is marked for all to see. This time of day the reflected light from the sun shines reddish gold off the roof. At night from the same place oil is burned in a large bowl. You can be sure that someone has been up there watching our approach."

"Then we are close!" proclaimed an excited Icarus.

"Very close," agreed Aadam.

"What is the roof made of?" asked the builder. "Do you know?"

"It looks like gold!" said Icarus.

"Polished bronze," replied Aadam. "There's a well-worn trail all along the ridge. The view is magnificent, well worth the climb."

"I want to see it!" Icarus exclaimed.

"What is bronze?" I asked, attempting unsuccessfully to hold back my eagerness. "I would like to hold a piece of it in my hands."

Standing on the stern deck with the pilot, Captain Nikolaos called for the sail to be taken in. Aadam was on his feet, scrambling toward the mast. Two more seamen joined him. Icarus watched from afar, wishing hard to be bigger, older, and stronger.

The *Pelican* began its broad turn into the channel between the two massive cliffs. It was like a huge open gate, Icarus said as he stood on the prow, watching their approach. Little by little the entire scene unfolded before his curious eyes.

"Tell me what you see," I pleaded.

"I see why they call this place 'the most beautiful.' It is everything they told us and more," replied Icarus, sucking in his breath at the wonder of the sight.

Icarus tried to describe a huge multilayered city above a bustling harbor, mantled across the green flanks of a broad mountain, all shimmering in the low-lying sun. On its verdant face an elegant waterfall cascaded onto a large fertile plain. Cultivation had turned the broad expanse into angular shapes and shades of green. There were lakes, streams, and gardens. An expansive palatial structure stood on the far side of the plain. The dome gleamed in the sun. Beneath the palace and the fertile fields, the upper reaches of the city extended out in all directions. Icarus spoke of row after row of great buildings and flowering trees and gardens. For the young boy, it was the most extraordinary sight there could ever be. And he had no words for it, just an exaggerated intake of breath.

Under the steady beat of its oars the *Pelican* reached the sea gate's outer edge, moving straight toward the channel beyond and pulling for home. The rowers had no choice but to face out to sea into the glare of the setting sun. The rest of the crew all stood and watched the approach of the majestic mountain, all but hidden inside a protective ring—everyone but Orion. Orion stood at the mast staring at me, his passenger; a man seized with an irresistible impulse to see for himself, who had lifted up the bandage that had covered his eyes until this point in the journey. I too, was looking straight ahead, transfixed by the sight of the inner island, bathed in the rose-colored twilight.

CHAPTER TWENTY THREE

His thick forearm balancing on the steering oar, Captain Nikolaos piloted the ship into the calm water of the huge inner bay. Orion strode down the main deck and met him there. While they spoke the captain's face took on a determined look. He turned the rudder over to his crew chief.

"Hold oars!" he bellowed to the crew.

Along both sides of the ship, the oars lifted out of the water. All around the ship questioning faces turned toward the Captain and the *Pelican* slowed, drifting towards the gleaming city.

"What's happening? Why are we slowing down?" I asked, anxiously pulling the blindfold back into place.

"It is not safe to land right now!" the captain declared. "We are bringing the ship about and taking her back out to sea."

A collective groan went up from all around; except for my own throat, which was filled with a rather large lump.

"Starboard oars, bring us around," the captain commanded. "Hold on the left. We have important business outside the wall!"

No one questioned his commands. Instead, the rowers on the right smartly returned to their rhythm. Just inside the cliff walls the *Pelican* moved through a tight turn with everyone, except me, watching the sanctuary of the harbor slip away one degree at a time.

"All oars," boomed Orion's deep, resonant voice, and the ship surged back into the channel, leaving the quiet inner waters of their home port behind.

Icarus was on his feet, looking at the faces of the crew.

"I'm going to go find Aadam," he said quietly, stepping past me and heading towards the stern.

"Don't go," I pleaded, adjusting once more, the makeshift blindfold. "Tell me what is happening."

"We're heading back out to sea," replied Icarus, his voice a whisper. For the first time since coming on board, I knew that he was afraid. It was something we had in common. I almost considered jumping overboard and trying to swim for it. But I would never get away from the ship. Orion would see to that, so would the weight of the gold and silver sewn into my tunic. There was nothing to do but wait. Begrudgingly, Icarus slumped down next to me on the deck.

The watch towers reappeared and then faded from view as the *Pelican* resumed the southeasterly course, paralleling the outer cliffs. One of the rowers took up a new song to give the rhythm, this one slow and mournful. Many of the crew took up the cadence and the ship sailed onward into the fading light.

The atmosphere on deck was sullen and dark.

"This place feels like a dam about to burst," Icarus blurted. "When will I ever learn? Adults cannot be trusted!"

Guilt ridden I tried to sound reassuring. "Icarus, it's all right. You can go. Find a place to hide. Or else search for Aadam and try to find out what is happening."

He quickly stood up and walked away, leaving me alone on the foredeck. My stomach was a hard empty pit. There was frustration and anger in the voices of the nearby rowers.

Even without understanding their foreign words, my instincts told me that I was part of the discussion. So I listened instead to the steady beat of the oars and disassociated from the gloom of the ship, trying to remember a dream from a long time ago, something about a gift. But I could not quite recall the details.

Sounds of activity brought me back to my senses. The ship was hardly moving. Crewmen were moving about near the mast on the main deck. Captain Nikolaos' voice broke the tension.

"Blind man! Come over here."

The tone was one he had not yet used on the voyage. Before this,

his voice had always carried an entertaining quality, a lightness of being. Now it was devoid of all that. There was only menace and a warning that he should not be challenged.

"Make your way along this deck!"

The words carried easily to the bow where I struggled to my feet.

"Young Icarus, wherever you are, do not assist him," the voice continued, softening a little. "Stay where you are! Let the man find his own way."

After that there was only silence, but I knew that every eye on the ship stared at me. There was nothing to do but obey. I felt their eyes following my slow blind man's shuffle toward the source of the words. I groped my way toward the mast and the crewmen parted, allowing me to pass and then closing ranks from behind, blocking any retreat.

Hearing movement ahead of me, I stopped and turned as if looking from side to side.

"What was that?" I asked.

Two strong hands pushed roughly against my shoulder blades, shoving me forward. My feet followed, rushing to catch my balance, until one shin collided with the stout wooden pole and I toppled forward. I crashed into the wooden deck with a thud and let out a garbled groan. Blood spurted from my nose. Sprawled across the wooden planks, I tried to reach up and stem the flow with the fingers of my left hand. But the spar came down hard against the nape of my neck, driving the side of my face back into the well-worn timbers. Blood ran onto the deck and down my throat. Someone grabbed the blindfold and tore it off my head. I found myself staring at a fit and muscular Minoan leaning into one end of a long wooden pole. He caught my eye and howled.

I placed my hands on the deck and tried to push, beginning a clumsy effort to bring myself up off the deck. Jeers taunted me. A well-placed foot slammed into my exposed ribs. With a resounding "Oooff" I dropped back to the deck. The seaman on each end of the pole renewed their efforts to grind my ear into one of the deck's smaller cracks. I could still see one of them far out of reach. His face was a mask of purposeful indifference. My breath shallow and quick, I grimaced and lay still, watching his calloused hands tighten on the pole. I felt the vibration of approaching footsteps and my body tensed for the next blow.

Icarus said nothing. He had heard the captain call me out, saw the crew gather, and listened to the thud of the blows. Now the young boy scarcely breathed. Like a jack rabbit being hunted by a hawk, he knew well how to hide and wait. Running like the wind was just not an option, especially in the confines of a sailing ship. In that moment he hated the ship and everyone on it, including Aadam, whom he had almost trusted. Now there was no escape, nowhere to run, and nothing to use to his advantage except his own small size. He burrowed deeper into the small space between the large cargo urn and the rail. Anger raged inside of him.

Slowly and without making a sound, the fingers of his right hand reached inside the lining of his tunic and grasped the smooth, blue stone hidden there. It was from an earlier time when his mother was still alive. She had told him that within it were powers that would watch over him and protect him from harm if anything ever happened to her. Inside his small fist he rubbed the stone between his thumb and fingers, stared at the backs of the men on the deck, and squeezed a little deeper into the shadows.

CHAPTER TWENTY FOUR

Captain Nikolaos walked over to where I lay sprawled on the deck. He stood over me without speaking, displaying neither concern nor urgency.

"Blind man," the captain began, his voice conciliatory once more, "you are quite the actor. The way you shuffled around and listened so attentively to all the sounds. You kept it up day and night for almost three days. It is a study in persistence. Bravo. I have been a trader for a long time and appreciate good acting. Bravo. Let us see how this story unfolds."

After a lengthy pause with no reply, the captain continued.

"Instead of a poor blind man traveling with his nephew, we have a man with something to hide. Perhaps he was an important man, a man of means, who fled from Athens in peril for his life? Perhaps he chose a ship bound for a distant land where no one would know him? This has the makings of a great story. Don't you agree, not–so-blind man? For that was his disguise, to be led about by a young boy from the streets. Tell me, Athenian, what is your real name?"

"You know my name. It is Daedalus."

"Then tell us, Daedalus, your terrible deed and why it was necessary for you to leave in such haste?"

"I didn't do anything to deserve what happened," I replied,

unsuccessfully twisting my head towards the captain. But it turned out to be the perfect position to get a glimpse of Icarus, opening the door to a cargo hold and climbing in behind. In that moment my heart swelled large in my chest, filling with sorrow and compassion for this youth. It hurt to know that I was responsible for bringing him into this.

The captain seemed to sense this new emotion, because in the next moment he turned toward the stern and spoke in a loud voice. "Icarus, we are still very far from land, too far away for even a strong swimmer like you. Stay with us on board for a while longer."

Turning back to me he said, "Aren't you curious to know what happens next?"

I felt as helpless as a beached whale, immobilized and bloated, full of fear and frustration.

Mustering as much determination as I could, I said, "There is gold in our bag. Take it. It is yours. But you must keep your word! Take us onto shore." As I spoke, I imagined that I could feel the weight of the spar on the back of my neck lessen a little, as if the burly sailors were considering the offer too.

With a malevolent grin the captain asked, "What can you teach us of promises and truth-telling, blind one?"

"You promised to take us to the island of Krete!" I responded, furious.

"Actually, I promised to take a youth and a blind man to Krete," the captain replied, drawing out the words and stepping into my line of sight. Slowly, he withdrew his jeweled knife from the protective sheath. "Krete is the next island to the south. If the winds hold, this ship and crew can reach its harbor by tomorrow evening. But there are two issues to be resolved before we can leave Kalliste. First is, whether or not you are a smuggler? And second, whether or not you will leave this place with your sight?"

"Pluck out his eyes!" shouted a sailor.

"There are pieces of gold wrapped in a linen cloth inside our bag," I interrupted, one cheek still mashed against the deck.

The captain nodded imperceptibly to someone in the darkness, who then turned and strode away to retrieve the bag. Nikolaos dropped to a knee along one side of me and, with the tip of his knife, poked at a small protruding lump in the bottom hem of my tunic.

"What about these?" Captain Nikolaos inquired.

"Take it. Take it all!" I cried out. "Just don't hurt the boy!"

The captain lifted his knife. Time slowed to a crawl. The knife seemed so real, so palpable; I felt that I could actually see it, poised above my back. Captain Nikolaos drove it into the deck, right between my arm and shoulder blade. Then he drew down on the knife, slicing through the tunic along its length, but drawing no blood.

"Do not move, smuggler," the captain cried, grabbing the collar of my tunic in his left hand and pulling back hard. He raised the knife again, slicing it across the shoulders in a smooth arc. "Rest assured, Daedalus, that we will take your gold," he said. And with that, he grabbed the torn garment with both hands and yanked it free from my back. "It is the tax upon your lies," he added.

As the captain lifted the garment, rings and small pieces of gold and silver spewed out the rends in the fabric like a fountain. Even in the semi-darkness, the metals gleamed as they flew, each one in its own separate arc. The precious metal rained down onto the deck, thudding onto the wood. Some of them rolled away and a few spun about like toy tops. The entire crew was transfixed. Then they were scrambling, lunging, and grabbing for the coins, knocking into anything and anyone who was in the way.

In the chaos of that moment I was released from the entrapment of the spar only to be caught in the center of the melee. I was kicked and pummeled as the sailors dove for the gold. But also, I was free again. With a guttural roar, I rolled and pushed myself away from the helplessness of the deck. A nearby sailor slammed a ferocious left directly into my chest, which dumped me rudely to my knees. Rough hands tore away the shreds of cloth still hanging from my neck. Anger surged. I regained my breath and stood up once more; this time with a closed right fist which I slammed into the mouth of the nearest man. Pain shot through my fingers as he fell to the deck. I stepped past, kicking and shoving my way out of the riot toward the relative isolation of the foredeck.

In only a few seconds my former pieces of gold and silver had found new homes in other men's pockets. It had seemed like an eternity, but at least I was no longer pinned to the deck. I was bruised and bloodied and sincerely hoped that nothing more than my nose was broken. Looking toward the mast, I could see the captain off to one side, returning the bronze blade to its curved sheath. We exchanged glances.

Then a mariner brought my traveling bag on deck. Wearily, I watched as the bag was turned upside down and the belongings spilled out: a mason's level and plumb line, spare clothes, rations of dried fruit, and a small rolled linen bag, which Nikolaos quickly took for his own. I leaned against the forward rail, hung my head and wept. Everything had been stripped away, every last vestige of life in Athens.

Safe on the stern deck, Icarus stood with Aadam. He looked across the length of the ship at the man who had promised to keep him safe and fed, now in tears and wearing nothing but a loincloth. He turned away as if searching for something in the water.

"That won't happen to me," Icarus said out loud. "If they come after me, I'm taking my chances in the water. I'll swim to the rocks or find a floating log out there."

"No one's coming for you," said Aadam. "You don't have to fear."

The captain stepped to the front of the crew, looking toward me and spoke again, this time in his entertaining voice. "Lounging around again on the deck of my ship?"

My chest still heaving, I looked up but said nothing.

"At the beginning of all this, I delegated the task of completing the story to you, smuggler." The captain paused, looked around the ship, and said, "We still have far to go tonight."

The crew surged forward, gathering in a loose group behind the captain. "If you no longer wish to be known as the smuggler, then tell us who you are. And explain why this new man should reach Krete with his sight."

I was stunned. A small voice inside of me complained loudly. "I have lost everything tonight. What is that demon asking for now?" Then I looked up and saw Icarus staring at me from the stern. The boy was trembling. I could feel his fear. Somehow it reminded me of the youth who fell off the roof in Athens. I remembered Aella's unremitting anger and the politician's driving greed — all of them actors in a play that had carried me step by step into this dark night. Then it came to me, the realization of what I still possessed. I remembered that I still had my life and my vision.

Facing the captain I looked into the eyes of the seamen around him and studied the circle of men. No one spoke.

Mustering the shreds of my confidence, I began, "There was builder that fled from Athens in a great hurry. His name was Daedalus, and I am that man. Once, I was an architect for Aegeus, the king of Athens. Now I aspire to be the architect and builder for your King Minos. Take me to your king. He will know of my deeds and reputation. And yes, not long ago an innocent youth did fall from the roof of a building being reconstructed under my supervision. He died. But it was not by my hand, even though his mother believes otherwise. It appears that she is a woman of some influence in Athens."

Feeling a growing sense of renewal and purpose, I looked into the eyes of the men standing in the arc of an audience that hemmed me in and said, "Even though I once tried to deceive you, do not take my sight. It will be put to good use. I am going to Krete to help rebuild the communities, temples, and homes that were lost in the last earthquakes. It is a worthy cause. Take us both to Krete. Send word to your king of my purpose. Arrange for a meeting. He might even reward you for bringing me from Athens."

The captain stroked his chin and said nothing for a long time. He turned to face the crew, trying to ascertain if any were in accord with my plea. I could see approval in some of their faces.

"Well said, Daedalus, builder of stone and wood," Nikolaos announced, clapping his hands. "I believe that you will do these things and more. For that, you will need your sight and a clear vision. But there is one thing more you must promise, before we can agree to finish this journey with you."

"Name it," I replied. From their murmurs, the crew appeared to be curious, as well.

"There are already too many orphans on the Great Green," the captain answered. "You must make room amidst all your ambitions to raise this one as your own." He gestured for Icarus to come forward. The boy acted as if his small hands were stuck to the rail. After a short struggle with Aadam, he released his grip. Walking together, they made their way to the cluster of men. The crew members parted, and Icarus was gently pushed forward to stand next to the captain, Aadam not far behind. "Make your pledge to Icarus right here right now and know that every mariner on this ship is listening. You will be held to your word."

I knelt on one knee to be at his level, and a great fullness rose into my heart and throat.

"Your instincts are probably telling you to run as fast and as far as you can as soon as this ship reaches land," I said. "But listen to me. Together, we have found a way through the danger, and it is over. There is no need for running anymore. More than that, I intend to keep the promise I made to you back in Athens. After today, I will not lie to you or to anyone else ever again. Icarus, I pledge to you that I will keep you safe, care for you, and see that you are never hungry. From this day on, I am, and always will be your father."

There were cheers and tears all around the ship.

PART III

Krete

Amidst the wine-dark sea lies Krete,
 a fair rich island populous beyond compute,
with ninety cities of mixed speech,
where several languages co-exist.
Besides the Kretans proper then are Achaeans,
Cydonians, Dorians of tossing crest and noble Pelasgians.
The capital is Knossos,
ruled by Minos who from his ninth year talked familiarly with great Zeus.

Odyssey, Book 19
Written by the Greek epic poet Homer
about 700 BCE

CHAPTER TWENTY FIVE

In the late afternoon heat, Naomi and Deena lingered in a patch of shade on a hillside decked with wildflowers. Hundreds of varieties of edible plants and herbs grew on the hillsides above their village, each one with a distinctive flavor or taste. Boiled and mixed with olive oil and lemon, the greens they collected in their aprons would soon become dinner. Maybe their mothers would ask where they had gone for so long. Or maybe each would just be assigned a new chore to complete before supper. Either way, the girls were in no hurry to return to the village.

Deena hummed contentedly, her head bobbing just a little too much as she pulled the petals one by one from a black-eyed Susan. She was full of music and rhythm and loved to mimic the calls of the bulbuls, blackbirds, and robins. Even at her young age it was a talent that set her apart from everyone else in the village. By adding overtones her calls sounded happy, fearful, or sad. Often the birds would answer back.

Naomi stared out at the calm clear water, combing through the tangles of her friend's long dark hair all the time watching a small fishing boat with a sun-bleached sail bearing for the village wharf.

"I'm sure that's his boat," Naomi said, adjusting the white oleander blossom that adorned her ear.

"Whose boat?" Deena asked, teasing her older and blossoming friend.

Naomi let go of the comb and pushed against her friend's back, laughing.

Although strangers sometimes asked if they were sisters or cousins, there was also a remarkable contrast between them. Deena had a noticeable length to her crooked nose. Owning this feature, Deena never attracted the looks quite like Naomi would. The one boy that seemed to keep Naomi's favor the longest was Salim, a handsome older boy with a ready smile. He and his father often fished along the rocks close to the coast where the fish came to feed. Everyone in the tranquil village knew that one day the boat would pass to Salim. That was the way things were done in this quiet tranquil place on the southwestern shore of the island of Krete.

One early evening not long ago Salim was by himself leaning against a rock near the water, reweaving a line from a net. Deena and Naomi had gone out walking the beach at dusk, looking for murex shells. And there he was just down the sand from them, watching their approach.

"Walk by my side," Naomi had whispered to her friend, and subtly, without even a pause, her walk became more. Deena changed course to keep up but without the graceful flow. As they walked past in silent recognition, Salim raised his free hand and waved, unable to either look away or speak. A few more strides and Naomi looked back, taking in his dark eyes. Then she turned with a sly smile and resumed her walk. Fascinated and distinctly removed from all of it, Deena broke into a perfect imitation of the bulbul's night song. Naomi listened and leaned her head and shoulder against her younger friend, and they both laughed for the sheer joy of it.

Separated from the fishing village by a range of high mountains, the *Pelican* and her crew were beached on the busy northern shore of Krete. Freshly bathed and groomed, Captain Nikolaos walked into the large hexagonal megaron of the palace, with its colorful murals and intricate ceiling designs of ceramic and terra cotta tile. Four stout pillars of massive cedar stood in the center of the room, supporting what was left of the roof and defining the corners of a large fire pit. Even though the day was waning, it was a busy place. Many citizens still waited with their disputes and their pleas for an audience with the king or some member of the council. Most carried gifts, believing that it would aid in their cause.

Nikolaos was arrayed in his finest saffron robe, cinching it, as always, with a finely tooled belt of leather and silver. The carved ivory handle of his knife protruded into plain view. The captain strode past the waiting citizenry without a glance. Two double doors beckoned at the far end of the room. Beyond it stood a semi-circular courtyard and garden with an expansive view of the surrounding fields. There, a young servant halted his approach, bowing to the man behind the well-weathered, impassive face.

"Just tell the king that the *Pelican* has returned from Athens with news of their defenses. If he's asleep, then you had better wake him up. Because Captain Nikolaos does not like to wait," he added, smiling for the first time, "and the king will want to hear this news."

King Minos came striding into the garden muscular arms extending from the sides of his long purple robe. A matching diadem of embroidered linen tied off the graying curls of his head. Minos quickly picked out Captain Nikolaos and walked straight for him, calling out his name. Soon each one was soundly thumping the other on the back.

"So good to see you, my friend," said the king, standing nearly a full head taller. "How long has it been?"

"Too long a time," replied Captain Nikolaos.

The king led the way toward a private section of the courtyard. In no time food and drink was served and the two men talked together long into the evening. The ruler was eager to learn about this most recent encounter with the Athenian king. The captain assured him that there had been no hostilities and that Aegeus had paid the time-honored tribute with a full chest of silver. At this news King Minos ordered more wine. He toasted both the captain and his crew.

"In fact," reported Nikolaos, "the voyage was without incident except for picking up two interesting passengers."

Minos happily listened to this unexpected and pleasant turn of events, enjoying how the wine effected both his mood and the tale.

"And you are sure that this man is really Daedalus the inventor and architect for Aegeus?"

"Quite sure," said Nikolaos, telling the story of the confrontation on the ship, and how his passenger had redeemed himself.

"You did not make land then on Kalliste?" Minos asked.

"I did not want to allow the man to be rewarded for his treachery," Nikolaos responded. "He only had a glimpse. We made sure there was no opportunity for him to view any of her fortifications."

"Tell me more."

"It was never his true destination anyway. From the start he made it clear that his goal was to come here, to reach Krete."

"There's a lot of work in Knossos for a man like him," replied the king. "Was he hurt in the fight?"

"Just some cuts and bruises. He will mend."

"Any of the crewmen hurt?"

"Nothing that won't heal."

"And what of the boy? What is his name?"

"Icarus. He's a quick study, that one. I'm still not sure what their relationship was before leaving Athens, but before the voyage ended the architect adopted him as his son. He made it through the entire voyage without complaint. He'll make a fine sailor someday, I have no doubt."

"All right then. I'm going to give your man Daedalus a chance to live up to his reputation. If he does, you and your crew will do very well by it. You have my word," Minos lifted his intricately glazed clay goblet.

"You've always been generous with us, my king," Nikolaos replied.

"Long ago when I needed men and ships for the assault on Athens, you were one of the first to sign on. You docked the *Pelican* and exchanged her for a war galley," the king continued, deliberately pausing for effect, "I will never forget that."

"We put on quite a show that day, didn't we?" agreed the captain. "Wave after wave of galleys and troops, we could have sacked the city before Aegeus was out of bed."

"We might have…and the vengeful father in me was salivating to burn her to the ground," Minos responded, staring into his goblet. "Athens was plump and ripe…waiting to be plucked in one swift stroke!"

"And Krete would have gained another sworn enemy," the captain countered, his tone low and conciliatory. "I am grateful to the king who had made the final decisions that day."

"I know all the reasons," said Minos, a touch of sadness in his voice. "The choices were difficult."

"For our nation to thrive, for our people to prosper, we must have reliable trading partners," Captain Nikolaos responded, his words energetic. "You, more than anyone, understand the greater wisdom of this path. It is what makes you a great king."

"Did Aegeus pay the bribe," asked Minos, "In full?"

"Yes, and it is safe in the *Pelican's* hold. I've already spoken with Belisario. He's on his way to the beach with a security force right now."

"Good. Very good," declared King Minos. "Thank you for your work, your counsel, and all that you do for our great nation."

He held up his goblet and drained it. Smiling at his guest, the king signaled for the performance to begin.

"How is the crew? Your second, Orion, is he well? Still plugging pirates with that oversized longbow?" he asked, a nostalgic twinkle in his eyes.

"He's greyer now, but still giving his all."

"Aren't we all?"

"Orion doesn't seek them out with nearly the same diligence that he once did, but the pirates still seem to find him or his arrows. It is a curious sort of attraction—" Nikolaos began before being distracted by the sultry movements of the seven nubile bodies coming into view.

"Oh, yes," he said, admiring the freshly oiled and glistening skin.

"More wine for the captain," ordered Minos.

"You probably haven't heard the latest. On our last stop at Lykia, he actually traded the longbow away."

"How is that possible? He treasured that bow. What could he have wanted more?"

"Another bow, genuine Phrygian," said Nikolaos, staring at the dancers, "Made of horn and wood and leather. I've watched strong young sailors try to string it and fail. It is a powerful weapon."

"I must see this bow someday."

"Come back with me to Amnisos then," the captain challenged.

"If only I could," the king replied, smiling as a dancer flashed by, catching his eye.

The captain continued, "There are a few oarsmen cashing out here. One wants to learn shipbuilding."

"Amnisos is a good place for a shipbuilder," agreed the king.

Nikolaos cupped his goblet in both hands and nodded, staring straight ahead.

"It won't be difficult to find replacements. There will be many to choose from, and Orion has a knack for seeing into a man's heart."

"What was that?" asked Minos, looking back and forth between his friend and the performers.

They both laughed heartily.

"I was just talking about the crew," said Nikolaos.

"Tell Orion that I appreciate his good works."

"He's offloading the Athenian trade as we speak."

"Then where are you headed?"

"First to Kalliste, for cedar, orichalcum, and perfume base. We'll trade the lumber for copper in Rhodos, and then on to Egypt."

"That could take most of the season."

"Only if the winds punish us."

A young dancer broke away from the group and stepped towards her audience of two with long, rhythmic strides. The conversation stopped. The dancer pulsed her hips slowly, provocatively, in time to a distant rhythm globe. She placed her hands on her hips and turned, bending at the waist. Her dark curls swept across the floor as she swayed back and forth to the rhythm, extending her gentle curves toward the sky.

"I would rather she did the punishing," said Minos, breaking the silence. "What do you think, my friend?"

Abruptly she stood up and faced them again, flipping her thick dark hair over her head. Hands on her hips, she voraciously eyed the captain. His jaw fell open. In the next moment, two muscular young men strode towards her from opposite ends of the stage. They grabbed her arms, dragging and pulling her back, away from her admirers.

"Do you like her?" The king asked while the dancers reformed their troupe and continued the performance.

"Unequivocally," replied the captain. "Yes. I do," he said, following her movements. Then she was gone and he picked up the thread of the conversation.

"It should be a profitable season. In the past, I've done very well trading with the Egyptians. They want our copper and will pay a good price for it. But the orichalcum, that's a completely different subject. They hunger for it," the captain said emphasizing each word. "From all my sources, I believe that our mines on Kalliste are still the only source of supply."

"I must be informed if that changes," said Minos.

"I understand," replied the captain.

"When you return from this next voyage, be sure and take time for a holiday here on Krete. I always enjoy your company, and your stories. I need men like you to keep me in touch with the rest of the world."

"It is my privilege. Much of the time," Nikolaos said, "I cannot imagine why any sane man would pass up a chance to sail the Great Green on a fine ship like the *Pelican,* with my steady hand at the helm. Then I have an experience like this, and I begin to see the appeal of life in the city."

"Perhaps you will have an even deeper appreciation as the evening progresses," the king replied, throwing back his head in a majestic wide-mouthed laugh as he thoroughly enjoyed the moment.

CHAPTER TWENTY SIX

A way from the bustle of Knossos, the *Pelican* sat beached on one side of a large, almost circular harbor. Grey and brown hills towered over the shore. Most of the crewmen were spread out around the remains of a cooking fire, gathered in pods of three or four, drinking wine, swapping stories, or gambling. I sat alone on the outskirts of the camp, well fed on fresh tuna and wine, watching the grey sliver of a waxing moon rise above the sleeping harbor town. My blindfold was gone. In its place were two black eyes and a swollen nose, but I felt content.

The bay at Amnisos was a sprawling accumulation of sun-bleached warehouses, stores, and shops that gave way to an assortment of nets, fishing boats, and galleys, all lining the beach. Interspersed between the smaller boats were six larger ships, framed and braced in various stages of construction, poised just above the water line. Looking to the horizon beyond the city, I lifted the remains of a wineskin and made a toast: "Here's to a new life on a fine island." Then, looking around and spying Icarus fast asleep on the sand, I added, "For both of us."

Sleep eluded me. Two days were gone since the struggle on the *Pelican*. Once it was over, the entire crew was ready to land. Everyone knew that sailing in the darkness was a fool's venture; too many tales of shipwreck and doom. Somehow the captain found a narrow beach at the base of the cliffs. We landed, built our fires, and tended to our wounds. For the injured, the ship's healer made an offering to the goddess of dreams and forgetfulness. He concocted a soothing blend of citrus, herbs, and honey to share among us. I remember drinking a few swallows, being carried to a place by the fire, but then the drink dulled my senses completely.

Too many thoughts jumbled for expression inside my head. I walked over the sand toward a stand of large rocks, trying to imagine the meeting that would take place between the king and Captain Nikolaos. There was so much to be done, much to learn about this new culture—and not just the language.

What had seemed like a remote possibility on the mainland only a few weeks ago was now almost at hand. To be seen by the king and his council, I had only to wait and be patient.

How strange that this introduction would take place, because the men I had once set out to deceive wanted to arrange it. They had challenged me. My face still bore the bruises. If there were lingering resentments among the crew, I was certainly not aware of them. Now they accepted me. We shared a common interest or purpose. Everyone certainly enjoyed having Icarus for company during the voyage.

I leaned against a large rock and looked around at the sleeping crew. Rubbing my back against it, I slid down onto the sand to find a more comfortable spot and a slightly different perspective. Icarus lay peacefully near the cooking fire, curled up on a sleeping hide near Aadam. Both were sound asleep. I couldn't help but smile.

So much had happened during the last five days, a complicated mix of tedium and beauty, of fear and release. It was so easy now to look back and see the choices made, so easy to judge the outcomes. I could have lost my life back there at the sea gate. I was very grateful that I hadn't. There was a discernible sweetness now in the beach's sand and the earth beneath my sandaled feet.

According to the original plan, the voyage was to be quiet and uneventful. How funny life can be. I had intended to travel unheard and unobtrusive, and instead Icarus and I became the center of the only drama on the journey. I knew I must talk with Icarus about this. Now that we were finally on Krete, I realized how important it was for Icarus to trust me. He was so vulnerable. He had no one else, no one but me.

With these thoughts and more filling my head, I gathered my sleeping gear and laid it out closer to the fire and to Icarus. Then I propped the empty traveling bag beneath my head, lay back onto the sand, and stared up at the stars, just as I had done every night since we left Athens. I was ready for sleep now, and the chance—just a chance—for the flight dream to return.

The captain sprawled on his back on a pallet of fine pillows, snoring loudly. His first day back in the palace had been massively enjoyable. With his good humor and generosity, Nikolaos was popular with the female slaves. In the crook of his thick arm, a big-breasted, blond slave nestled her head, sleeping quietly. Next to her lay another one, dark skinned with huge eyes. The king was nowhere to be seen. His wine had been watered. After the entertainment he left the captain to his own devices, choosing instead to follow the drum of his own ambitions.

Minos had gone walking in the moonlight along the cobblestone road, the one that would someday stretch all the way to Zakros on the eastern coast. Behind him, at a respectful distance, a scribe and a servant followed. The king was lost in his thoughts, mumbling and gesturing with his hands. It was not unusual for sleep to elude him. Usually he made the most of it. Sometimes he was just too busy for it, other times too filled with worry. On that night he was genuinely motivated, making an inventory. Soon, there would be a new, particularly skilled set of eyes to consider the restoration of the palace and the city. A whole new phase of rebuilding could begin, assuming that the man in the harbor really was Daedalus the engineer, and not just another spy sent by the crafty pale-skinned Aegeus.

With the sun on the eastern horizon, Minos returned to the colorful gardens and to the huge, intricately carved, high-backed chair with gold inlay. He was finally ready for sleep. He was a large man. Naturally, his chair was the largest one in the complex. No one else would dare to use it. Once, it had occupied the center of the megaron where the King and his advisors held court and dispensed justice. But with the gaping hole in the roof, that room had lost its power. Spread over a huge wall mural behind the dozing king, mythic creatures sat upon rolling hills beneath a summer sky. Just before drifting off to sleep, he reasoned that this was just the right location for meeting the newcomers.

CHAPTER TWENTY SEVEN

On the north shore of the island Icarus awoke to the early morning light. He looked around at the sleeping crew scattered on the beach and walked to the water's edge. Pausing there, he took off his sandals and dug his toes into the smooth wet sand. In shallow water just a few feet off shore, large grey rocks beckoned him to come further. So he did, jumping from one to the next, watching the shadows shift beneath the water's surface. In the shallows between the rocks tiny fish of electric blue and green floated motionless as the boy leapt across the gaps between the rocks. At the furthest point from shore he stopped, balanced on the rough sloping surface of a prominent rock and relieved himself, shooting warm urine from his pressured bladder in a high arc, splashing patterns into the water below.

Returning from a predawn walk engrossed in my thoughts, I walked down the strand line among the sandpipers and tattlers. The flight dream had not returned, but I knew that it had to be more than just a random event. The memory was still very fresh, and I believed that the dream was a rare and precious thing, something to be nurtured, even protected. I was still trying to understand it, confident that it was somehow connected to all the changes my life was going through. If only I could experience it one more time.

My train of thought was interrupted by the sight of Icarus' artistry from the rock. Then I realized that he was motioning to me, inviting me to join him. There was a lightness in my chest as I left the shore behind, following the same course of rocks in a series of awkward jumps. In Athens, I might already have been at work at this time of the morning. But this was a very different place and a brand new day. I had nothing to do, no deadline to meet, and no project to work on, except perhaps for building a relationship with an eight-year-old boy.

I certainly did not miss the busyness of my life in Athens.

I was on a different journey now, and it was just beginning. I had a vision to follow and there was just no room, no place for lingering on old resentments.

"What do you see down there?" I asked, stepping onto the last rock.

Icarus looked up and pointed into the water, saying nothing. Slowly, I made my way to the edge and peered into the sea. We stood on an immense block of stone, most of it underwater. Hundreds of silver and blue fish hovered in the crystalline depths, all of them gently following some unseen guidance.

"Beautiful!" I said, glancing at Icarus and kneeling down for a closer look.

As I lowered myself onto one knee perilously close to the edge, I lost my balance. I threw one hand up into the air to compensate, waving it back and forth as I teetered over the water. In slow motion I tumbled over the side, but not before receiving a stout push from my newfound son. Instantly, the fish scattered. Icarus laughed, jumping up and down with glee, and pointed at me as I splashed about in the water.

He stood on the rock outside of splash range. Treading water I called out, "What a difference a day can make!"

More than the words that were spoken, there was ease in the sound of my voice.

"Oh, yes," he replied. "How much longer do we have to wait here?"

"Until the captain returns. We don't know where the palace is or how to get there. Better to wait and let him provide the introduction. All I know is that good things are coming our way, and soon."

Icarus stepped a little closer, taunting me. I responded with a flick of my hand, quickly sending a spray of water in his direction. It fell just short of its intended target.

"You missed me!" Icarus quipped. "Watch this. I'm going to leap off this rock and skim across the water, just like a skipping stone," he announced.

Taking two quick steps toward the edge, he faked a jump and then abruptly turned back.

I splashed several more times at the dodging, laughing figure. Then I took a deep breath, raised both arms over my head and slid beneath the water's surface into a light-shaft chapel of pale blue shadows. Slowly I exhaled, gradually descending into the drifting mass of silvery fish. They circled about me in an endless spiral, reminiscent of the dream of flight. I held my breath, watching the obsessively curious fish circle around me, until I could wait no longer. With two sharp thrusts I kicked toward the surface and broke through like a dolphin breaching. I gulped a lungful of air, rolled over onto my back and swam back to shore.

The sounds of our play attracted an audience, and a rower named Panos met me at the water's edge.

"Nothing like a morning swim for a complete wake up," he said.

"That's for sure!" I replied through labored breath. "Panos, how long is the hike to the palace at Knossos from here?"

"If you left now and didn't dawdle along the way, you could easily be there in half a day. There is a good road." He pointed a thick, muscular forefinger to a spot on the hillside where a river descended through a maze of greenery, before cutting a curving channel into the bay. "Up there, in the hills above the beach. Once you find the road, you really can't miss it."

"I can't wait to get there," Icarus said, joining us.

"And I hope to be taking you there," the sailor announced. "What would you like to do there?"

"See the palace. Meet the king. Lots of things," Icarus insisted.

"Well, there is a lot to see there," Panos replied with a wink. "You will like it, both of you. I can promise you that," he continued, making no effort to downplay his pride. "It's not at all like Athens. It's so much better."

"Aren't cities and people pretty much the same, wherever you go?" I asked, taking the bait. "How can it be so different here?"

"Krete is like no other place. You will feel it soon enough, once your soul begins to grow. The gods are very close here," Panos insisted. "The priestesses call it a force, vital and beneficent that rises up out of the land and into our veins. It does not discriminate. You will see. It is lucky for you that you came to Krete."

"I heard the same things about Kalliste, and getting there almost killed me!" I joked.

"A little misunderstanding," said the oarsman with a laugh. "Look how much the swelling has gone down already. The area around your eyes and nose has turned a lovely shade of greenish yellow. You'll be good as new in no time."

The bruises on my face were still tender. I couldn't help but laugh at his description.

"Whenever I look at the city of Athens all that I see are shades of white, gray and brown. It reminds me of old bones, all the color bleached away from standing too long in the sun," the sailor said.

"It's the only place I've ever lived," I replied.

"In Knossos, there are gardens everywhere." The seaman spoke with swelling satisfaction. "Even the walls are decorated in the colors, patterns, and shapes of the earth and the sea. We have large public arenas for festivals and athletic competition. I have sailed all over the Mediterranean. There is no better place to come home to!"

"So you were born on this island?" I asked.

"Of course," said the seaman, in mock reply. "This island is my home and I've journeyed far enough for this season. I will guide you as far as Knossos."

CHAPTER TWENTY EIGHT

Three days later Captain Nikolaos appeared back on the beach, beaming and full of goodwill. With him came a small caravan of merchants and entertainers to make the last evening at Amnisos more enjoyable. He even brought a seamstress and cloth to make new tunics for Icarus and me. The captain announced that tomorrow the *Pelican* would sail again for Kalliste. But this time, Icarus and I would not be on board. Our journey was inland for a meeting with the king. Panos and Xanthus, both with young families in nearby villages, would accompany us as far as the palace.

That night Icarus and I had our first taste of bougatsa, a mouth-watering Kretan pastry made from several varieties of nuts and seeds mixed with honey and folded between thin layers of dough. We had several contests to see which one could savor the sweet goodness the longest without swallowing as the tasty morsel dissolved in our mouths. I can still see the smile on Icarus' face as he licked his fingers, honey dripping down his cheeks. It was the food of the gods.

Much later, Nikolaos invited me to share some wine. As always, he spoke freely and with confidence, rambling on about the long pull to Egypt that lay ahead. Then, without notice, he changed the subject.

"You know, we have to clear the air about what happened at the sea gate."

"What about it?" I stammered, my voice betraying disappointment at the change.

"About what happened to you," he said, patting his open hand against my cheek. "Even though the swelling has gone down, I can still see some of the bruising," he continued, turning his head so that we were face to face. "From my side of the ledger, I could not let you enter these islands that way, all secrets and smuggling. You understand that, right?"

"And if I hadn't found my voice that night, what would you have done?" I asked pointedly.

"But you did," the captain said.

"You could have killed me or had me thrown into the sea."

"Those were possibilities. You could also have been struck by lightning. None of those things happened," Nikolaos responded, throwing an arm around my shoulder. "You showed us the man underneath the mask. And you, Daedalus, are a good man. In your heart you know what is right. And you touched us all that night, the way that you strove to accomplish it. You understand these things, yes?"

"When you put it that way, yes, I do," I replied, nodding.

"And it was a good outcome. Don't you agree?" prodded the captain.

"Of course. I'm alive. We're both alive. And we're both leaving for Knossos in the morning?" I said, seeking final confirmation.

"The king wants to meet you. You have a marvelous opportunity here," the captain insisted. "Continue to do what is right, and he will welcome you. Good fortune has already smiled upon both you and the boy, just not in the way that you planned."

"You know what, captain? It *was* the right outcome. Not just right, but good."

"Yes, it was. And the next time we meet, it will be as friends. You can do that too, can't you?"

"Certainly," I replied from my heart. "Yes, I can."

"These islands are a good place for you, my friend. You'll do very well here. I can see this in you. You will be a rich and influential man, if that is what you want. So, if you ever need a good ship for another transport, don't forget the *Pelican* and her crew."

"Oh, I won't forget," I replied with an uneasy laugh, remembering all the gold and silver already lost to the captain and his crew. "The fee has already been paid, right?"

Nikolaos threw a thick forearm around my shoulder. "Of course, my old friend, of course," he replied with a grin.

CHAPTER TWENTY NINE

Naomi wandered alone through the hills above the village. The easy finds near the village were all picked over. It was late in the day. A hot wind from the south blew against her back. Why hadn't her mother planned this better? Naomi had called out to her friend to come along, but Deena's mother had had other plans. Now she had to climb higher, alone, and walk much further to find edible wild greens, horta, for her family's dinner.

She froze in her tracks and listened. It was a snorting sound, carried on the wind, like an animal looking for its own dinner. Only then did Naomi realize how far from home she had traveled. She scanned the hillside above. Nothing moved. Then she heard it again, closer this time. Her heart raced. She ran toward the top of the hill for a better look.

"Snorrttt!" it sounded again.

She nearly jumped out of her skin. Then came a wave of reassuring laughter. She looked around and saw Salim, coming out from the shadow of a large rock. Sudden relief swept through her, then happiness, then anger. She shook her fist at him, but he just stood there staring back at her for the longest time. She dropped her fist and smiled, returning the look.

Most everyone in the village at one time or another had noticed something about her eyes. Perfectly matched on each side of her slender nose, some described them as so dark that the pupils were barely visible. Salim had certainly noticed. He said that looking into them was like falling into a deep well.

"Come over here. I want to show you something," he said, gesturing toward her.

Her heart beating like a drum, she started moving along the crest of the hill towards him. Then she stopped and pulled herself back.

"We can't be seen together like this," she said, trying to sound convincing.

"Come down off the top of the hill," Salim reassured her. "No one will see us here."

"You have to leave."

"I know," he said, smiling and gesturing for her to come closer.

She moved until she was standing right next to him, enclosed by the sloping hillsides and out of the wind. Gazing into her eyes, he reached down and picked up her hand, holding it in both of his. Naomi swallowed hard. She wanted to speak, but found no words. There was an intense quickening deep in her abdomen. He placed her hand upon his chest and held it there. She felt the beating of his heart fast and rhythmic just like her own. Salim reached out his hand and placed in on her chest. He felt the beating of her heart. He caressed her very young, budding breast until she gasped and quickly pulled away, severing the connection. Without a word she crossed her arms over her chest and stepped away.

"Wait!" he pleaded. "I will go," he continued, bowing to her and smiling once again. "And do not worry. One day soon, we will marry."

Then he waved to her in that same way of his, and headed back down the gentle slope towards the village. For a long time she watched, waiting for him to turn around and look again. And he did, twice.

We stood on the shore at Amnisos, saying our farewells. I was more than ready to start over in a landlocked, inland city. Icarus though, was clearly torn watching Aadam leave. I invited the young mariner to visit us in Knossos anytime and to stay for as long as he liked.

"The *Pelican* is my home," Aadam had replied, "I will stay with her until I've found a better one."

The words had such a practiced sound to them. It must have been a line said many times over by other crew members. We watched the crew

launch the ship for the last time. Then it was gone, heading north out of the
harbor, bound for Kalliste to pick up the remainder of their trading pod of
ships, and then on to Egypt. It was sad watching the ship depart for the last
time, but I had had enough of the seagoing life.

We gathered our few belongings and followed Panos and Xanthus
up the hard-packed trail that led out of town. The earthen road traversed
through tall stands of oak and cedar, ascending to the top of the pass and
a rocky ledge overlooking the harbor. A few leagues further the trail led
into a cobblestone road. There at the junction was a large distinctive stone
marker, carved in the shape of a double-bladed ax head.

"It's the sign of the realm," explained Xanthus with a grin. "One of
the many ways our king marks his territory."

The road ahead was wide enough for a two-wheeled cart or for two
people to walk side by side.

"Were you here for the last earthquake?" I asked Panos.

"Depends on what you mean by the last one. Sometimes we don't
feel them on the ship." The sailor shrugged. "The sea has other storms for
us to face. We often only learn about the damage after we return home."

"We certainly have them in Athens," I replied, "the earthquakes."

"Of course, it's a fact of life all over the Great Green."

"When I was Icarus' age, we lived on a small farm outside of
Athens. We had a few sheep and goats, and a garden to keep them away
from. One dark night, a quake rumbled through and shook the house so
hard part of the roof fell in. I still remember as if it were yesterday."

"Where were you?" asked Icarus, who had been silent up to this
point.

"I was lying with my brother and sister like spoons on a large pallet
on the floor of our house. Something woke me up. It was very dark, and
in the distance I could hear a low rumbling sound, coming closer. Then
the ground began to rise and fall. The sound grew louder and louder, like
a huge bull charging toward us. Earth fell from the ceiling. Then there was
a crash. We all screamed as the roof fell in on top of us. The sound moved
on as quickly as it had come. The shaking stopped. I wanted to get up, but
I couldn't rise off my knees. I was trapped. I couldn't move."

"Was anyone hurt?"

"I couldn't see or feel anyone. I tried to call out, but my nose and
mouth were full of dust and dirt. I heard sobbing. After a short time or a
long time, there was no way to tell, I heard my father's voice, calling for us.
It sounded far away, but I knew he was searching. He had always told us,

'I will always be here for you.' So I just lay there with my hands cupped in front of my face, holding open this small breathing space."

"You were blessed that night, my friend," said Panos.

"Then what happened?" asked Icarus.

"They dug us out, one by one. I remember bathing in the stream that night and sitting around the fire for a long time, drinking tea. Some of our goats heard us and began to wander back, all on their own," I continued, smiling at the memory.

"I have a wife and a small son," Panos responded, "And the supporting beam in our house has held. But some of those who lived in and around the palace have not been so lucky. In the city, the buildings are multi-storied, with walls and upper floors high in the air. When they began to shake and sway, there was much damage. Many were hurt, both the poor and the powerful. All that anyone can do is endure, be grateful when it's over, and then start rebuilding."

CHAPTER THIRTY

While our guides led us to the palace a beautiful woman named Naucreta quietly ate her breakfast on the balcony of her room within that very compound. Dressed in a green flowing robe edged with gold thread, she sat on her veranda drinking her morning tea. Great magenta sprays of bougainvillea bedecked the balcony. About to turn thirty, she chatted with her servant and listened expectantly to the early morning bustle of the plaza below.

Naucreta's servant, Filia, was older and she took great pride in the gardening. She had a way with plants and enjoyed spending her early morning hours on the balcony, nurturing those in her care. Like her, the flowers were at their best in the early mornings, before the heat of the day extracted its toll. Filia was the one keeping the pace in the ongoing competition between homeowners for the most elegant display. She sang to them regularly, watered them, and plucked the withering blossoms. And she would do it all over again today as soon as she finished combing her mistress's hair into long thick curls drawn back to reveal the stunning face.

The morning air was already full of the sounds and smells of hundreds of people on the courtyard below, setting up shops and stalls and displaying their merchandise. Soon, shouting and arguing would be heard as accompaniment to the buying and selling of everything from this morning's catch of fresh fish and octopi, to the normal carpets, tools, and fine jewelry, handcrafted by the residents. Sequestered within the green vines and blossoms, Naucreta's quarters had a view that took in all of it. Through the years she had received many presents, precious stones, fine pottery, and jewelry. Once, the king of Naxos had even sent a gift of ivory from far-off Carthage. And she had been clever enough to use them, to trade her way into possession of one of the highly valued, east-facing apartments.

Naucreta understood that the longing looks she had once easily inspired in men were no longer given so freely. She knew that their gazes were going to younger, fresher-looking women. Even though she and the king were no longer lovers, he still valued her company, her insights, and her conversation. Once he had moved on to the body of another, Naucreta had continued to cultivate their relationship, and remained a trusted advisor. That was how she had learned of the pending arrival of the Athenian architect, even before most of Minos' so-called aides knew. She still had access to the palace whenever she wanted. And foreign men with power and influence were often very clear about their desire for the services of the king's mistress, even a former one. Some were willing to pay her price and usually they shared their secrets.

"You must return to the palace today and watch for the Athenians," she told Filia that morning. "I want to know as soon as they arrive at the gate."

We followed the road through hills and forest, always climbing, until we came to a rocky plateau with a fine view. There, we rested on the high ground. Below us a shimmering river, still swollen with run-off from the snow-capped mountains, curved across the valley. Our path seemed to follow its course at a respectful elevation. To the east were rolling hills of pine and juniper, covered in dull shades of green. Far to the west lay a large patch of cleared ground built into and spreading out across gently sloping hillsides.

"It's beautiful," I said, admiring the landscape and studying the distant complex of buildings.

Panos had been right. This island was more appealing. The center of Athens was a towering natural fortress that overlooked a crowded city, all surrounded by decaying outer walls. Here, nothing suggested a boundary or battlements. This was a growing city, expanding outward into the verdant green of the surrounding fields and hills. Even from this distance I could make out patches of green within the complex of structures, some of them filled with wild color.

"You can see the maze of terraced buildings, right?" asked Panos, pointing with his calloused hand.

"It's so far away," Icarus remarked.

"It's also our destination," said Xanthus with no small amount of desire. "That's why we need to keep going."

"And we will," Panos replied, adjusting his seat on a large flat rock, "after a little break." He took another swallow from his water skin. "Do you see the high point of the structure?" he continued. "It's called the palace. That's where the original citadel was located. Legend has it that it marks the entrance to a large underground cave."

"It's would make a good defensive position," Xanthus added.

"With lots of storage," Panos continued. "Anyway, the foundations there are ancient," Panos continued. "The citadel has become the king's megaron. All around it, the old buildings are used as treasuries or offices for the council."

"And that's where you're taking us?" I asked.

"A couple old salts like us won't be goin' all the way up there," answered Xanthus. "People get lost in that maze…and they never come out."

"Are you talking about the caverns below, or the politics above?" I asked, trying to make a joke.

"I'm talking about the caverns," Xanthus insisted. "They're a cold dark maze of blind passages and twisting paths. When Minos' father had a thief or a miscreant to deal with, he'd make a spectacle out of throwing him into the caverns. None of them ever came out again."

"That's why we call it the labyrinth," said Panos.

"Because there's no way out?" asked Icarus.

"Only one, the same way you went in."

"Does King Minos do the same with his enemies?" I asked.

"He couldn't, even if he wanted to," answered Xanthus.

"Why not?" I asked.

"It's flooded now," answered Panos. "So they say."

Descending into the valley, we passed lumber camps on both sides of the river. All around them trees had been cut away, fodder for the maritime fleet. Above the cuts, a canopy of tall trees covered the hillsides. Ahead of us there were pastures, fields, and farms. We passed row upon row of domesticated grape vines and large groves of olive trees. I had never seen so many farms, and we encountered more and more people. There were merchants, farmers, and slaves; some hauling goods in pushcarts and many just walking along with a bedroll and a water skin. Nearing the city, the road became even wider with room for the four of us to walk together.

"What are those things?" Icarus asked.

There were sculptures, regularly spaced along the tops of the palace and the city's highest buildings. I was curious about them too. They looked like giant sentinels that were keeping watch from the roof lines.

"What do they look like to you?" asked Zanthus.

"Like horns," Icarus replied.

Then I saw the resemblance, larger-than-life replicas, upright and projecting their power outward.

At last, the road we had followed all morning, diverged into two, both of them still inclining. Xanthus explained that one way led south over a distant mountain pass and eventually to the southern coast. There was another fertile valley and a large city named Phaistos. We took the busier road, turning west toward the heart of Knossos.

We passed through huddled buildings, small stone walls, more people, and a variety of languages. These were the homes of the poorer inhabitants, the servants, and lesser craftspeople. They worked in the dye trade or as processors of fish products, and in places the air was ripe with the byproducts of their labor. The road narrowed as it climbed higher. Neighborhoods, shops, and shrines began to appear, enveloping the road on both sides. These were the homes of a wealthier class, the merchants and skilled artisans.

Finally the road led to a huge, imposing threshold, the gateway to the city. Beyond it lay the palace and the homes of those with power or influence. The gate was actually an open portal constructed of two rows of thick red pillars, holding up a long, flat terrace. Painted on the walls behind the pillars were large frescoes of rolling hills against a sun-filled sky. Here the cobblestones ended, replaced by a beautiful floor covered in intricate mosaic tile. I had never seen anything quite like it, and had to stop to admire the craftsmanship. Even Icarus unconsciously traced the unique spiral patterns in the floor with his bare toes, humming to himself.

Inside the passageway and shaded from the heat, a clean-shaven young man wearing an ivory-colored kilt waited and watched. Blue stone bracelets adorned the dark skin of each wrist. We said our goodbyes to the two seamen, thanked them, and wished them well on their journeys. Both were eager to get back on the road and return to their homes and families. The young man would guide us for the rest of the way. It was Icarus who took the initiative, taking me once again by the arm and guiding us both into the shade of the colossal east entrance of the city of Knossos, the center of commerce for the Minoan empire.

Chapter Thirty One

Icarus and I followed the athletic strides of our broad-shouldered guide through the shade of the passageway into the hot and crowded plaza. More than once Icarus hung back, drawn to the displays of protective amulets or weapons, but I kept a close watch and never let him fall too far behind.

Our guide then led us into the cool of a twisting passageway, up a huge flight of stairs and into a brilliant inner courtyard festooned with flowers and huge richly-patterned rugs. Oil lamps of hand-wrought gold hung suspended from poles. Men and women in layered colorful robes gathered in clusters, busily chatting with one another. It was easily the most luxurious display of furnishings, clothing, and accoutrement that I had ever seen and all of it outdoors. A group of seven stone chairs filled the center of the space, arranged in a large arc. Each had its own uniquely decorated cushion. One, of course, was distinctly higher, broader, and set back from the rest. A large man with disheveled hair and an unkempt beard occupied it. His pure white linen robe was offset by his dark skin. He sat silently, resting his graying head upon his hand. Maybe he was sleeping, or perhaps just bored.

The brand new tunics that Icarus and I wore were undyed and plain. In comparison with all these colorful richly adorned people, I felt distinctly out of place. Icarus felt it too. He stood directly behind me, looking out at the gathering from behind my waist. I'm sure that he preferred the hustle and bustle of the open market to this. Out there he had avenues of escape, places to hide. In this place there would be no hiding.

Our young guide scanned the room, eventually signaling to an older man with a scholarly air who was standing at the edge of the gathering. His face was a mask of composure as he chatted with a bronze-skinned woman wearing a flowing yellow robe. She wore a ruby red necklace. I could not help but notice her, especially her smile. The dignified companion, a translator, nodded to our guide and walked purposefully toward the gray-haired man in the center of the room. Almost at once the courtyard grew silent. King Minos turned towards us, the newcomers, and every eye in the room fell upon us.

I could feel Icarus behind me trying to shrink even further away, as I returned their gazes, trying to make a connection. Walking around the perimeter of the courtyard, the woman with the radiant smile approached us and extended her arms in welcome. First glancing at me, she knelt down to Icarus' height, met his gaze and said hello. He went to her easily, without as much as a backward glance. Meanwhile, the king beckoned, urging me forward. As I stepped into the limelight, I could feel his gaze, taking me in, making his assessments.

I had spoken with a different king on many prior occasions, labored for him over many years. I reminded myself that underneath the purple diadem crown, King Minos was just another man.

After a moment's pause the king greeted us in a rich and resonant voice, easily projecting so that the entire room could hear. "If you are Daedalus, the famous inventor, then welcome to Krete and to Knossos! Do not feel anxious. You are among friends here."

I looked around the courtyard and smiled.

"We know of your fame as an engineer and builder," the king continued. "There is much need in Knossos for a man of your talents." Then he paused, looking down from his elevated, elaborate chair, and waited for a reply.

"Hopefully I can use them in service to this community," I said. Hearing a few approving tones from the crowd, I continued, returning to many of the same ideas and feelings from a few nights before on the *Pelican*. "I am Daedalus, the inventor, and I appreciate this gracious welcome. We are very pleased to be here at last. My young son and I have traveled a long way to offer our services, however they can be used, to help rebuild your magnificent city."

King Minos literally rose to the occasion, dominating the room. Sweeping his open hand across the room, he asked in earnest, "Knossos is a shell of what it once was. Many of our fountains, pillars, and walls tumbled to the ground in a series of earthquakes. We are still rebuilding years later. How can you make these things right, when so many before you have failed?"

"You say you have heard my name before today, so I will confess. It is true that I designed and built a large temple in Athens, along with many fine homes," I answered, wanting to address the entire gathering. "The techniques and designs are in my head, and I will gladly share them." Then I had a moment's inspiration and continued, "Perhaps your engineers look at the city, and see from the perspective of what it once was. If so, then their efforts become constrained to restore what was there before. I am not bound by their preconceptions. Why limit the palace to restoration, when it could be recreated into something more than just its former splendor? I can look with fresh eyes. I can see the potential, for what the city and your palace can become."

"Wonderful," said King Minos, clapping his hands and returning to his chair. "Give me an example."

"Well…" I replied, suddenly improvising. "What about a dance floor? Your island is blessed with an abundance of forests. We passed by so many tall trees on our journey today. Long planks could be cut and fit together like the decking on a ship into any width or length. It could stand near the center of the plaza," I paused, "for ceremonies and celebrations."

The king nodded, obviously pleased with the concept. "I have never heard of such a thing," he replied, stroking his chin. "And I'm quite sure that neither have any of my colleagues. This could be a useful device for performances and celebrations. Several of my daughters are dancers. I have no doubt that they would approve of anything to do with a stage."

"It will require many axes, saws and strong backs," I said.

"We have all those things in great supply. Plus forges and skillful alchemists to make more tools, as needed," replied the king. Then he stopped himself. "How long must the people of the city wait for you to prove your worth?"

It was a fair question; by his having asked it, I knew that the job was mine. "Give me one cycle of the sun to build the dance floor, and to demonstrate the value of my ideas. In that time I assure you, you will know from the progress of the work whether I have the skills to rebuild the rest of the city to your satisfaction."

"One cycle goes by quickly. What if I am displeased?" Minos asked.

"You can fire me at will," I assured him. "And we will leave Krete, if that is your wish. In return, do you promise to give us one full sun cycle before passing judgment on the work?" I asked, hoping for a reciprocal commitment.

"We have an agreement," King Minos announced. "If you can accomplish these things, then you and your son are welcome to stay as long as you like. You shall live in the palace and make your home in this city."

Icarus was holding his hands together, looking very pleased and smiling up at his elegant, graceful companion. I knew that he had heard and understood.

I watched them walk together around a large circular bowl, filled with colorful blooms. From the conversation I had just learned that the Minoan word I had understood as meaning "palace" actually referred to an entire complex of buildings and apartments. It meant a whole system of adjacent structures designed to house a community, many more than just one or two noble families and their servants. Apparently, Icarus and I were now a part of that community.

As the meeting progressed, I felt my confidence returning. King Minos had done much to restore a sense of satisfaction and purpose, refilling a void created the night of the struggle on the ship. In a very short time I had gone from being a prosperous builder in Athens to a penniless man far from home. Now, I was a builder again, this time with a small family. I was grateful.

Tea was served in delicate clay cups, and then a midday meal for everyone in attendance. The king continued our conversation with many other nobles joining in, explaining their wants, ideas, and priorities. It was a collegial exchange of ideas, and with the translator's assistance, I listened thoughtfully to their competing interests.

Then, just as I thought the meeting was ending, the king rose to his full height and walked over to my chair. His face wore a different look, one that was hard and uncompromising. He announced to those still remaining, "Daedalus, I know why you left Athens, and I know what happened to your former apprentice. Serve me with devotion and I will forget your past. And," he continued in slow measured tones, "if it turns out that you still serve Athens, then, both of your lives are forfeit."

It took every ounce of composure I could gather to prevent my jaw from dropping. No words came to mind. I simply stared up at the aging monarch, startled by the sudden and unexpected exercise of authority. Instantly his face transformed back into a mask of composure, but his presence still commanded the room. He calmly returned my gaze, reinforcing the message. Then he showed yet another face, and became the master of ceremonies. He returned to the elevated center of the courtyard and in deep resonant tones announced, "Master builder, you and your son are indeed fortunate. The articulate and talented Naucreta has volunteered to assist you both with your move into our city and in becoming its newest citizens." He gestured toward the beautiful woman who had kept Icarus company throughout the meeting. "For the work you are undertaking, it is critical that you consider yourselves a part of this community."

I was stunned by the king's ease with duality. But looking around the room, everyone within earshot was nodding their approval. Apparently such displays were not unusual. And the king went on, "Naucreta can be a marvelous resource. She knows the city and its people as well as anyone. If you are willing to receive her guidance, she will prove very helpful. Rest in the comfort of your new home. Refresh yourselves, and tour our wonderful city. Master Builder, two days from now, return to this courtyard and ask for me. I am an early riser. We will speak of plans for the city, your needs for a work space, and of things to come."

CHAPTER THIRTY TWO

"I learned about the minotaur today," Icarus said in halting Minoan. We were sitting together on the patio of our new home, intending to speak only in the new language. "He's a half-man, half-bull that lives under the palace."

"He sounds scary. How did he get down there?" I replied in slower broken Minoan.

"No one knows for sure. He just did," Icarus insisted.

"According to Panos, the caverns under the palace are flooded," I answered.

"Maybe he's half-fish too!" Naucreta added, laughing at her own joke.

She had been listening patiently to our efforts. Learning the language was our first real step towards becoming part of the community. At first Icarus had held back, unsure of how to respond to all the attention. But it didn't last. Naucreta found ways to get through or around his fears and make a connection. Then, all it took was a simple gesture for the gangly young boy to respond in kind, reaching around the folds of her long robe and sinking into her warmth. Once he began to trust, he became curious about everything. More than once I heard him ask if she had any children, or when she might move into the apartment.

Naucreta had arranged for a housekeeper. Next, a language tutor appeared. And for an entire cycle of the moon, our lovely guide returned nearly every day. She listened to our questions and offered her suggestions. She brought language and culture lessons, food and good company—and her smile. In return, Icarus and I dedicated ourselves to mastering the intricacies of life in Knossos. It was satisfying for me to watch him blossom.

Our new home faced south, with a view of the hillside and sky. It wasn't dramatic or impressive, but it was comfortable, and only a short walk to the central courtyard and the business of the city. This would be our home, at least until the dance floor was completed, maybe longer. We had a kitchen area, two pallets for sleeping, and a table and chairs. There was even a large oil lamp on the patio. It was a perfect place for me to sit and ponder the *why* of things. Sometimes when it was quiet, I could sit and watch the shadows fall across the flanks of the mountains—and dream of things to come.

Icarus and I certainly had our disagreements. He was not drawn to concentrating patiently over puzzles or using inventive skills, things that I enjoyed. He was high-spirited. Just learning the language was not enough. Once he gained confidence, he made it very clear that his goal was to sound like, act like, and be like every other eight-year old Minoan on Krete. He wanted so much to belong. After he received his first linen kilt, he would wear nothing else, even when the weather grew cold and wet. It pained me when other children teased him about his accent, or called him stupid. But Icarus would just try that much harder. Whenever Naucreta visited, Icarus insisted on as much alone time with her as she would allow. They practiced pronunciation, idioms, and conversation, and he basked in her praise. I too, enjoyed face-to-face time with her, practicing my language skills or learning about the latest palace intrigue. More than that, I just wanted to be near her.

There were many lessons for both of us in this new culture. Icarus started attending day school. I spent hours attending meetings and studying the infrastructure of the city, and coming up with a reasonable model for the construction of the dance floor. After much discussion, the planning council adopted my recommendation to build it on the edge of the plaza, overlooking the sporting arena.

I was careful not to let the work occupy all my time, because I looked forward to going home and spending time with my son. The challenges were mostly good ones, and one thing we both enjoyed was testing our language skills by exploring the neighborhood. That was how we met Georgios the baker who lived nearby with his family. They ran a tea shop and from their small storefront came an endless variety of delicious pastries. Exploring was even better when Naucreta came along. She had a remarkable ability with names, faces and making people smile.

One of my early goals for the king was to study the city's plumbing and irrigation systems. Over many generations these islanders had constructed an intricate system of irrigation canals and aqueducts that delivered fresh water to Knossos from the melting snows in the nearby mountains. Much of it was collected and stored in cisterns and spring chambers lined with water-resistant plaster. The rest was channeled into baths and pools, with overflow drains that allowed the excess to run down through gutters lining the streets or inside some key buildings and homes. This complex system of culverts and drains provided an effective means of keeping the city both clean and cool in the hot summer months—at least that was the way it had worked before the earthquake.

The destructive vibrations of the aftershocks had wreaked havoc on the high walls of the buildings. Roofs and floors had failed. Many buildings still stood with jagged edges of unfinished reconstruction open to the sky. During the hot dry months the sun poured in through the damaged roofs, bringing light and midday heat into many places that had once been in cool shadow. The wet winters were worse. Following a storm, a good rain turned the city into a giant funnel, collecting and channeling water downward into the lowest places. Some of it would evaporate. Some would be collected by servants and slaves in urns or anything else that would hold water. For all of its beauty, Knossos had the smell of a city in decay.

Politicians and street performers told colorful stories of the water bearers filling their ornate and colorful urns not with clear, life-sustaining water, but with dark and murky fluids, and passing the clay pots along long lines to the closest outside wall or working drain. The planning council had even considered commissioning a muralist to commemorate the work of the water bearers. The Minoans loved their murals. It was their way of recording history.

The remaining water would percolate, drip, and follow gravity's relentless pull through fractures and crevasses into the depths of the limestone caves beneath the surface. Panos was right. The large cavern complex under the city had partially filled with an immense underground lake. No sunlight ever danced upon its surface. The water was stagnant and cold, and the air above it took on the smells of decay and decomposition. Sometimes when the wind was right, the obnoxious smells drifted up into the palace of the king. Draining the caverns would become my second recommendation.

To restore the labyrinth, I proposed to dig a tunnel into the sloping hillside underneath part of the city. The plan was complex and would require considerable time and labor. King Minos and the council unanimously agreed that this project should receive the highest priority. So I set to work, studying the fracture patterns in the surrounding rock and mapping the gently sloping hillside; all to establish the optimal location for the tunnel entrance. Just about that same time, Naucreta told us with tears in her eyes that her charge of integrating us into the community was complete. The king had other duties for her now, ones that would prevent her from spending so much time with us. It was a very sad day for all of us, especially for Icarus.

CHAPTER THIRTY THREE

Our first year on the island had its challenges. Icarus was part of a household now, a family, albeit a small one. He had to relearn how to live life as a young boy with enough food to eat, friends to be with, a school to attend, and a father who cared that all these things were happening in the right order. The lessons of scarcity he had learned in Athens, how to survive as a beggar and a thief, would not serve him as well in Knossos. During our first few cycles of the moon on Krete, Naucreta had been a wonderful teacher and a stabilizing influence. The announcement that our time with her was ending was difficult for him. Icarus stormed out of the house, tears running down his face. I was up very late that night.

For a few days afterwards our lives seemed to return to a stable flow. Then one quiet day, while many slumbered in their afternoon repose, the baker began his preparations for afternoon tea. To draw people into the shop, he set out displays of bread, honey cakes, and other delights. Then he returned to the kitchen for more. At precisely the moment that Georgios turned from his task to look out the window into the street, two small hands reached up and snatched two pastries. An empty plate rocked back and forth on the counter.

"Stop, thief!" yelled the portly baker, shaking his fist and rushing into the street.

The boy didn't stop. He ran like a jackrabbit. Around the corner he dashed, slowing just enough to bite down on the first piece of sticky goodness. Angry words filled his ears. He swallowed hard and kept going.

"I know your father! I know where you live!" The baker's shouts reverberated off the gypsum walls and the cobblestone street. "There is nowhere you can run."

But he didn't stop. Instead he ran down one street and then the next, finally pausing long enough to jam the last of the bougatsa into his mouth. He savored the sweet flavors. Then he was off again, legs pumping, all the way to my workshop. Georgios followed, much slower but relentless in his pursuit.

My breathless son burst through the door.

"Icarus. What's happening?" I said.

Breathing hard, he paced around the small room, saying nothing. He ran to the window and looked down the street. I got up and joined him there. Together, we watched the baker about twenty strides away, muttering to himself and making a bee line for the workshop. Looking down at his cheek, I saw small bits of honey and dough. Without saying a word, I reached down and lifted his wrist, checking the palm. He tried hard to pull away, the baker only a few seconds from the door. Somehow I held onto his wrist, searching his face.

"Don't run away," I said, in as calm a voice as I could muster. "Stand behind me. We'll do this together."

Just as the baker reached the door, I opened it for him and held it, gesturing for him to enter. Panting, he walked across the threshold, one hand holding his side, the other stridently pointing a finger towards Icarus. Several bystanders had already gathered outside.

"The boy is a thief!" the baker gasped. "He stole my pastries."

I could feel Icarus' hands on my waist, pulling on my tunic.

"Georgios, take a breath. Please."

Then I turned around, knelt down and looked at my small son.

"It's not true!" the boy declared in our native tongue and though his cheeks were streaked with honey and tears. "I didn't take his pastries. I didn't," he repeated.

"Look at me, Icarus," I said, holding onto his small shoulders. I gave them a gentle shake and repeated the words, "Look at me."

Tears were forming at the corners of his eyes. Then they began to flow, as if somewhere inside a dam had burst wide open.

I took Icarus into my arms and held him there for a while, until the baker finally coughed.

"Did you take this man's pastries?" I asked.

"Yes," sobbed Icarus, in perfect Minoan.

"You know that he is our neighbor. He has daughters about your age. If you steal from him, you are stealing from your friends," I reasoned.

Nodding, Georgios looked at Icarus and said, "We are living on the same island, son."

"What can we do to settle this?" I asked the baker.

Still staring at Icarus, he turned towards me with an open palm, saying nothing.

"We are new to this neighborhood," I said in my best Minoan, trying to sound conciliatory. "We want to be good neighbors," reaching inside my tunic and taking several copper rings from a small leather bag. "And we want to continue to drink your tea and eat your fine pastries." It was a generous offering and after some handwringing, Georgios accepted the money.

Pushing Icarus in front of me to face the man, I said to him, "Icarus, you will be repaying this with chores at home."

Before long Georgios was thanking me and explained that he had to get back to his shop. He even patted Icarus on the shoulder, gave us both a nod and left.

Closing the workshop, I took Icarus for a long walk away from the noise and the vibration of the city. We followed the main streets downhill and eventually came to the main road and the open fields beyond the city. Our path led us to the river. We walked along the bank until the channel curved. There was a large sandbar with some good-sized, smooth stones at one end. Right away, Icarus bent down, picked up a stone and threw it into the current, as far as his arm would allow. After it splashed, he bent down to pick up another and another.

"Somehow, this thing with the bougatsa takes me back to what happened on the *Pelican*. It's uncanny, Icarus. You don't have to repeat my mistakes," I said, bending down to pick up a stone and flinging it into the water.

We threw together in silence for a while.

"What do you mean?" asked Icarus.

"I was jumped, beaten up. They took all my money, our money."

"I remember, but…"

"If I hadn't pretended to be blind, if I had been truthful from the beginning and just told them who I was and where I wanted to go, then maybe the fight with the crew would never have started."

"Well, I'm sorry," said Icarus.

"It wasn't your fault. You didn't do anything wrong," I said, reaching out to hug him around the shoulder.

"I'm talking about today with Georgios, the baker," observed Icarus from within my protective arm. "What were you talking about?"

"Oh," I said, realizing that we were coming from two very different perspectives. "Well, about our voyage on the *Pelican*."

I picked up another rock and threw it into the current.

"All I know is that on the voyage I made a promise to you, to Captain Nikolaos, and to the world that I would always be here for you. I meant those words. You reminded me of that promise today."

"I remember," Icarus said, splashing his next rock. "You know, it was fun on the ship sometimes. Remember Aadam?"

"Yes, of course. I liked Aadam."

"I wish that I could see him again. Will he ever come and visit us?"

"I hope so. Next time I'm at the palace I will ask about the *Pelican*. Find out if there is any news. And do you know what I want to do now?"

"What?"

"Go home and have dinner, just you and me."

CHAPTER THIRTY FOUR

During that first winter on the island, I completed a model and the plans for tunneling into the caverns under the palace. The actual site for the portal was on the outskirts of the city. Conservatively, I estimated that the whole operation would take five cycles of the sun to complete. The king and his counsel approved without hesitation, allocating both the materials and an immense amount of labor.

Before the digging and chiseling into the earth could begin, custom and ritual demanded that the location for this forceful entry into the earth be blessed. Right away our local priestesses began to meditate and pray over the site, and the people of Knossos supported them by bringing food and drink. Word of the coming event was spread far and wide. King Minos sent emissaries to Kalliste to request a special delegation from the matriarchs of high priesthood. I was not asked to accompany them, but I was pleased that they did transport my model of the site and use it for their presentation. It was a high honor.

More priestesses began to arrive, traveling on foot from faraway places like Phaistos, Malia, and Zakros. Many wore the traditional bell-shaped patterned skirts, close-fitting blouses, and low cut, open bodices. Finally, with the moon waning away, three matriarchs arrived from Kalliste. There was a brief welcoming ceremony at the central plaza, and they went directly to the site. Townspeople followed, bringing cut flowers, firewood, or food. The ritual would begin on the night of the new moon. By the end of the day preceding it, mounds of flowers dotted the hillside in piles of riotous color. Three large open and level plots had been dug out of the hillside with firewood stacked at each end. The ground was tamped firm.

That evening, the earthmonks set up a wide perimeter around the area to keep the curious at bay. Large fires were built on the two outer spaces. The priestesses filled the middle one, spilling out onto the hillside and surrounding the fire pits. They chanted and sang, their sounds filling the night. Over time, large circles of glowing coals formed beneath the fires. With the flames still crackling, the priestesses freed themselves of their restrictive garments and began to dance. Bathing themselves in fragrant oils, they transformed into a writhing cluster of feminine energy, singing and chanting. Late into the night their bodies shimmered in the firelight.

At dawn, a bull was sacrificed. The meat would later nourish a crowd that was already beginning to assemble. Clothed in her ritual garb and with pendulous breasts, the high priestess from Kalliste stood on the level ground. Thousands were gathered all around her. She danced, she sang, and she spoke to the crowd. Snakes were not native to Krete. Yet, she had two of them, one in each hand. The crowd had gasped when she pulled them from a basket. She captivated us with her movements, her words, and the sight of these flexible serpents, writhing in her hands. To complete the ceremony, she freed them both at the site of the incision to be cut into the earth. Instantly, they disappeared into the grass. The crowd responded with a collective gasp.

The air heavy with the mixed aromas of roasting meat, the priestess encouraged King Minos to join her on the makeshift stage. She pointed to a nearby pick, inviting him to take the first cut into the earth. Easily gripping the wooden handled tool with his large hands, he took a wide swing and sunk the point into the earth, all the way to the shaft. Leaving it embedded in the ground, the king surveyed the crowd, nodding to some and searching. Then, he called for me to join him on the stage. There, in front of the entire gathering, King Minos introduced me as the architect and chief engineer for the project. I had no idea, no forewarning that he was planning to make a public announcement. Somehow I stumbled over a few words of thanks in my heavily accented dialect. The crowd roared their approval. Icarus was right there, with his classmates from school. Vivacious Naucreta was there too, clapping and cheering. It was such a memorable experience, signifying that the different aspects of my life were finally coming together. It was a wonderful feeling, like I had come home.

CHAPTER THIRTY FIVE

Much later that evening, after all the celebration, Naucreta and I sat on large pillows on the veranda of my home, talking and sipping wine under a starry sky. I was truly grateful for all the support she had provided since our arrival at Knossos and told her so. I also told her how much I enjoyed spending time with her. I even found the courage to tell her in her own language how much I cared for her.

Naucreta smiled and took my hand in hers. "Thank you for sharing these feelings with me. I can look into your eyes and know that it is true. It touches my heart."

I moved closer, wanting to take her into his arms. Fragrances of lavender and scented oils filled my nostrils.

Stroking the back of my hand, she continued in a matter-of-fact tone. "You don't hide your feelings nearly as well as you think you do. They have been on display for viewing for some time."

"What are you talking about?"

"Your desire, of course. Whatever you call the way you look at me when you think no one is noticing."

After all that had happened, her words, her touch, the moment, it was like standing on the threshold of a sensuous garden; one that might vanish at any moment. I wanted to be closer, to feel her next to me. I freed my hand from her grasp and slid closer, sliding my arm across her neck and shoulder. But she receded into the pillows, backing away from my touch.

"Daedalus, you want so much, too quickly," she said, her voice moving into a subtle challenge. "You have come very far, very fast in your time in Knossos. But you are still an outsider here. You are an Athenian, a pale-skinned foreigner." I withdrew my hand and pulled away.

"You want nothing more than an evening's pleasure with a palace courtesan," Naucreta scolded.

"That's not true. You are so much more than that. Naucreta, you are like a radiant light and have been ever since I arrived here."

"The man has found his tongue tonight," she replied, smiling at me with her green eyes in the glow of the oil lamps, as if reconsidering something. Then she lowered her head, dark curls falling across her face. I watched every move, hanging on the next words. When she looked up again she said, "But still, you will not be using it for more than words tonight."

My face flushed, I asked, "Why not tonight?"

"There is so much you do not know about the ways of this island. This place is my home. I am Minoan."

"I know that," I said plaintively.

"But you do not understand it!" she countered sharply. "There are many spheres of influence in the palace, different roles and rules in each one. You, my friend, seem so busy with your work and your son, to even notice or care about the social order that is all around you. Yes, you have the king's ear from time to time, but only when it comes to your buildings and waterways. I assure you, he has many other interests."

I sighed and rolled back into the pillow, turning away and looking up into the sky.

Without a word she raised her knee beneath the robe, exposing a shapely ankle and shin. Immediately I turned my head to watch, my eyes unabashedly tracing the lines of her thigh and narrow waist.

"My friend, you are so easy to read," she quipped.

Once again, I blushed.

"And to manipulate."

Blood coursing into my cheeks, I said, "I've really had about as much fun as I can handle for one evening," staring at her stonily.

"So quickly your moods swing," she said with a coy smile. "I will leave if that is what you want. But I promise you, it would not be a good way to end such a memorable day. What if tonight we settle for honesty with each other instead of passion? Could you accept that?"

I opened my mouth to answer, but she hurried on into the next words.

"You cannot always have the one that you want. No one knows that better than a courtesan. There is something I must tell you about, before we go any further tonight. Can we stop playing games?"

Leaning in towards her, I said softly, "Parts of the game have been exquisite, and you are such a good teacher."

"That sounds so much better," she said, smiling and dropping her gaze toward my loins. "I have several priorities to consider. You, my friend, have only one."

Soundly rejected and wanting her as much as ever, I rolled onto my back, still thoroughly enjoying the evening.

"If you want to be my lover, Daedalus, first show me that you can be my friend. Listen to me. I promise that I will tell you only truths for the rest of the evening. If you want this relationship to develop into something more, you must be strong enough to hear them."

My desire rapidly fading, I looked into her eyes and said, "Go on. I am listening."

"Daedalus, if tomorrow the king told me to stop coming here, then you would never see me again. You have no idea what a forceful controlling man he can be. He is certain that everyone around him is there for no other purpose than to follow his plan for their life."

"I saw that side of him at our first meeting," I replied.

"So you can be sure, Daedalus, that he has a plan for both of us. You are living in Knossos, sitting on these comfortable pillows, sharing wine with this exciting, stimulating woman of the court, because that is part of his plan for you. He has blessed all of it. But what if tomorrow something goes wrong with your construction plans? What if you make a costly or embarrassing mistake? What if you say the wrong words to the wrong person at the worst time? If you displease him, because you have no connections here—no support—then you will be gone just as quickly as you arrived. That is what it means to be a foreigner here. Worse still, you come from Athens. That complicates everything."

I stared back at her, puzzled.

"You really have no idea, do you?"

"No, I don't. What are you talking about?" I asked.

"You remember Ariadne, the king's daughter? She is the child of Minos and Queen Pasiphae, a few years older than Icarus. There was an older brother once, Androgeos. He was a great champion, the golden son, and heir apparent. We all loved him. He had strength, endurance, and so many athletic skills. He even spoke well at public gatherings. Androgeos would have made a great king."

"You say this as if he is gone."

"He is. And to us, it was a great loss! The queen has not been the same since his death. Now she chooses to live in a sanctuary in the high mountain valleys. No one has seen her in Knossos for a very long time. Minos still visits her, when he goes off to Mount Ida each year to speak with the God of the Sky. It surprises me that you don't know this story. Then again, I can see why you Athenians don't want the history remembered."

"Once again, I have no idea what you are talking about."

"Androgeos traveled to Athens as our champion to participate in one of your Olympiads. Before leaving, there was a huge ceremony for the athletes with dancing and speeches in the central court. A large platform stood in the center of it all. One by one they took the stand and stood before the crowd. Everyone threw flowers for their favorites. Handsome Androgeos was the last. I was a young woman then. You can trust me when I tell you how tall and beautiful he was. And the roar that went up from the cheering crowd! It seemed to go on and on. We showered him with flowers, and adoration."

"You saw all this?"

"I watched it. I heard it, and I felt it. Yes."

"What happened to him?"

"He competed in your summer Olympiad. And he won all the events."

"That should not be fatal."

"No. But celebrating afterward with those you have defeated, apparently was."

"What does that mean?" I responded.

"There is so much more," she said quietly. "After Minos learned of his son's death, he was overwhelmed with grief and rage. He assembled a huge fleet of war galleys and support ships. They sailed to Athens for revenge."

"Yes, and I remember when they arrived," I said thoughtfully. "But it was a long time ago."

"It was exactly the summer when the full moon rose right after the longest day of the year," she replied. "An event that only happens once every nine cycles of the sun. It was a very favorable omen by the way, for Minos and the fleet. "

"And how many seasons ago?"

"Let me see," she replied, counting in her head. "Twelve, maybe thirteen seasons ago, by my reckoning."

"Naucreta, I don't want to minimize the history here, and I'm truly sorry for the loss of Androgeos. But it was a long time ago," I repeated, wanting to be reasonable. "Athens was not plundered. Surely, they must have worked something out."

"Our mariners tell us that when Aegeus saw the Minoan fleet filling the harbor and our armored men sharpening their daggers and spear points on his beach, he immediately soiled himself. Next, he concocted a fable to explain Androgeos' death; which he used to weasel his way out of a confrontation with the might of the Minoan nation, standing on his doorstep. Then, your good King Aegeus agreed an onerous settlement in order to save his own worthless behind."

"Sounds to me like he saved the city," I responded, enjoying the repartee.

"And you in the process," she countered.

"I can't fault him for that. It must have been an interesting tale."

"You decide. He explained to King Minos and his captains that it was all a tragic accident. According to Aegeus, Androgeos was killed several days after winning the Olympiad, trying to capture a fierce bull on the plains of Marathon. Aegeus also produced seven virile young men willing to back up his story. And then, he offered a chest of silver to compensate for the loss of the Minoan prince."

"Did that settle it?"

"No, it certainly did not. Minos was in much pain over the loss of his son and heir. Nothing could make him whole again. Yes, he took the silver. And then, he took the seven athletes. There is a reason the other sovereigns call him the lawgiver. He had the men bound by the wrists and hauled onto his war galley. Right out from under cowardly Aegeus' nose."

"All seven! King Minos does drive a hard bargain."

"Yes, he does. But the story does not end there. The fleet had sailed for plunder. His captains—your friend Nikolaos among them—were not satisfied with the prize. They wanted more. Minos pressed his advantage. He demanded seven young women as well, the best and brightest of Athens, to share the same fate as the young men."

"And Aegeus agreed to this?"

"After much wringing of hands and deliberation, yes, he did. But it had to mean that the conflict was truly ended. Aegeus would provide seven young women in return for a guarantee; that all Athenian merchant ships would be free to sail anywhere on the Great Green, without being preyed upon by the Minoan fleet."

"Surely that ended it," I said.

"Not quite. The captains and the king would only agree to the free passage of the Athenian ships for a fixed period of time."

"So the bribes had to continue. Is that what you are saying?"

"In Knossos we refer to them as tributes. And yes, every nine cycles of the sun another one becomes due, on the celestial anniversary of the Olympiad. Aegeus must deliver another chest of silver… and a bounty of seven young men and seven young women, all healthy and strong, to the Minoan fleet at Pireaus harbor."

"This explains a great deal," I answered, sitting up and taking a swallow of wine.

"Then prepare yourself, my friend," she cautioned. "Because the day is coming when fourteen more of your countrymen will be paraded through the streets of Knossos in their ropes and chains, the defiant ones bruised and bloodied."

"That's barbaric," I said.

"I don't disagree, but that begs the question," she responded pointedly.

"Which question is that?" I asked.

"Will you still want me when that day comes?"

"Of course, I will want you," I insisted. "My life as an Athenian is over. I have left all that behind. It means nothing to me now."

"Well, I cannot stop being Minoan," Naucreta calmly replied. "Your words come easily tonight. We will see when the time comes."

"What will we see?" I said mockingly, trying to sound indifferent.

"Only this," she replied, forming a triangle over her sex with her forefingers and thumbs. "My garden is the playground of kings. If you want to be welcomed," she stopped, "no, honored, then you must prove yourself. It is that simple."

"Tell me what you want," I said returning her candor, "and I will do it."

With a flash of her sparkling green eyes she answered, "I am counting on it," she said reassuringly. Naucreta paused, then reached for my hand and continued, "All that I ask is for you to care enough about the rest of your own life, to become a trusted member of Minos' council.

You should want that much anyway, if not for yourself, then for the sake of your son. He will still be here long after both of us are gone. And know that behind the scenes, I will be assisting, promoting you in any way that I can. Once you have gained the king's trust, then it will be safe for us to be lovers. That is, if you still want me."

"Of course I will want you," I insisted.

"Easy to say now, but everyone changes with time. A handsome, creative man like you may find that as your influence grows, you attract the attention of other admirers. Most of them will be younger than I. A few might even be as alluring." She smiled and dropped her gaze. "No one really knows what the future holds, Daedalus. Those are my terms."

"Minos is not the only one who drives a hard bargain."

"Once again my clever friend, I agree with you," Naucreta replied, her red lips curved in a sensuous smile.

CHAPTER THIRTY SIX

Spring arrived in a rush. In only two or three days the hillsides and fields were suddenly covered in wildflowers. There were birds everywhere. Undulating lines of migrating storks croaked by overheard in a pure blue sky. Down here on earth, crews of skilled craftsmen steadily worked to fit and assemble the wooden planks of the dance floor upon the smooth and level foundation. It had to be complete by the equinox. The deadline was my own. On that day thousands would gather on the well-trodden ground of the open-air arena in plain view of the central plaza. The king and his friends would gather to watch the ceremony unfold. I wanted the smooth and well-oiled surface of the dance floor to be plainly visible for any and all to view.

I'm told that in the days of the early kings wild bulls roamed all over Kalliste and Krete. They were easily the largest of all the islands' animals, and the Minoans worshiped them. Their raw and prodigious power symbolized an elemental vitality present in all forms of life. They could be playful and, at other times, almost willing sacrifices, notwithstanding their size and formidability. It was inevitable, especially on Kalliste with its limited size, that as the human population grew, it would compete with the bulls for the same territory.

At one time there had to be uncounted numbers of these huge, dominating beasts, marking and defending their territories on most of the inhabited islands. That is, until they became a threat to the harvest, or to the safety of the citizens. After that the bulls were hunted, to almost total eradication. To preserve their elemental nature in the wild, the ruling priesthood of Kalliste decided to confine the survivors on a large plateau of land, cut off from the rest of the island by deep, steep-walled canyons. A handpicked group of dedicated hunters trapped and captured the remaining animals from all over the island. One by one these earth monks led them to their high and remote range where fences and natural barriers safely sealed them off. Ever since, the earth monks have managed the number and welfare of the bull population, working in concert with the feminine priesthood to ensure a ready supply of masculine power for the major events and rituals.

One of the most significant of these events came with each spring. At the end of a cold stormy winter, these sea people looked to the heavens and to the god of the all-encompassing sky in order for the earth to bloom again. On the day of the equinox the priestesses would lead the people in prayer to this deity, inviting him to return to the earth and bring an end to winter and fertilize the lands. Always, he appeared in the form of a virile and vigorous bull with a strong, muscular neck and back, a great heart, and massive testicles. Stout horns protruded from the sides of his relatively small head.

The Rite of Spring was both a festival and a community prayer. It was a core invocation summoning the warmth and growth of summer followed by an abundant harvest. It began at dawn and continued long into the night. Everyone attended. Everyone had a part. Of course, only the most agile and athletic youth actually participated in the bull leaping. Ariadne, the king's daughter, was among them. She wore with pride the blue stone amulets that set her apart as one of the acrobats. Injuries were not uncommon in this very specialized endeavor. All the athletes wore the amulets on their ankles and wrists to ward off broken bones and sprains. It was a mark of distinction, a point of pride for them.

Early in the day and while the bull was fresh and alert, hundreds of hand-picked and practiced dancers surrounded him at a respectful distance, chanting, singing, and moving in opposing spirals. Behind them, less agile but still loyal practitioners continued the colorful patterns, encircling the bull within a living fence of athletes, dancers and citizens. Hundreds more chanted and watched from a safer distance. It went on like this all through the morning, while the animal snorted and pranced as only a bull can, watching the colorful, graceful, nubile youth parading before him. He pawed the earth. He bellowed. He circled right along with them. Occasionally, he would throw his head, slashing a horn across empty space. Sometimes he just stood and watched, as if appreciating the moment.

Eventually the hours of persistent effort, lack of water, and the day's heat combined to drain away his energy. Once the mighty head began showing signs of fatigue, one by one the acrobats would test his vigilance, slowly wearing him down. Behind them, the chanting intensified.

Finally, when the neck drooped low enough, one acrobat rose to the occasion. Instead of just feinting with her hands, she dived toward him as if aiming to butt heads. The crowd cheered wildly. Fingers flexed, hands wide open, she threw her weigh directly onto the horns. Shocked into awareness, the tired beast instinctively threw his head, flinging the agile young woman high into the air and into a long vault over its broad, muscular back. Arms outstretched, her breastplate of golden filigree shone in the sunlight. Minos recognized it at once. It was bold Ariadne soaring through the air. The king was on his feet at once, clapping and cheering at the first leap, and for his daughter. The entire audience cheered. Her teammates rushed in behind the horns to spot the landing. Others distracted and disoriented the bull. And another young athlete aligned himself for the second leap.

By the end of the day, everyone was exhausted, especially the bull. As the shadows extended into late afternoon, the bull finally collapsed. His head, lying to one side, exposed a broad expanse of neck. One by one the athletes departed, replaced by earthmonks and priestesses. They sank to the earth, bowing to the beast and praising his prodigious efforts. Silence reigned. The high priestess in her colorful headdress approached the fallen animal. Behind her, two attendants waited and watched, carrying between them a great earthen bowl. Standing next to him, she withdrew a curved bronze blade from its sheath. The bull did not seem to notice her. But his eyes opened wide in the shock of his final gasp, as the knife plunged deep into the muscles of his neck and severed the artery. He tried to rise, but the mighty legs would no longer hold. Like a dancer, the priestess grace-fully stepped away as he collapsed again to the ground. Then she returned, gripped the handle, and withdrew the knife. Blood spurted like a fountain, splattering everyone within reach. It quickly became a sanguine flow, and the bowl was aligned to catch as much as possible.

In my entire life, I had never seen anything quite like it. The bull was sacrificed, his blood fertilizing the earth, and the entire community had participated, slaves, citizens, and royalty alike. On this day the Minoans were one people. They had danced, prayed, and sang together. Even the air seemed to resonate. All around me, people bowed to the earth and prayed. Others simply meditated. On the fringes of the gathering, couples that wanted children copulated together. Above us the sky filled with vibrant shades of blue, orange, and pink. There was no doubt, that the community was receiving a magnificent blessing.

Even I, a stranger in a foreign land, felt an incredible sense of belonging to something larger than myself. I too, wanted abundance to flow into our lives in the coming year. I wanted to taste and be nourished by the roasting meat. Dragging Icarus, I slowly weaved through the crowd to the bloodstained earth at the heart of the ceremony. All around us, priestesses and their followers praised the bull for his strength, his gifts, and his sacrifice. They prayed to the immortal god of the sky, now freed and returning to his celestial home. Tears running down his face, Icarus spoke of how sad he felt for the fallen animal.

CHAPTER THIRTY SEVEN

Not long after the solstice came the anniversary of our arrival in Knossos. It was the end of my trial period, and no one seemed to notice. No one with any influence even raised the question of whether or not I should continue on as the architect for the reconstruction. I just did. With the dance floor as a well-established attraction and the tunnel underway, I turned my focus and attention to other projects.

I was already working on other ideas. The new designs and models were filling the workshop. I met regularly with the members of the planning council, and I patiently and thoughtfully responded their questions. We discussed materials, priorities, and schedules, all the while monitoring the progress on the tunnel. Minos approved project after project. Laborers, servants, and slaves were committed to a series of rebuilding programs. The sights and sounds of reconstruction appeared all over the city.

Over the next cycle of the sun it became clear to the citizenry of Knossos that their city was undergoing or enjoying a transition. The king's walking tours of the city were now made by day, and he reveled in a resurging popularity.

Many cycles of the moon had passed since our arrival. My last flight dream was a distant memory, remote and inaccessible, overshadowed by the events and demands of our first seasons on the island. Gone were the times when the power of the dream could infuse a day with a sense of vitality. I had other priorities now. The flight dreams were simply something that had happened once—a moment in the sun, long ago. With my newfound responsibilities, I scarcely noticed the many varieties of birds that nested in the island's forests and fields. Had I been a bird watcher then, I would certainly have appreciated the eagles, vultures, and even the occasional albatross that flew high above the city. Every now and then, the sight of a large soaring bird still caught my eye.

But, they had to compete with the newer, more immediate visions for life in Knossos. I had grown comfortable, living together with Icarus in our new home. It was fascinating that the satisfactions of being a father felt as rewarding as those that came from completing the design of a complex building project. They allowed me to see the better man that I was becoming.

Our days became filled with new sets of habits and routines. When I dreamt at all, it was of building designs, canals, and supporting beams— or those unforgettable green eyes of Naucreta.

Far from palace, on the other side of the snow-covered peaks, Naomi and Salim were married. Their world was a narrow strip of land between the mountains and the sea, far from the bustle and noise of Knossos. There were no roads into Platanos, only footpaths and walking trails that led to other nearby villages. Those who arrived from the outside world, traders, pirates or shipwreck survivors, always came by sea.

Embraced by their small fishing community and driven by their passions, these two young lovers readily followed their people's encouragement to marry. In a village of this size, weddings didn't happen that often. The people of Platanos would take time to savor the event. Everyone would be there. It was a time of transition, a time for the man to leave his boyhood home and with the assistance of family and neighbors, build another. It was a time for the woman to leave behind her life as a young maiden and move into that home as his wife and, someday, the mother of his children.

As the oldest surviving son of his family, Salim's home site had been selected long ago. With the blessings of the village elders, he and many male relatives had already begun the task of constructing the couple's new home. It would be an elegant and egalitarian two-room hut of stone and wood with a magnificent view of the sea. The building did not stop there. They went on to construct a fine courtyard with an east-facing threshold. The new home and patio would be one more link in the picturesque agglomeration of snow-white homes wrapped around the arc of their small harbor.

Naomi spent the final few days with her life-long friend, her mother, and a few other female relatives, preparing for the wedding. Offerings were made to the goddesses of virginity and transition, an old toy and worn clothing. There were gifts to be presented, memories to share. With the heat of the final day past, she was bathed, purified, and perfumed. Naomi dressed in a full, flaxen robe and veil, a garland of flowers adorning her long dark hair. With her mother on one side and Deena on the other, Naomi left her childhood home behind and walked solemnly along a well-trodden path to the new home where Salim nervously waited with his uncle.

With dignity Salim welcomed the three women into the courtyard. A small altar piece was built into one corner. The couple made joint offerings, this time to the goddesses of the home and fertility. Then they all walked together along a flower-strewn path to the village center. A priestess received and blessed them both and presided over another round of offerings, this time for health and wisdom. There was a short ceremony. She led the entire village in blessing and honoring their union.

Only then did Naomi happily remove her veil. Salim gazed at her proudly, warmly, and they kissed. They drank fresh wine together. There was a series of toasts and many well-wishes. The couple received all of it graciously. There was laughter and gaiety. Many local delicacies were offered by the attendees, and were graciously received and shared by the husband and wife. Next came more wine and more offerings, this time for harmony and pleasure in their bed, and, of course, for children. Naomi hugged Deena and told her how grateful she felt for all the good memories they had made together. Tears filling her eyes, Deena agreed. Her gift to the couple was her music. She serenaded them both with a composition she had prepared from a lifetime of memories, which inspired the melody. The gathering of family and friends fell silent, appreciating the moment.

Side by side, Naomi and Salim gave her a standing ovation. Jubilant once again, the entire gathering joined in. The new couple thanked everyone for their part in the celebration and said their goodbyes. Deena and Naomi hugged again. With torches lighting the way, the newlyweds turned their backs on the gathering and returned to their new home. Deena did not follow. Holding her flute in her hands, she sat amidst the remains of the crowd and watched emotions play across their faces. She slipped the instrument into the fold of her apron for a solitary walk under a blanket of stars. A few revelers were already ahead of her on the beach, preparing the stage for the evening's activities. She knew that when she returned many of her community would still be gathered around the small fire, sharing its comfort and warmth.

CHAPTER THIRTY EIGHT

B esides the progressions of the sun and the moon, there were many ways for me to measure the passage of time. It was there in the gray hairs of my beard, the steady progress in the tunnel, and the increasing sturdiness of Icarus' legs and arms. His height was rapidly approaching my own. In our time together we had grown very accustomed to each other. Looking back, the days appear like a seamless web, filled with time spent being a father, the designing of public works projects for the king, and the summertime treks into the remote places of the country.

At work, I focused my energies on a redesign of the larger buildings, including light wells to bring light and air into the dark, unventilated spaces. New wall construction now included an elaborate system of horizontal beams, to provide increased stability during earthquakes. The wood came from the trunks of tall trees, mostly cedar, cut from the thick forests that covered the hills beyond the city. They were shaped and cut into usable lumber with long sharp saws and dried in the sun. Teams of laborers carried them one by one into the city where they were installed into the floors, walls and ceilings of the new apartments and homes. Fortunately, I was able to visit the foundries and observe the entire process of creating a saw from a mixture of copper and orichalcum.

In just a few short years of renewal, the city had taken on a new look. Minos could walk down the streets of Knossos during the daylight hours and receive grateful cheers as a benevolent sovereign. It was not unusual for members of the planning council, or even Minos himself, to stop by my workshop. Sometimes we would walk together and tour the reconstruction while discussing plans and progress for each project. During one of our walks, the king spoke to me about how much he was looking forward to the next gathering of the sovereigns on Kalliste. Knossos was reclaiming its prominence as a magnet for adventurers, artisans, and travelers. Once again the city was perceived as a work of art on the world stage. Traders and merchants from North Africa, Italia, and all across the Great Green returned home, telling of the wonders of the thriving Minoan culture and the beauty of Krete.

After the devastating quakes, the king's status among the other sovereigns had suffered a bit. Reputation was of paramount importance to him. He understood that these recent successes were due in no small part to the successful repairs, and he was not remiss in conveying his praise and appreciation, both in public and in private. My stipend was dramatically increased. Icarus and I received a larger, much more scenic apartment. We said goodbye to the old neighborhood, to the baker's family, and to all the others who had befriended us in those first years on the island. We moved on. That summer we took a long holiday together, just Icarus and I, trekking into the nearby mountains, exploring the caves and waterfalls, and returning by the shore.

Sometime after the end of that trading season, Aadam arrived in Knossos, alone in a strange new city. He found the megaron of the palace without any difficulty. The expansive room was half-filled with construction materials and workers. Shields and double bladed axes covered the walls. The laborers were busy building a scaffold beneath the central dome. The rest of the room was taken up with waiting people, most seeking an audience with the king or some member of the counsel. All of them carried food or wine, many had gifts as well, chickens or doves in wicker baskets. One even had a small dog. He complained to anyone who would listen, the man not the dog, that the king had not granted a single audience that day. Two tall warriors armed with spears and shields guarded the entryway. Friendly faces were few.

Actually, Minos was busy conferring with Meriones, king of the island of Naxos. In the vibrant light of the courtyard, Minos noticed once again how fast his friend was aging. Always thin, this day he appeared even more drawn and haggard. Meriones' wife, a queen, had for many years suffered from the wasting disease.

"I have watched her weaken and wither for so long," Meriones confessed in confidence. "It is not an easy thing to stand by helpless and watch a loved one leave like this."

"You and Eva have been together for a very long time."

"The healers are saying that she won't last much longer," Meriones replied. "I wonder how it will feel when it is finally over."

"Everyone commends you for your devotion."

"She was—is—a good woman, loving and kind. It's sad that we never had children. She always wanted them."

"Perhaps her illness prevented it."

"I've often wondered that," Meriones continued. "And somehow, I have become old, with no son, no heir."

"You are still King of Naxos."

"How can I continue to rule? Without an heir, the king has not provided for the future of the island. Naxos will suffer because of me."

"My friend, you just told me that she cannot last much longer. After she is gone, you will find another queen, someone that you can address the issue of not having an heir with. Come on," the king chided him, "there must be someone on Naxos that interests you."

"Perhaps," said Meriones, without humor. "But my eyes seem to have grown tired of all of them. There is, however, one I have admired from afar for a very long time.

"Only one?" Minos laughed.

"This one is special."

"Tell me, you old fox," Minos insisted. "Who is this lucky future queen? The suspense is killing me."

"You know her quite well. At least, you used to."

"Naucreta?" Minos guessed.

"Of course, Naucreta!" declared Meriones. "She is like no one else on these islands. She is a breath of fresh air."

"Ahh," replied King Minos, pausing to nod and consider. "You are right about that, and she'd make a fine queen. But she has duties here on Krete. She is a trusted advisor. I cannot let her go."

"Minos, you and I go back a long way," Meriones responded in his slow patient manner. "Remember your first gathering? Remember how you placed your noose around the bull's neck too soon, and there was no one ready on the other side to oppose that force?"

"Meriones, I remember all the bulls we have faced together."

"Then you should remember how angry that one was."

"That he was!" said Minos, smiling at the memory. "We have shared some interesting times together, you and I."

"Then you remember how he hooked his horn toward you as you dropped your stave?"

"I can still see the tip of it moving right past my belly."

"As I pulled you away," Meriones completed the story, "saving you from injury."

"What is it that you are asking, my friend?"

"I'm asking you to release Naucreta from her responsibilities on Krete," Meriones insisted.

"And she is willing to go?" asked Minos. "Have you asked her about this?"

"Kings do not ask," Meriones insisted.

"Yes, that is true," Minos agreed, "but have you spoken with her about this offer?"

"Many times," Meriones responded, irritation creeping into his voice.

"She is aware that you want her to become queen?"

"Of course," Meriones answered.

"This will be a major change for you," Minos said. "When do you think, you will be ready for this? She is a rather strong-willed woman."

"She is a beautiful, loving woman."

"And I advise you to prepare well for her arrival."

"Once Eva has passed, I will be ready," Meriones calmly replied. "And when she arrives in Naxos to be the queen, then it is I, who will be in your debt."

Looking up to the sky Minos responded, "Then I will assist in every way that I can.

Unaware of what the two kings were discussing, Aadam was fortunate to find one person in the midst of the chaotic room, willing to take the time to listen to his questions. She was a barefooted servant with a kindly face. Her black hair was short and unruly. It was Filia, and she was willing to be distracted from her own priorities to stop and talk with the polite young man. By the merest of chances, she did know Daedalus, the architect, and his son, and knew exactly where they lived. She said that if her mistress would allow, she would take him there herself.

The years had not changed Aadam that much, except that he was taller and broader and more confident in his manhood. He still had the boyish grin and a dream to one day captain a ship of his own.

Upon seeing Icarus, Aadam noticed that Icarus had changed a lot. To begin, Icarus had grown from a boy to a man. He no longer openly talked about becoming a sailor. Instead he claimed that he wanted to spend his time playing sports, camping in the mountains, or fishing along the beaches. Icarus proudly showed Aadam his school and the practice field where he wrestled and raced with his friends and other students and honed his skills with the bow and the javelin. To Icarus' delight I invited Aadam to stay with us for as long as he wished.

Aadam had traveled to Krete with Xanthus, the sturdy handsome oarsman from the *Pelican*. The older seaman had a growing family that lived on a large farm, just a two-day walk from Knossos. Xanthus had a young daughter, and he wanted Aadam to meet her. Every year when the trading season ended, he returned there to his wife and children with his share of the proceeds. Awaiting his arrival as well were the constant chores of tending the goats and the sheep, the grapes and the olives.

But there was no magic in the meeting. She barely looked at him. Aadam could think of little to say, and she had many cousins. Most of them treated him a newcomer with little understanding of country life. He was an easy mark for their pranks. One of the older ones treated him like an intruder, someone who had to first prove himself. After a short and awkward time, Aadam began to yearn for his life at sea. Or at least, he realized that he wanted something more than to cultivate children on an inland farm. Xanthus had invited him to stay the whole rainy season. But Aadam packed up his small satchel, said his goodbyes and began the trek to Knossos, alone.

For the rest of the winter he was our guest, helping out when and where he could. Icarus was glad to have Aadam, someone closer to his own age, for company. Whenever there was time, the two youths trained together, developing their muscles and athleticism. Under Aadam's tutelage, Icarus' endurance grew, along with the size of his arms. He honed a talent for wrestling, and as his athletic prowess developed, I enjoyed watching Icarus' confidence blossom.

Of course, the spring arrived as it always did, with migrating birds and hillsides carpeted in flowers. When the lupines appeared with their purple heads, Aadam knew it was time for him to depart, in order to rejoin the crew. He was grateful to me for the hospitality. He would be a welcome guest any time and I told him so. It was a sad day for all of us when he left for Amnisos, promising to return someday. Envious, Icarus walked with him all the way to the city gate, wishing he could go along. They exchanged promises to meet again.

Aadam was an oarsman now. He could trade his experience and endurance at the oars for passage anywhere on the Great Green. He had only to choose. The *Pelican* waited at Kalliste, with a new sail and rigging, for her crew to return. Her hull would be scraped clean of barnacles, resined, and tarred. The merchant galley was the most stable and dependable home he had ever known. Her crew was the closest he had ever come to having a family. Orion, Captain Nikolaos, or perhaps an amalgam of the two, the father he had never known. Aadam's loyalty to them was beyond measure.

Chapter Thirty Nine

It wasn't even a stream, just a rivulet with no name, running down the hillside between the backfill and the debris. Its moisture seeped into the earth long before reaching the valley floor. That is, until one hot mid-summer day when a miner drove his chisel hard into just the right crack. A jet of cold water forced the tool from his hand. He screamed as it knocked him off his feet. All down the line haulers and diggers dropped their loads and tools and fled for safety out of the narrow opening filling fast with elbows and knees. Somehow they all made it out and one-by-one returned to the portal, grateful to be alive. They stood together and watched the greasy, gray slurry pouring out of the earth.

For many cycles of the moon and sun, they had labored in the tunnel, digging and drilling into the hillside, boring and chiseling, and carrying away the broken rock. Early in their labors, water had begun seeping from the cracks and fractures in the roof of the tunnel, mixing with the sweat and dirt of their backs. To drain it all away to the outside a straight trough was cut along the length of the tunnel. Once through the portal it became a brand new stream laden with crushed limestone and cutting a sinuous course into the hillside.

Word quickly spread that the caverns had been breached. Icarus found me at the workshop, just as the crew chief was arriving with the news.

All of us had been waiting for this moment for a long time. Exhilarated and expecting a show, we hurried to the site of the portal into the earth. A crowd was already assembling, and there we waited for the rest of the day, growing listless and bored as the flow of water steadily diminished.

After a time, the townspeople began to disperse, returning to their homes. Icarus had already wandered off with some friends, looking for treasure recently freed from the earth along the new stream bed. The crew chief sent all the miners home, telling them to come back in the morning for work as usual. Then we waited on the hillside with a few other stalwarts, unwilling to give up. As the sun descended over the western mountains we were rewarded with a loud crack—something like thunder but not from the sky. It was shallow and very close, like a great beast stirring down below. There was a low rumbling sound and a torrent of water gushed from the hillside. Debris, rocks, and bottom-dwelling creatures jetted from the bowels of the earth and roared into the air. For the rest of the night turbid water flowed out of the portal in an exuberant rush, freed from its confinement inside the caverns. The waters surged down the hillside in a desperate flight to join with the River Kairatos and then on into the clear waters of the Great Green.

By dawn most of Knossos had returned to the scene, King Minos and his entourage among them, watching the murky flow still erupting from the hole in the earth. Overnight the cascading water had eroded a deep channel into the hillside, cutting a nearly straight course and flooding its way into the river. The king strode over to where I stood. I've never seen him look happier. He heartily thumped me on the back, proclaiming it as an engineering marvel and a great moment in Minoan history. We had restored the labyrinth!

The lover in me was mindful that Naucreta was close by, and presented a congratulatory smile and kisses on both cheeks. She wasted no time in introducing me to a delegation of visiting dignitaries as Daedalus the famous inventor and engineer. Then she prompted me with an open-ended question about the project.

By midday the flow was done. The king wanted to explore the caverns at once. He and his party would enter the caves from the lowest level of the palace and descend. A reliable miner, the crew chief, and I entered from the cool moist air of the tunnel. All of us carried ropes, resin torches, and oil lamps. If the fates smiled on us, we would all meet in the middle.

The sound of dripping water filled the air. At the end of the passage was a jagged hole where the water had broken through. We tied off a rope and boosted one another into the deep darkness of the twisting caverns. Right away I was on my hands and knees, squeezing through a tight passage. All around, the surfaces were hard and unforgiving. In a loud voice I tried to make a joke about my bruised and bleeding knee, wanting the others to hear. Up ahead, the miner cursed the gods. When one torch began to fail, we quickly lit another. We stayed close. We did all the things that people are prone to do when surrounded by rock walls and darkness, which lights and sounds cannot penetrate.

It was not easy keeping track of time inside the limestone vault. When I found myself thoroughly exhausted from all the crawling, stumbling, bumping, and backtracking, the two teams met in a cavernous room somewhere in the middle. It was a huge space. I was soaked, dirty, tired, and yet very happy to have completed this mission. There was rope enough left to tie together and mark our passage. We rested, planning our return to the palace for clean dry cloths and celebration.

"King Minos!"

It was Belisario's excited voice breaking through our collective reverie.

"King Minos!" he called out again. "You will want to see this for yourself." His solitary torch defined the edge of outer darkness.

It seemed incredible to me that anyone would have left the group to go off by themselves and explore the expansive space. But that is exactly what the chief of palace security had done. With slow measured steps and a lot of grumbling and cursing, his group heeded the call. When I caught up to them, Belisario was holding onto the stout bronze link of a rather short chain. He jerked on it, hard, but there was no give in it. The ring was well-anchored about waist high to an oaken beam secured somehow, into the rock face.

"What do you make of it?" asked the king.

"I have no idea," replied Belisario. "But it's strong enough to hold a bull."

"How could anyone lead an animal that size down here?" Minos asked.

"Unless there was another way inside," I proposed.

Holding our torches high, we split into pairs and explored the cavernous room for clues that might reveal some history about the ominous device. No one found anything, not that day. Whatever clues there might have been were gone, washed away by the departing waters.

On the southern coast of the island, Deena wandered alone into the small grove of olive trees. She had always known that her friend would one day marry Salim. And that had not just been her belief. Long ago, their fathers had come to an agreement. Everyone in the village had said so.

Before the marriage, Naomi's mother had constantly talked about making things for her dowry. Before that she had never tired of telling and retelling the story of how Naomi and Salim had first met. Both were infants; Salim was only just learning to walk. Naomi had been such a beautiful baby. When their young mothers had gone together to pick olives from the ancient grove, the tiny boy had stumbled away from his own mother in order to see the other baby, just as Naomi opened her very dark and perfectly symmetrical eyes. For the rest of that day, Salim would not willingly leave her side. When Deena had asked her own mother about a dowry, her mother smiled and told her to be patient, that there was plenty of time for such things.

Deena knew that the adults in the village did not look at her in the same way that they looked at her friend. Naomi got everything she ever wanted, no matter how vain or melodramatic she became. Even towards her best friend, Naomi could be unreliable and infuriating. But she was also supportive and trusting. Many times Deena had benefited from Naomi's soft-hearted side, usually well hidden from the others. They were best friends.

Everyone Deena had ever known had been born right there. She was terribly discontent, but had only ever told Naomi about this. For Deena, nothing ever changed, and everyone eventually died within a few stadia of that same place. The only exceptions were a few fishermen, a few poor souls unlucky enough to go to sea and never return.

Many times since the marriage Deena had sought out solitude in the same grove of olive trees where Naomi and Salim had first met. She felt herself aging, growing old before her time, and she appreciated the company of the ancient trees. Looking up into their blackened and gnarled limbs, she wondered if she had been born in the wrong place or time. She felt overlooked, misplaced. None of the villagers, not even her mother, had ever told her a story about a young boy searching for her through the olive grove, or anywhere else for that matter. Perhaps it made her realize that she too was near the place where she would die.

Running her hands along the bark of the old limbs, she felt the tree's living memory of the countless scores of people who had come to that same grove for generations to pick the fruit. Each one of them had used the oil in their own way, even to light the night. She wanted so much to belong to that lineage, but she had no idea, no sense of where she could fit in. Naomi certainly had a well-defined role. She was the wife of Salim. Soon they would have children. Naomi would become a matriarch. She was already part of the lineage. Deena could only conclude that she was on the outside of a warm, comfortable village scene, looking in.

CHAPTER FORTY

Solstice was approaching; it was the beginning of another hot dry season. On Kalliste it would soon be time for another gathering of sovereigns. Before leaving for that event, King Minos decided that the timing was ripe to declare the work of draining the caverns completed. Always enjoying the public eye, he held a ceremony to celebrate the restoration of the labyrinth and to honor the leaders of the project. A large crowd assembled in the main courtyard for the event. Minos addressed them from an elevated dais. I stood nearby on the smooth planks of the dance floor with many of the crew leaders. Minos went on for some time that morning, praising all the good work that had been done by so many.

As the sun rose higher I began to sweat, barely listening to the words. Naucreta and Icarus were standing together in the audience. He was growing so fast. His upper body had responded well to his persistent workouts. They were about the same height now. The king was calling for someone, or maybe everyone, to rededicate themselves to the completion of the work that remained. Naucreta was so pretty that morning. Her smile so composed. I watched her drape an arm across Icarus' shoulder and give him a squeeze. It was an easy spontaneous display of affection, something she had been doing ever since we first arrived on the island. I could not help but notice the way his eyes lingered on the shape of her breasts beneath the deep blue fabric of her robe.

"Daedalus, will you please come up to the dais," the king called out.

My face flushed as I watched the faces of so many turning toward me. There was scattered applause. I took a deep breath, exhaled slowly, and walked to the king and the stage.

"This morning I want to recognize someone, a recent arrival to our community, who has been a guiding force throughout this restoration," the king said, dramatically pronouncing the word. "As leader of this island I am very grateful to you, Daedalus, for your leadership, your tireless creative energy, and your dedication to rebuilding this city." Minos spoke in his grandest voice. "I decree that henceforth, you shall enjoy the rights and privileges of a free and full citizen of this island. To bear witness to this new status, I am presenting you with this fine amulet."

In his large hand he held up, for all to see, a polished stone of deepest blue connected to a colorful, braided necklace.

"We are so grateful for all your efforts here," the king said, placing the piece around my neck. "Thank you, Daedalus, for your service."

I turned to face the cheering assembly and waved. Naucreta was walking toward me, Icarus trailing behind. It's difficult to stand and wait while people are cheering, but that's what I did, waiting for the two of them to make their way through the crowd. We walked away from the stage together.

"Such a lovely piece," she said, admiring the highly polished stone that hung from my neck, "And this is truly a high honor. I have never seen the king make a public presentation like this. The news will spread. Everyone who sees this stone will know of you and your deeds."

I shrugged, barely able to speak. All I really wanted in that moment was to take her in my arms and kiss her.

She looked around to bring Icarus into the conversation and continued. "Icarus, this is a stone of power. Heads will turn when your father wears this."

My tongue felt tied with the knot of all the feelings from so many days of desiring her. She placed her hand on my chest and grasped the stone. My breathing slowed a little.

"What kind of power?" Icarus asked.

Slowly turning it over and examining the stone, she continued, "Look at the inclusions in this one. They are like rays of sunlight trapped inside. A stone like this has many names. Here, we call it lapis," she instructed, her scent filling the space between us. "It has always been one of my favorites. The jewelers say that it comes by camel train from a range of distant mountains far to the north and east, a place called Badakhstan. For that stone to be placed into your hands this morning, it had to first travel countless stadia, pass over high mountains and survive encounters with bandits, border guards and thieves all along the way. It is the rare stone that makes it all the way to Knossos, which is not necessarily a bad thing, as the ones that do become imbued with very special qualities. Their charms protect the wearer from the trouble and darkness of the evil eye. Daedalus, if you honor it and keep it safe, the stone will return the favor."

Watching her face while she spoke, I finally said, "I'm so glad you were here to be part of this."

"Oh, I wasn't about to miss it," Naucreta answered. She grasped my shoulders with both of her hands, pulled me toward her and kissed both of my cheeks, one after the other. Then she affirmatively pushed me away, creating some space. It was all so abrupt that I had to take a short sideways step and keep my balance. She returned my gaze and said, "It's about time that you received some recognition for all your dedicated work here."

"You mean more than our fine home, friends, and lifestyle?" I quipped.

"Yes, I do," she answered calmly, looking from my eyes to the blue stone and back again. "You deserve this…and more."

With those words I wanted to take her in my arms and feel her lips against mine. I wanted to pick her up and carry her away. Instead I responded with my head and said, "This is only the beginning. I still have much to hope for."

"It pleases me to hear you say that," she said with an approving nod. "What is next for you, Daedalus?

"Now that Icarus and I are citizens, what should be next for us?" I wondered aloud. "I want to find out about the privileges the king was referring to. That makes me curious. Then again, a bigger grander apartment would be nice; something with a view to rival yours."

"You'll have to talk with Minos about all that when he returns. He's leaving for Kalliste tomorrow with some of his favorites."

"So am I," Icarus interjected. "But only to Malia. We're leaving early tomorrow morning, me and four friends, to enter the regional athletic games. With luck I hope to be ranked among the top contenders, maybe even win a price."

"How nice for you, Icarus," she replied. "What contests will you enter?

"Wrestling and the javelin."

"Be safe, do your best, and make good memories," she replied. "I want to hear all about it when you return. But today is about your father," she continued, changing the subject and turning her green eyes back towards me. "All of Knossos has watched this city transform itself. Your father has been honored for his role in making it happen. You have come very far, both of you."

"But is it far enough?" I asked.

With an intake of breath she ignored the question and continued, "In this specialty of yours, invention, design, public works—whatever you call it—you, my Athenian friend, are without peer. You have demonstrated that your ideas are sound and that you can turn them into useful plans. Best of all, you complete the projects you begin. Do you know how rare that is?"

I blushed at the praise.

"Look around this city. Minos has, many times. You should be proud and happy for all the good works you have created here. And I thank you, Daedalus, for all you've done." She reached up and stroked my head with her hand. "Don't stop what you're doing. But do revel in this praise for a day or two. You've earned it."

Realizing that this was one of those rare days in which everything seemed destined to go well, I continued. "I will. We will. But Naucreta, what about you and me?"

"Oh, that," she replied with a flirtatious smile. "Why don't you stop by the megaron tomorrow after your work is done for the day? We can visit more then. I would love to hear how you intend to reconstruct the dome. Or do you have other plans already?"

"No. Of course not," I said, a little too earnestly. "Tomorrow after work would be perfect."

"I am looking forward to it," Naucreta replied, turning on her heel and walking away, her long robe swaying back and forth. I stared silently at the retreating feminine form, until Icarus interrupted my reverie. "Da, Naucreta was flirting with you," he said, giving me a playful shove.

"Yes, she was," I replied, returning the push on his shoulder, and wanting her more than ever.

CHAPTER FORTY ONE

There was nothing like falling in love to feel young again. For the rest of that day, all the pieces of my life seemed to be in perfect balance, moving together in a synchronous wave towards some distant, ineffable goal. The gods were indeed very close here.

For the longest time sleep eluded me that night. I sat on the balcony alone, looking out onto the central courtyard to the river and beyond and thought about the day's events. It felt like such a milestone on this adventure of my life. Watching Icarus grow and mature was stirring up in me a host of long-forgotten memories from my own past. He was energetic and high-spirited. I tended to be thoughtful and deliberate. He didn't want to spend all his time cooped up in the city focusing on the endless details of a long-term building project. He wanted to be in nature, whether hiking the canyons, hunting in the mountains, or trekking along the coastlines. In these wild places, Icarus was at his best. The surprising part for me was that increasingly, I wanted to be there as well and share the experiences.

I saw the threads of my life woven together with his into a deeper and richer cloth. He would always have a place in my heart. And I wanted Naucreta to become part of that fabric. She seemed to be considering the very same thing. I had reached the point in my life on Krete where I dared to hope for even that relationship to blossom into something more.

I could see the shadowy courtyard illuminated by starlight. On three sides it was bounded by gray stone blocks of gypsum and limestone. Strong vines descended from the balconies of the upper floors, adding texture and color to the otherwise drab walls. That's when the idea of the grand staircase came to me. It would be the final piece of the master plan to redevelop the city; a staircase connecting the upper level of the palace to the central court, three floors below. It had purpose and could also serve as a wonderful entry or stage for dramatic entrances into the public areas for musicians, performers, and speakers. A grand staircase could be my masterpiece, the crowning achievement of a life's work on Krete.

Chapter Forty Two

The dome was the highest point of the city. With the king gone to Kalliste, the expansive megaron was nearly empty. The last of the workmen were all cleaning up and going home. The central hearth stood directly beneath the dome completely surrounded by scaffolding. Naucreta was nowhere in sight. I paused to inspect the maze of poles and ropes. After testing several of the joints I began to climb.

Above my head the light was growing dim. I wanted to see the layout of the roof and the view beyond. Reaching the top row of scaffolding, I looked out at the city and the sprawling fields below. The western sky was streaked with pastel swaths of orange and pink.

"There is still so much to do," I said aloud, "So much to see. How fortunate it was that the Fates brought us to Krete."

"What's that you say?" an inquisitive voice called up from below.

Shaking myself from my reverie and recognizing the voice, I turned with a hopeful glance to the floor below.

"Who are you talking to up there?" she called again. "By the way, did you know that you have very attractive legs?"

"Talking to myself, as usual," I replied, "and thank you for noticing."

"Is there room up there for one more? I'd like to see the view."

"Yes, of course. Come up."

Untying her sandals, she climbed up on the scaffolding and joined me at the overlook, stepping so close that our shoulders and arms touched. The contact was electric, and I leaned gently into it.

"It is so lovely out tonight," she said softly. "From up here, it looks like we're on the edge of something magnificent."

"That's very poetic," I said.

"Let's climb out onto the roof and watch the stars come out. Would you like to?"

"Very much," I said.

It was a long step from the scaffolding to the roof, one that ended with her leaping up to grab my extended hands and arms. From there, it was only another short step forward into an embrace. My heart raced as she gracefully took that step, placing her arms on mine and pulling herself past the edge. Then, we were facing each other, unwilling to let go. My breath coming quickly, I reached around her waist and drew her close. I could feel her arms wrapping around my back as our lips met in one wild, very long-awaited kiss.

For a long while we stood on the rooftop, exchanging tender kisses in the twilight. Below us, the megaron was still. I took her by the hand and led her away from the opening, toward what I hoped would be a more secluded spot. There, she took the heavy shawl from around her shoulders and laid it out across the hard surface. We stretched out side by side.

With a gentle touch she traced the lines of my face, closing my eyelids. She ran her fingertips down the bridge of my nose to the tip, and then onto the contours of my mouth. I kissed her fingertips and drew her close, kissing her cheek and ear and telling her, "I have loved you since the very first day. I can still remember how you looked in your golden robe, standing there in front of the wall of flowers."

"I remember it well," she said, propping herself on one arm.

Opening my eyes I said, "I can still see it so clearly. We had not even spoken then, not until much later."

"You have such a strong, handsome face," she said softly, "One that has occupied my thoughts for a very long time."

I reached for the ties of her bodice and she began to hum softly. The scent of lavender wafted into the air. She nodded yes, and her breasts came free, full and exposed. I nearly lost myself in them, moving my fingers down across her stomach, slowly caressing the length of her waist and hips.

"Yes," she said again, loosening the remaining ties and exposing the brown curves of her waist and legs. She reached for my waist and chest, holding onto the tunic. "You must take this off and lay it here."

I quickly complied, rising up just enough to pull the tunic over my head and exposing the lapis amulet against the soft, pale skin of my chest.

Naked and kneeling on the hard surface, Naucreta arranged her shawl and the discarded clothes into a cushion while I stroked the smoothness of her calf and thigh. She turned her head to watch and smile, and then lay back upon the makeshift blankets. I looked into her deep green eyes and then down across the length of her body. She was irresistible. She beckoned me closer with her hands, reaching for me.

"What a memory we will make tonight," she whispered as her legs spread apart and her eyes closed. A low moan sounded from her lips.

Several floors below, Filia searched for her mistress. The servant had made a reputation for herself by preferring to go barefoot when nearly everyone around her wore sandals. Some wrongly assumed she was slow in the head. Actually, she preferred having the soles of her feet in contact with the earth, which she did even on the coldest of days. Filia didn't care what others said about her behind her back. And she enjoyed feeling invisible as she moved soundlessly through the shadowy hallways of the palace.

That night, the barefoot chambermaid had a mission, one that took advantage of her natural stealth. She was tasked with the chore of finding her mistress and discretely leaving the pillows and the wineskin that she carried in a satchel on her back. She knew to begin her search in the megaron, but was more than a little anxious about what to do if there wasn't any sign of where the lovers had gone. Thankfully, it was not long before Filia found the sandals at the base of the scaffolding. It didn't take her long to guess that her quarry was on the outer dome. She smiled at the thought of the two of us groping for the beast with two backs on the palace roof. Tucking her mistress's sandals into her waist sash, Filia climbed to the top of the scaffolding and admired the view. The stars of evening were already filling the sky. She was too short to climb up, but certainly tall enough to stand on the platform and feel the gentle breeze coming out of the west. The same breeze carried the sounds of our coupling. She opened the wine and took a swallow or two. She stacked the pillows on the edge of the roof and looked out at the night sky, enjoying the view. When all was quiet, she took one last sip, descended the scaffolding and was gone.

CHAPTER FORTY THREE

Naucreta and I lay in each other's arms on our roof-top perch. With immense satisfaction, I sighed and opened my eyes.

"Such a beautiful night," I said, animating the stillness.

"And you, my love," Naucreta softly replied.

"What a delightful surprise you made of this. I did not expect any of it. Not here. Not tonight. At least not until you suggested climbing up to the roof."

"So you were surprised?"

"Yes."

"And you liked it?"

"Yes, more than I can say."

"Those are good things. Maybe I can make it still better."

My expression must have betrayed my doubt.

"Go over to the scaffolding, my lion. See if a goddess of love has left us some pillows and refreshment."

I hesitated, uncertain of her game.

"Just go and look."

I got up and walked over to the hole in the roof, where I quickly found the wine and pillows. All at once I felt naked, exposed, and very amused. I could not help but laugh.

"How is this possible?" I asked, returning to our nest.

"Perhaps we both have a talent for invention," Naucreta declared. "And I have a question for you."

"Yes?"

"Was it worth the wait?"

"Oh, yes."

CHAPTER FORTY FOUR

In the afterglow of our encounter on the rooftop, we walked together in a contented flow through the darkened streets, making our way toward the apartment I shared with Icarus. Neither one spoke much, but we moved in a graceful, unspoken compromise, matching each other's stride, shoulder to shoulder, hip to hip, in perfect counterpoint. I was thinking how nice it would be to eat a little something and make love all over again, this time in a softer, warmer place.

"What have you done to me, Naucreta?" I asked.

"We just made love at the top of the city, though I doubt that anyone except Filia noticed. Have you forgotten so soon?" she replied, feigning a pout.

"Yes. I know. We did, finally. It was wonderful. And do you know that a few hours ago I was telling myself how content I was to be a father and a builder for the king—how complete my life felt. Then you came along, batting those long lashes, throwing your arms around me and then your legs," I laughed. "There goes my theory of being in some kind of balance. Of course, I do feel happier than I've ever felt before."

"You're funny," she replied, "And an excellent father to Icarus. That is one of the many reasons why I am choosing you."

"What?"

"I am choosing you," she repeated, "Just as you have chosen me." We reached the doorway to the apartment. She waited while I went inside just long enough to light an oil lamp. It was not long before the entire room took on a warm glow and I returned to the doorway.

"What do you mean, choosing me?" I asked, holding out the lamp.

"We can discuss this later. Right now, there is something I must do." Naucreta took the lamp and set it on the table. I watched curiously, as she removed a roll of dried green sage from her bag. "It's for cleansing this space," she explained in a calm voice, "and you and me." She held the sage over the flame until it burned with a blue flame. "You still have your clothes on," she complained.

Then she blew it out, leaving behind the pleasant scent of smoldering embers. Placing one palm on my chest, she languidly passed the fragrant smoke in front of my face, my chest, and my stomach. Then she knelt to pass the fragrant smoke in front of my groin, my legs, and my feet. She turned me around and repeated the process, eventually returning to her feet. She handed me the burning smudge as her robe fell to the floor, and bade me do the same with her.

While I knelt in front of her and passed the smoke from the glowing embers over her stomach and abdomen, she asked, "Have you ever heard of the island of Naxos?"

"I know of it," I said, as I knelt in front of her, eyeing her legs through the moving smoke. "On the maps it's a big island north of Kalliste. But I have never been there. Why do you ask?"

"It's complicated. An aging king lives there. He is named Meriones. You may have met him. He travels often during the trading season, and comes to Knossos from time to time to visit with Minos. They are old friends."

I turned her around and blew softly on the embers. Gray smoke wrapped around her heels and legs.

"Meriones is the one with the long nose and large nostrils that have too much hair growing out of them. It's not a pretty sight. Not like your strong face and straight Athenian hair," she concluded, starting to turn back around.

"Not yet," I said, placing my hand on her waist. "I'm not quite finished here."

"As you wish," she said in a most assuring way.

"What about this Meriones?" I asked, a tinge of jealousy creeping into my voice. Standing up again, we faced each other. I held the smudge stick behind her, tracing the smoke across her shoulders and the back of her head.

"His wife has recently passed. She was ill for a long time. They have no heir. And he has fancied me for a very long time. Meriones wants me to couple with him, and make the baby that will preserve his line. But the thought of him lying next to me makes my skin crawl."

"Why are you telling me this?" I demanded, angrily turning away and searching the room for somewhere to crush out the smudge stick.

"My love, look at me," she said with compassion. She stepped toward me and carefully removed the glowing sage from my hand. She thoughtfully crushed the embers into a small clay dish. "My love, look at me," she repeated. "Unlike you, I have no child."

"But," I interrupted.

"Let me finish," she protested. "And I am getting older. The time is coming when men will not be so eager to spend their time and their fortunes on me."

"But I want you to stay here on Krete with me," I pleaded.

"His wife has died. She had the wasting disease. He wants me to become the new queen."

"I will marry you."

"You are so sweet to say those words. Thank you, my love. Now hear me out, please."

"All right, I will listen," I replied.

"As the queen of Naxos, my future is secure. And if I provide him with an heir, then my child lives the life of a princess," she paused, letting the words sink in, then added, "or a prince. Daedalus, I chose this courtesan's life. As a young woman, I had a proposal very similar to the one you just made. I could have been a fisherman's wife. But I was young, full of life. I wanted more than that. I wanted to see the world or at least a different part of it than I could see from my village. By the Fates, Minos and several of his ships landed on our beach one day. Before they left, he gave me that chance."

I frowned and pulled away.

"Don't be so judgmental. He didn't steal me away or force himself on me. He has never been like that. I wanted to go with him! And he promised the village a brand new fishing boat before the next spring, fully rigged with sails and nets. My family, the elders, almost everyone was pleased and proud."

I just shook my head, avoiding her eyes. "So why did we just become lovers?"

"Only for the most basic reason of all," she said provocatively, grabbing me by the hips and pulling me back into her embrace. "Don't you remember the night on your veranda at the beginning of all this, the pillows and the stars? You tried to seduce me that night. You wanted to make love with me. Did it occur to you to stop and explain why?"

"No," I replied, with an embarrassed laugh. "There was no reason to. There was no need to explain."

"Of course not, you are a man. You have seeds to sow."

"I don't understand."

"Why does everyone say that you are so smart?" she teased, gathering up the pillows from around the room. "I just told you why." She arranged them into a large cushion. "Meriones wants an heir," she said, nestling onto the cushions. "And, he wants Naucreta, queen of Naxos, to provide him with one." She turned onto her side. "I won't disappoint him," she said, her voice becoming languid and sultry, "but it is your seed that I am after. You are a caring, intelligent man, the kind of a man who is at his best when he is creating things to benefit others. I have chosen you," she said, extending her arms and hands toward me.

I understood that she was playing me like a musical instrument, but there was nothing I could do or say to resist. I was completely under her spell.

"Daedalus, it is your child that I want," she repeated, meeting my gaze as I crawled onto the makeshift bed. "But I cannot marry you. That is not something I have to give."

My eyes downcast, I tried to take her into my arms. She pushed me away, laughter spilling from her lips. Disappointed and confused, I sat back against the pillows and the wall. Silence filled the smoky room, until she stirred and began stroking my head with her hand. She knelt beside me, holding my head against her breasts, and said in earnest, "So will you please do that thing that you do so well, one more time?"

CHAPTER FORTY FIVE

At the north gate, Icarus and his friend said goodbye. They had walked together all the way from Malia. They were both tired. It was late. Icarus just wanted to get home, have a cool drink and sleep.

When he opened the door to the apartment, he was greeted by the smell of fragrant oils. The empty room was illuminated by the warm orange glow of an olive oil lamp, burning on the table. Beyond it, Naucreta and I sat on the balcony with our backs to him, cross-legged at the low table. We were sharing a plate of fish and fruit. Icarus froze in the threshold, silent. Naucreta was wearing my robe. He tried to leave, but the door creaked. Both of us turned almost in unison. Naucreta smiled and waved, simultaneously closing the top of the robe's collar with her other hand.

"Umm... Hello," Icarus said. "Maybe I should have knocked?" He looked embarrassed and more than a little irritated, but instead of displaying either emotion, he joked, "Well, well. Looks like I just can't leave you two alone, without you getting into some kind of mischief."

"Icarus! You're back," I responded. "I mean, welcome back! Come out here. Come in. Say hello to Naucreta. How did the games go?"

Icarus sighed at the mention of the games, but no words followed.

"Uh-oh," said Naucreta. "That doesn't sound good. Come out on the balcony where we can see you. Tell us about it. You must be hungry.

Have you been traveling all day?"

Dropping his shoulder bag onto the floor, he walked towards the balcony. "You're right, I am starving."

Naucreta stood and offered him her place at the table. "Here, sit," she said, placing her hands on his shoulders and giving them a squeeze. "I'll get more food and tea. Sit. Be comfortable."

Barefoot, she stepped away, discretely picking up her skirt and blouse as she made her way into the bedroom.

I still wonder what she was thinking about as she dressed to leave, standing next to our bed on that last evening together. Every night for the last five she had entered this apartment, pushing the door shut and latching it behind her. Each time, no matter how late, I waited for her in the warm glow of the oil lamp. Each time, she had stepped out of her clothes and slid naked and cool into my arms.

"You're back early," I said, smiling at Icarus. "I wasn't expecting you to return until tomorrow."

"Yes, I can see that," he responded with a smirk, reaching for a piece of tuna. "Truly, I am very sorry for barging in on you like that. I should have understood, back when I took the first step inside the room. I'm just going to eat something quickly and then go to bed."

"Oh, no," said Naucreta, returning with a welcoming smile, a plate of fruit and an amphora of honeyed tea. "I want to hear about Malia. What happened?"

"It's rather boring."

"You didn't want to stay for the awards and the closing ceremonies?" asked Naucreta, a quizzical look on her face.

"Aaah…that's a rather long story," he stammered. "I don't know if I can talk about it like this."

"What do you want to talk about?" I asked.

"When did you two start, you know?" Icarus began. "I'm just curious, because if it's been going on for a while," he stopped himself, "really, I had no idea, and——" again he hesitated, "I'm surprised is all."

Stumbling for words, I replied with an embarrassed laugh, "I think that you have known Naucreta even longer than I. We've all been friends for a very long time. But what you see tonight is a rather recent development."

"Your father is a smart, kind, and handsome man," Naucreta added. "I could no longer resist his charms."

"Well, congratulations then. To both of you," Icarus said, guardedly.

Naucreta and I looked at each other, neither one responding.

Finally, she broke the silence.

"Welcome back, Icarus," she said. "One day soon you must tell me about the games. But now, it is late. I'm going to leave you two alone and go back to my home. You have much to catch up on, I'm sure."

I stood up too.

"I have an early day tomorrow and must get my rest," she said. Walking towards the door, she gathered up a few remaining items and put them in her shoulder bag.

Watching her leave, I had never felt so torn.

"Let me walk you back then."

Turning back toward Icarus, I said, "I'll just be a little while. We will talk."

"No. You stay with your son," Naucreta implored. "You and I can say our goodbyes at the door."

"This is no way to say goodbye," I said as we walked out the door together and stepped into the twilight. We were alone once again.

"There isn't a good way," she answered.

I reached for her waist and pulled her body against mine in a tight embrace.

"When? When will I see you again?"

"I don't know the answer," she replied, cuddling into the embrace. "Here, you must take this back," she said, removing the lapis amulet from around her neck. She placed it back over my head. "I can't go back to the palace wearing it. I am touched that you want me to have it, truly, but it would give too much away. From now on, you have to be my co-conspirator with this secret love of ours."

"But I want you to have it."

"You've given me everything that I ever asked of you," she said. "That makes you a wonderful friend. And we have some wonderful memories."

"Let me walk with you part of the way," I said.

"Stay here with Icarus. He needs you right now."

For a few short days, we had created a passionate fantasy in which we were the only two people on earth. I had known all along that it would not, could not last. But I never guessed how tragically complete the separation would be, how sad the ending. Naucreta pushed herself gently away from our embrace. My arms gave in. We shared one last look.

"When the child is older and all the speculation has become moot, come to see us in Naxos," she said.

I could not answer. My heart was in pieces, parts of it filling up my throat.

Shoulders stooping, Naucreta walked away down the cobblestone path. Her head was moving slightly from side to side, and I watched as she hesitated for a few moments. On one side of her was a wall mural of many fish schooling in blue water. She reached out with her hand for the place where dolphins played. Then, she straightened her shoulders and walked away, again. With a long breath, I wiped my face and stepped back into the apartment.

The first half of Icarus' life had been spent in Athens, the other half on Krete. For him there was no question which life had been the better one. Since settling in at Knossos, much of his energy and time was devoted to the singular goal of adapting to the ways of the islanders, their speech, mannerisms, and culture. He had wanted nothing more than to re-create himself and be just like all the other boys on the island. In many ways, he had succeeded.

Outside of our home, Icarus moved and spoke with the air and the sound of someone who had lived on the island all of his life. Inside our home, he wore a slightly different persona. At the end of the day when we were alone, I often relapsed into our shared Athenian tongue. Sometimes Icarus responded in kind. Other times, he would just listen to the old words and not contribute much at all. He lived in two places, the world of his peers and that of his home. In the former he wanted to thrive. From the other, he wanted to fly away or at least emancipate.

CHAPTER FORTY SIX

Icarus was sitting on the balcony, sipping on a wine skin, when I returned from saying goodbye. His back propped against the wall, he looked out at the moonlit valley far in the distance and asked, "Is it alright if I help myself to some wine?"

"I'll join you," I answered, sitting down nearby.

Smiling, he took a swallow from the bag.

"I just let the love of my life persuade me that the right decision was to let her walk out the door," I said, launching the conversation.

"That sounds very sad, Da. I'm sorry," Icarus replied. "You know, when I came in the door this place looked and smelled like Aphrodite's gymnasium. I should have realized what was going on right away, closed the door and left. If you want to go out and find her, then you should. Really. I'm fine right here."

"You know what?" I declared. "She was right about one thing."

"What?"

"That you and I need to talk. We need to talk about the games. What happened in Malia? Why are you home early?"

"It's a long story," he said. "I'm sure that your week has been much more eventful and enjoyable."

"Come on, tell it."

"Well, the first part of the trip was good. We camped on the beach, met a lot of interesting people, and arrived in Malia in plenty of time to enter the games. It was fun. Everyone was getting along. Then the games started." He paused and took a deep breath.

"I didn't make it past the first round in spear throwing. None of us did. These were regional games. There were competitors from all over the eastern provinces. But in wresting, I won my first three matches."

"Good for you," I replied.

"And that meant that I advanced to the semi-finals, where I lost. That's when Demitrious and I decided to leave. The rest stayed until the games were finished."

"So you didn't want to stay for the closing ceremonies?"

"Not really. Demitrious and I, we were both eliminated. We didn't want to stay."

"I'm guessing that there's more to this story," I said, prompting him.

"People were betting. After the first few rounds of competition, there were some fights. One of the fathers, he didn't want me to compete in the wrestling competition."

"What did he say to you?" I asked, feeling shocked and defensive.

"Everything was fine until I started advancing. Then he started complaining to the judges. He said that these were Minoan games. When I won my last match, he booed. He called me an Athenian cheater, and, oh yes, an Athenian dog. He definitely had a good time with that one."

"But why?"

"His son's name is Avram. We're in the same weight class. The father wanted to have me ejected from the games."

"That's ugly," I said.

"He was yelling about it, making a huge scene."

"Weren't there any judges? What did they do?"

"Nothing," Icarus replied.

"They must have done something!"

"Well, they told him to sit down. Then they started the next match."

"Did you ever wrestle the other youth. Did you ever wrestle Avram?"

"Not exactly, I think Avram was pretty embarrassed. He wouldn't even look at me. But the father, he kept following me around, pointing his stupid finger in my face. I kept walking away and telling myself that I didn't care what he said. Then, he called my mother a whore—"

"Ouch. Then what happened?"

"I hit him."

"Who did you hit? Were you hurt?" I asked.

"No. Demitrious was right there. He saw the whole thing. He was helping me with the crazy father the whole time."

"Remind me to make a present for Demitrious," I said. "Who did you hit? Avram, or his father?"

"The big fat father. He kept coming toward me, shaking his fist and waving his finger up and down. Telling me to go home. Saying that I didn't belong there."

"That's insane. He had no right to treat you that way."

"According to him, the games weren't for Athenians."

"I can't believe people didn't help you out," I replied.

"People were watching. They were talking about him, but you're right, no one did anything! That made me mad, too. I was afraid. I really wanted to run away."

"Is that when you hit him?"

"Are you going to get mad at me?" he asked.

"No, I promise," I said. "Finish the story."

"He was big and slow, and backing me into a wall with that finger pointing thing. I knew that he expected me to run for it."

"But you didn't?" I asked, surprised.

"No, not then. I let him back me up a few steps and head-faked to the left. It's my strong side. That's the way he expected me to go. But I cut back to the right. When he adjusted, I kicked him in the crotch with my left foot, just as hard as I could."

"Did he go down?" I asked, smiling for the first time since the story started.

"Like a tree felled by an ax."

"Well, good for you," I said, clapping him on the shoulder.

"Where did you learn that?"

"You remember the winter that Aadam stayed with us, don't you? We practiced moves like that, all the time. He was always showing me ways to defend myself against someone bigger. Are you sure you're not mad?"

"Very sure, and right now I'm proud of you too."

"All I remember is the pig-faced man lying on the ground and swearing, his hands between his legs. That's when people started to gather around. Demitrious grabbed me by the arm, and we took off running as fast as we could go. Nobody tried to stop us. We just kept going."

"Until you found your way back home," I said. "I like the ending. You did well. You both did, to get out of there without getting hurt. Icarus, you didn't do anything to deserve that kind of treatment. You didn't do anything wrong."

"Thanks, Da."

"You were attacked by an over-zealous, misguided father. The man sounds possessed. What else could you have done?"

"You might get a little more judgmental, Da. You know, put some feeling into it," Icarus teased.

"You're right," I said, raising my voice in mock anger. "He was an over-zealous, misguided, stupid, ugly, pig-faced, ass of a Kretan."

"Do you think it was all about helping his son win at the games?" Icarus wondered.

"There's no logical explanation for what he did. I guess that's as good as any," I answered.

"His face was so angry, all swollen and dark. He really did look like an enraged boar!"

"I'm sure he did," I said. "And I'm sorry, very sorry that I wasn't able to be there."

"That's alright," Icarus replied, reaching toward me and pulling on the blue stone that hung from my neck. "So I'm a citizen now. We both are. That's what this shiny piece of blue stone means, right?"

I shrugged my shoulders and said, "Had you won at the games, the judges would have given you a shiny trinket too—"

"Da," Icarus interrupted, his voice becoming intense. "There was a lot of talk about the arrival of the next round of Athenian slaves this summer."

"The things that you can carry in your hands eventually lose all their glory," I continued, not wanting to hear the part about Athenian slaves. "All that really matters, all the important things are you ones you hold in your heart. People like the pig-faced jerk are still waiting to learn that. His heart is so constricted and buried so deep, it can't hold much at all."

"Father, he's not alone!" Icarus declared, his own anger returning, "Hating Athenians is coming back into fashion this season."

"You're exaggerating," I said. "Anyway, you were out in the provinces. It's different here in Knossos."

"Oh, really?" he said sarcastically. "They are being brought to Knossos! This city will be the heart of the abuse. People are already talking about it like it's some kind of holiday."

"I haven't heard that."

"That doesn't mean it won't happen," Icarus replied. "Father, I mean no disrespect, but your head is in the clouds half of the time. The rest of it you spend mooning over Naucreta."

"Tell me what you have heard," I said.

"That King Minos will have them dragged through the streets. That he'll have them thrown into the caverns to break their spirits. He'll sell them. He'll give some away to his friends, and keep a few for his own entertainment."

I reached inside my tunic and pulled on the blue stone amulet, nervously fingering it in my hands.

"And what's incredible to me—no—infuriating," Icarus continued, "is that I really don't care about where we came from. Being from Athens means nothing to me, less than nothing. But the islanders won't let me forget it."

CHAPTER FORTY SEVEN

I walked aimlessly through the darkened city that night, replaying in my mind the conversation with Icarus. I could not sleep. Too much had happened that day. Seven seasons were gone since leaving Athens, seven cycles of suns' worth of effort and energy into making a new home here. And for what? Digesting my son's perspective, I felt overloaded and burdened far beyond my ability to cope. So I walked, gradually making my way downhill, inexorably drawn to the river.

Was I really unaware of the talk around the palace about the arrival of the Athenian slaves? Or was I just ignoring it? Either way, they were about to burst onto the scene. Some of our former shipmates might even be transporting them, trafficking in their slavery. Naucreta had told me it was coming. It had been so easy for me to feign indifference to their fate as we were drinking wine and flirting with each other. That was long before Icarus' assault at the Malian games. It seemed so obvious now that all of our fates were connected by some invisible design.

One thing was constant, the authority of the king. Minos controlled all of our destinies, and he was a man prone to many excesses. I was his engineer. I should have known. I should have seen the risks inherent in the king holding that kind of power over us.

There was some comfort in remembering that, back in Athens, I had faced a similar challenge. A younger man, I had risked everything in order to sail across an unknown sea, far beyond the comforts and routines of the life left behind. It had been a great leap of faith, something I looked back on with pride. On Krete, I had become a successful builder all over again. But any sense of satisfaction was gone. Almost in the flash of a moment, I became certain that the work was no longer enough.

Leaving the city, I followed the river road's cobblestone course to another proposed building site. Minos had promised the priesthood a new temple. Looking across the unbroken landscape, I felt no motivation. I didn't care about designing or building it. Instead, I vividly remembered the dream from so long ago. I recalled the tablet and the promise made that night. Icarus coming into my life was a gift. So was the chance to build for King Minos. But neither of those had set me apart from other men. Minos was just another man following his own dreams, another man, who happened to wield incredible power.

As for Icarus, at nearly sixteen, the child had grown into a strong and healthy young man, striding purposefully toward his own independence. Each day he asserted his individuality more and more. He was certainly not a gift to be received or possessed. One day, he too would leave, and it would be my role to bless that transition as best I could. So if there was a promised gift, then it just couldn't be Icarus. Nor was it Naucreta. Our time together was over. So if this grand and wondrous gift was real, it simply had not yet arrived. I would have to continue to wait.

Remembering the dream in the midst of all the discord proved to be a welcome relief. It made me realize that I had had a fine run in my time on this island. There was much to be grateful for. I had a home, my health and a job. I had something to do, people to love, and I had hope for the future.

I tried to imagine myself working on the design for a new temple, but there no excitement, not even much interest. It wasn't my dream. It was only the opportunity to fulfill King Minos' dream.

When morning came, I decided to go and see the king. I had gone to an administrative aide that morning and demanded an audience. Yes, I had to see the king right away. Yes, it was important. And no, I didn't care to tell them what it was about. Sweat forming on my brow, I waited anxiously for the unscheduled meeting.

CHAPTER FORTY EIGHT

Passing through the shaded entryway, I reconsidered the opening I planned to use. As if for the first time, I noticed how large and imposing the king's chair was. Hard stone benches protruded from the walls on both its sides. Bored-looking council members adorned them, arrayed on plush pillows. The fourth wall was open to a blooming courtyard and framed by heavy columns. Hummingbirds flitted among the bright flowers. Lifting my eyes, I looked upon the painted images of indifferent griffins gazing out from the walls.

The king looked up from the deliberations. He watched and waited, probably reading my attitude from all the silent cues. Then he spoke first, as was the custom. I was sure he sensed my unease.

"Welcome, Daedalus. A lovely morning, isn't it? Have you come up with any new ideas to show us today?"

"Good morning, King Minos. No, I have no new designs or inventions to show you. I have other topics on my mind."

"Then what brings you to court today? You appear to be troubled."

"I do have a significant problem."

"Then tell it," replied the king. "You are among your most ardent supporters."

"Many years of work went into restoring the caverns underneath the palace. Now, I am regretting it."

"Go on," replied the king.

"Were you planning all along to use it as a dark holding pen for imprisoning the Athenian slaves this year?" I asked, going straight to the heart of the matter.

"Are you feeling competing loyalties today, my friend?" asked the king calmly, offering a palliative smile.

"The Athenians have committed no crime. Their imprisonment will be an injustice."

Several members of the council began a private conversation. Minos said nothing and looked off into the open sky, as if collecting his thoughts.

"If I had known that from the beginning, I could have taken my planning in other directions," I continued. "The caverns would still be flooded."

"And the caverns would still be flooded?" Minos interrupted, shifting his gaze toward me. "Who is this man today?" he asked looking around the room, probably already aware of an angry fire beginning to smolder inside his spleen. "Yesterday, you were my architect. Today, you try your hand at politics. Daedalus, if you aspire to be an advisor…you are off to a poor start."

Many people came before the king in this fashion, seeking his intervention into their personal matters or for assistance in resolving a dispute. From long experience the king knew that his decisions were better when he remained emotionally detached from the outcome. It was not always an easy thing. On another day Minos might have let his anger get the better of him, but not yet. The day had begun so well. He was already looking ahead to a pleasurable encounter with an old friend. Besides, the king did value my work and wanted it to continue. So, he listened as patiently as he was able, allowing me to make the points that I apparently needed to make.

"There are already so many servants and slaves," I said. "Why not just keep the silver? You have nothing to lose by letting these fourteen men and women go free."

The council members looked at one another in amusement.

"You are well paid, Master Builder. Why are you not satisfied?" Minos inquired honestly, gesturing toward me with an open palm. "Why can't you just be content with your living situation and your pay, without troubling me with these trifles?" The council nodded their agreement.

"Trifles?!"

I bridled at the word.

"These are lives!" I said, struggling to regain my composure. I took a few breaths and continued. "I am asking you to spare the lives of the young Athenians. I am deeply troubled that their days may end in a labyrinth of my own creation."

Minos haughtily raised an eyebrow. Hearing me refer to the caverns as my own must have touched a nerve. Clenching his fists the king squirmed in his chair.

"With your past, I am surprised to learn that watching Athenians die is such a problem for you," he lashed out sarcastically.

The words stung. All I could see was my own feet, still standing on the ground.

Seething, Minos looked blankly across the room and began to rant.

"I am not going to change! Aegeus and I have an agreement, a contract. If I stop the slaving, then the king of Athens will conclude that I am getting soft with age." Shifting into a strident voice, he added, "That is a perception I will not allow!"

I felt the king's rage surge against me like a wave. I had nothing to gain by resisting it and much to lose if I responded out of my own anger. Still looking down I took another breath and reconnected with my own sense of purpose, gathering my strength.

"My work here is concluding," I replied. "Your palace and city are nearly complete. When I first arrived on this island, I promised to serve you well. I have done that. I think that it is time for new challenges."

"Finally, he arrives at the point," Minos said aloud. The king seemed to grow calmer. "What are you saying, Master Builder?"

"That surely there are other islands, other kingdoms in need of roads and new buildings."

"And what of your son?" asked the king. "He has grown up in Knossos. The only life he knows is on this island. From what I know of it, his memories of Athens are not good ones. It is to your credit as his father that you were successful in making this island his home. Are you ready to leave all that behind? Or will he go with you?"

Despite my earlier conversation with Icarus, I was not sure that I knew the answer. Clearly, Icarus was upset with the current situation. But was it so bad for him that he wanted to leave? With these questions, the king had found the heart of the issue. Minos wielded indiscriminate power. His reach was wide and I had been put on the defensive. I simply had no faith in Minos on the subject of Icarus' future. So I deflected the question and simply said, "He will go his own way when it is time."

"Daedalus, let's take a step back from the precipice," said King Minos. "You and I have a history together. We have accomplished many fine things. You have wonderful creative ideas and a knack for giving them form and substance. I have the power and the means to facilitate your work. We can still support each other. Look at all the work that is still left undone. Are you really ready to throw all that away?"

"If I stay on as your architect and builder, will you stop the torment of the Athenian slaves?"

"Are we back to that again?" the king demanded, furious once again. Glaring at me, he rose to his feet and roared in a commanding voice, "You cannot stop being my builder, any more than I can stop being king. Know these truths, Master Builder, and know them well. You can no more leave this island than you can fly. I rule the land. I rule the sea." With each "I," he thrust his thumb, which extended from a clenched fist, into his chest.

I felt his voice washing over me like a wave in a storm.

"There are three reasons why you will stay on my island," he raged on. "First, you have nowhere else to go. Years ago you left Athens in shame. You cannot go back, and no one else will have you. Second, you and Icarus are living a very comfortable life in my court. You cannot replace that anywhere. And third, as I told you when you first arrived on Krete: you and your son are welcome here, as long as each of you serves this community. When that ceases, your lives are forfeit."

Minos shook as he made his threats. Then the aging king sat back down upon his throne, breathing hard, his ornamental headband askew. In the silence that followed, one of his aides approached and whispered a message into his ear. The king smiled and said in response, "Tell Naucreta to wait in the queen's room."

My heart ached, hearing her name like that. Queen Pasiphae was cloistered in her mountain retreat. It was common knowledge that the king preferred using her apartment for his sexual assignations. There was even a private bath. My knees felt weak.

Seeing my distress, the king changed tactics. Affecting a smile, he opened the palms of his hands and gestured around the room.

"Daedalus, can you be reasonable?" he asked. "You will never find another place like this; one that gives you the kind of opportunity to do this work that you enjoy so much. You're more than just a builder. You are an artist. And there is so much more to be done to glorify my reign. No one else can provide you with the resources, the materials, and the labor you need to do your work. We have accomplished much together, you and I, in rebuilding this city. You, better than anyone, have to know that."

He was trying to flatter me with words of praise, comfort and security. But it was far too late for that. I barely even heard the offer.

"Here is my proposal," Minos babbled on. "Take Icarus and leave on a long holiday. Take a full cycle of the moon. Take the rest of the summer. Tour the island, from Knossos to Zakros, to Phaistos and back again. When you have finished, you and Icarus can return to your lives here. You can begin your next project. If it's the new temple, then it's yours to design and build from start to finish. This could be your life's work, your masterpiece."

Aware that he was finally finished, I struggled to make eye contact. Somehow, I blurted out that I needed more time to consider. Minos cut me off with a wave of his hand. Like smirking young boys on a school yard, I overheard one white-haired councilman say to the other, "He's going to ensure that King Meriones has a proper succession plan in place."

"You have my answer," the king said, sounding indifferent to my distress. "This concludes our meeting." With that the king rose again to his full height and looked about the room. "I have another matter to attend to," he said, smiling to several individual members of his counsel.

CHAPTER FORTY NINE

I stumbled my way out of the palace. Nothing had come of my efforts. I had completely caved in, right in front of the counsel.

I walked straight to the workshop of the best alchemist in Knossos. He looked up from his sweetened tea and greeted me warmly. His hands and forearms bore the scars of a lifetime of minor burns. He was a craftsman, a creator of bronze and other metals. Perhaps he recognized me, or maybe it was the lapis amulet that he recognized. Charred holes covered his stained and ancient tunic, but his face bore the countenance of a true artisan. Right away he began to describe in loving detail the fine quality of the products of his most recent casting—and the understandable demand.

"Fortunately, one of the finest products remains," he said, reaching inside a large reed basket. The alchemist brought out a well-oiled leather scabbard with the bone-handle of a knife protruding from the open end. He offered it to me to inspect.

I withdrew the curved bronze blade and ran it back and forth across my palm, admiring the edge and the workmanship.

"This blade is the highest quality bronze," he said with great sincerity. "If it breaks, bring back the pieces and I will make you another. You have my personal guarantee."

"You made this knife?" I asked.

"Yes, I did," he said with obvious pride.

"How?"

"From the ores of copper and orichalcum," he replied.

"You made this from rocks?" I asked.

"Yes and no," he replied. "The actual process is very complicated. And it is very secret." Looking me up and down he continued, "I love this knife. It pains me to think of losing it, but I will give it to you for five silver rings."

"Five?" I responded, wishing that I had worn an older tunic, "Perhaps another day. Actually, I came here seeking advice."

"Do not ask about the process of making bronze," he said resolutely. "Ask me anything else."

"All right," I replied. "How do you get the ore?"

"That I can answer," he said with a smile. "I buy it of course."

"Where?" I asked.

"There is a huge warehouse in Amnisos, more than anyone could use in a lifetime of this work," he assured me.

"Can anyone purchase it?"

"Anyone with silver or gold rings," he said candidly.

Still holding the knife in my hand I asked, "Do you have another one of these?"

The alchemist nodded.

"Good," I answered. "For six silver rings, I'll take both of them."

CHAPTER FIFTY

It was already mid-afternoon by the time I walked back to our apartment near the main courtyard. I was drained, exhausted, but had no interest in napping. There was too much on my mind. Perhaps I should have tried harder to find some common ground with the king. Without it, the subject of the slaves would be impossible to bring up again. By the end of the meeting, the king's position had been cast. There would be no bringing up the subject again, not without some new facts or circumstances. His only concession had been to offer the opportunity to build the new temple—all of it in the presence of his council. Now, the two unrelated topics had become linked. If I began the work at all, the council would regard it as acquiescence to the harsh treatment of the Athenians.

I wanted to talk with Icarus about all these events and developments, but he wasn't at home. He was probably over at the gymnasium working out, or spending time with that girl who had recently caught his eye.

All alone in the apartment, I made some tea and began making preparations for a long trek. I found our rucksacks and began filling them with sleeping gear, a copper cooking pot and a brand new knife, all the things we would need to make the task of living off the land more enjoyable.

Icarus returned around suppertime, hungry and surprised to see the rucksacks packed and sitting next to the door. He had already heard several versions of my meeting with Minos. It was the talk of the town. But I didn't want to discuss the meeting itself. I had more important things on my mind.

Somehow and within a few short days, all the fun, the satisfaction had vanished, smashed on the rocks of my tempestuous love affair. My heart felt like it had been ripped into pieces. It would be easy to despise her. But how could I harbor that kind of resentment for the woman who might bear my child? And when would I even learn the outcome of the pregnancy? On top of everything else, the slaves from Athens would soon arrive. How could I stand by and watch fourteen of my countrymen go to their doom at the hands of my benefactor, King Minos? It was too much. Some of them would not be much older than Icarus. It was an impossible situation. Minos had refused to listen to reason, and his mocking words were now etched in my brain, "You can no sooner leave this island than you can fly!"

I remembered the recent dark night, walking alone by the river. Wistfully, I began to speak about how simple and balanced life on Krete had once seemed. In the early years, I'd wanted nothing more than to do the work of reconstructing the city. Not only did I enjoy my career, it was part of being a father and fulfilling my promise to Icarus. The work had so much value then. "Watching you grow and become a young man, Icarus, has been a great source of satisfaction."

"So what are you going to do now?" Icarus asked.

"Well, the one thing I can't do is pretend to be numb and look the other way."

"What's the rucksack for?"

"Another suggestion from the king," I replied. "In a conciliatory moment he suggested that I, no, that *we* leave Knossos before the slaves arrive, and go trekking around the island."

"For how long?"

"As long as we want."

"But what about my friends, my athletics, my school?" Icarus asked.

"What about the pig-faced man from Malia?" I responded, "Calling you an Athenian dog. He's not alone, you know."

"Dianna says that he's just a stupid farmer," Icarus responded. "She says that I should just forget about him."

"Minos is expecting me to take a holiday and, frankly, I like the idea. Let's explore the canyons on the western side of the island. No one ever goes there. And while we're at it, maybe we can look for a good boat and crew to take us away from all this. We could go to Sicily, or back to Athens, or anywhere else for that matter."

"What are you saying, Da?" questioned Icarus. "I don't want to leave the island."

"Oh, I'm just thinking out loud. But there are other places we could live, you know."

"How could you even consider going back to Athens?" Icarus asked, judgmentally.

"I understand that all your friends are here in Knossos," I responded, avoiding the question.

"My whole life is here!" Icarus said.

"And it's been a good life," I calmly responded. "We're comfortable and secure. But how long can it last? What if, when the temple is completed, I'm no longer useful for Minos? What will happen to us? What will you do then?"

"I don't know, but that will be years from now," Icarus said. "What if next winter Aadam returns and stays with us again? In the spring I could go on a trading cruise, maybe even join the *Pelican's* crew. Captain Nikolaos already said that he would have me. Remember?"

"Yes, I do," I answered, not willing to take the conversation in that direction. "Icarus, there are so many things you can do with your life. But I'm not talking about next spring. I'm trying to talk about right now."

"So am I," he replied.

"The slaves from Athens are coming soon. Do you understand that for us to just stay here and do nothing different is a choice? It's a choice to become small and compliant. If we stay in Knossos after that, then we will live our lives like tethered eagles. Minos will let us fly around a little. He'll let us soar over the palace from time to time, but we will be stuck here, always tied to a very comfortable tether. There will never be any more freedom here on Knossos, for you or me, than Minos will allow."

"What if I want to stay?" said Icarus defiantly.

"You can do that," I slowly replied. "Just understand the decision you are making. From my perspective, that way will go hard for you. The king is showing us what eventually happens to Athenians on this island. We serve at the pleasure of Minos, and that is as much of a life as we get. You and I have been fortunate. We live amongst the nobles of the island, birds in a gilded cage. But only for as long as Minos appreciates my work and wants to spend his time and money on reconstruction."

"Why now?" asked Icarus.

"It is comfortable here, even beautiful at times," I continued, thinking wistfully of Naucreta. "But it's still a cage. What will you do after I'm gone to set yourself apart, so that you get better treatment than the other Athenians?"

"Da, I have no idea what I will be doing in five years, or ten, or even one! What I know is that I am happy now. The future can take care of itself."

"What about his daughters, Ariadne and Phaedra?" I teased, watching the discomfort spreading across his face. "You might marry one of them. That would ensure your future. Maybe mine, too."

"Dianna's more to my liking, she's more my age," he replied with certainty. "Besides, the king's daughters will marry someone rich and powerful, you know that."

"I agree, because Minos will manipulate and control that too," I answered.

A frustrated Icarus didn't respond. He probably wasn't comfortable having a conversation with me about his blossoming preoccupation with young women. I mercifully took the discussion in another direction.

"Icarus, when we left Athens behind, I thought that my life was in ruins. I decided to take a chance then, because I believed there was nothing to lose. I had no knowledge of Krete or its people, only a hope in a better future. But in order to do that, I had to step into the unknown. Looking back, I sometimes wonder whether or not I could have made that choice alone. There I was, standing on the edge of that threshold, too despondent to move. That's when you appeared in my life, and we made the journey together."

"Why are you bringing up all this?" he asked.

"Ever since then, our lives have become intertwined, but for how much longer? Maybe we're approaching another decision point, you and I, a fork in the road."

"Maybe," he said defiantly.

"Soon you will be moving into your own life. I just hope you choose wisely. If we stay in Knossos and try to make the best of things, I warn you, it will be at the whim of the king." I paused to look at his face and see what impact the words might be having. "In this time of your life you can go anywhere, be anything. You have so much freedom now. So much more than any of the young slaves will ever have again. We have to start making our own choices."

I wondered if I could leave without him.

"I will never go back to Athens!" Icarus fumed.

"I'm not exactly sure where I want to go," I replied, trying to stay calm. "All I know is that I can't stay in Knossos right now. And I don't want you to stay here either." Frustrated, I tilted my head back and looked at the ceiling. Turning back to the youth, I continued. "I'm saying that one day we should leave the island, you and I, so that each of us, especially you, can have a real future. I fear for us here. I fear that we are both destined for the king's labyrinth unless we choose another path. Come with me, Icarus. And you're right about Athens. It's not a good option for us." Finally the words I had been searching for arrived. "Do you know what it comes down to for me? I don't feel any hope here. When we first arrived, there was hope. Now, I can't find any."

"Is that because of the Athenians?" Icarus quipped, "Or because of Naucreta leaving?"

"Probably both," I answered. "Icarus, you are my golden son. Do you realize that? You are so smart, so strong and vital. You can go anywhere, be anyone, do anything; you have only to choose. There really is no one like you in the whole, wide world. There will never be another time in your life when you will have so much freedom, so much energy with which to carry out your choices. Here in the palace, you will never be more, have more, or do more than Minos will permit. Come with me. Think of what you can do. Icarus, I promise you that this journey will make you a man, and me, a better one."

Icarus had only vague recollections of those times back on the streets of Athens when I first proposed that we leave and go on this journey together. After his mother was taken, his life had become a constant search for food, safety, and warmth. Without her, he had no attachment to Athens; not a healthy one anyway. It had been an easy place to leave. In that way, our first journey across the sea was a gift. And I had kept my word. I had always been there for him, with the possible exception of the trouble in Malia.

"About this camping trip," Icarus said, beginning to acquiesce. "When do you expect to leave?"

"Soon. But there are several things I need to finish before we can go. Let's plan to leave in a three days. That way, each of us has time to prepare and say our goodbyes. After the meeting with Minos this morning, it's what everyone expects. We'll walk out of the city together, right under the king's nose. Are we agreed then?"

"I can be ready to leave then. But Da, if you go looking for a way off the island, we still have to decide on the destination, right?"

"That's fair."

"And if I decide that I want to return to Knossos, then you have to promise not to stand in my way. It will be my choice."

I placed my hand on his shoulder and said, "I can make that promise."

"You won't get angry or hurt? We'll say our goodbyes and then go our separate ways."

"Have you been taking lessons from Naucreta?"

"Not like yours," he replied.

"Icarus, I promise that when the time comes for us to part, you will have my blessing."

CHAPTER FIFTY ONE

The next morning there was a knock on the door. My heart leapt at the thought that it might be Naucreta. I hurried to the door, only to find three well-dressed young women. They all wore their long chestnut hair in carefully combed coiffures, held in place with delicate coils of small, beaded shells. One of them looked familiar, but I wasn't entirely sure who she was.

Smiling awkwardly I said, "Good day. If you are looking for Icarus, he's not here right now. But I'm expecting him to return very soon."

"Good day to you, sir," replied the closest one. She had sparkling eyes and a warm smile. "Actually, we're looking for his father, Daedalus. That wouldn't be you, would it?" she nervously asked.

'Yes, I am Daedalus," I responded with a slow smile. "What can I do for you?"

"I heard you in front of the council yesterday, advocating for the plight of the Athenians," she said. "That was a courageous thing to do, to argue with my father like that."

"Of course. Now I remember," I replied, "you are Ariadne."

"And this is my sister Phaedra and my very good friend, Dianna. I've told them all about it."

I nodded to each in turn, just in time to notice Icarus rounding the corner of the cobblestone street. He smiled, looking the three striking young women up and down, and approached.

"There's Icarus now," I said.

Dianna turned and smiled in his direction.

"There aren't many willing to confront him like that," Ariadne continued, her friends nodding in support. "Believe me, I know how intimidating he can be."

"Do you know my son, Icarus?" I asked, changing the subject and inviting him to join the group. "Please…go on. What were you saying, Ariadne?"

"We all agree with you," she continued. "Yesterday, after you met with my father, we went looking for the old entrance into the labyrinth, the one you made on the hillside. It's covered over with stones and dirt, but easy to find. We made a lever out of a long, straight branch and used it to pry some of the stones apart."

"Did you go inside?" asked Icarus.

"I did," said Dianna. "I crawled inside, stood up and felt around a bit. These two wouldn't even do that much," she said, gesturing to Ariadne and Phaedra. "Inside, the light doesn't penetrate very far. The darkness becomes thick after just a few steps."

"That's why we've come to you," interjected Phaedra.

"What is it that you want?" Daedalus asked.

"We want you to take this cord," Ariadne replied, holding out a large skein of thread wrapped around an ornate clay cylinder. "Take it back inside the labyrinth from below and mark the way to the access door beneath the palace."

"Are you serious?" I queried.

"I heard what you said. So I know you want to help them," she insisted. "You do, don't you?" Ariadne asked, sounding quite unsure. "You've been through the labyrinth before. You know the way. Here, take the skein. Please!" She pushed the large spool towards me.

"Will you do it?" Phaedra and Dianna asked together, looking from father to son.

"You're the only one who can do this," Adriana pleaded.

"Once the cord is discovered, your father will reach the same conclusion," I said cautiously. "What then?"

"Yes. He will know," replied Ariadne defiantly. "Just as he will know who supplied the thread, especially if you leave this spool inside the entrance. But by the time it's discovered, you will be gone, won't you? You'll be off on your holiday, while my father deals, not just with their escape, but also his daughters' complicity."

"And that of her friends," Dianna joined in.

"You know what, Father? I think we should do it," Icarus responded.

"The king will be furious with us," Daedalus replied. "If we take this step, Icarus—"

"We will support you any way we can," Ariadne interrupted.

"I can see that some planning has gone into this," I said. "But before this talk goes any further, I want to discuss this with my son, alone. Can you come back later? And here, take this spool with you."

On board the *Pelican,* a young Athenian man sat alone on the foredeck, his back to the wind. A beaded strap of leather kept the thick brown hair from blowing into his face. Coarse ropes bound his muscular arms tightly behind his back, not quite hiding the jagged scar that ran across his right arm.

"I have a bad feeling about that one," said Orion. "He is going to be trouble. I know it."

"Once he gets to Krete, perhaps," Captain Nikolaos replied. "But by then, it will not be our worry. Besides, he gave me his word. Our charge is to get him there, as intact as possible."

"Still, I'll feel better with an arrow and a short bow in my hand, and twenty paces between us."

"Then go and get one out of the hold. Every warrior on the Great Green knows of your skill with a bow. But remember, he has no value to us with an arrow in his chest."

"I can aim lower."

"Look at the size of his shoulders," said the captain. "He will bring a hefty price in the markets. I do not want 'Golden Hair' damaged."

"I'm not certain he'll make it that far."

"I told you, Orion. We have an arrangement. He told me that he actually wants to go to Krete, and I believe him. I promised to take him there, safe and unharmed."

"Then I won't shoot at him until he's about to club a crewman over the head. What did he say his name was again?"

"Theseus," said the captain. "He calls himself Theseus."

CHAPTER FIFTY TWO

B ack in Knossos, we walked through the city reminiscing, and eventually found our way back to the old neighborhood. Georgios, the baker, was in the same shop, a little older and rounder. He greeted us warmly, looked Icarus up and down approvingly, and served us tea and freshly baked bougatsa. Then he left us to our discussion of the day's events.

"I'll tell you what's changed for me," Icarus said.

"Other than the fact that it was a pretty girl asking you to sever your ties with the kingdom, instead of me?"

"I'm serious father, listen. This is important."

"Then tell it. I'm listening."

"Long-forgotten memories have started coming back to me," Icarus said, "waking me from my sleep. Lots of them."

"When did they start," I asked.

"Right after I came home from Malia."

"What kind of memories?"

"Remember the little place where I used to live with my mother? I took you there once, a long time ago," Icarus answered. "Last night I dreamed that we were hiding together in the fruit cellar again. She shushed me with a finger to her lips and then held me tight. She held me warm and close, and said to be still. And I was, just as quiet as I could be."

"What happened?"

"I heard the sounds of the door crashing down, and she held me even tighter," he said with a sigh. "The fruit cellar was the first place they looked."

"Who?"

"The bad men. The trapdoor flew open, and a man was staring down at us. He had wild eyes. I can still see those eyes. He grabbed my poor mother by the hair and dragged her up the steps. She was screaming and kicking, with me still holding on."

"No wonder you became so angry in Malia," I said.

"There was one with a face like a donkey. He grabbed me and tore me away from her," Icarus said flatly. "I was screaming and she was reaching out for me. The third one kicked her in the chest. She went down, and just lay there gasping for air—"

"Is this the dream," I asked.

"He had a knife. He held it right here against my neck," Icarus responded, gesturing with his hand. "I can remember his foul breath, and the smell of his leather breastplate."

"That's terrible," I said.

"That's not all."

"What else?"

"They tore off her robe and held her down. I couldn't watch," he sobbed. "They did it right in front of me."

"I'm so sorry."

"When they were through, they tied my mother's hands in front of her and dragged her out of the house by a rope," he said, tears running down his cheeks. "I followed at a distance, all the way to the promontory, the place where you can look down and see the harbor."

"I remember it. We talked there once a long time ago."

"Yes," he said, "That place."

"What did you see?"

"The curve of the bay was filled with ships, hundreds of war galleys and ships," he said, making a large sweeping motion with his hands. "The ships were drawn up so tightly, there was not an arms-length between them. The beach was covered with tents, fires, and men. They were sharpening knives and axes, playing dice and sleeping. Their breastplates were bronze."

"That had to be the Minoans' attack on Athens," I added.

"There was a tall pole with a pennant and a small, tired group of men and women huddled around it," Icarus continued. "That's where they took my mother. I tried sneaking into their camp to get close to her, but I was afraid. Finally, I went back to the promontory to watch and wait. It was cold. I stayed up there for a long time."

"Your mother was one of the first group of slaves."

"I think so too. And I feel so bad for her," Icarus continued. "Her entire life was torn apart that night."

"That is very sad," I said.

"She was nothing to them, just a young woman, vulnerable—expendable," Icarus said warily. "Da, the men that took her that night, they were Athenian." Icarus said warily. "Those men that raped her were supposed to be protecting us."

"She fought as hard as she could," I said, "And she never deserted you."

"I know that," Icarus replied. "Sometimes I have to wonder though, what if she's still alive somewhere?"

"I suppose it's possible," I said.

"The king probably sold her," Icarus declared, "From the slave markets at Zakros."

"She could be anywhere," I said, sympathetically. "She might even still be here on Krete."

"Right now," Icarus said. "I hate everything about this place!"

"So you don't care if we are caught?" I asked.

"What's the worst they could do to me?" he replied. "Turn me into a slave?"

"I don't know," I replied, as honestly as I could. "How long have you known, remembered these things?"

"I've always known pieces of it," he said. "But after the fight in Malia, the memories started coming back in waves. I've never been more ready to leave Knossos."

"Good," I said. "Then we agree on that."

"And I'm not going back to Athens," he said stridently, "unless it's to burn it down."

"If that's how you feel about it," I said earnestly, "then before we leave, let's do this quest for Ariadne, and the rest of the Athenians."

"Thanks, Da," he replied. "I was hoping you'd understand."

CHAPTER FIFTY THREE

After waiting for darkness to fall, we left the city for the entrance to the tunnel. We each carried a rucksack. Mine was filled with torches, extra water, and dried food. Icarus carried the spool. Everything we were about to do was treason, and I was glad to have his company. None of it made any sense, but there seemed to be no other way. It was best to just not think about the consequences.

The portal into the earth was just as Ariadne and her friends had described. I picked up a small rock and pounded on one of the entrance stones. The dark hole was black and foreboding. Some unknown creature might already be inside, using the tunnel as shelter for the evening. In any event, Icarus and I were standing on another threshold. For as long as I could remember, all I ever wanted to do was build things out of stone and wood. First, it was a calling. Then it became a career and a good one. But now, with Icarus nearly grown and my heart full of longing for a woman I would never see again, none of it seemed to matter anymore.

I took off my rucksack and set it on the ground. Inside were the two bronze knives.

"I want you to have this," I said, handing him one and tucking the other inside the sash of my tunic. "A man should have a good knife."

With no more explanation than that, I crawled through the gap in the stones.

A small goat's horn hung from my neck. Inside I carried several small smoldering coals from the remains of a burning log. Still kneeling, I carefully opened the horn and shook a few of the coals out onto a small piece of cloth saturated with pine resin. I bent forward and blew gently until the coals glowed red, igniting the cloth into bright flame. The inside of the tunnel flashed into illumination, but it quickly faded. Through squinting eyes I lit one of the resin torches from the cloth. The small space filled with shadowy fumes and light. Then Icarus crawled inside and we set off on our mission, a small circle of light glowing from the torch in my hand.

Halfway to the ceiling at the end of the tunnel there was a large, gaping hole in the limestone wall, large enough for just one person to squeeze through. It opened into the labyrinth. Complete darkness waited on the other side. I handed the torch to Icarus. He took a look inside.

"There should be a small pile of stones, a cairn, just to the left."

"I see them."

"I'll go first," I replied. "You hold the torch until I'm inside." Then I wrestled my way through the opening, noisily banging my head on the rock wall.

"Are you all right?" Icarus asked.

"I'm fine," I answered. "I've got my first bump. At least I don't have to wait any longer," I joked.

It was slow going. We squeezed and scraped our way through confining passages of cold, grainy rock. Every step made a shuffling sound. By the time the first torch began to dim and grow hot on my hand, we were well inside the limestone caverns. It was not like walking on the surface. Here, there was very little ambient noise. Every little sound became intensified. Somewhere in the darkness, a single drop of water sounded, falling into a larger pool. I lit a second torch off the first.

It made me sick to think of all the energy and work that had gone into transforming this place into a coffin. I pressed forward, knowing that each uncertain step had the same effect as re-flooding the labyrinth, one cup-full at a time. When the trail opened into a large chamber, we took a break and stood next to each other. I told Icarus how grateful I felt to have him along. He didn't answer. Instead, he put his finger to his lips for silence, sniffed at the air and peered all around. We moved on. On the other side, a large cairn marked the next passage. I moved carefully, by memory and by guess, until we reached the stout wooden door. There was no handle, no way to open it from this side except perhaps with a stout axe. But those kinds of dramatics were for another day and a different kind of hero.

Lighting another torch, we looked around for just the right place to tie off one end of the guiding rope. It had to be within easy reach of the door and high enough for someone to stumble into, groping in the dark. To the left of the door, a tall stalagmite rose out of the floor. It was perfect. With two half-hitches, Icarus secured the end of the stout thread. For the newly arrived Athenians, it would be a constant effort to keep the panic at bay. One lucky prisoner stumbling around in the darkness could find this rope. And in that moment, find hope. If they allowed themselves to act on it, they would be rewarded with a pack filled with supplies that we positioned nearby. Then, if they kept their wits, the slaves might find their way out of the giant labyrinth. I hoped that there would be a strong leader among them.

Leaving most of the resin torches behind, we began the return trip. With a much lighter load I led the way, back toward the open air. It was better to be moving away from the intrigues of the palace. Icarus followed behind and lay out the heavy cord.

"There it is again," Icarus said softly.

"What?" I asked.

"That shuffling sound," he said.

"I don't hear anything," I said.

"It sounds like something following us," Icarus said. "It stopped when we stopped."

"Are you coming?" I said, thoroughly breaking the silence. As soon as I stepped away I banged my head, right in the same spot. My ears rang. I quickly stopped and knelt down, rubbing my poor head with my free hand. Warm blood ran onto my fingers. I watched Icarus lay down the spool of thread on the grainy rock. He sat down next to me.

"Shhhhh!" said Icarus softly. "Just rest a while."

I sighed and learned back against a solid wall. All that I could hear was the sound of the flame consuming the resin-packed torch. Moving into a kneeling position, he put his ear to the ground.

"What is it?" I asked, breaking the silence.

"Something else is down here," he said.

"It's nothing, just the sound of the torch," I said. And we waited together, breathless, hoping it was true.

"No, there's something, or someone," replied Icarus. "All those stories about a half-man, half-bull had to come from somewhere." I listened hard to the heart of darkness and felt the depths of my unspoken fears.

There, I imagined us being pursued through the caverns by a mythical creature, a snorting, grunting half-man, half-bull. He had picked up our scent and was even now following close behind, hunting us, chasing us out of its lair. Without another word I stood up, reached for the cord and gave it a tug. Then we kept going, step by step through the dank caverns. More than once, I was sure that we had missed a turn. More than once, I was sure that we had gone too far. But at last we reached it, the gap in the rock wall that connected the caverns to the outside world. It felt like a lost and precious thing, now found.

While I held up the torch high over my head, Icarus threw what was left of the skein of thread into the hole. It clattered against the rocks, filling the cavern with sound. Neither of us moved, not until the silence returned. I lit the last torch and with the triumphal look, peered into the gloom. I half expected to see another pair of eyes, peering at me out of the gloom. But there was nothing, nothing but darkness and ever deepening shadows.

Icarus eased himself feet first into the tunnel. I quickly followed. It was an intense relief to be back inside the straight-walled passage with its low ceiling and unobstructed view. Icarus jogged toward the portal. Without a moment's hesitation he got down on his hands and knees and scrambled outside. I stayed behind for a last look and a few breaths of the stale, tainted air. Then I knelt down and crawled through.

My son was waiting on the other side, lying on the ground, all limbs extended. He was clearly enjoying the starry wonder of the night sky, the feel of the warm earth, and the fresh air. He raised both arms towards the heavens and shouted, "I am Icarus." Then, he looked around and smiled.

"What's that about?" I asked, speaking softly in the cool night air.

"Try it," he said. "I feel like I left my old, scared self inside. This is a new, grown up Icarus. I'm telling the world. Really, you should try it."

I couldn't resist. I lay down in the grass and extended my arms and legs just as he had done. I closed my eyes.

"It's better with them wide open," he instructed.

Starlight glowed above us. I could feel my own life force pushing against the inside of my skin. The skin of my back and legs tingled. Reaching my arms towards the sky, I called out, "I am Daedalus." Then, I anxiously looked around, half expecting someone to reply. "No one cares."

"Just, do it again, Da," Icarus said, "This time with feeling."

PART IV

The Flight

Beneath their flight the fisherman while casting his long rod, or the tired shepherd leaning on his crook, or the rough plowman as he raised his eyes, astonished might observe them on the wing and worship them as Gods. Upon the left they passed by Samos, Juno's sacred isle; Delos and Paros too, were left behind; and on the right Lebinthus and Calymne, fruitful in honey. Proud of his success, the foolish Icarus forsook his guide, and bold in vanity, began to soar, rising upon his wings to touch the skies; but as he neared the scorching sun, its heat softened the fragrant wax that held his plumes; and heat increasing melted the soft wax—he waved his naked arms instead of wings, with no more feathers to sustain his flight. And as he called upon his father's name his voice was smothered in the dark blue sea...

Metamorphoses Book VIII
Written by the Roman poet Ovid
43 BCE - 14 AD

CHAPTER FIFTY FOUR

Krete was long and mountainous; its border, a panorama of endless beaches and rocky cliffs. The seas surrounded it like a warm, soft blue desert. It was summer. The sun always seemed to shine out of a serene and luminous sky. Wherever the right combination of water and soil existed the vegetation was lush. Tiny settlements dotted the coast—small communities in close connection with the sea and the land. Icarus and I were in no hurry, and by mid-afternoon the air began to bake. Then, we found a place to rest and speak with the people, the farmers and the villagers. I was looking for just the right person, someone with discretion, skill, and a good boat. Icarus had a different mission. He asked about an older woman that spoke with an Athenian accent, probably a slave. Was there anyone like that in the area?

In the last days before leaving the city, I had decided that the best use of my time was to stash away a nest egg of orichalcum ore. I knew of a secluded cave, high in the hills above the coast road. The alchemist had agreed to travel to Amnisos and purchase as much as I could afford. I met him and his porters at a prearranged site along the road and spent the rest of the day carrying sacks of ore up to the cave, alone.

I really didn't mind that Icarus had wanted to stay behind in Knossos. I had never spoken of my arrangement with King Aegeus of

Athens. Icarus would not have understood. Besides that, he wanted the time to say goodbye to his friends. It was late when I finally returned to the apartment that evening. He had spent most of his last day with Dianna. In the evening they shared a meal together, and said goodbye. He wouldn't talk very much about it, which was fine with me because I could barely keep my eyes open. Still, I couldn't help but notice the new blue stone bracelet on his wrist.

The coast road was paved and bustling with traffic. It went all the way to the harbor at Zakros, the gateway to Egypt. Our plan was to stay together and keep moving from one small settlement to the next, never staying long in one place. My search for a way off the island might have been more productive if we had visited the larger cities along the northern coast. Icarus agreed with the plan. He had no interest in returning to Malia, or for plodding along the windswept cobblestones to a distant city known for its slave trade.

Besides, our profile was too memorable. We were travelers with Athenian accents, a father and son. It was just a matter of time before Minos placed a price on our heads. Best to act as if he already had. His people would be watching the northern harbors. We could be recognized without even realizing it. That would mean detention, and eventually, being dragged back to Knossos in disgrace.

After a few days we turned south, crossing a high plateau into the majestic valley of the Letharios River. It was the heartland of the island, the fertile Messara plain. These were the fields where the God of the Sky took human form and after great effort, seduced Europa, a princess of Phoenicia, to create the island's original inhabitants. Here, the gods still seemed to be very close. We followed the river through abundant olive groves, vineyards, and pastures. Often, we were stopped along the way by generous, hard-working and inquisitive people. We admired their fertile lands. They were gracious and hospitable and very interested in talking with travelers from Knossos. They shared their food and drink, made no judgments, and never showed any animosity toward us.

Many times I thought wistfully of Naucreta and our times together. With the exception of Icarus, I had known her longer and far better than anyone else on the island. I would never forget her, and truly wished for her happiness on Naxos—doubly so if she was carrying a child.

On that last morning in Knossos, it was Filia who waited at the North gate to say goodbye. She had a message from Naucreta. Both of them had made offerings to the Goddess on our behalf, for a safe and memorable journey. They were leaving Knossos very soon to meet with the ship that would take them to Naxos. Much packing still had to be completed; more arrangements had to be made. Her mistress regretted that she was not able to be there in person.

"Naucreta wishes you well in your travels together," Filia continued. "She wants both of you to know that her memories of the two of you are very sweet," she said, "and always carried close to her heart." Then Filia motioned for Icarus to move away so that she could whisper something to me. When I leaned over to hear the words she said, "Memories are not the only thing that she is carrying."

"What are you saying?" I asked.

She just laughed until her side began to ache. "You are a smart man," she finally said in reply. "You figure it out."

CHAPTER FIFTY FIVE

To this day I wonder how long it took for King Minos to learn that his captives had escaped from the labyrinth. Luckily for Icarus and me, we were already gone.

"What fool is pounding on my door?" demanded an angry Minos, sitting up abruptly and throwing the blanket aside.

"Belisario, my King!" the chief of palace security obediently bellowed. "There is trouble. You will want to know of this."

Under his breath Minos replied, "This had better be good." He rubbed his head, massaging the scalp and bringing himself back into awareness from a very pleasant dream. Next to him, the young girl moved to the edge of the bed, her slender back toward him. The day before, he had culled her out of the freshly arrived Athenians. Soundlessly she withdrew deeper into the blankets.

"What kind of trouble?" he yelled at the door.

"The slaves have escaped, my King."

"Impossible!" Minos roared. Imperceptibly, the young girl lifted her head off the mattress.

"Sire, the report is accurate," Belisario stridently replied.

Minos looked over to the reclining feminine form on other side of the bed and said with cool conceit, "Not all of them." The girl did not move.

"Then why aren't you busy hunting them down?" the king shouted at the door.

"It's not that simple, Sire."

The king rose from the bed and put on a fresh robe.

"What does that mean?" he asked through the door, fully aware of the young girl's glee.

"King Minos, the situation is complicated," Belisario repeated.

Returning to the bed, he gripped the blankets in his thick muscular hands and threw them back, exposing the smooth, olive-colored skin and long dark hair. She held her breath. One of the same hands reached for her shoulder.

"Your daughter is involved," said the voice from outside the door.

The king sighed audibly.

"Which one?" he asked.

"Ariadne," replied the warrior.

"Ariadne has been taken? She's their hostage?"

No answer came from the other side of the door.

"Answer me!" Minos bellowed.

"Sire, the situation is complicated," replied Belisario.

"Meet me in the inner courtyard," he ordered, pacing across the room. When he stopped, he was directly across from her. Looking down at the slave, Minos folded his arms across his chest, and in deep resonate tones said, "Look at me." Obediently, she turned toward him covering her breasts, her face a mask of purposeful indifference. "Refresh yourself. Eat, drink, bath…and be here, waiting for my return."

The river led us to the city of Phaistos and to the expansive beaches on the island's southern shore. From Phaistos, another well-traveled road led north, winding across the mountains all the way back to Knossos itself. Krete was a narrow island. Our old lives were only a two-day walk away. We chose a different road, one following an undeveloped path to the west. It led to the remote, mountainous, and sparsely-populated half of the island. By then, we had been trekking for almost one full cycle of the moon.

We found our way onto beautiful secluded beaches and scenic places where the land dropped precariously into the sea all around us. The country was magnificent, but our westward progress was rather slow. The steep terrain often compelled us to go inland onto the high ridges. We spent most of the summer trekking up and down canyons. Finally, we found a secluded gorge of astonishing natural abundance on the western edge of the island. A freshwater stream coursed through it, cascading onto the beach and then into the sea. Along both banks citrus and olive trees and wild grapes and berries thrived, along with the native birds and animals that fed on the lush vegetation. Recessed into the wall of the gorge was a large cave protected from the prevailing winds. It bore no sign of human habitation. From there, it was an easy scramble up to a craggy point that offered a commanding view of the shoreline and a borderless expanse of sea and sky.

It seemed the perfect place to stop and rest. The bounty of the land and sea would sustain us. The nearest village was many stadia behind. Without regret I watched the days growing shorter and turn into moon cycles. The cave's isolation would protect us from the wandering eyes and reach of the king. I suggested passing the wet season right there. Winter was approaching. I figured that we could resume our trekking in the spring.

Icarus was not so sure. He certainly enjoyed exploring the countryside and roaming across the rocky ledges high above the sea, but he was restless for more. Sometimes I watched him stand on the edge of the cliff and become the very intersection of sea, sky, and land. I was still young enough then to remember being that age and its irrepressible attraction to distant lands and experiences. From his youthful perspective, excitement and adventure awaited him just beyond the wavy haze of the gray-blue horizon. He was bursting with eagerness and anticipation to find it.

I, too, enjoyed the view from our rocky perch. There was even a comfortable place along its contours to spread out my sleeping skin. I could spend hours there, gazing across the sea to the west. The sunsets were often magnificent. Watching them, my mind would fill with strong memories of times shared with Naucreta. I missed those carefree days.

Other times, I thought about Athens, about meeting Icarus, and about all the changes that had unfolded in the wake of that one encounter. Dreams of that city pulled at my heartstrings, like an undeniable call from my ancestors, reminding me who I was and from whence I had come. In the wildest one I returned to Athens a hero, with a ship brimming with orichalcum ore. Of course, if I brought up the subject of Athens with Icarus, he would spit on the ground and walk away in disgust.

All along one side of the palace courtyard, rich and glossy grapes dripped from sagging arbors. Belisario plucked one and rolled it between his fingers and thumb while he waited for the king. He tested the firmness, knowing that it was too young for eating. It would leave a bitter taste. In the distance the king's footsteps approached. He tossed the grape aside.

"Warrior, tell me the day's important news."

"King Minos," he replied without hesitation, "the slaves have freed themselves from the labyrinth."

"That's not possible!"

"Yes, it is. They're free. The one called Theseus is leading them. He has a knife, and they are on the coast road, headed back toward Amnisos. Unless we stop them soon, they will be there before sundown."

"How many are there?"

"The scouts count fifteen."

"How is that possible?" asked Minos. "We started with fourteen, and one of them is in my bed."

"Sire, I have twice that number of fighters and bowmen trailing them. If you say the word, I will have Theseus' balls delivered to you before dawn."

"First, tell me the rest of the story," said the king.

"Ariadne is among them. Phaedra, too."

"Oh, no," the king moaned. "Not Phaedra! How could both be taken?"

"Sire. Perhaps you should sit down."

"Out with it," the king roared.

"They do not appear to be hostages."

Unable to prevent his tears, Minos turned away. For a short time he sobbed in silence. Finally, he composed himself and said, "Ariadne always was a willful child."

"She is guiding them, Sire."

"Like a bitch in heat, I'll wager," replied the king, clenching his fists.

"What is your command, King Minos?"

"You are quite right in your assessment, Belisario. This is complicated. Give me time to think."

Clasping both hands behind his back, Minos paced back and forth alongside the greenery. He finally came to rest beside a small orange tree and motioned for Belisario to join him.

"Have your men follow at a distance. No one is to be hurt. Let them reach Amnisos," he said disdainfully. "Let them steal a ship, if they can manage it. I don't care. With only fifteen sets of shoulders, it will be a very long pull back to Athens."

"What about Phaedra and Ariadne?"

"They have made their choice," said the king with a bitter smile. "Let them sail off with Theseus, if that is their wish. If the Fates allow it, my grandchild will one day sit on the throne of Athens. Their city will be conquered without spilling a drop of blood."

"A pleasing outcome," said the warrior.

"Time favors Minos," replied the king.

"I will relay your commands to the runner," Belisario said.

"Yes, and follow behind him. I want you there, to ensure that my words are carried out," continued Minos.

"That will take time my king," said Belisario.

"Time favors Minos," repeated the king, pleased with the pith and moment of his words. "And while you are gone, I will figure out how they managed to escape."

CHAPTER FIFTY SIX

In the time since leaving the palace, most of our nights had been spent in the open air. Our senses were heightened, more attuned to the animals, birds, and to the natural elements that shaped our days. We rose with the sun, nourished ourselves from the bounty of the land or the sea, and slept when it became dark. It was a slow, steady drum beating twice each day, imposing an ancient rhythm onto our lives.

In time, I began to enjoy the company of a large, densely packed colony of brown-backed terns just a short distance down the beach. I could identify individual birds from their markings and their nests. Somehow, I had even grown fond of their harsh, single-noted call. For countless hours, I watched them circle and glide through the air. They were different from the gulls, much more elegant in flight, and with pointed beaks. During the daylight the terns were in constant motion, circling in the sky above the rocky ledges and swooping down to the sea in a never-ending search for fish. They had webbed feet, but rarely seemed to use them for floating on the surface. They preferred to dive out of the sky directly into the water and then swim after their prey using their feet for propulsion. Only then would they regain the surface and frenetically flap away, regaining the sky with a small fish caught in their beak.

And there were pelicans, graceful masters of flight, skimming low across the water in their precise formations and searching for food. Usually they flew with great serenity. It was a beautiful thing to watch. Gliding low above the water, they imperceptibly lifted their wings just enough to stall. Their legs extended gracefully to splash through the surface as their wings folded. They then paddled away, buoyant now, still searching for food.

All along the shore, there were birds of every color, size, and shape— long-legged waders, diving cormorants, and long-beaked skimmers. Each one seemed to have its own special utility with which to thrive, and I admired them all. Of course, I did have my favorites. I envied the long-winged ones most. They used the thermals and the air currents to circle higher and higher into the sky and then glide effortlessly away, wherever they wanted to go. From those elevations even Naxos would not seem very far.

Of these, the albatross was like no other. It soared endlessly, majestically across the sky. It was rare to see two such birds together, sharing the same high altitudes. They seemed to prefer a solitary existence. I had to wonder if these large graceful birds became so absorbed with the joy of flight that they just didn't care that much about each other's company.

The condors, with their large black bodies and larger wingspans, were more common and much easier to spot and observe. Even in the higher altitudes they dwarfed the other birds. I wondered if one day I would go in search of their rocky perches in the high crags of the island.

Icarus, on the other hand, rarely joined me as I bird-watched. He did not enjoy sitting still for long. He preferred to be moving, doing. His days were spent hunting, fishing, and exploring this new section of the island. He kept himself busy learning every game trail, tidal pool, and source of fresh water that the land had to offer. It became a source of great pride to him that in this wild place, he was the one who supplied most of our food. He could scramble up and down the rocky trails between the sea and land all day long, never seeming to tire.

Of course, there were many things we enjoyed doing together. One activity was building a shelter using only native plants and our wits. Near the cave there was a tree that grew out from the hillside. With ropes made from the fibrous inner bark of the tall cedars, we lashed neighboring tree trunks against it, to form the outline of a roof. We filled the spaces in between with long stakes and earth. Then, we constructed a soft and elevated floor out of logs, covered over with sand. For the longest time, we were so pleased with the results, that we made a contest out of improving it. A rock projecting from the hillside became a fire pit. Smoke rising against the face of the grey rocks above it was difficult to detect from even a short distance away. Our home half stood, half hung on the steep hillside, all but impossible to notice from most directions. Because of its shape we affectionately called it the egg. And because we could, we built it large enough to sleep five or six with some comfort.

One day I noticed that some of the birds in the neighboring colony had begun to molt. I collected their feathers, starting with the easy-to-find ones. Soon, I had gathered together a sizable collection, which I stuffed inside the folds of a spare, well-worn tunic. In a few more days we each had a pillow for our heads at night.

The search extended into other nesting areas. Sometimes I found tail feathers with colorful hues in elegant designs. Other times, I was drawn to their unusual shapes or sizes. I kept the best ones stored inside the cave. If I became bored, I expanded the search again, collecting an even greater variety, including my favorite, a single long black feather. It had to be from one of the condors.

After a time, the recesses of the cave became filled with piles of feathers, sorted by size and shape. Sometimes, when the wind was low, I laid them out in intricate arrays. A few of the designs became wall hangings and masks, quills bound together with beeswax and string. I hung my favorites from trees all around the camp to blow in the wind. In a competitive way, this even tweaked Icarus' interest, and he joined in the hunt for the most elegant of tail fathers, the long ones from the tails of the elusive predator birds. Both of us appreciated the beauty of these powerful birds in flight, and prized the long feathers that stabilized their wings when aloft.

One restful day I found myself pensively gazing out across the sea, holding the quill of a long, black feather in one hand, and stroking it across my thumb and forefinger. For some reason I was thinking of Minos and our last meeting. By now, I was sure that the king was hunting for us, sure that we each had a price on our heads. I remembered our confrontation, and how the king had angrily responded to my reasonable requests with threats and intimidation. I could still hear his words: "You Master Builder, can no sooner leave this island than you can fly."

After all this time and far from civilization, I was willing to consider that anything was possible. Using a stick to carve the moist sand, I covered the beach with pictures of pairs of wings from many different angles. Then, one morning I awoke with a very different idea. Rather than a bifurcated pair, it was a design for a single symmetrical wing, one with a gently curving arc, and a span much greater than my own height. Right away I found my drawing utensils and committed it from memory into the sand. It was time to begin the search for the materials to build a strong and resilient frame.

CHAPTER FIFTY SEVEN

Later that night as I slept inside the egg, the flight dream returned. I hadn't had one in all the time living in Knossos, but it all came back, vividly. I walked across the familiar green field. It was a lush fertile place. The rolling hills surrounding it were covered with the soft green of Mediterranean pine. The breeze was strong and steady. Barefoot, I walked to the crest of the knoll and waited, closing my eyes. I felt a tingling in my knees and a vibration from the ground passed into my bones. Warm air flowed against my face, resonating with the energy filling my chest and shoulders. I lifted my arms effortlessly and felt the energy of the sun.

The uplift was coming—one that would pull me out of the shadows and into the light. This time, I did not wait for the converging energies to draw me away from the earth. This time, I eagerly dropped my weight onto my thighs and pushed myself upward, leaping into the sky as high as I could possibly go, arms outstretched, beaming, trusting that the air currents would catch and hold me. And they did.

Once more, I flew.

In the morning I awoke with a vitality that would not be refused. The experience of the flight dream filled me up, topping off every cell. It was the song in my heart and I could not stop from singing it. I walked, bounced, and skipped onto the path that led from the egg house, around the cliff face and down to the sea. There, I swam and bathed with gusto. Sitting on my rumpled clothes next to the water and warming my skin in the early morning sun, I looked up into the sky and saw the dark silhouette of a large soaring bird. Silently I marveled at the bird's graceful, effortless glide on the currents of air. It was very low, close enough to see the white markings under the broad black wings.

"That bird is huge!" I cried out. "How can such a large bird glide through the air with so little effort and so much grace?" Reaching for my clothes, I simultaneously walked and stepped into them, hurrying back to the camp, one eye on the sky and the other on the ground. There, I grabbed a few things that I would need—the bladder to hold fresh water, my knife, and my sandals. Then I was gone to find out if the bird would show me its nesting ground.

Much later that same day, I was bent over my next project inside the cave. The distinct smell of seawater and sweat wafted through the air. Looking up, I had to smile. Silhouetted by the sun, Icarus' golden brown skin seemed to glow. His dark hair was pulled back from the high forehead and tied with a frayed leather cord. He smiled back in greeting, his dark eyes flashing, and I nodded approvingly. Around his wrist Icarus still wore the blue stone amulet, held in place these days by a stronger, more practical braid.

"You're looking rather serious today," I said in greeting. "How was the fishing?"

"See for yourself," he replied, holding up a string of cod, and beaming. "The terns showed me where these were feeding."

"It appears that we'll eat well tonight."

Icarus looked down at my latest project arrayed across the ground. He walked slowly along its length, his face growing somber. "Is this what I think it is?"

"What does it look like?" I asked, trying to engage him in a little conversation.

"A large wing of course," he replied. "And who are you making this for?" he asked.

"I haven't decided yet," I replied, "maybe for Minos."

"Why waste all this work on a fat king?"

"At the moment, he happens to be my inspiration," I said with a laugh. "Those last words of his have been resounding in my head for days. You remember, back when we lived in the palace and slept on real beds."

"Oh, yes. I remember, but I don't miss that part of it one bit."

"Really, not even the sports? What about Demitrious? Dianna?"

"The year that we left and the slaves returned, Knossos changed," Icarus said. "I couldn't stay any longer. Dianna understood that." His features softened. "But, I would like to see her again, someday."

"I feel much the same way," I replied. "I can still see the glare in Minos' eyes, the anger and the rage." Then I dropped my voice into its lowest range to mimic the king and said, "You, Master Builder...*and your son.* You can no sooner leave my island, than you can fly!"

"So you've decided to take him literally," Icarus teased in response.

"I have been studying the birds, especially the condors, for a long time."

"And dreaming of flight," interrupted Icarus.

"It's an old favorite of mine, yes—soaring, gliding on the currents of air like the condors," I said, feeling more animated with each word. "What if it just came down to having the proper equipment and technique? Would you try it?"

"Maybe," said Icarus, definitely not ready to promise anything at this stage of the project.

But I knew that my enthusiasm could be entertaining. Besides, who wouldn't want to soar like an eagle? For a long time he stood there and looked down at the intricate weave of the feathers, saying nothing. Finally, he remarked, "That wax is no good for wings. It will crack and break if you put any weight on it at all."

"You're right. Wax is far too brittle," I replied. "Good thing this is only a model. For the prototype, I'll need something much stronger; something to bind the feathers together into a strong and flexible weave."

"Where are you going to find this substance?" Icarus asked, his interest growing.

"Well, I haven't really given that part of it any thought," I replied, crossing my arms and considering the next step. "But there has to be a decent adhesive somewhere on this island."

I was just about to propose that we begin making plans to leave the camp and continue our trek in search of materials, when Icarus spoke.

"Maybe I can find something that will work."

"What did you say?"

"Father," he said with a resolute stare. "I want to go in search of the adhesive, the glue for the wings."

CHAPTER FIFTY EIGHT

"You want to leave?" I asked, shocked at the unexpected development. "Everything anyone could ever want is right here."

"But not the glue," Icarus replied.

"You're leaving on your own?" I asked, incredulous at the suggestion.

"It will be fine. Besides," he said confidently, "it's boring being stuck out here all day, every day. Yes, it's beautiful and unlike anywhere else we've ever been. But we are all alone out here."

I didn't know what to say. Looking into his intense dark eyes, I saw that the once eager-to-please boy was completely gone. In his place stood a willful, strong, and competent young man, one with incredible endurance and thorough self-sufficiency. It was a bittersweet moment. Every passing day since leaving Knossos, I had acquiesced to Icarus taking over more and more of the responsibility for our daily lives. He was so willing, and so good at it. Now I could see that my son was keenly aware of his competencies, of how much he had grown—and that he wanted more.

Part of me felt betrayed. We were a family, albeit a small one, a community of two. Icarus wanted to break that unity apart. It felt like resistance or rebellion, something to defend against, but I knew that there was much more. Icarus was becoming a man. He was asking to be tested.

He wanted, he needed a quest. Somehow I understood that it was my role to encourage this fire, not dampen it, even if it hurt.

I tried to remember my own emancipation from family. It was a futile exercise. I couldn't remember any particular recognition by my own father that I was ready, that I was good enough. I wished there had been. I had no memory of a specific event to commemorate it. Had there been one, a ritual or an initiation, then I might have some kind of guide for this transition with Icarus, something to go by. Tearfully, I realized how important it was to make a good memory out of the event, his passage from boy to man.

So, for two more days, we talked and planned, waiting for the new moon night, the time for new beginnings. Icarus caught a fine sea bass that day. With the sun setting we feasted on fish, fruit, and wine on the lee edge of the rocky promontory. We reminisced about the many shared times. It was enjoyable.

Before the evening got away from me, I placed both hands on my son's shoulders and said, "We have been together for so many years that the idea of parting is very difficult for me. But Icarus, you and your readiness have convinced me that it time to embrace this change."

His deep brown eyes softened as he smiled.

"Da, you really surprised me when you agreed to this," Icarus said in reply. "And tonight, my practical father, you surprise me again with your words—"

"Then let me finish," I interjected. "I honor this calling. Go. Search out the material I need. It is a quest, an adventure, and I know that there is no better man than you for the task."

"I really don't understand what you're getting so *official* about, but thank you," Icarus said.

"I am glad. That is all," I replied, "And don't worry about me. I am content right here."

"I know what you'll be doing," Icarus said with a grin, "you'll be working on how best to build a wing."

"You're right about that," I said. "And I'm going to need your help to test the prototype. I'll build it long enough and strong enough to hold even your weight."

Icarus stood up and walked past the firelight to the edge of the cliff face. He stood there for a long time, staring out across the moonlit sea. When he returned to the fire he said, "I won't return until the glue is found."

"Return when you are ready, with or without the glue," I said.

"Then I won't be ready until I've found it," Icarus said.

"No matter what happens, I'll be here to welcome you. Where do you plan to start?"

"I don't really have a plan," he said, "other than to start walking into those white mountains over there. They have been calling to me ever since we arrived. From there, I'll see where my feet take me."

"Mountains can be a great place to seek inspiration," I said, "but I do have one word of caution."

"Only one?" Icarus teased.

"When you're out there all alone, you may be tempted to go back to Knossos," I cautioned. "Don't do it," I said. "Go anywhere but there."

"Da, I can take care of myself," Icarus said dismissively.

"I know that," I replied, wanting to sound reassuring, "but hear me out. We left before the Athenians arrived. When we left we were trusted citizens."

"And tell the truth, Da," Icarus began in earnest, "wouldn't you like to know what happened to them?"

"Not as much as I want to keep my head on top of my shoulders," I replied sarcastically. "Whether the slaves escaped or not, we have to assume that our efforts to help them have been found out. Knossos can no longer be the safe place that we left behind; not for you, or me."

"Da, you're exaggerating."

"No, I'm being realistic," I said sternly. "I'm assuming that there's a price on our heads, a hefty one. I'm also assuming that Minos is just like an old cat, waiting patiently for his prey to come out from the safety of their hiding place, ready to pounce. Icarus, you have to act as if you don't have any friends in Knossos."

"So I can't trust Demitrious," he said, the words taking on a challenging tone. "Is that what you're saying?"

"Or Dianna," I responded, nodding. "That's exactly what I'm saying."

"And you're just wrong about that!" Icarus exploded, stomping away from the fire and into the night.

I laid awake in the open by the fire that night, second guessing the many words I hadn't said. I could have chosen any number of things to worry about. Why did I have to pick returning to Knossos? Lying back on my sleeping skin, I cradled my head with my hands and looked up at the night sky. The simple truth was that on any given day, either one of us could be hurt or injured, and not be able to return to the camp. Anything could happen out there, but that included good things too. Icarus might just as readily find someone with a stout boat, someone eager to leave the island for his own reasons, and ready and willing to take two passengers off to a new life.

With all the talk, feasting, and wine, I stayed up much later than usual. Though we had argued, I was also relieved. I had found the right words and given Icarus my blessing. That was what mattered most, to me. When I finally fell asleep, it was with a vision of the two of us in flight together, gliding over the sparkling sea.

The next morning, we drank warm tea and shared a breakfast of dates and oranges. When we spoke, it was of practical things.

"Where did you sleep last night?" I asked.

"Down at the cove, by the water," Icarus replied. "I don't know why I became so upset."

"That's all right," I replied. "Let's agree to end this on a positive note. I shouldn't have been judgmental about your friends."

"Agreed," Icarus replied. "And Da, if for some reason you decide to move on, be sure and leave a trail."

"I will be waiting right here, ready to welcome you and listen to your stories," I said, repeating myself and tearing up again.

"Seriously, if you have to leave, build cairns," he said sternly. "Mark each one with a feather, and you will be easy to follow."

"I will," I replied. "Until then, let's both just stay safe and healthy."

Icarus looked so fit and full of life. I looked him up and down. A reliable water skin hung over one shoulder. Tucked into his waistband was the knife I had given him, a fire-starting kit, and a proven fishing line. Tied to his wrist to ward off injury he wore Dianna's blue stone gift. His well-worn sleeping skin was rolled up and lying the ground. Rolled deep inside a hidden leather pouch he still carried the blue-stone keepsake from his mother. And somewhere in his heart, he carried my blessing.

Reaching around me with both arms and squeezing tight, he said, "Thank you, Da, for everything."

I hugged him right back, wondering if it would be the last.

Turning an affirmative push into a wave goodbye, Icarus said, "May the Fates be kind to us both."

CHAPTER FIFTY NINE

Icarus walked into a wild magnificent country. In earlier treks we had camped together in many fine places, usually with the sea nearby. Perhaps he was preparing for this adventure all along. Now the youth wandered through huge stretches of green fertile plains and onto high plateaus bordered by barren, craggy ridges and distant peaks. During the wet season the mountains had a weather all their own, often shrouded in clouds. When the sun did break through, their tops would reappear covered in white. I like to think that his spirit longed to stand among them.

Occasionally, he later told me, Icarus saw signs of hunting parties long past. Otherwise, he was completely alone. It was life, raw and elemental, in a majestic land. With each day's trek into the island's inner passages, he became an integral part of that nature. He became a hunter, an eater of goat's flesh and venison. For warmth he wore their hides. He was wild and free and fully realizing forgotten boyhood fantasies—those dreams of exploring steep-walled gorges, unmarked snow fields, and standing on mountain tops. And practically speaking, no matter where he might wander, he would never be more than a few days' walk from the sea. If he could reach the sea, he could find his way back to our home.

Icarus took on greater and greater challenges, testing the limits of his endurance and his will. One night, while camped within a stand of small trees on the rocky soil of a steep walled canyon, he awoke to the rolling thunder of a distant cloudburst. As dawn broke, he rose to the subtler sound of water rushing by. The nearby stream was rising. A large branch swept by in the current. Without a moment's hesitation he was on his feet, rolling his few belongings inside the sleeping skin and running. He searched frantically for a way off the canyon floor. The sound of roaring water filled the air. It spilled over the low banks of the stream. The canyon was flooding, and he was climbing up an offset fracture in the wall. Below him, dark water surged. Gulping for air, he strained against the rock, punishing his hands and feet. The water's unrelenting roar filled his ears. He kept moving, gaining elevation and the crack developed into a narrow ledge. He crept along it slowly until it became a wider place. Icarus plopped down with huge sigh, sitting back into the comfort and security of the cold, hard, and immovable rock. Down below him, well past his feet, the water churned with whole logs and rocks.

Somewhere below the surging water lay his former campsite. The trees where he had slept were gone, torn away by the high water. He watched, mesmerized, his back propped against the rock wall and until his eyes were no longer able to fight off sleep. When he awoke, sunlight filled the canyon. The water had begun to recede. By midday the canyon floor glistened in the sun, filled only with an innocent looking unobtrusive stream and bare cobblestones.

Sitting by a small cooking fire, I dined on octopus cooked in lemon juice and wild herbs, and watched another vibrant sun fade into the sea in a panorama of orange, pink, and blue. I was catching and cooking my own food, making my own wine. Self-sufficiency was turning out to be a rather pleasant development, now that Icarus was gone. It was different without anyone for companionship, without anyone to look to for help with the basic necessities. Those were the raw edges of being alone. Despite the loneliness, there was also a deep sense of wellbeing in rediscovering the freedom and independence that now characterized my life.

A wave of sea air blew into my face. The coals of the fire glowed. The evening was so peaceful, so serene. I had that sense of being in the right place at just the right time. I could not remember the last time that I slept on a bed, but I could feel a growing connection to the earth and its rhythms. Certainly there were hardships that came with living alone, but having all this beauty more than compensated. I sliced off another piece of sinewy octopus, savoring the flavor of each bite.

A few days before, I had found my seldom used fishing cord, placed it around my neck and body like a sash, and gone for a swim in the late afternoon. Following a shoal of meandering fish some distance from the shore, I passed over a great slab of rock that lay just an arm's length or so beneath the surface. Directly above it, the water was surprisingly warm, and I lingered there, floating on my back. Eventually, the drift carried me into cooler water, where I noticed a shadowy gap between two undersea boulders. The fissure was deep and perfectly clear.

Just the way Icarus had showed me, I checked that the large piece of gray cloth was securely tied to the weighted end and let it drift down into the water, angling the line into the watery stillness. It was not long before the sinuous tentacle of a curious octopus slipped out to examine the bait. Another tentacle soon followed, and I, architect turned fisherman, gently coaxed it out with the line. The octopus responded by grabbing on with greater authority and several more tentacles. I slowly drew the creature to the surface, the line spiraling upward into the light, my reluctant quarry still clinging to its prize. Every day since my initial discovery, I returned to the same spot. Every day I found another octopus already occupying it, as if waiting for the air-breathing neighbor to arrive and for the baited line to drift down into the shadowy depths.

As I finished the last morsel, I recalled the thin sliver of a moon from the night before. Tonight it would not appear at all. Substance and form would be gone, leaving only potential for what was to come. I walked to the edge of the cliff and hung my toes over the edge. Dark sea stretched out in every direction. I had become detached from everything I once believed was important. Balanced in the gentle breeze, I raised my arms and extended them, palms upward.

"Here I am," I said, closing my eyes and leaning forward as far as I dared. I imagined a pair of long, dark, elegant wings in place of my shoulders and arms. "Right here," I said aloud, "no longer just a builder of wood and stone. I am a builder of wings."

A warm glow filled my chest. It was too fine an evening to sleep indoors inside the egg. Instead I returned to a sheltered place under some nearby trees. I thought of lovely graceful Naucreta and our times together. She was the only woman to ever say to me that she wanted my child. It pleased me to think that one day soon she might give birth. Was she healthy? Was she content? What about the baby? How would I ever know any of it, now that she was gone to Naxos? I missed our times together.

There had been so much change and too many farewells. I remembered my last days together with Icarus. The memories were like a rich tapestry. I smiled to think about my efforts to warn him against returning to Knossos, realizing that now he was almost sure to go.

It was out of my hands. Icarus would do whatever he was drawn to do. All that I had left was confidence in his abilities to figure it out. Rolling onto my back, I turned my attention upward to the panoply of stars. Wherever he was tonight, I hoped that he was warm and dry and happy.

CHAPTER SIXTY

Since leaving on the quest, Icarus' physical body had become even leaner and harder. Inside, his confidence had grown. His physical presence was changing, a gravitas developing. Given the chance for a rematch, he had no doubt that he could overwhelm Avram, the wrestler from Malia. It was not just the obvious matters of greater suppleness and strength. Here in the wilds he had found a core of inner vitality unlike anything he had ever known before. When he choose to strike, he was like an eagle, sudden and swift, and with a ferocity that could not be overcome, short of his own death. Avram and his father were mere city dwellers.

These days, Icarus was fully engaged in the present. Being well supplied with food and water took most of his efforts. Drawn by a distant snow-capped peak, he spent an entire day approaching it across a fertile high plateau covered with citrus, oak, and olive. That night he camped on the low flank in a grove of ancient cedars. These were the last trees he would see for a while. The next day's climb would take however long it needed to take. Food and water would become available when he was ready to find them. It was an overriding and fearless belief in his own destiny that fueled him. When the moon was right, he let out his own high invocation, singing his song into the starlight, an integral part of the island's natural balance.

The next morning Icarus rose early and hiked to the lower saddle.

The last of the vegetation was behind him. He followed one ridgeline into another, gradually making his way up the flank of the mountain. He was high enough to watch the soaring predator birds from above, the eagles and hawks.

Trekking further still, Icarus was high enough to enjoy clear vistas in every direction. The long narrow island spread out before his eyes. To the north, the sea stretched away from the mountainous ridges like a blue carpet, all the way to the smoldering summit of Kalliste. Its broad gray volcanic cone was the only land to break through the distant boundary of sea and sky. It had long been on his list of peaks to climb someday.

He crossed snow fields and followed windswept ridges until the ground leveled off and there was nothing any higher to reach for. Sweat and warm sun filling his face, Icarus sat down on a large rock, his back to the wind, and caught his breath. Lifting his water skin in silent celebration, he drank deeply. The summit was a scattering of large angular rocks, swept by the wind. There was a surreal quality to it, as if he had intruded into the home of a god. Limitless sky stretched in all directions. Far and away he could see into a few billowy white clouds. The ascent was the culmination of a personal challenge, but he did not remain on the summit for long. The winds were too intense for that, too cold. Walking to the leeside of a large outcropping of rocks, he rested and ate some dried fruit. Hard granular snow covered the ground. It crunched beneath his footfalls, adding to his sense of isolation and a growing sense of discontent.

To the east, barren ridges of gray and brown blended into an endless array of snow-covered slopes and peaks and stretched as far as he could see. He saw no roads, no cities—no hallmarks of a civilization. All of the Minoan Empire lay hidden behind a mountainous wall. Icarus toyed with the blue stone bracelet still tied to his wrist, missing all of the people and things he had left behind.

CHAPTER SIXTY ONE

Wearing his goatskin leggings and tunic, Icarus sat outside the western gate of Knossos. He watched a steady stream of travelers, merchants, and porters coming and going through the broad gate. With his disheveled hair and beard, he looked like a shepherd or a hunter. Few would recognize him for the young student he had once been, or so he hoped. My warnings weighed on his mind.

The gate was exactly the way he remembered it. There were no sentries, and he was hungry for a warm meal and companionship. Entering would be the easy part. He had a sack full of lichens, hand-picked from a moist rock wall on his way down from the mountains. Makers of fine oils and scents used the flowerless plant to craft perfume base. Icarus could trade them for a good meal or a few copper rings.

He decided to stay where he would have the least chance of being recognized. So he approached a few travelers and asked them where a poor visitor could find a bed and food. Carrying his few belongings, he soon found a tanning business on the edge of the city willing to take him in. There was a small room with a tiny window overlooking a fenced pasture. The bed was rickety; the smell of the room, intense. Icarus did not care. He would only be there long enough to find out what happened to the Athenian slaves, to his friends, and, most importantly, to Dianna.

His search began at the public baths. There was no better place for catching up on the important news and gossip. He learned from a talkative bather that Daedalus the builder had disappeared with his son. Neither one had ever been seen again. But it was just a matter of time before the guards caught up with them. Anyone with information leading to their capture would be paid ten golden rings. At that price the pair could not possibly go unnoticed forever.

I had been right.

"What could those two have possibly done to warrant such a reward?" Icarus asked, disbelieving the sum.

A shrug of the shoulders was the only reply. What did it matter? The king, the lawgiver, was offering the prize.

The gymnasium where Icarus had spent so much time training together with Aadam was close by. Icarus waited at a local tea shop at the end of the day, hoping that Demitrious would pass by on his way for a workout. But his old friend was not to be found so simply. So he asked an official, for information about where he might find him.

Following the man's directions, Icarus walked along the sloping streets away from the palace. Knossos was not a single city. Its burgeoning wealth meant that it was growing fast, spreading out over the surrounding hills. He did not marvel at the magnitude of the changes. All of it was still too familiar. Instead he stroked his beard, wondering how effective his disguise would prove to be. He found himself in front of an anonymous apartment house in the lower town with a shaded courtyard and flourishing greenery. There, on a stone bench facing the western sun he saw his old friend. Seated next to him was a young woman Icarus did not recognize. She was quite pregnant, and her feet were elevated, nestled right in Demitrious' lap. They looked so handsome together, and somehow that was enough. Icarus could not bear to interrupt the scene.

Finally, she rose from her seat and went inside the building. Icarus knelt down, picked up a small pebble and tossed it at his friend. The first did not come close enough, but the second one hit him right on the arm. He jumped and turned, and stared.

"Is it really you," Demitrious said, rushing out into the street. "What are you doing here?"

"Yes," Icarus replied with a huge grin. "You were expecting someone else?"

"Come inside," he said. "I want you to meet my wife, Sophia."

"I can't," Icarus replied. "You two look so happy together. But I can't come inside, and no one else can know that I'm here."

"I understand," Demitrious replied.

"Just tell me this," Icarus asked. "What happened to Dianna? Is she alright?"

"Ariadne and Phaedra are gone. They left for Athens with the runaway slaves. You know that, right?" Demitrious asked.

Icarus nodded.

"Well, Dianna didn't go with them. She stayed behind. I've heard that she's studying to become a priestess, living in their quarters near the palace. I haven't even seen her since you left. But don't go looking for her. They'll catch you for sure."

"Who's that you're talking with?" a pleasant voice called from the courtyard.

"Aaah," stammered Demitrious, "Just a lost shepherd looking for his flock."

"Be serious," called the voice.

"I'm leaving now," Icarus said resolutely. "Not a word about this to anyone," he said, shaking his friend's hand and trying to look into his eyes to connect one last time. But Demitrious had already turned to smile at Sophia. Without a glance in her direction, Icarus waved politely and walked away.

The next morning as Icarus walked toward the north gate, he saw a man ahead, hooded and cloaked, watching the street. Crowds of brightly dressed citizens thronged the marketplaces near the portal. Instinctively Icarus touched the handle of his knife with his fingertips, feeling for the position. The man turned away sharply and disappeared down a side street. Icarus' heart beat faster. Just outside the gate was a good place for an ambush. How many would there be?

As he closed the distance to the gate, Icarus saw another cloaked man angling around behind him, blocking his retreat. A man in a dark hood stepped from the crowds, leaping forward. A knife flashed into his hands. Instead of dodging away, Icarus leapt in to meet him. He grabbed the knife wrist with one hand, and thundered a blow into the man's eye with the heel of his other hand. All around the crowd scattered. As the man fell back, Icarus kept hold of the wrist and spun him around, twisting the arm savagely and dislocating the shoulder. With a scream the assassin dropped his knife. His cloak fell away, revealing underneath the bronze breastplate of a palace guard. Icarus kicked and pushed him roughly toward the pursuing comrade who caught the stricken man with one arm. Off balance, he tried setting him onto the ground. Without a sound, Icarus swept up the fallen knife and charged, glaring at both men.

Too late, the would-be assassin recognized a murderous fire in Icarus' eyes. Too late, he threw up his forearm to defend against violent assault, his own knife useless. The blade plunged into his throat. Too late, he attempted to scream for help.

Releasing the handle, Icarus let the second assassin crumple to the earth. Chest heaving, he dropped into a low crouch and spun around on the cobblestones, scanning the market place for the next threat. Nothing came. He grabbed onto the handle of his own knife and pulled it away from its sheath. With an angry roar of defiance, he plunged into the gateway and out into the light of the far side. He found no opposition there either.

Returning the blade to its sheath he began a cross country run away from Knossos and all of its intrigues. He soon settled into a steady pace with the occasional backward glance. He crossed fields and pastures, backtracking occasionally to lay down a confusing trail, and, generally, he put as much distance between himself and the city as he could. By early afternoon Icarus was following a stream channel up into the hills above Knossos. Eventually it would lead him back into the relative safety of his mountain highlands.

Seen from below, the soaring bird in mid-flight was fast developing into a distant black speck. I trailed along behind as best I could, finding and following game trails for large distances over the uneven ground. Every few steps I looked up and scanned the sky for another glimpse. The bird, of course, was in its element, easily maneuvering over fields and shoreline. On earlier hikes I had sighted these majestic, soaring wonders, effortlessly rising on thermals above craggy ledges far to the north of the camp. Today I would go there in hopes of finding its nest and watching the bird close up. I wanted to see for myself where it lived on the ground and how large it could actually be.

Several times it circled back and overflew the path I traveled, encouraging me onward. Dripping with sweat, I set my course into the hills and watched for the flashing patches of white. They marked this bird with distinction and willed me to keep going.

This was not a sea bird. I had seen the clawed feet. The bird would eventually land upon the earth. It was the take-off that fascinated me. I wanted to watch firsthand that initial moment of letting go. I wanted to see how such a large bird transitioned from walking with feet firmly planted upon the earth into flight. If I could just get close enough to witness that leap of faith, this would all be worthwhile. Interminably, I walked toward the distant seaside cliffs. Once there, I would search for a good spot to discreetly observe the bird and study its ways. There might even be a whole colony of them. There was no reason to assume that the bird's lifestyle was as solitary as my own.

In late afternoon the condor began its circling descent. There were so many things that could go wrong with a landing, so much technique involved. I felt no small amount of envy for the soaring birds. It descended toward a desolate headland, a windy edge where the land met the sea. Far below, I sat in shadow on the edge of the high plateau, with what I hoped would be enough of a vantage point to have a view of its final approach. I watched for the subtle maneuvering of the wings as they interacted with the wind. I saw them retract and pull up, stalling the flight as the bird dropped below the face of a high cliff and into some hidden place along the rock wall. I sat spellbound, grateful for having come this far.

The next day I would try to find a better approach to the high crags where the bird made its home. For now, I needed to find my own protected place and to tend to my own needs. Exhausted from the long day's journey, I soon fell into a deep sleep with visions of the soaring bird in my mind.

While I slept, the flight dream returned without the green field. This time, I stood in a shaft of sunlight on a thin strip of rocky beach next to a high cliff wall. I listened to my own breath, relaxed and deep, over the sounds of the water and wind. The warmth of the sun radiated onto my chest. Without effort, the muscles around my sternum seemed to enlarge and spasm in the sunlight, as if large wings were enveloping my shoulders. I shook them briskly and then relaxed. An overwhelming energy poured into me. Whatever it was it filled me up, pulling me into an upward spiral and freeing me from the earth.

In the slow ascent I passed a series of long horizontal fractures along the face of the rock wall, some of them wide enough to become ledges or caves. The sounds of the sea and the surf dimmed as greenery came into view. There the wind greeted me, blowing against my face and chest and lifting me higher as I extended my arms completely. I looked down to see the land transform into a fine patchwork of textures and colors bordered by the silken carpet of deep green sea, spreading outward in all directions.

High above the island, the wind was steady and strong, forceful enough to push me upward and back when I faced into it. I found that when I kept the right balance, I could use the wind to soar higher into the sky. In those brief moments it seemed effortless. But it was so very easy to overcompensate. Sometimes I became distracted. Other times, the wind shifted unexpectedly, roaring in my ears. When that happened, the wind buffeted me about while I tumbled through the sky like a drunkard during an earthquake. It took all of my effort and concentration, like learning to walk all over again. And so it went for much of the dream, until I found a sense of comfort with the constant adjustments that were necessary to maintain that elusive equilibrium.

To one side, I spied a protected bay. I looked toward it, not by turning my head but by slightly adjusting my shoulders, arms extended, banking my body and allowing the wind to bring me around. Descending in the turn, I found myself in a river of wind, deep and wide, which lifted me from below. I soared into its current, maintaining balance, and allowed the warm uplift to carry me higher into the sky. Mindfully, I realized that the wind made no sound carrying me aloft, and in that satisfying moment I began to understand why the great white albatross might choose to live in solitude.

High above the island, I banked into a gradual descent toward the picturesque bay far below. I remembered my first flights in the dreamtime, how the winds had pushed me about, graceless and awkward, wherever the opposing forces conspired to take me. I was a gangly intruder then. This time it was very different. I was beginning to realize that there was more to flying than just being blown about by forces greater than myself. In a glide low to the water and slowing, inside, I felt my confidence growing.

For many days afterward, I contemplated the lessons of the dream. I stayed near the craggy headlands where the condor made its home. Unobtrusively, I observed and studied its ways. I soon located where the nest was hidden, far up on a sheltered ledge overlooking the sea. I also found new vantage points and learned that there were actually three birds living there, all very large. The two biggest ones both carried the white patches on the undersides of their wings. The smaller one, apparently their offspring, was all black. I guessed that it must be waiting to come into its first molting. Because it was so easy to distinguish from its parents, the small one became the first to receive a name. I called it Bashia.

When extended full out, each one had an incredible wing span. I observed how much they relied upon the wind when taking off and landing. The longer I stayed and watched, the more it became apparent that Bashia was indeed the apprentice. Her sorties were more frequent and much shorter in duration. Often she practiced pre-flight calisthenics on the ledge of their home, taking short jumps to test and strengthen her muscles, extending her wings and quickly retracting them. After spending entire days watching and thinking about the birds, the flight dreams would fill my slumber.

I stayed with the condors until the weather turned, always watching, always learning. If they noticed me at all, they did not seem to mind. When the first winter storm blew down from the north, I had already returned to the camp by the sea.

CHAPTER SIXTY TWO

Pushing himself to the limits of his endurance, Icarus went back to the highlands and eventually returned to the same summit from which he had departed for Knossos. The wind and the cold had eased since his first ascent. That was a blessing. Emotionally drained and physically exhausted, this was more than just one of the highest points on the island. Icarus was standing at a turning point. On the one hand, he could continue to the west, come back to the egg house, and resume the routines of our familiar relationship. Or he could press on; he could rejoin his adventure and embrace the ambiguity of life in the wilds.

More than just a place, the peak was a portal. Standing on his mountain top in the light and warmth of the sun, he had to do something to commemorate the remarkable turn of events. He had just killed a man and injured another. What did it matter that they were also assassins? Icarus had been unjustly attacked. But in the eyes of their king that would be a distinction without a difference. Icarus could never go back to Knossos. He would never see his friends again.

He would never be able to talk with Diana again. How could he forget her face, her smile as she'd handed him the blue stone talisman? Icarus had worn that same stone on his wrist ever since leaving Knossos. And what about Demitrious? He had been a loyal friend on the long walk home from Malia. Had his old friend just betrayed him for a few pieces of gold? There was no way to know. What about Naucreta? She had always been there for him. She practically taught him the Minoan language. He remembered the way she looked inside the shimmering yellow robe, the one she had worn the day that the king had proclaimed their citizenship. Icarus had loved her from afar, as only a young man can.

Whichever way he traveled from here, Icarus would never see them again. They were passing from his life. He wanted to create a symbol, something to commemorate the completion of this part of his journey. There were certainly enough small stones exposed on the northern face. After a few trips back and forth he turned a pile of freezing rocks into a small conical pyramid, marking the summit. Sealing all these childhood memories inside the blue stone, he untied it from his wrist and placed it within the center of the pyramid. Someday when he was old, Icarus intended that he might turn these events into a meaningful story for telling others around a campfire. In the meantime, the cairn would be a memory and a link between himself and the next one to pass this way.

Comfortable now, Icarus leaned against the large rock, a cool breeze on his brow. He waited there for a long while, listening to a distant song. To the south, the land sloped away into snowfields and gray ridges, leading to a huge brown plateau transected by gorges and ravines. Scanning the landscape, one particular valley stood out from all the rest. The brown and gray colors of the rocks bled into warmer shades of green as the valley widened, deepening into lush vegetation. All of it portended flowing, fresh water. That meant edible plants, more wild game and perhaps even people. The thought of it brought a smile. It had been too long a time since he had enjoyed a conversation.

Billowy white clouds were beginning to gather. Gazing into the pyramid of smooth gray rocks, Icarus took one last look at the blue stone keepsake. Its color and texture were completely out of place. Turning eastward he began his descent, away from Knossos and ahead of the clouds.

The wind died away as soon as he left the summit. In no time at all, the snowfields were behind him. His food was gone. Small sprouts of vegetation began to appear along the game trail he followed. Gradually the air became warm again. Breathing through his nose, he sucked on a small smooth stone, conserving the scant moisture. He wanted to reach the gorge that had caught his eye on the mountaintop, and to be off the high plateau before darkness fell.

Just before sunset, he stood on the ledge at the top of the canyon.

Although tired from all the exertion, he would not allow himself to rush ahead. Instead, the young hunter waited in the shadows and looked for movement below. He smelled the upslope breeze and listened for any warning sounds. Nothing seemed out of the ordinary. Only then did he drop below the edge and descend a steep trail into the stillness. Soon it became easy going, walking along the rounded stones that covered the descending base of the gorge. Clumps of grass or dittany marked the few areas of sparse soil. Occasionally a tamarisk or pine found a way to struggle into the light. As the walls grew higher, water seeps arose. There were pockets of herbs and flowers. Then the stream appeared.

The canyon became his own private garden. His senses were wide open, fully alert to every sight, sound, and smell. He had no doubt that the right place to camp for the night was just around the bend. As he passed deeper into the gorge, pools of water dotted the rocky floor, some with tadpoles and algae. Plants burst out of every cranny in the rocks. There was even the occasional olive tree. In the sand or silt he saw the record of the rabbits, deer, and goats that had passed this way before him.

Then he saw it, a sight that fixed him in his tracks. He bent and placed one knee to the earth to examine more closely the marking in the soft silt. Unmistakably, it was a human footprint.

CHAPTER SIXTY THREE

Icarus followed the stream to a rocky ledge and a flowing waterfall where he stopped for the night thoroughly tired from his long day's trek. To the sound of falling water, he quickly drifted into a deep and peaceful sleep. The next morning birds came to bathe and drink in the nearby pool. He slept right through their songs. The rays of the sun edging toward the rim of the gorge finally woke him. Rousing himself, the young hunter extended his long arms and stretched the well-muscled shoulders as he looked out across the canyon floor in the light of day.

Many days' worth of grime covered his body in thick layers. He stripped off the heavy tunic and the goat-skin leggings and boots, all of them hand-made for his sojourn into the mountains. There would be less need for the heavy garments in the more inviting clime of this elevation.

Standing at the edge of the pool, he dipped his toes into the cool water. He knew that this would be a favorite spot for game to water at the end of the day. His next meal might already be making its way to this place, drawn, just as he had been, to the sounds and smell of fresh water. It was not just frequented by animals and birds. A carefully constructed dam of rocks and logs backed up the stream to form the deep pool. Below the pool a quiet stream flowed on, both sides lined with the husks of old, dried flowers.

Scanning first left and then right, he gazed down into the surface of the water. Reflected back was an image of dark eyes and hawk-like nose behind a scruffy beard. He smiled, recognizing himself only after a moment of examination. He removed his kilt and waded in, slipping naked into the wet coolness.

Lying on his back in the solitude, Icarus looked up into a narrow frame of cloudless cerulean sky between grey canyon walls. Silence surrounded him until he broke it, leaning forward and rising up onto his hands. He tipped his head back and heard the sound of the water draining into the pond from his long dark hair. He untied the leather strap and threw it to the shore.

After so much time trekking, Icarus was ready to come out. The thought of contact with others pleased him. It was time. He missed the comfort and pleasure in having others nearby. Someone had left the footprint. To find that person, Icarus had only to follow the stream and the companion trail toward the sea. The day awaited him, an empty canvas in a place and time for myths. He scrubbed himself with clean sand, rinsed it away and rose up into the warm sunlight, drying himself in its rays. He was primed to enter into this new world.

He hid his mountaineering clothes under a pile of rocks near his last night's camp, wondering if he would ever use them again. Then he filled his water skin from the waterfall, looped it onto the waist kit with a few other essentials and headed down the valley. The trail led him into stands of palm trees and citrus until the gorge ended, and he stood on a windy plain that sloped gently toward the sea.

The stream meandered across the plain, curving through a cluster of large trees and then winding back on itself and making for the shore. Hidden within the trees sat a small cluster of brown and gray cottages, a large courtyard and an elegant shrine. Down from the village, a straggle of bare wooden scaffolding for drying fish lined the shore. There were nets strewn across humps of rock and an assortment of small boats. Icarus stood on the threshold beyond the edge of the gorge and took it all in.

The nearby fruit trees still wore the barren look of winter. But the air seemed to carry the smell of baking breads or some other warm delight, inviting him to hurry along. Then he heard it, a melody played without inhibition, something so lively and free that it brought a smile to his face just to hear it.

He set off in the direction of the sounds and smells. Ahead lay a green hillside and grazing sheep. As he reached the base of the hill, a

long-haired dog began to bark, silhouetted on the top of the hill. At once
the music stopped. So did Icarus, not wanting to arouse suspicion or
challenge the dog, which was now running down the slope toward him,
intermittently barking and baring its teeth. Icarus stood still and waited for
a chance to demonstrate that he meant no harm.

It was not long in coming. A young woman with long dark hair
soon appeared. Icarus stared at her, unable to speak. There was a wooden
flute tucked into the dark sash that wrapped around her slender waist. She
also carried a stout staff, balanced on both shoulders. Icarus watched, spellbound, as she walked over the crest of the hill and toward the still barking
dog. She held her head high, balanced, as if walking to a melody that played
inside her head. She felt his gaze and looked back at him curiously.

She called to the dog. Faithfully, he returned to her side, but looked
back once or twice; just to be sure the newcomer understood who had the
high ground. Icarus didn't care. From his perspective, the dog was hardly
even noteworthy. The young woman directed a half-smile at the speechless
youth. He had the good sense to return her smile and call out, "Hello. My
name is Icarus."

The dog responded with a growl. She frowned at the animal and
told him once again to hush.

"What is your name?" Icarus persisted. "And what is this beautiful
place called?"

Regaining her composure, she replied, "Hello, Icarus. Welcome
to Platanos. I am called Deena and this is my home." Taking hold of her
staff with one hand, she beckoned for him to come up the hillside with the
other. "The goddess teaches us to welcome travelers."

The thick braid of her long dark hair splayed across her shoulder.
Barefoot, she wore a simple gray blouse and a dark wraparound skirt. He
had not spoken with a woman his own age for far too long. Carelessly, she
tossed her hair back. He watched as if frozen in time, caught up in that
uncertain place between intense desire and fear. He didn't want to stare, but
couldn't keep his eyes away.

"Well, are you coming or not?" she asked. The dog began to pant,
taking on a much friendlier demeanor. Icarus had no idea what to do or say,
but he was absolutely certain that he did not want to leave.

Mercifully she broke the silence, "Icarus, are you hungry? There is
some bread and fruit that I can share. How long has it been since you ate
something?"

"Too long," he replied.

"Well, come on then," she said, retreating back across the hillside and waving for him to follow. "I must get back to the sheep."

Icarus trailed behind, filled with relief. That smile, the innocent trust that the beckoning wave revealed, was enough, much more than enough, to turn his indecision into longing. His feet fell in behind hers to the top of the hill. She gave him food, she gave him a radiant smile, and then she began to talk. Listening carefully, he scanned the angular features of her face, content just to be near her. Her nose was beautiful, long, and straight as an arrow. Pointing to the various sheep by name, she explained the ways in which they spoke to each other. There was one that always led, another that was smart, and a third one was stubborn as a child.

"Icarus, it's your turn," Deena said with encouragement. "Where did you come from and how did you get here?"

"I came from over the mountains," he replied, "from Knossos. I am looking for an older woman who spoke with an Athenian accent, probably a slave. Has there ever been anyone like that around here?"

"We have no slaves here, of any nationality," Deena answered matter of factly. "Just work that needs doing."

"That's good to hear, despite the fact that it doesn't help to find her," Icarus replied.

Deena blushed at the enthusiasm. "Why are you looking for her?" she asked cautiously.

"She was my mother."

CHAPTER SIXTY FOUR

The village of Platanos was a cluster of huts made of stone and wood in the shape of an arc, connected with each other by narrow stone paths and built around a common courtyard. Its residents numbering slightly over two hundred, there simply wasn't enough room for everyone to gather on the plaza. Instead, in the evenings they gathered in several makeshift, concentric circles centered on campfires and watched the stars come out. In the enveloping darkness, they told stories, they sang, and they danced.

Deena made sure that Icarus understood that he was welcome in these evening circles. She reasoned that as he was already the principal player in most of the village gossip, he might as well have a say in what everyone else was talking about. Most were curious, some suspicious, some both. His accent was different and he came from a distant land, far beyond the confines of their village by the sea. But for anyone with eyes to see, there was one thing about him that was true, his attraction for Deena. Their shared glances were not lost on anyone, even the children. As the days turned into moon cycles, it served as a continuing source of interest and speculation. Seeing the way that Deena returned his gaze, the villagers of Platanos could not, would not turn him away.

About that same time, spring arrived. The earth became covered in anemones, asphodels, and wild gladioli. Birds appeared, returning to the southern coast from their winter migration to somewhere over the sea. Since Platanos was without a doubt the most beautiful place Icarus had ever been, it made sense that few would ever leave. Of course, this conclusion was inevitable and directed by the fact that he had fallen so completely in love with Deena. Almost all the villagers were related to one another in some fashion. All of them had been born right there. Within the connections of their egalitarian community slavery simply did not exist.

Icarus wanted to make a good impression on them. He was young and strong. He was willing to work and to learn about their ways. At first he thought that he might make the best impression by demonstrating his independence and self-sufficiency. For a time, he went out alone to hunt for his own food. But it was not long before younger boys from the village wanted to go along and learn to hunt and shoot a bow. Icarus taught them well. In the process, he discovered that what impressed the villagers most was not so much the results of his hunting, but his willingness to share his knowledge and experience.

One day a villager named Salim invited Icarus to come fishing on his boat. His father had passed away a few years before and ever since Salim had fished alone. But he was tired of that now. He wanted the company and sometimes he needed help. His wife, Naomi, supported the idea and encouraged her husband to offer the newcomer this place on the boat. Besides, their own children were still too small to learn about the ways of the sea. So Icarus went along on the next trip and the one after that. He and Salim became good friends. After a short time, Icarus began sleeping on the sand by the boat instead of alone in the gorge far from the village.

Deena often played her flute around the evening fire. When she played, she would close her eyes and begin to sway, lifting her chin and exposing her long and slender neck. Her profile was exquisite. Icarus loved to listen to her music and watch her perform. He asked her how she had learned so many songs. She replied that the bird songs inspired the melodies, and the rest was just improvising.

At first, despite kind encouragement from all, Icarus didn't say very much at the gatherings. But after time, one night the rugged youth opened up and related some stories of his life. It was not long before everyone in the village was enraptured with the story of Icarus and Daedalus. They learned about his growing up in a great city on the other side of the mountains, and how Daedalus worked there as an architect and builder for a king named Minos. But Icarus never told anyone of his most recent return to Knossos.

Later that same evening, Icarus and Deena left the fire together to go walking. Her young cousin went along. While they walked, Deena tripped and to catch herself from falling, her hand reached out for his shoulder. It might have been the first time they ever touched. They both felt the same longing for more.

She told him stories about growing up in the village. She had many good memories of family and friends, and though times were difficult for her right after her friend Naomi was married, she explained that she was quite content to live in the quiet village between the sea and the mountains.

"Sometimes," she confessed, "when traders sail into our harbor, they bring with them stories about great cities in distant lands. Apparently the cities all have royalty."

"Of course," replied Icarus.

"Well," she responded. "None of those kings or queens have ever come to Platanos. Here, they would just be ordinary people, far from home."

"That sounds like me," replied Icarus.

"It is exactly like you, prince Icarus."

"Hmmm. I like that," he replied gratefully. "And who would you like to become?"

"I've become quite content just being who I am," Deena answered, a placid smile on her lips.

CHAPTER SIXTY FIVE

For safe sustained flight, any wings I constructed had to imitate a gliding bird, as I would never be able to flap them. For my first test flight, I would have to use the morning thermals that rose up off of the island in the same manner as the birds of prey. My wings would have to derive all their power from the air currents and wind. My body would hang from the device, my torso supported by a great wing. It would be at least twice the length of my own wingspan. I needed the lightest and strongest native materials and a means to attach them in a framework to my own chest. The goal was straightforward and clear. I intended to duplicate the condor's ability to sail for hours through the currents of air.

Now that Icarus was gone, I relished the evening hours of reflection. I often found it amusing that for all my skills as a builder of fine homes and temples, when given the choice, I chose to live under an open sky.

Here, there were no more construction projects to be managed, at least none subject to another's approval. There was just one plan. Building the wings would put to test years of design and building experience. Upon my first safe landing, they would prove to be my masterpiece.

It was a vision I had shared only with Icarus. Even Naucreta did not know. I missed them both. There were empty spaces in my heart for both of them. I deeply missed the easy companionship Icarus and I once shared, and I hoped often for his safe return.

Bedding down once more, I dreamt another flight dream, but this one was very different from its predecessors. This time I stood on a rocky ledge with a beautiful set of wings at my feet. High above, Icarus soared in the moonlight, long white wings on his shoulders and arms. For a long time, I stood and watched, proud and at peace.

Then, I hurried to join Icarus in the sky. After a lot of fumbling and effort, I leapt up and away from the land, wings extended. The air currents lifted and pulled me higher and higher. Once more, I felt the invigoration of soaring in the winds. Gaining elevation, I could plainly see Icarus' profile far ahead against the night sky. Try as I might, I could not shorten the distance between us. I became disappointed, frustrated, and hurt.

Waking in the morning, I remembered the dream with clarity and sadness. I believed that I understood his desire for independence. It was a natural and inevitable part of life. And it was no accident that the timing of Icarus' quest to search for and find the missing, yet necessary material came right on the heels of my own separation from King Minos. In a way, I had modeled the behaviors for him. Both of us were making leaps of faith, only at very different stages of life.

Over the years I had made my share of promises and kept them as best I could. It was becoming clear that when Icarus returned, he would not be the same. I resolved to expect that and support the changes whatever they were. If he was empty-handed, hungry, or hurt, I would welcome him and celebrate his return. On the other hand, if he came back with a fine boat and all the riches of a king, I would welcome him and celebrate, just the same. All I wanted and hoped for was for him to be safe, healthy, and content.

I imagined Icarus moving into his own life, a vital and energetic young man, here on the island or wherever else he chose, walking or sailing, or even flying. Icarus was moving on, and though my own emotions some-times got in the way of it, I understood in the deepest parts of my soul that I wanted him to flourish. Our paths had coalesced for a long time, the journey fruitful and satisfying. But self-reliance and independence had begun to flow out of him. Before he left I could see all too clearly the man he was becoming.

He would certainly follow his own path. I must not lose sight of mine. Building the wings had become the greatest challenge of my life. I had only to close my eyes to imagine myself soaring through an azure sky high above the island.

As the days grew shorter and the weather cooled, Icarus and Deena explored many beaches together. The late evening walks had become quite routine. No one bothered to direct the little cousin to follow along anymore. Many nights the young lovers sat side by side on a secluded patch of shore and watched the moon pass overhead. There were many long and passionate kisses.

They enjoyed walking by the sea. There was always something to watch or do there. But on one clear, starlit night they decided to take a different turn. They went inland to the waterfall in the gorge. Alone with each other by the pool, he gently stroked his fingers through her long dark hair and said, "Deena, this feels so right."

"I feel it, too."

"I didn't know what happiness was until I met you."

"I feel the same way for you. Just tell me why I had to wait so long for you to appear," she teased, nestling her head a little deeper into the crook of his arm.

In reply, Icarus gazed into her eyes and smiled, running his fingertips gently over the smooth brown skin of her face. She smiled up at him in return. His hand traced the straight lines of her neck down to her collar bone and lingered at the boundary of her gray shirt. She closed her eyes, inhaling deeply as his free hand gently moved across one breast and then the other. He undid the ties of her blouse, easing it away from her neck and shoulders. His fingers played across the delicate contours of her nipples and the smooth expanse of stomach.

On other nights before this one, Deena had always found some inner reserve and slowly but firmly took his wrist and stopped the explorations from going any further. Many times she had lovingly explained that she could not become pregnant. The elders were putting their trust in her, in both of them. She would not betray that trust, and he should not plant his seed until after they were married. Each time, Icarus had stopped, reluctantly.

The last time, after the kissing stopped, she grew serious and had asked him about his father. She asked him about the great inventor who was living in a cave in some far away part of the island and waiting for his son to return with a mysterious adhesive so that they could carry out their plan to build wings and fly away.

"Is that what you really want," she had cried out, tears running down her cheeks. "To plant your seed in me and then fly off to another island far away?" Hands on her hips and tears brimming in her eyes, she taunted him. "Surely the wingbuilder expects his son to be part of that plan."

Icarus only hung his head and said nothing.

"What about your dreams, Icarus?" she persisted.

Icarus had no answer for her.

On this night by the waterfall, however, as his fingers played across her belly, she did not reach for her defenses as his hand slipped beneath her gray skirt. Instead, she moaned quietly, pushing her hips into his tender caress. It was a most seductive sound. Hearing it, Icarus wanted to be even closer. He wanted to feel the skin of their bodies touching and to hold his stiff erection against the warmth of her skin. Lovingly, he set her head down and began to rise on one knee in order to be closer to her.

In that brief moment of separation, his mind leapt away from the quiet pool and back to Athens, into the memory of his mother's efforts to cover herself with her torn dress, while one man slapped her repeatedly across the face and two others held her down. Once again, he was a small, fearful boy, hearing two coarse and angry men swear at him, yelling at him to leave and get out of there. Once more, he watched in horror while the man who had been hitting his mother undid his tunic, exposing a tumescence that to a small boy was quite immense and unnatural. Once more, he heard her crying out and sobbing.

"Where'd you go?" Deena asked.

The sound of her voice brought him back to the pool. But his own erection, the one that had been a nearly constant companion the whole evening, was gone. The images had been so vivid, the look on his mother's face so real. It sickened him. Taking his hands away from Deena he sat up and placed them on the sides of his head.

"I'm so sorry-I," he hesitated, "we cannot do this now." He rose up and stumbled into the darkness of the cold water.

Deena sat on the bank, perplexed. She watched and waited while he lay back in the water and looked up at the sky.

"How can you stand that cold water?" she asked, trying to keep a conversation going.

Icarus only sighed in response.

In the still of the night, they walked back to the village together. Several times he started to tell her about it, but could not find the right words. Eventually, he just became sullen and irritable. Finally, as they reached the village, she turned to him and said, "Someday soon you must tell me what happened up there. Let's not talk anymore tonight."

"You're right," Icarus replied. "I want to have time to think."

"Goodnight, my love," Deena answered back.

CHAPTER SIXTY SIX

In the next flight dream, the winds in the high altitudes were very strong. Erratic and gusting, they became a sort of ceiling, kept me in the lower elevations, and prevented me from pursuing what I had hoped would be a test flight over the sea. Contentedly, I remained at lower levels, skimming over the trees and gliding low across the rocky plateaus. The moon was bright, casting shadows across the landscape. I could see the terrain spread out before me. Up ahead a herd of wild goats descended into a gorge no doubt searching for their evening water.

They would not hear or smell me approaching. Nor would they tend to look up into the sky. I angled toward them, directing my flight toward a large male at the back of the herd. The alpha buck suddenly perked his head up and swiveled it around, as if he had sensed my thoughts. He rotated his ears in different directions, scanning the earth all around. He watched the ground, looking down into the canyon. The temptation to fly close enough to tweak one of the dark pointed ears was irresistible.

I dropped quickly, keeping my speed up and descending directly toward the animal. His pointed ears loomed large in front of me. But reaching out to touch the soft furry target instantly decreased the lift on that side. I went into an unexpected turn, completely missed the goat, and lost airspeed and elevation at the same time. Sensing danger he instantly bolted away, sending the herd into a sympathetic sideways rush. When the wings finally leveled, I was skimming over rocky ground. Slowly, I limped back toward the shore, desperate for a thermal.

After regaining some elevation, I reversed my course and overflew the winding canyon, searching for the herd. They were long gone, scattered and hidden. The buck had provided me with a good lesson, a demonstration that I still much to learn about flight.

Finding another thermal, I spiraled higher into the night sky and to my surprise saw that I was no longer alone. In the distance was a winged figure so far away that I could barely make it out, but from its shape and the way it moved, it could only be another human.

Whoever it was had seen me, too. I tried to approach, but each time I came closer, the other figure receded, maintaining a respectful distance. It went on like that for a while, matching my speed and maneuver, and always remaining far apart. Then, I changed my strategy. Instead of the direct approach, I maneuvered into a broad arc that took me over the sea and steadily away from my flying companion. As I'd hoped, the other figure began to give chase, still keeping its distance, and taking us both further out to sea. The distance between us was closing. The other flyer was right behind me, matching every maneuver and forcing me onward and away from all of my familiar landmarks. We were moving out to sea as fast as the wind allowed, but it no longer felt as if we were children engaged in a game of tag.

Whatever the game, the novelty had given way to anxiety. Another island appeared on the horizon, one with a large volcano in the center. We were heading straight for it, and gradually the other glider closed the distance between us. After all that time and maneuvering, a face came into view. I recognized her right away and was shocked. It was a woman. Not just any woman, but Talos' mother, Aella, the person who more than anyone else had been directly responsible for driving me out of Athens. It was all a painful memory, resurrected out of the long past. I rarely thought about those times anymore. What was she doing there, I wondered?

We stared hard at one another in recognition, fascinated but wary. We flew together that way for a time, matching each other's speed and direction. No taunts or insults were exchanged, but neither did we speak. To venture too close would be disastrous. There was too much at risk. Even the smallest of collisions would cause both of us to lose hard won elevation. I was not about to end the dream with a fall to the earth.

Without so much as a sign or signal Aella descended, moving

rapidly towards the smoldering cone. I pursued her cautiously, and was thoroughly relieved when she rose into a natural ascending arc. The air above the cone was filled with a rising fountain of heated air. She had led me to the mother of all thermals and I was soaring right into it. Gratefully I followed, slowing and staying just inside Aella's artful loop. At the top, we were side by side, able to look across at one another and smile. Then, it was descending race back to the cone, to do it all over again.

Soon we were carving out parallel trajectories above the volcano, something like a dance. Several times we climbed into curving spirals, weaving our flight paths together into a giant helix, and all of this coordinated without a single word. High above the island I banked away and looked for her. There was the island we had started from, far in the distance. I circled in a quiet equilibrium, realizing that the lesson was over, and Aella was gone. But I had more than enough elevation to reach my own destination. It was just far away in the distance, the green field of my home island. I banked away from the warm luxury of the rising air and into another broad arc, heading for the soft earth of the landing, alone.

The next morning Icarus spotted a flight of terns feeding in deep water. The two fishermen set out after them, but the birds dispersed before they could get close enough to set their nets. From his place on the bow, Icarus looked back towards the shore and saw a large black bird soaring high above the island.

Salim was a brown-skinned man with an easy laugh and a full head of dark, curly hair. He had strong shoulders and thick forearms from long days in the sun, pulling on nets and lines. Watching the circling bird, he and Icarus talked while the boat drifted lazily on the sea. Salim was a few years older, probably about the same age as Aadam. He was a caring man with two small children and a lovely wife who doted on him. Talking with him on the water that day, Icarus realized how rich Salim's life seemed. "That bird has found something worth descending for," observed Icarus.

"Maybe we should go investigate," his friend replied, raising the sail.

"Salim, we are friends, yes?"

"Of course," Salim replied, extending an open hand toward him.

"Well, something happened last night, between Deena and I," Icarus continued.

"She finally let you in! Congratulations."

"No," Icarus interjected, shaking his head. "We didn't. But something rather unexpected did happen."

With a light breeze pushing them towards their quarry, he told Salim everything. At least, he described what had happened the night before with Deena. He knew that much of what he said would soon be repeated to Naomi, who would tell Deena, but what difference did it make? He would soon be having the same conversation with her, anyway.

Salim's response was to assure him that everything he could ever want in life was right there in Platanos. The villagers had already accepted him. Placing an arm around his shoulder, he squeezed Icarus hard and said, "You and Deena are perfect for each other. She loves you. You love her. Once that happens, you are stuck my friend, gloriously stuck."

"What about last night?" Icarus asked.

"Don't dwell on the past. You have too many good nights ahead of you for that. From now on, there can be no other happiness for you. Not until you marry her. That is what I think about all this."

"You make it sound so simple," Icarus said.

"Why make it complicated. Promise me Icarus, if you ever need my help with anything, you have only to ask. You will ask, yes?"

"I promise," said Icarus. "And Salim, I will do the same for you."

"It's all a brother can do," Salim replied.

The bird went into a rapid spiraling descent. It was not long before they saw the broad carcass of a whale, beached on a lonely stretch of sand. The tail of the bloated creature was stretched out flat, half of it still in the water. Astride its immense back stood the huge, bald-headed condor. If it had noticed the men, it made no sign. The long wings folded into its body, the bird calmly fed on the exposed flesh of the whale's back.

In the stern, Salim steered the boat downwind, looking for a protected place to beach it. When the crystalline water grew shallow enough, Icarus slipped over the side with the lead rope and hauled the boat onto the sand. Then he was gone, dashing off toward the site and leaving his friend to secure the sail, stow the tiller, and catch up. Few words were spoken for any of it.

Taking his time, Salim vaulted over the side of the boat. He sauntered across the sand, his eyes betraying his curiosity. There were no tracks in the mixture of hardened sand and pebbles, but Salim kept going in the same general direction, following behind his friend, until the overpowering odor of their quarry stopped him in his tracks. Icarus stood a few strides ahead of him, staring at the large, black bird perched on the beast's back.

The bird was dwarfed by the sheer bulk of the dead leviathan, and the smell was intense.

Turning in the direction of the approaching footsteps, Icarus said, "Look at him up there, so pleased with himself. He wants us to think that he rode the beast right up onto the sand, and now it's his."

"It's possible," Salim joked.

It was such an unusual sight that the two of them watched for a time, not wanting to disturb the contentment of the feasting bird with its meal. Strong talons held fast to the whale's flesh as the bird's curving beak tore out large chunks. With each gulp the bird looked up and cocked its head, returning their gazes with a corresponding intensity.

Guessing that more carrion eaters were en route, Salim took three large strides towards the huge bird. The bird somehow intensified its gaze. In response the fisherman waved his arms and lunged forward, breaking into a scream that overwhelmed all the other sounds on the beach. Instantly, the bird extended its massive wings and flapped, stretching its long neck and shoulders in a broad expanse of black and showing off the distinct white pattern underneath each wing. It was clearly meant to soar on the winds. Stretching for takeoff, the bird's body was easily as tall as a man.

Right before their eyes the great bird braced its legs, digging the claws even deeper into the whale's flesh. It launched itself from that fixed position straight upward, several arm's lengths off of its meal. Salim jumped, too, but with far less grace. He quickly fell back to the earth and called out for the huge bird to take him along.

At the very top of its leap, the bird energetically flapped into the face of the onshore breeze. It quickly gained elevation. Wings fully extended, it flapped twice more, looking down at the intruders. Spying Salim, it dropped toward him and loosed a discharge from its tail, offering a last word on the subject. Then, the bird was off, catching a breeze and allowing the wind to push it away from the beach, the intruding men, and its meal. It glided away faster and higher than any pursuer could possibly go.

The two men stood on the beach in silence, watching the bird soar away. The wings were longer than the sail of their boat and what a beautiful sight to behold! To have seen such a huge bird leap into the air like that, so close at hand. Both were filled with awe.

That night, back at the village, strips of whale blubber were cut away from the carcass and boiled down into an oil that would have many uses. Icarus did not stay to be part of the dancing or the drumming that would follow. The events of the day had taken him inward, and he wanted some time alone.

So many new people had come into his life since beginning this quest. It was as if he were carrying a great weight. He had made so many promises, spoken and unspoken. There were the intensely passionate ones made to Deena, the unspoken ones made to Salim, and the implied ones communicated to the rest of the villagers, which indicated that he wanted to be one of them. And of course there was the one spoken to me, the foundational one that lay beneath so many of his actions and decisions over these many cycles of the moon: his pledge that he would find the material for building the wings and one day return.

Had he forgotten the promise or just misplaced it? Deena was right. Certainly he had a role in his father's dream of flight. It was to find the right glue. Icarus had designed the quest. The words were his own and now, he winced at the thought of his unintended duplicity. If only his father could understand how sweet life was in Platanos.

There was no going back to the wilds for him. His desire to live alone was sated. The freedom of that lifestyle had been good for a time, until the fight in Knossos. Salim and the villagers had showed him another way. Deena had opened his heart. What he wanted most was right in front of him. He wanted to be with Deena, make love to her in a garden of flowers by the sea, marry her, make a home with her, live in this tiny village, and become part of the community—even if that meant that he would never again venture more than a few miles from this place.

Of all the possibilities, this was the one Icarus kept coming back to, again and again. He stood on the threshold of a new and very different quest. More than anything he wanted to become a fisherman, a husband, and even a father. With that clarity, Icarus found peace within himself. Surely, in those terms, he could persuade even his own father to understand the change of heart.

The condor and its flight into the sky had been a very powerful reminder of his own father. The bird was a messenger, demonstrating that it was time to reconcile and then move on with his own life. One full cycle of the sun had passed since they'd left Knossos together. So much had happened. There would be many stories to tell. Spring was upon them. It was the perfect time to travel.

Icarus walked alone under the stars, remembering all the events and choices that had brought him to Platanos. He walked long into the night, flooded with ideas and far from the village. Icarus was still out walking when the sun and the birds awoke and the day appeared. He had two things to accomplish. First, he would ask Deena to marry him. Second, he would persuade Salim to lend them the boat.

CHAPTER SIXTY SEVEN

By the spring equinox migratory birds had already begun their annual processionals. In the clear blue sky over Platanos, undulating lines of storks passed overhead, croaking their peculiar calls and generally announcing that the storms of winter were past. All across the Great Green, the trading season was beginning, and it was time for the newlyweds to begin their journey to find Icarus' father. Salim even offered him the use of the boat as a generous wedding gift.

For much of the first day they sat together in the stern, exploring the hidden coves and inlets of their island. Deena often played on her flute, letting the music flow into the wind. Two heavy urns rested in the bottom of the boat, aligned for balance. One held extra food and water. At the tiller Icarus glanced at the graceful outer curves of the other container. He wondered if its contents were sufficient to carry all the hopes and visions that had been poured into it.

On the first night they camped on a long sandy peninsula far from Platanos. Deena had never been so far away from her home, a community where all the houses were linked together into a cluster of similar structures. There were few secrets. Sleeping together on the edge of the land with water nearly all around, it was as if they had their own private island. They spent the night cuddled together in luxurious comfort and warmth. It made a fine memory and perhaps one day a good story.

On the second day their small sail boat rounded the southwest corner of the island. Right away they picked up a hot wind from the south. It bellied the sail, blowing them smartly across the water and directly into the shallows of a large sandbar. The safety of deep water lay much further to the west. The uncompromising beauty of the brown sands drew them in, covered as far as the eye could see with thousands and thousands of blossoming sea lilies. In a shallow inlet they beached the boat on a colorful shoreline streaked with pink and red sand. They made love on a bed of vibrant white blossoms and spent the second day exploring the endless dunes.

When they finally returned to the sail boat, they were parched, exhausted, and very grateful to have each other. As the sun set they replenished their water supply and made a vow to devote the next day to the search for the father and the rocky promontory where he made his home.

In the morning a favorable breeze came up to take them further out to sea. By midday, they rounded the sand bar. There were high cliffs in the distance and Icarus was eager to make headway. But the breeze was no longer as favorable, and the day began to drag. One gray cliff looked very much like the last. There was no end to them.

"How much further, husband?" Deena had to ask.

"I have no idea," Icarus replied, a touch of boredom in his voice. "It has to be somewhere along this stretch of western shore. I'm sure I'll recognize it."

"I'm excited for you to see your father again," she replied. "Just understand that I'll be meeting him for the first time. I'm getting rather nervous about all this."

Scenes and words from the last days with his father flooded into his head.

"I want to see his face when he realizes that I not only found what I went searching for, but something even better," said Icarus.

"And what would that be?" she played along.

As she spoke the words they came to an inlet that had a familiar look. Icarus rose to his feet and scanned the shore, recognizing the familiar outline of rocks and trees and confirming that they were getting very near. She looked out across the water, hoping to see some sign of habitation. But there was nothing.

"I want to see this egg house of yours," she said. "It had better still be there."

"Don't worry," said Icarus. "We'll find it."

With the sun waning and the breeze picking up once more, Icarus spotted the footpath he had so often climbed leading down to the familiar stretch of shoreline and sand. He pointed toward the beach full of excitement and relief and said, "This is it, Deena! This has to be it." He angled the bow toward the shore and the sail followed, the boat surging forward. Standing in the stern Icarus shouted, "Father! I'm back!" Then with a wink at Deena, he corrected himself and said, "We're back! Father, are you there?"

But there was no response, no movement from the shore. The small boat glided past the high cliff that marked their inlet. They took in the sail and let the momentum carry them into the same tidal pool where Icarus had fished so many times before. He jumped in the shallow water and grabbed the lead line, pulling the craft onto the safety of the sand, just as a distant and joyful cry rang out. His wife looked up to see a small figure jumping up and down on the top of the neighboring cliff, waving intensely. She waved back, calling to Icarus at the same time.

"Is that him? Turn around, quick."

Still waving, I let out an unintelligible, exuberant shout. Then, I tore through the brush, making for the trail that led to the shore as fast as my legs would travel. Up ahead, Icarus was securing the mooring. Then, he took her by the hand, and they walked together towards the trailhead. That's where I came bursting into view, rushing along the trail like a racer coming to the finish line.

"You move well for an old man," Icarus called out, laughing as I ran down the final stretch. I had not moved like that in many sun cycles.

This was not the homecoming I had envisioned. I had always believed that Icarus would return; except that in my imagination, it would be over land, the way he had left, with a goat or an antelope over his shoulders to feast upon. But here he was down on the beach with a sailing boat, and a young woman—a happy, smiling young woman.

"Who knew you could sail?" I said, breathless and slowing down just enough to throw my arms around a slightly taller, much broader Icarus.

There were so many things I wanted to know about this man I was holding in my arms, but there was no hurry. I was thrilled. Tears of joy streamed down my face.

With some difficulty I finally managed to say, "Welcome back, welcome back! I always knew that you would return one day," I said, stepping back and placing my hands over my heaving chest and beating heart. Looking from one to the other, I continued. "You make a very handsome couple," I said. "You must introduce me to her someday," I joked.

Without responding, Icarus knelt and wrapped his arms around my waist. He picked me up and swung me around as if I were a rag doll. She watched and laughed, happy to bear witness to the moment.

After setting me down on the sand he looked over to Deena and said proudly, "There's someone you have to meet."

Deena was already stepping forward, a small blue stone hanging from her neck. Placing her hand on Icarus' shoulder, she extended the other hand to me in greeting and said, "You must be Daedalus. I'm very pleased to finally meet you. I am Deena."

The smile on Icarus' face spoke volumes.

In my wildest dreams, I had never anticipated that he would marry; but in hindsight, why wouldn't he marry? I easily adjusted and warmly included Deena in the welcoming. At the same time, I had reached the obvious conclusion that my concept for flight had been altered. There was no longer a need for two sets of wings—possibly three—but definitely not two. The realization created a pang of regret, even in the midst of this joyous moment. Fleeting, the feeling was quickly overpowered by an outpouring of love for them both. Icarus was healthy and happy, and he had returned. That was all I needed to know in that moment. The rest would come later.

"Clearly, much has happened," I said, "and we have a lot of catching up to do. Come, both of you. Come up to the camp. You must be thirsty, hungry. I have some wonderful tea we can brew. A little homemade wine that is quite good. We will make a fire and feast just like the old days. And you must tell me everything that has happened."

"You go ahead, father. I need to go back and get some things from the boat."

"Let me help then," I offered.

"No. Not yet," he said. "You will ask too many questions. Deena and I will follow in a minute."

Smiling, I returned to the camp and stoked the fire. There was much I wanted to say, but I didn't know where to start. I decided to let Icarus be the center of attention and listen to him, and hear his young wife tell her story. I was eager for all of it. Counting all the seasons I had been without company, I looked up to see my son, walking up the narrow trail with an enchanting young woman, and carrying between them a large, colorful urn.

"They move well together," I said, with an approving smile.

CHAPTER SIXTY EIGHT

"We were married on last new moon," said Icarus, reaching for Deena's hand. "It was a beautiful thing, Da. You would have enjoyed it."

"Yes. I'm certain of it," I replied. "How did you two meet, anyway?"

"Da," Icarus replied, taking a serious tone. "There is something I have to say, and it is best just to begin. After that, we'll talk about the wedding and all that. I promise. This is important."

"All right," I responded, "Go ahead."

"Even if you're ready to show me how to fly, I won't be joining you in the sky. That's your dream," said Icarus. "I have found my own, and it is with Deena in Platanos."

"Somehow I knew that from the moment I first saw you together," I replied, returning Icarus' serious expression with a smile.

"Do you know how long I have dreaded this moment?" said Icarus. "I was afraid you would be hurt, even devastated."

"Would you settle for disappointed?" I replied earnestly. "I am disappointed but I'll get over it. I'm also very pleased and happy that you've come back. The rest of it just doesn't matter that much. So tell me, how did you two lovely people meet?"

Icarus told of leaving our camp and picking his way through a series of valleys and ridges to a high plateau, with many antelope, goats, and deer. He described trekking through these wilds for many days, until it became apparent that he was being drawn toward a high, snow-capped mountain. Of course he just had to climb it. From its heights he discovered the trail to a gorge that led to the sea and to Platanos where Deena and her people lived. Icarus started to describe the village and its people, how they lived, and how beautiful and fertile the land was.

"Wait, please," I interrupted. "You just jumped over the good part. I'm most interested in hearing your story," I said, extending an open palm towards Deena. "How did you two meet?"

Icarus smiled as Deena picked up the cue and responded. She explained how she was tending her flock on a hillside one day when a gentle and handsome young man walked out from the canyon by the stream that brought fresh water to their village. She had her flute with her that day. The young man followed the sound of the melody all the way to the hillside where she played to her sheep.

"With his handsome face and rugged vitality, his proud nose and his appreciation for good music, I knew from the moment he began to speak that I was in trouble, the most delicious kind," Deena said, laughing at her confession. "He told me that his name was Icarus. It is a fine name."

Her listeners applauded, rising to our feet and toasting her story with wine. The fire danced and crackled. She gave us both a radiant smile.

"She stole my heart that day," Icarus said. "You know what that's like, don't you?"

"Yes. I do," I admitted, "and I'm so glad that you came all the way out here, Deena. It warms my heart that you made this trip. There is great happiness in both of you. It is so good for me to see and witness in both of you." Lifting the wine skin, I stood and made a toast to their long and happy lives together. "Now tell me about the wedding."

Deena continued the story. She began by explaining that weddings don't occur that often in Platanos.

"When they do," she continued, "it is a process. The village enjoys taking its time with the ceremony and celebration. It's more than just the transition of a young maiden into another home as a wife. It's to create a union recognized by all. But with a newcomer like Icarus, we had to improvise. The elders selected a proper location, the site was blessed, and the men constructed a beautiful two-room house and courtyard. It's everything I ever wanted in a home," Deana said, smiling and turning toward Icarus. "There were many offerings and rituals. But I won't bore you with the details."

"Tonight, you couldn't possibly bore me," I candidly replied.

"I was bathed and perfumed, and dressed in a full-length robe and veil—"

"She was so beautiful," Icarus interjected.

"I felt beautiful," Deena replied. "We walked together, Naomi, my best friend, and I, to the new house. The path was strewn with spring flowers. Icarus and Salim, Naomi's husband, were waiting there. Then, there were more flowers, all along the path to the center of the village. Everyone attended—the young and the old. There were more offerings, blessings, and many toasts."

"It sounds like you did your best to announce to the entire countryside that a marriage has taken place," I answered.

"To the entire earth and sky," she responded.

"Yes, and consider this," Icarus continued. "We want you, father, to return to Platanos with us. The villagers will welcome you. The elders have already extended the invitation."

Deena nodded.

"It is a place like no other and I know you could be happy there," Icarus went on. "You don't really have to leave Krete anymore, do you? You could return with us tomorrow—or whenever you are ready—and make it your home."

I smiled and said nothing for a while. I tried to imagine myself as a fisherman in a small village by the water. Even then, I could tell that it wasn't a good fit. Closing my eyes for just a moment, I remembered all the flight dreams and the grace and elegance of soaring on the winds. I had already seen the shadow of my winged figure moving across the water, even if only in a dream. I did not belong in a tranquil village, not yet.

"What if Minos somehow learns that I am there? If I know the man at all, he is already hunting for me, possibly for both of us."

"Knossos is on the other side of the mountains," said Icarus. "There are no roads. How could he ever find us?"

"He has wealth and power," I replied emphatically. "That gives him a very long reach. We helped his slaves escape from the labyrinth, remember."

"What is he talking about?" Deena asked, a worried look on her face. "What labyrinth?"

"It's a deep cavern, a maze for holding prisoners," replied Icarus. "I will tell you about it later tonight."

Apparently, there were a few things she didn't know about his past.

To lighten the mood, I rose to my feet again and walked around the fire until I could place my hands on both of their shoulders. Kneeling a little, I gave them each the strongest hug I could manage. I made Deena blush by telling her how much I had always wanted a daughter. Then, I embarrassed Icarus, too, by telling him how proud I was of him.

"It warms my heart that both of you have come home," I gushed.

I returned to my seat by the fire and began talking about wings, flight, and my fascination with the soaring birds, especially the condor I called Bashia. Icarus' face lit up when he heard the description.

He responded with a story of his own, telling about finding a black condor with similar markings, feeding on the carcass of a beached whale.

"I wonder if it was her," I replied. "There are hundreds of them on this island. Probably silly to think it was the same bird."

"Unless she was playing her part in bringing you two back together," Deena concluded.

For a while, we sat silently.

I had been alone by the sea for many cycles of the moon. In that time, I had missed him greatly. Many times I had hoped for his return, and there he was. I had no doubt that on his quest, Icarus had been tested in ways that I would never know. Yet, he was back with a design for his own life. By all appearances, Icarus had made some fine decisions. This was not the same youth who had left our home so long ago. We had said many things to each other before separating. Some of the words were hurtful, some of them kind. The important ones I still remembered. I could never forget saying, "No matter what happens, healthy or sick, rich or poor, you must return. When that happens, no matter how or when, I will welcome you and listen to your stories."

I had had no idea how prophetic those words would become, but it was certainly coming home to me now. With the moon high overhead, we were still awake, laughing, and sharing.

Eventually though, I started to yawn. Feigning impatience, Icarus pointedly asked, "Aren't you even going to ask about the quest? You do remember the quest, don't you?"

"I thought you reinvented it and brought back a girl, I mean, a woman instead," I replied, completely serious.

"No, father, there's much more to talk about," he continued. "So you had better stay awake. The glue that you sent me to find is there in the urn. It's also true that I would have never found it without Deena. She and the villagers made all this possible."

Icarus stood and retrieved the heavy clay urn, setting it right in front of me by the fire. I ran my fingertips over the hard, dark shell that had formed on the top. I rapped on it with my knuckle. Tears running down my cheeks, I reached out and steadied myself by placing a hand on my son's shoulder.

Icarus had been waiting for this moment for a very long time. I was savoring it. Sitting back down, he began his explanation by talking about fishing from the boat with Salim. In good weather they might venture far beyond the sight of land to go after tuna. For that, the boats had to be seaworthy.

Deena and I nodded.

"Whenever the villagers are able to gather together enough of the right materials, they make a sealant and apply it to the hulls of the boats to protect the wood from splitting. Not so long ago," Icarus continued, "they were able to do this."

Icarus explained how the villagers had boiled down slices of the whale's flesh to make a fine oil. Some of it was set aside for burning in their lamps. The rest of it was mixed with pine tar, finely ground sea urchin spine, and other ingredients that Icarus could only guess at. Everything was heated into a bubbling liquid in a huge copper pot. The elders took turns. They added ingredients and stirred some more, until it was finally ready. Then the boats were hauled up onto the sand, and the keels painted with the hot, sticky liquid. All the while, the villagers chanted and drummed for the safe return of the boats and everyone in them. It was a beautiful thing watch.

"It sounds fascinating," I replied.

"There's more," Deena continued, smiling at her husband.

"When I saw the hot liquid transform into a hardened shell, I knew that it had to be the perfect substance for your wings. Many times around the fire, I had told my stories of growing up in Knossos. How we once lived as caged Athenian birds in the palace of King Minos. Finally, we had to leave, in order to discover our freedom. The villagers wholeheartedly approved of your choices and of what we did."

I could see a look of satisfaction on Icarus' face. My throat grew tight with emotion. I could not speak, so I nodded, encouraging him to continue.

"Of course, I told them what had happened to us afterward," Icarus continued. "How we came to live on the far side of the island near a cave that you stuffed full of feathers, your study of birds, and your dream of designing and building wings for flying off of this island."

"They must think that I am crazy," I said.

"Some of them do. That's true. But they have never met a flying man before, so it is difficult for them to believe." He slapped me on the shoulder. "And the best part is this. Whether they think you are crazy or not, all of them want to support you. Everyone wanted to help."

"We made a big batch for you and your wings," said Deena, "but not in the usual way. Yours was very different. After the tars and the oils were heated together, we added other ingredients, special ones, for you and your flight over the water; dried powder from an eagle's heart, small bits of tail feather from a condor, and other sacred items only the priestess would know."

"Da, it was such a beautiful sight," Icarus said. "The entire village was singing and dancing around the fire that night, chanting and praying."

Speechless, I stared into the fire.

"It will be a lonely journey," Icarus said, with pride and sadness.

"And like no other," Deena agreed.

My vision of flight was coming true. All I had to do was reach out and take it. Icarus walked around the fire and stood behind me. Placing his strong youthful hands on my shoulders, he gave them a squeeze. "Da, if you won't come back with us, then accept this gift from us."

CHAPTER SIXTY NINE

I offered them the egg house, but the newlyweds choose to return to the sandy beach and sleep near the boat. I sat by the fire, unable or unwilling to sleep. Their invitation to return with them to their village definitely had its appeal. Of course, it also meant changing the course of my life. But how satisfying it would be, to watch Icarus keep on growing into the man he was becoming. How enjoyable to bear witness to the birth of grandchildren. Surely, it would not be long before Icarus and Deena had a child. These were very pleasing ideas. With all my heart I knew that I would enjoy being a grandfather.

I had to ask myself, "Did I really want to end my days living in a quiet fishing village, surrounded by people I had never known before?" I knew the answer without even seeing the place. As appealing as it sounded at first, life in the fishing village was not my path. My life hinged on a singular pursuit, a calling that I had felt for a very long time. My soul had challenged me to soar upon the winds, on wings of my own design. There would never be another time like this one. All that remained was to assemble the pieces. It was just as the dreams had foretold.

But there was another, more pragmatic reason to persevere with the wings. Just one sun cycle ago, we had aided and abetted the escape of the Athenians from the labyrinth. That history was still very recent, and

Minos was not one to forget or forgive. Not until he had a good reason for it. By now there was surely a reward for both of us. If I returned to the village with Deena and Icarus, how long would it be before some traveler or sailor visited? How long before that traveler stayed long enough to learn that Daedalus, the inventor, was living there? Minos had many eyes and ears. Eventually, word of my identity and location would travel back to the king, particularly if the way was paved with gold. I could not give Minos the pleasure of plotting our demise. He would send ships and warriors, and that would be the end of my life. The entire village could end up destroyed as well.

I could not let that happen. Icarus and Deena deserved a chance to have a life together. More than that, they deserved a chance to have a safe and stable place to live and raise their family. They deserved the opportunity to have hope for the future. I would give them that much. When I finally dozed off to sleep, my dreams were of small children playing happily in the sand near a tiny fishing village.

On a patch of level ground at the base of a nearby hill stood two almost identical pyramids of stone, half the height of a man, and separated by a length of three strides. Balanced between them and supported in the middle by a wooden frame lay a narrow length of carved wood, straight at the center and with gently curved outer edges. Slender wooden ribs with doweled ends were mortised along its length, suggesting the internal structure of a bat's wing. As soon as they saw it, however, they knew it was my wing—the first of its kind.

I had been waiting for a very long time to make this presentation to someone, and I was excited. For too long I had had only myself to talk with about the vital connection between the wings and pilot's body. That day, I stepped into the inventor's role, relishing it like never before. I explained that early on I had discarded the idea of designing articulated wings. That was for the ducks and the gulls. It was too complex for this stage of my studies. First, I would master the art of gliding. Considering the mighty thermals that arose from the island during the dry season, hanging from a fixed wing and soaring like the condor was more than enough for the first flight.

To support my weight, I had constructed a foreshortened plank platform centered below the structure to hold my body. It would mount to the wing with a harness of bone and leather. Missing were the feathers. There was nothing stretched between the ribs, nothing to hold the wind.

With a wink to Icarus, I said, "You know, there are two of these frames. I have the parts for a second wing stored down in the cave."

"Deena and I have other plans, remember?" Icarus replied.

"Yes. I remember," I answered, with a smile and a nod to each of them. "But times do change, whether you expect them to or not. Now, will you help me test this one?"

"Da, what about the feathers?"

"You can incorporate those improvements into the next one," I replied with a laugh. "For the longest time I struggled with the feathers. The pinions are so short. They dry out and lose their strength. I tried, I really tried to figure out a way to join them together into some kind of intricate weave, and mimic the design of the bird's wing. Nothing seemed to work."

"How will you cover this entire frame?" Deena asked, running her fingertips along the smooth ribs.

"Linen," I announced, "Finely woven fabric. Just like the sail on your boat."

"How did you get it?" Icarus asked.

"From the plants with the blue blossoms," I replied. "They're everywhere in the springtime."

"You did all the retting and combing yourself?" Deena asked.

"Well, I was waiting for someone. Let's just say I had a lot of time on my hands," I teased. "Actually, the weaving part was rather enjoyable. That's how I made the cloth for this stylish tunic," I said, showing off the fabric.

"So, you have a loom?" Icarus asked.

"In the egg house," I answered. "It was easy to build, much easier than this frame."

"Do you even need the sealant?" Icarus asked, disappointment creeping into his voice.

"Absolutely!" I quickly responded. "It is very critical to the construction. Without it, there is no way to solidly fix the ribs into the crosspiece; no way to fasten the cloth to the wing. I am rather stuck without the glue," I said, unable to resist the bad joke.

"Ouch Da'," he said. "Did you have to?"

Wasting no time, we built a fire in a small hole in the ground and buried the urn right next to it. Eventually, the stiff, tarry mixture gave way to a glossy black liquid that bubbled in the heat. We spent the rest of the day gluing the frame together. Next, we labored to stretch, shape, and affix the fabric to the curved surfaces. The assembly required several days and all six hands. It was the culmination of a lifetime of experiences, focused now into a single challenge. And what a joy it was, to be able to share it with Icarus and his new wife!

In the end, the three of us produced a huge, magnificent wing. It was late afternoon, but otherwise a perfect day for flight. Balanced between the three of us, we carried our creation to the treeless top of a rocky hillside. With Deena and Icarus each holding up an end, I wriggled into the harness. I had taken off and flown so many times in the dreams. Suddenly, however, doubt thickened like never before. Who was I kidding? How could lessons I had learned from dreams actually help me to fly? My stomach churned. My mind raced. I looped my feet into the leather stirrups. There were a hundred reasons to stay, a thousand things I had not yet considered, all flooding into my head at once.

The wind was strong and steady and blowing directly into my face. The memory of a dream came back to me, one from long ago. Not a flight dream exactly, but a dream about a gift and a commitment that I had made; to be ready and willing to receive a great gift whenever it arrived. I had promised not to be too busy, too tired, or too afraid.

CHAPTER SEVENTY

With Icarus and Deena steadying the ends, I placed my arms into the leather straps and slowly raised my chest, lifting the wing into the wind. When it began to shudder for the first time, I quickly backed away. Then, I regrouped and repeated the process. Each time I took the expansive wing a little closer to the point of lifting off. When I felt the uplift on my back and shoulders act like a kite wanting to gain elevation and saw that the wing held together, I knew that it had passed the first test. Even the fabric seemed to sigh.

"It was beautiful to watch," said Deena, breaking the silence of a pleasant end to a long day, filled with work, cooperation and hope.

"It was good, but we were not meant to fly today," I said. "For me to reach my destination, we must have the morning thermals."

"And where is your destination?" Icarus wondered.

"Help me take this wing back to the mounts at the base of the hill," I answered. "We can talk about my plans over dinner. I want hear your ideas."

For our last meal together, we feasted on sea bass and fruit, shared wine, and watched the sun go down from the top of the cliff. It was a magnificent sunset, the sea sparkling like a huge diamond against the backdrop of a primrose sky.

When the sun was nearly gone, I announced, "I have a gift for the newlyweds."

"You have already given us so much," said Deena.

"Back in Athens when you were a little boy, Icarus, I promised to keep you safe. I have a plan to carry out that promise."

"What are you talking about?"

"King Minos, of course," I replied.

"He has never come to our side of the island," responded Deena.

"But he could, for the right reason," I said. "I want to make sure that he never has a reason to start looking for you. That will be my gift."

"How will you do that?"

"Tomorrow, the wing will carry me across the sea to Kalliste. The summit of the volcano is like a giant forge, sending columns of heat into the sky. Once I reach it, I plan to use the rising heat to regain whatever elevation has been lost. There are many islands to the north of Kalliste. I will continue on until I find the right one."

"The right island for what?" Icarus asked.

"For mischief," I replied. "As much as I would love to reach Naxos and visit with Naucreta and our child, it's not worth the risk. Meriones would not take kindly to a flying man visiting his island, especially one wanting to spend time with his queen. Besides, Naxos is right next to Kalliste and that's much too close to Krete."

"Da, what mischief?"

"The news of your untimely death," I replied as sincerely as I could.

"But I've never been better," Icarus replied.

"I get the picture," Deena said.

"How about you, Icarus?" I asked, "Are you following now? The right island will have enough people to notice the landing, and yet be far to the north of Kalliste. Once there, I'll explain that we both took off on a warm, sunny day from this beautiful island in the middle of an azure sea. But you, Icarus, overcome with youthful exuberance, disobeyed my guidance to be patient and prudent. You, my dear son, crashed into the sea and drowned."

"And were never seen again," Deena said, concluding the story. "I like it, but are you sure that your King Minos is really worthy all this trouble and deceit?"

"I'm afraid he is," Icarus replied for both of us.

"It's more than just the business of helping the slaves to escape from the labyrinth," I said, apprehensive about saying too much. "The king of Naxos and I were in love with the same woman. There may be a baby now, a light-skinned baby."

"Oh," Deena said discreetly. "That is complicated."

"Wait," Icarus said in a defensive tone, "both of you. Even that is only half of it."

Staring at her husband, Deena pointedly asked, "What are you saying?"

"Something I've needed to tell you about for a long time," he replied, resolutely this time, "both of you."

Shocked and surprised, Deena and I just looked at him, waiting for the explanation.

"That business about not following your advice, Da, not heeding your warning, that much is true," Icarus said dramatically. Turning to Deena he said, "There was a girl in Knossos. Her name was Dianna."

Deena looked toward him, nodding her head but saying nothing.

"Before you and I ever met, he tried to warn me not to go back to Knossos," Icarus continued, returning her gaze. "But I did. I was hungry and tired, sitting on top of one of those mountains right over there. I shouldn't have gone. I know that now, but I missed her, and the city, and everything else about it." Looking first at Deena and then at me, Icarus concluded, "You're right about there being a reward for us."

"Did you find her?" Deena asked.

"No, I didn't." Icarus said emphatically. "In fact, I found out that she has joined an order. Dianna is studying to become a priestess."

"Go on," she said, with obvious relief.

"I asked a lot of questions in different places," Icarus continued. "I found out about the slaves and Ariadne, Phaedra and Theseus. And I found Demitrious. He told me that Minos was offering ten golden rings, just for information about us."

"Why didn't you tell us any of this?" I asked.

"Because I killed someone leaving the city, one of the palace guards," Icarus replied flatly.

"How did that happen?" I asked.

"I was trying to leave the city," Icarus continued, "return to the mountains. It all happened so fast. They wore cloaks over their breastplates. One of them cut off my retreat. Another one came at me from out of the crowd. He had a knife. They even had a lookout."

"And you could have been killed," I said, a tone of disappointment hiding my concern.

"It was planned," he said.

"Do you have any idea how Minos found out?" I asked.

"Someone recognized me," he said. "I don't know who or where. This has been troubling me for a long time."

"What about Naucreta?" I asked, "the baby?"

"Sorry Da, I don't know anything new about either of them.

"And now that you have told your father and me, it can go no further," Deena declared with a look only a matriarch can make, a face that says; do not make me explain all the reasons why. "No one in Platanos can know. Not even your friend, Salim."

"She's right," I said.

"Not even Naomi," Icarus added.

"Especially not Naomi," Deena agreed.

CHAPTER SEVENTY ONE

We sat on the hillside together, next to the wing, drank warm tea, and said one last round of goodbyes. If I was going to do this thing, it was time to begin. The sun was warming the earth. The morning thermals would soon begin rising off the land. I would go from one to the next and ride them higher and higher, like the eagles and the condors, until I was high enough to see the distinctive profile of the northern volcano. That was the first leg of the journey.

"This invention of yours is quite remarkable," said Icarus.

"It is rather inspiring, isn't it?" I agreed. "You know, Deena, looking back I can truthfully say that some of my greatest joys in my life have come from the acts of raising the fine young man you find yourself married to. When you two sailed up onto the beach the other day, I became the happiest man on earth."

"That is a very sweet thing to say," she said softly.

"This wing," I went on, "will have to carry me very far in order to compete with that."

"If that day you were the happiest, then today you must be going for the title of the luckiest," Icarus quipped.

"It's quite possible," I replied. "If not for you, Icarus, I might have buried my head in the sand, drunk too much wine, and let the Athenian slaves solve their own problems. But for a few simple twists of fate, I would still be back in Knossos, building a temple for King Minos. I would have been bored, restless, and wondering where all the satisfaction went."

"Don't you remember?" replied Icarus with a smirk. "It left with Naucreta for Naxos."

"Ah yes, Naucreta. She is a fine woman," I said with a sigh. "And I will be close to her new home today. But I want to talk about you, Icarus," I continued, refocusing the conversation. "In order to stay the course, I've had to reach deep inside. You were always a large part of the motivation behind those choices. I want to thank you for that. And I hope that in your time, both of your times, you can experience a similar kind of fulfillment. Make a memory of me to my grandchildren."

As I spoke, I could see in his moistening eyes that my words and the moment were combining to conjure memories about how he had ended up standing there in front of me and listening to a farewell speech. Once a street urchin and an orphan, he took a leap of faith and became my son. And no matter how much I had bumbled the task, he had grown into a fine man. This was the day of our first flight and I was a happy man. As much as I might want to take credit for the accomplishments, I knew—he knew—that we had done it together.

Tears filling her eyes, Deena found words more readily and said, "We will."

For all his physical prowess, Icarus wasn't able to manage the emotions that stirred within him. He returned to talking about my plan and implored me to come back to Krete after Minos was gone and it was safe again.

"We will be the ones waiting for you this time," he said.

"You will always be welcome in our home," Deena rejoined.

"And when you come back," Icarus said, "We'll throw a three day celebration for Daedalus—the first man to fly!"

One last time, we embraced at the top of the hill. It was tearfully clumsy, but heartfelt. A breeze was coming in off the sea, rising from the shore. It flowed around us like a welcoming breath.

"Let's do this thing." I said with a glance at my partners. "I'm going to fly!"

My heart pounded as I wriggled into the harness beneath the wings.

Once again Icarus and Deena stood on each end, elevating the ends of the wing. With slight pivots we adjusted it to face directly into the wind. The wind was strong and steady, and full in my chest, assuring me once more. It was a perfect day for flight. I placed my arms into the leather straps and felt the uplifting force pulling at my shoulders. I straddled the pallet that would soon hold me above the earth and called out that I was ready. Lifting my eyes to the horizon, I launched myself forward with two quick steps, pushing away from the slope as if I were diving from a cliff and onto the pallet. At first, all that I could feel was my body falling, dropping down toward the rocks below. But then the wing shuddered with a blast of warm air that filled it, lifting me skyward. I countered the shifting forces with the mass of my own body, just the way I had done so many times in the dream, finding equilibrium.

I soared.

Below, in the distance, I could hear the unmistakable sound of Icarus and Deena clapping and cheering.

I spiraled upward on a rising thermal, a subtle bursting of warm air carrying me aloft, higher and higher above the island. It all happened so quickly. By the time I finally looked down, Deena and Icarus had become two small round specks on a gray patch of earth. "Farewell," I called out as loud as I could as I continued to ascend.

CHAPTER SEVENTY TWO

The sun was up, rising over a magnificent green island, the snowcapped mountains, and the beautiful brown beaches. Finally airborne, I had to confess that my first impression of flying was that it was a lot more work than I expected. Luckily, there was no option for failure, besides death. So I allowed visions of grandeur upon my successful landing to abate the unplanned workload. I rode the thermals high above the island, moving from one to the next, using them to follow the coast all the way to its northern edge. Far below, the water sparkled beneath the low angle of the sun. At just the right elevation, I was able to see my companion on the water below, the moving shadow of a flying man. The silhouette moved across the sparkling surface, and I watched with fascination.

Far ahead, the gray sloping mass of Kalliste was already visible on the other side of a deep blue, early summer sea. Instead of striking out across the water, I stayed in the rising air above Krete. I kept my altitude and moved steadily east toward Knossos. The sun felt warm and inviting. I could see the city and the central palace basking in the morning light. The sight of it brought back a flood of memories. A ribbon of gray followed along the coastline, reaching all the way to Malia and beyond.

Nearing Amnisos I felt the *meltemi* winds coming out of the north, and banked into them. Balancing against the force, I used them to climb

high as I began the over water flight to Kalliste. While the day was young
the experience was sublime. My body seemed to find ways for rest from
time to time and the coastline of Krete slipped away. I soared across open
water, midway between the azure heights of the sky and the great depths
of the sea.

All morning long, I watched the mountain ahead loom larger and
larger. Like a protected jewel, the gently sloping volcanic peak sat inside
a much larger ring of gray and brown cliffs, off-center. It rose to heights
many stadia above the water. If the winds held, then I might still be high
enough to soar above it. Sunlight surrounded me, warmed me, and helped
to keep my spirits up. Far below and up ahead I could see that there was
actually a second, smaller ring, lower in elevation and concentric with the
first. Straight canals cut through it, each one leading to its own harbor, with
dock works and densely crowded buildings. A vast array of ships and small
boats filled the waters of the inner ring. I had never before imagined that
so many ships could all come together into such a confined space. Seeing
so much activity and people, I wondered if anyone below had noticed the
unusually large and slow-moving bird passing overhead.

Beyond the harbor steam oozed from multiple vents on the mountain's slopes. I chose one of the larger ones and gently banked toward the
visibly rising heat. As soon as I reached it, I found myself surrounded by a
malodorous sulfur smell. Spiraling upward, eyes watering, I held my breath
and rapidly gained elevation in the warm grip of the hot column of air.
Feeling light-headed, I rose into wispy clouds. When I finally looked down,
I saw that I was passing over the glowing red fire of the caldron. It was an
ominous sight, powerful and thoroughly foreboding.

To the north were many more islands, arranged like pieces in a
giant puzzle. The nearest one was quite large, with an inviting shade of
green. I headed straight toward it, while the *meltemi* held me aloft. It had
to be Naxos, still well within the Minoan empire. Once I was beyond its
northern shore, it was just a question of how much further to go.

Nothing had prepared me for the breadth of the selections. It was
something like choosing from a banquet table. If the number of choices
wasn't shocking enough, I realized that I had had nothing to drink in too long
a time. The flight was beginning to finally take its toll on my body. My joints
were growing stiff, not to mention the particular weariness I felt in my chest
and shoulders. Through the grogginess, I reminded myself that in order to
carry out the plan, the island had to be inhabited. I needed others to see with
their own eyes that a winged man had flown to their island and to be curious

enough to want to hear my stories. I would keep going until I found it. If the winds held, I might be able to stay aloft for the rest of the day.

It was hot and I was alone in an endless sky. The stimulation and excitement of the takeoff, the splendor of the morning's flight, those things were now a distant memory. I felt a growing fatigue, especially in my chest. I wanted badly to move but that was impossible. Gliding alone in the heat of the afternoon was not at all the way it had been in the last flight dream, the one in which Aella had put me through my paces.

I could not let go of the memory of that dream. The more I thought about it and the double helix we had created over the volcano, the more sense it seemed to make. With the next island coming into view, there was a growing awareness that I was no longer alone, but it was not Aella this time. Instead, I saw a vision of Naucreta, rising above the island directly ahead. I could see her face, the green eyes and radiant smile. I wanted to be close to her again.

Flying over the center of the island, I felt her presence as if she were there alongside me. Drawn to her, I scanned the ground for a place to land and began to descend. Right away, she appeared in a vision far ahead. Her arms were outstretched and she was moving away, beckoning me to follow. Thinking became difficult. I was so tired, but I had to follow my guide away from Naxos. King Meriones would not welcome me.

After Naxos, I saw a compelling chain of islands close by and trending to the northwest. But the winds in that direction were not so favorable. To turn toward the island chain meant I'd have to lose life-giving altitude.

"Tell me which way to go, my beloved," I said, scanning the sea and sky in all directions.

Almost at once, I could feel her returning and scanned the sky for her image. There she was, far to the northeast and rising above what might be a gray and very distant island.

"Tell me that is the one," I said. Naucreta only smiled and beckoned me onward.

By the time I could see the harbor and the small town that inhabited it, I was tired, very tired. My chest and shoulders were leaden and all that I could feel was the desire to stop and rest. My eyes burned from the glare and I blinked them constantly. Nothing took away the dry ache. The sun was far to the west, long past its zenith.

"This has to be the one," I said to the smiling image. She did not disagree.

As the distance closed, I watched anxiously as the island took shape and grew larger, taking up more space upon the water. The details of the topography slowly came into view. I could see green forests and hills. A river channel beginning in the high peaks at the island's center was also visible. Square patterns of farms appeared, grouped around a decent sized village. Right next to it, two tiny fishing boats were making their way into the harbor.

"This is it," I said, feeling a wave of relief. "It's time to land."

With the sun on my shoulders, I set a mark on the center of the village and continued my gradual descent.

Still tens of stadia away, I slipped down through the layers of air in a broad arc, just like I had seen the condors do so many times before. Somehow, the condors seemed to enjoy the maneuver. For me, it was a tremendous amount of work. To make matters worse, my speed was increasing. At first, I was just too tired to respond to the downward acceleration. Nonetheless, the unforgiving earth was filling my field of view. I knew that I could not ignore it for long. All around me the air was steadily growing warmer. I knew what had to be done. I tried to turn my shoulders back and down in order for the wing to brace against the air beneath it and slow the descent. There was no strength left in them. Curiously, I watched the land coming towards me as if in some kind of greeting.

So much time and effort had gone into planning for the flight; now I realized that I should have spent more time conceptualizing the details of the landing. Most of the time my mind had jumped right to the ending, an image of me dropping in for a graceful and dramatic finish, all amidst an excited village full of trusting people. In this optimistic plan, the villagers recognized right away what was happening and welcomed it. And it would be something so unusual that they would tell of it for years to come, the story of the flying man and how he landed on their island.

In that moment, however, it became clear that in order to reach the intended outcome, I first had to survive the landing. Ditching the flight far out at sea was just not an option. There had to be people watching it all unfold. I tried to level the wings and hold some elevation. If only I could slow the downward descent, regain some control, and find my way into a downward spiral. But each time I tried to hold back, weariness gripped my back and shoulders. My muscles were heavy and barely responsive. I was coming in like a star falling from the heavens.

I was so close. With the earth rising faster, I realized that the quality of the landing did not matter at all, so long as I made one. All the rest was my own vanity. I just needed to finish and survive. That would be enough, and it was all that really mattered. Icarus and his young family were depending on it.

As the distance closed, I could make out individual homes and see people moving about. If only I had the wings and the strength of a young condor, I could simply slow myself to a stall, then pull up for a graceful drop to the earth. But that was completely out of the question. I was coming in fast. The best I could hope for was to avoid a fatal crash by landing in the sea.

Directly over the village's main street, I found the strength to roll my exhausted torso into a banked turn. The wing held together and I soared past the roof tops, gliding into the uplift of an offshore breeze. The wind was a lucky break, giving me just enough altitude to complete the turn and head for the water just beyond the harbor.

And they saw me! As I passed overhead, the few people in the street looked up into the sky. I actually heard them shouting to one another. I watched as they pointed. I could even feel their sense of wonder as it reached up and out toward me, even as my own heart went out to them, thanking them for being there.

More people joined in, coming out of their homes to see what was happening. They were cheering and calling out to others. Some of them were following along below, running to the harbor, trying to catch up.

Beyond the shoreline I found another breeze and tried to use it as a kind of brake. But I was too tired to properly balance against it. The opportunity was lost. I felt myself giving in to the fatigue. Before closing my eyes, I had just enough time to see a fishing boat not far off, the setting sun directly behind. What a pretty sight it was!

As I glided over the water, an image of my father as a young man came to mind. I could picture his face and feel his presence nearby. Behind him, I saw another shadowy figure, my grandfather, a man I had never known. There were other deeper shadows, more grandfathers and ancestors, all gathered around me, guiding me through the descent. They were holding me up, just as they had all through the flight that day.

Very low to the water now, I shot past the last of the shallows and rocks. Still burning, my eyes were shut tight. I thought that I could hear the sound of someone close by, calling out to me. The water was very close. I could feel it pulling me in, but I was much too tired to look, too tired to do anything except trust in the choices I had made. Then, everything went black.

Epilogue

The fire had grown smaller and smaller. Still, there was plenty of light for the audience to see me, an old man, alive and well, drawing out a pause at the climax of the story. Yet in the brief span of that pause, many still wondered if the wingbuilder would live. It was a precious moment, built upon the wonder of what an amazing gift life is.

My student, Agapios, sat nearby, watching the faces in the crowd. He preferred to sit where he could see my profile and still watch the audience without drawing attention to himself. Turning an upraised palm towards him, I said approvingly, "Agapios, my student and friend, will tell you the rest of the story."

"Gravity finally prevailed," Agapios began, standing up and shaking my hand. "One of the fishermen later explained that the left tip of the wing hit first and took much of the impact. It broke apart and shattered into pieces. The fishermen stood up in their boat, staring in disbelief as Daedalus cartwheeled across the water, right in front of their eyes." Smiling to the crowd Agapios confided, "Of course he was a few years younger then, and a lot more flexible." For the longest time, neither of them moved.

Then, the best swimmer or perhaps just the boldest, dove into the water after the sinking man. Strong steady strokes pulled him toward the point where bits of broken wing littered the surface. The swimmer paused to fill his lungs and then dove into the clear depths.

Unsure of what he had just witnessed, the rescuer was relieved to find not far below the surface this man, along with the bone and wood remains of some kind of harness wrapped around his torso. The rescuer swam in from behind, grabbed his limp body by the armpit, and made for the surface in quick, deliberate strokes. When he finally broke through the surface, the swimmer rolled the stricken man onto his back, and pulled and kicked for shore. It was not long before a friend waded out into the water to help. Together, they dragged the flying man out of the water and onto the gentle slope of the beach.

While the fishermen worked to restore his breathing, curious villagers made their way to the beach. It was reassuring to learn that a man, and not some kind of monster, had flown over their village. He was breathing on his own now, and after some gurgling and retching, seemed to be sleeping.

They decided to make him as comfortable as they could right there on the beach. A few caring villagers went back to their homes to retrieve blankets and sleeping skins. The village healer prepared a soothing concoction of citrus, herbs and honey, filled a colorful urn with it, and brought it to where Daedalus lay sleeping. She pulled the remains of the harness away from his chest and held her hands over his heart for a long while, slowing her breathing to match his.

Everyone wanted to get a look at the flying man. For a long while, many of the villagers stood circled around the makeshift bed, keeping a vigil until long after nightfall. Finally, they began drifting away. In the end, only the fishermen and the healer remained, the ones who had pulled him from the sea. The next morning when he awoke, the people of the town responded with all that they had, bringing the finest fruits and cheeses, and the freshest breads on the island.

Everyone in the village shared in the bounty of that morning meal. His body bruised and battered, Daedalus wanted nothing more than to sit on the blankets and pillows, drink the delicious thickened teas and replenish himself. But, the townspeople would not let him rest. They could not resist peppering him with questions. It was inevitable that with most of the villagers gathered around, the builder began a new vocation as a storyteller.

A man had constructed wings and used them to fly all the way from Krete. The news of the incredible feat just kept going, heard and repeated by merchants, traders and mariners who sailed throughout the Great Green. Like ripples on a pond moving out in all directions from the impact of a single stone the story spread. Their stories went something like this:

> A well-known architect and inventor named Daedalus was born in Athens. He later sailed to Krete with his son, Icarus. There, he restored the city of Knossos and created an underground labyrinth for Minos the king. But eventually, politics and palace intrigues got the better of him and Daedalus fell into disfavor. To escape impending imprisonment in the very same labyrinth, the father and son fled together from the palace into the island's countryside.
>
> Minos tried to prevent them from escaping from the island and kept a close watch over all the ships leaving from the island. Somehow, the great inventor Daedalus created working wings for both of them, made from the feathers of seabirds and wax. With these wings, the father and son were able to successfully fly away from the island. The sensible father warned his son to fly in the middle passage, far enough below the heat of the sun and high enough above the sea to be safe. But young Icarus, enamored of the newfound freedom, flew too high, the wax on his wings melted and the wings broke apart. Icarus was lost at sea."

Agapios paused, nodding to the crowd. "Countless times the story was repeated, just the way the wingbuilder intended, just the way he and Icarus had planned. Inevitably the news reached Knossos and the ears of the powerful king. Minos was furious that Daedalus had escaped. He swore angry oaths to the god of the sky that no matter what was required, he would hunt Daedalus down," Agapios mockingly thundered, careful to emphasize each word. "Immediately, the enraged king began plotting the pursuit, capture, and punishment of his former builder. But he never gave Icarus another thought."

Nodding to an approving audience, Agapios concluded, "And that is how this man, this father, perfected his plan and kept his son's family safe, right under the nose of the tyrant king. Despite all the strength and the might of Minos' army and navy, they were powerless against the words of a simple story, told by one man living from his higher purpose."

THE CATACLYSM

Volume Two of The Minoan Trilogy

Dangerous pressures develop underneath the volcanic paradise of Kalliste. Naucreta gives birth to a child, and an equally dangerous build-up of pressure begins to develop within King Minos. His well laid plans for revenge against the Wingbuilder become a reckless pursuit. All the while the children of Icarus and Deena grow into maturity in the tranquil beauty of their remote fishing village.

The King's dark quest to destroy Daedalus takes on epic proportions. Only one can survive. The children of Icarus, now grown, are swept into the fray. Agapios bears witness to all these events, picking up the storyteller's torch to carry on this chronicle of the rise and fall of the Minoan empire.

ACKNOWLEDGEMENTS

I am immensely grateful to the foundation of family and friends, colleagues and supporters, who have made this book possible. There are many. This mixture of biography and historical fiction has been a work in progress for a very long time. The people of the island of Crete have been a welcoming and reliable source of motivation and inspiration throughout.

The writing began in the oral tradition of telling stories around a fire to a gathering of interested people. An early version of this story was first told at a weekend men's retreat in the mountains of Colorado during the winter of 2006. Telling it was a powerful awakening, and I'm grateful for the receptive and supportive group of men who provided both the venue and the fertile soil for the seeds.

It has been a process of expansion and revision. I am grateful to the artist, Benjamin Hummel, who developed the means to present the work to the reading world, and for a beautiful cover and map. For lively discussions and technical assistance with all things related to flight, I am grateful for my friend and editor, Pete Deakon. More editing thanks go to Dr. Bob Rich, author and psychologist.

There have been many more readers along the way, offering their insights and suggestions. These include Kathleen Schulz, Joan Heller, and Wayne James. The list would not be complete mentioning the unwavering support of Gina Bolton and Porfiria Medina. I am grateful to the Toastmasters organization for introducing me to the world of public speaking, and particularly to the members of District 26 for their universal support, evaluation and guidance. They were always there, whenever I needed direction. And surely, I could have completed this without the loving guidance and support of my partner and wife, Marceil Case. Hurrah for families.

ABOUT THE AUTHOR

Robert has always been fascinated with the goddesses, heroes and gods of Greek mythology, and especially the very human legend of Icarus and his father. As a young reader, the author remembers a picture-book image of the helpless youth, feathers flying everywhere, falling through an endless expanse of deep blue sky. Even then he knew that there had to be more to the story. Dropping out of college in the early 1970s, Bob traveled to the Aegean and eastern Mediterranean for the first time, drawn to the land and its cultures, the beauty and the turmoil.

Returning to the USA, his journey led back to college, then marriage and fatherhood. Through it all, the fires of the ancient legends still smoldered. He studied the geology of the Aegean, the history of the Minoan people and the legend of Atlantis. After his children had grown into their own lives, Robert discovered improv, Toastmasters and an inner creative writer that was tired of waiting. Drawing inspiration from the stories of Daedalus and Icarus and their first flight, his first book, *Daedalus Rising,* was published in 2008. Now, the journey continues with the publication of *Icarus and the Wing Builder*, the first volume of a trilogy of historical fiction about the rise of the ancient Minoan civilization and its fall, in the wake of a cataclysmic volcanic eruption and the destructive tsunamis that followed.

Robert lives in Colorado with his wife and two Boston Terriers. Visit his website at (www.robertwilliamcase.com) or follow his Pinterest Page (www.pinterest.com/daedalusr/).